HAWK

A DARK & DIRTY SINNERS' MC: SEVEN

SERENA AKEROYD

DEDICATION

TO CLAIRE.

I never met you, and now I never will.

But... we *have* met. In a fashion! Through Anne. :)

You might have wanted her to be a doctor, but I'm so glad she's not! May you rest in peace, finally free from pain, with those you love, knowing full well that your goddaughter isn't working in the porn industry just for a very naughty author. Either way, she's a woman to be proud of, so keep on watching over her. <3

Much love to you,

Serena

xoxo

WARNING

Please be advised this book may contain scenes that are disturbing to sensitive readers.

It also may contain scenes that make you grin.

That make you cringe.

And that make you think.

All are acceptable responses. :)

- History of human trafficking,
- Grooming,
- Kidnapping,
- General violence,
- References to sexual abuse

AUTHOR NOTE

DO you read my author notes, dear reader?

Do you skip right past them to get to the good stuff? LOL. I bet you do, but you shouldn't! ;) I have info for you.

So, this story is about Amara, who is Ukrainian. During her POVs, she's thinking in Ukrainian, even if it's in English because, ya know, this is a romance set in English! I just wanted to clarify that. <3

Here are a few curse words you'll see:

Korva - shit

Suka - bitch

Khuy - dick, but can also mean 'fucking' as in, 'He's a fucking asshole.' (This is an important one lol.)

Pizda - cunt/whore

Poshel na huy - fuck you

Blyat' - bitch

Zalupa - dickhead

Musor - trash (can refer to the police)

Pederasti - pedophile

Idi v zhopu - go to hell

Chyort - damn

Zhopa - asshole

Anyhoo, I hope you're ready for a Serena-style romance. Weird shit's about to go down. ;)

Much love,

Serena

xoxo

UNIVERSE READING ORDER

FILTHY
FILTHY SINNER
NYX
LINK
FILTHY RICH
SIN
STEEL
FILTHY DARK
CRUZ
MAVERICK
FILTHY SEX
HAWK
FILTHY HOT
STORM
THE DON
THE LADY
FILTHY SECRET
REX
RACHEL

FILTHY KING
FILTHY DISCIPLE
THE CONSIGLIERE
THE ORACLE
LODESTAR
SILENCED
END GAME
FILTHY RICHER

PLAYLIST

If you'd like to hear a curated soundtrack, with songs that are featured in the book, as well as songs that inspired it, then here's the link:

https://open.spotify.com/playlist/4vS25LZlQIOCQvK4JcL1Ki

ONE

HAWK

"I SEE YOU, LITTLE BIRD."

She jumped, much as I expected her to.

I wasn't sure where the endearment came from, but to be fair, my options were either a bird or a mouse, both of which she resembled in nature, and I didn't think any woman would appreciate being likened to a rodent.

A sky rodent? Sure. They had wings. That was much cooler than mice who shit and pissed in your hand if you held them.

Okay, I had issues with mice. Issues with most animals to be honest, so, little *bird* it was. I couldn't exactly hate on birds when I was named after one.

"Of course, you can see me," Amara whispered huskily. "I am visible."

I wondered if she forgot that sometimes.

Couldn't blame her if she did.

"You're very visible," I said, "but I meant you can't sneak around when my eyes are on you."

An interesting flush kicked up around her cheeks, one that made her pretty face that much prettier.

In all honesty, she was beautiful. A little wrecked, a lot broken, but somehow, all the more beautiful for it. Which was fucked up, I knew that, but I didn't have a say in how I responded to her, did I?

The porcelain doll look had never been my thing. I tended to go for stacked bitches, all hips and ass. Give me a chick who could twerk while she was riding my dick, and I was as happy as a fucking clam.

Amara, on the other hand, was only just starting to gain some much needed weight after being starved.

To death.

Insane, right?

Starved to death. Left to die. Sold into slavery. The rape doll of the rich.

Four descriptions. Each described her, but I knew none defined her.

Even if she didn't yet.

Pursing my lips at her, I murmured, "I saw you last night too."

Her bright brown eyes flared wide in surprise. "What?"

"I saw you last night too," I repeated easily. "Nyx'll kill you if he catches you spying on them again."

She swallowed. "You told him?"

I snorted. "No."

The tension around her mouth and in her shoulders lessened some. "Thank you."

I'd known she was hot for Giulia, my baby sister, but spying on them while they fucked was the opposite of cool. In fact, it was creepy as hell.

My twin, North, always did say that I liked the freaks. Not that he could judge. The fucker.

With my feet kicked up on the railing instead of the coffee table right in front of me, I peered over into the distance. There were the faint noises of construction work going on, but that was to be expected. The compound had been destroyed and the Satan's Sinners' MC were having to rebuild it. That was why we were here, at the MC's lawyer's home, just a stone's throw away from where the clubhouse used to stand.

It meant I was looking onto a sea of lawn, some flowerbeds, an herb garden of all fucking things, and my ass was in a comfortable porch swing, one of those fancy schmancy ones that probably cost more than I earned in three months.

For all that this place was like a palace by comparison to the clubhouse, I'd prefer to look onto a sea of bikes, but that wasn't an option right now.

My gaze drifted wide as I waited for Amara to make a decision. Maybe she was more of a mouse than a bird, because I knew I'd just laid a trail of crumbs that I was hoping would lead her into taking a seat beside me.

She wasn't skin and bone like she'd been when she'd arrived at the compound all those months ago, and what there was of her was covered in an oversized sweater and jeans, but she had a delicacy about her that made me want to protect her.

As well as shove an extra-large burger down her throat.

She reminded me of a skinny Mila Kunis, which was really saying something because Mila Kunis, my spankbank material of choice, was the opposite of plump, but in comparison to Amara, she was.

Big almond-shaped eyes peered out onto the world like every avenue heralded danger, those plump lips of hers were always tightly pursed with a bitterness she couldn't hide. Her cheeks were gaunt, but they exposed cheekbones that belonged in front of a camera. Her hair had, once upon a time, been brittle and dull, but now it was starting to get glossy and thick. She had it slicked back, tight to her head with gel, which kind of reminded me of how a ballerina wore theirs, only without the bun.

The thought triggered something in my head, something that was confirmed as Amara took my trail of crumbs, nibbled on them, and sat at my side on the porch swing. As she did so, she crossed her legs, and her foot, instead of just swinging free, extended. The arch was high, her toes pointed, and all her calf muscles, even beneath the skinny jeans, became delineated.

"Did you learn ballet as a kid?"

She turned to me with a frown, but in her eyes, I had my confirmation before she stiffly nodded.

Okay, so that just made her even hotter.

Fuck, as much as I loved twerking bitches with more ass and hips than J-Lo, ballerinas were like my 'thing.' Every dude had one. A special case. A certain sumthin' sumthin' that got our dicks hard. Some liked being walked on by bitches in high heels or having their toes fucking sucked. Others were feeders or got off on female wrestlers.

Me?

I had a thing about ballet dancers. Had done ever since Giulia had gone to a ballet class when she was a kid. I'd only been twelve at the time, but that teacher was my legitimate first crush. Man, no wonder Amara had me jonesing after her even if she was a creepy little freak. Something about being so frail and strong all at the same time sank right into my goddamn bones.

"Giulia did ballet as a kid," I said offhandedly, wondering what her reaction would be.

This crush she had on my sister might have made sense considering she was probably going through a 'I hate every person in possession of a dick' phase, but it had to stop. Giulia was very much straight, very much pregnant, and very much attached to a psychotic cunt who'd slay an army to protect my sis.

"She did?" Amara asked, her eagerness clear as she stopped staring out into the distance, and instead, twisted to look at me. That she wanted to know more was evident.

"She did," I confirmed, a smile twisting my lips as I remembered how North, my twin—the bastard—had bitched and whined throughout her classes about wanting to go home, while I'd been enthralled with the instructor.

"Was she good at it? I bet she was," she gushed.

I arched a brow. "My sister wasn't made to be a ballerina," I said dryly. "She didn't have the temperament." Her shoulders sank with disappointment, but I carried on anyway, "She went to two classes. The first time, she hurled her shoe at the mirror, which cracked it." Amara gasped in surprise, but I just grinned. "Even as a kid she had a temper on her. Then the second, she tore off her tutu and stomped on it."

The teacher, Ms. Hottie, had had no idea what to do with Giulia, so Mom, fuming at spending two hundred bucks on a tutu that was ripped, on classes Giulia refused to take, and then having to pay for the mirror too, had dragged her out of the studio by the ear.

Because my baby sister was a bitch, she'd smirked all the way out of there.

"Oh dear," Amara whispered sadly.

"I get why Nyx likes her. I mean, she fights fire with fire, you know?" And if ever a motherfucker was a raging wildfire, it was Nyx. "But you? I'm not sure I see the attraction. Like, I could see you with Lily. Or even Tiffany, Ghost, maybe. But Giulia? She's way too..." I pondered my next choice of word, eventually settling on, "...strident for you."

Amara blinked. "You have thought about this."

I'd thought about nothing else since I'd walked into Rachel's kitchen to find some kind of trial by combat going down with the 'new' Old Ladies of the club.

Ghost, or Alessa as I should call her now, had been smashing Amara's face into the fucking table, trying to get her to talk.

See, Amara had been discovered in a pit of hell with Alessa, a dead girl, and a chick called Tatána who'd died in the blast that had destroyed the clubhouse. We'd recently discovered that Tatána was a treacherous cunt, and my sister and her new Posse, being the fucking insaniacs they were, had decided to ascertain if Amara was guilty of betraying the MC too—the table had been their weapon of choice.

I shrugged. "I think."

She frowned. "You think? What do you think?"

"I mean, I *think*. If I'd been another guy, in another time, in another culture, I'd have been a philosopher." I grinned at her, seeing her confusion. "Ya know, trying to figure out why humans do the shit they do? Trying to understand the reason for our existence? That's my jam."

"It is?" she asked warily. "What is this jam?"

"Well, depending on where you come from, it can be like the jelly you put on toast, or it can be the 'scene' you're into," I reasoned, and determined then and there that I'd stop using colloquialisms until I could ease her into them.

Amara was Ukrainian, and for the longest time, we'd figured she couldn't speak a lick of English but she'd been lying about her command of the language.

It was natural to wonder what else she'd been lying about, but I wanted to take things at face value. Especially after seeing her being beaten by Alessa. Everything about that, after what both women had endured together, put me on edge. They should be allies, not enemies.

Sisters, not foes.

"So, your scene is to think? Don't we all think?"

"Yeah, but not like Plato or dudes—I mean, guys like that. I enjoy thinking about why people do the shit they do. Why a sex slave would crush on a snippety bitch is one of the things I'm wondering about right now."

Her nostrils flared. "*Ex*-sex slave."

I dipped my chin. "Sorry."

"Don't be. Just do not do it again."

Raising my hands, I grinned. "I won't. Pinkie promise." Leaning over, I placed my hand in front of her and extended my pinkie. "In the US," I explained, "we wrap our pinkies around someone else's and make a promise."

"Why?"

I shrugged. "It's tradition. We do it as kids. If we break the promise, we can break the finger."

A gasp escaped her. "Your children break each other's fingers?"

Snorting, I shook my head. "It's more figurative than anything else."

"I should hope so." She reached out, extended her finger and watched as I wrapped mine around hers. She stared at the way they coiled about one another before she asked, "This is strange?"

"Plenty still that's stranger in the US, little bird," I said cheerfully. "Take-out drinks that contain a bottle of soda. Sales tax... I think pinkie promises fit right in."

She hummed, but still didn't detach her finger from our light clasp, and I wasn't about to encourage her to let go.

"Is odd, is it not?" she asked huskily.

"The promise? I guess. Odd is a synonym for strange, after all. But gaining trust through violence is never right."

My pointed words had her peering over at me, and I knew she was well aware I wasn't talking in general terms but of what I'd witnessed in the kitchen a few days back. "Thank you for standing up for me."

I shrugged, and squeezed her finger.

"You didn't have to."

"No, I didn't."

"Then why did you?"

"Because I didn't like to see you being put through that."

I let my gaze drift to our simple union, wishing it was more, even as I accepted that it might never be. My dick was a miracle maker, but I couldn't turn a lesbian straight. Funny thing was, I'd never wanted to.

Until this chick here.

"Why not? I might have done all the things they accused me of," she rasped, her tone blank even as her voice conveyed so much more emotion than she probably recognized.

"But you didn't. Link had already spoken with you. They didn't have to take matters into their own hands."

"I wasn't mad at them."

"No? Well, you must be more of an angel than me, because I'd have been wicked pissed."

"Wicked pissed?" Her smile made an appearance.

"Sorry," I muttered sheepishly. "I'm trying not to use, like, our sayings and shit, but it's hard."

"How will I learn if I don't hear them in context?"

"True." I pressed my booted heel to the coffee table in front and started to rock us. Softly, so as not to spook her. "I wasn't sure it mattered."

She shot me a look. "What?"

"If you learned more of the language. I got the impression you were going back to Ukraine."

"No. There's no place there for me anymore." Her lips tightened. "If Rachel can get me a passport or green card or whatever, then I'll stay here. If she can't, I'll hide out somewhere else.

"She said there were only a limited number of visas given to women in my position, so it is unlikely I will get one, but until then, I have nothing but time on my hands to learn your language."

"You already have a good grasp of it. Why did you hide it from us?"

We'd all thought she couldn't speak a word of it, but here she was, conversing with me. Her accent was incredibly prominent, but she spoke well. Each word held the lash of a Baltic whip to it, but I got off on that too.

She hummed under her breath. "People say things around you when they don't think you can understand them. It came in useful."

I grimaced. "I'll bet. But, Amara, we weren't the enemy."

"No, you weren't," she agreed. "But it was a very hard habit to break."

Plucking my bottom lip, I murmured, "Amara?"

"Yes?"

"We all know what it feels like to have a crush on someone that doesn't reciprocate it, but Nyx is going to be like a bear with a sore paw now Giulia's pregnant. You don't want to get on his bad side."

"I was curious. I only did it once—" She winced when I arched a brow at her, skeptical to the last. "Two times."

"Why?"

"I don't know. She sounded..." Her brow puckered, before she turned her face back toward the view of the city in the distance. "I suppose she sounded in pain."

"Pleasure *can* sound like that, can't it?"

She shrugged. "The first time, I was concerned for her. They were so busy with each other that I opened the door and they didn't notice. I watched, saw how they were doing *that*, and realized I'd made a mistake."

"Did you like watching?" I asked uneasily.

"Not particularly." She bowed her head. "But I saw she was enjoying herself. The complete opposite to what I'd expected, and I was curious."

"About what?"

"How she could enjoy it."

"Ah." I winced. Figured she'd have issues. "Were you a virgin before—"

"Before I was sold?" She surprised me by maintaining eye contact with me as she arched her brow. "Yes. I was. My..." Her lips pursed once more. "What is it called? The thing. The virgin thing?"

"Virginity?"

"No. There is a thin skin. Deep inside."

I rubbed my chin and sheepishly admitted, "Little bird, I ain't got a clue."

"Never mind. It was sold to the highest bidder." She blinked. "It hurt."

Grimacing, I stopped rocking us and leaned forward. "Every time?"

"Yes."

Jesus.

Blowing out a breath, I muttered, "Can I ask you something?"

"That is question, is it not?"

It was, but like my namesake for her, I kept thinking she was going to flutter away.

"It is," I answered wryly, "but that wasn't what I wanted to ask."

"Continue."

I almost smirked at the command. I knew it was a language thing, but her being bossy was hawt. "Are you gay?"

"I do not know."

"What do you mean? You have to know." Didn't she? Confused, I asked, "Well, do guys or girls turn you on? I mean, arouse you. Or do both?"

"Both sexes forced me to do things that I never wanted to do. I like neither."

"You like Giulia," I pointed out.

"Yes. She is strong. She is kind to me. She looked after me, and talked to me, and said nice things even though she didn't know I understood her. When Tatána was a brat, or if I was difficult, she never got mad."

I snorted. "Giulia is the opposite of an angel."

"This, I know. However, she was patient with us. Kind. I liked that."

Pondering that a second, I murmured, "I get it."

"This 'get' word is very confusing."

I cleared my throat. "I understand."

"Ah." She frowned. "What do you understand?"

"I understand that you wanted more of that in your life. And when you thought Nyx was hurting her, you wanted to protect her from him. Like no one did for you." She turned away at my words, staring at the view before woodenly getting to her feet as if she was about to leave. The urge to stop her was so strong that it was like a hit to the solar plexus, so before she could return inside, I blurted out, "You don't have to leave. I'll go."

She paused. "You were here first. That is not fair."

"Life isn't fair." If it was, then my brother would still be in West

Orange, he wouldn't have run off with our stepmother, and 'allegedly' wouldn't have killed our dad in the process.

"This is true."

I got to my feet, being careful to go around the coffee table toward the right, so she could slip back in toward the left and didn't have to touch me.

As she took a seat, I hovered by the patio railing, knowing I should leave, but some little devil made me say, "Amara, if you ever decide you want to know what pleasure feels like, not just looks like, I'll show you."

She reared back at that, which made the porch swing jerk into a ragged, swinging motion. "What?"

"You heard me." I shrugged. "No fucking. I wouldn't have sex with you. I'd just make you feel what—" Well, *this* wasn't awkward. "Giulia felt."

Ukrainian spilled from her lips like I'd made her lose access to the English language, but I was okay with that. I preferred that reaction to the wooden stiffness of before. The garbled Ukrainian didn't sound pissed, more confused than anything else. I didn't blame her, either.

I was confused too.

What would I get out of that? Fuck all. But I didn't mind. It wasn't something I offered out of pity, just, well, humanity. To have been used, to have been sold, to have been hurt... no wonder she was so frail and delicate.

An orgasm was the least society owed her, and I was willing to take one for the team—not that I expected her to say yes.

A guy had to throw out an offer every now and then though, right?

I didn't hang around, just carried on to the doorway, intending to head back to my room, but she stunned the fuck out of me by murmuring my name, "Hawk?" It was so loaded with her accent that I swore, it sank right to my dick.

"Uh-huh?"

One hand on the doorknob, I turned to look at her, and saw she was flushed and pale all at the same time. Her temples were clammy like she'd been sick, but her tits were bobbing with how hard she was breathing. Her visceral response to my question stunned me, but what shocked the shit right outta me?

Her answer.

"Yes."

I blinked. "Yes, what?"

"If you can show me pleasure, I would like to know it."

TWO

AMARA

WHEN NYX GRABBED Giulia's hair, tugging it around his fist as he hauled her up onto her knees, she didn't cry out in pain. She didn't moan with distress.

She growled.

That growl was something I'd remember forever.

Something that, as I looked at her older brother, a man who'd offered me something that no one else had... I wanted to experience.

I wanted it so much that I felt hot and sweaty because of it.

I wanted to growl.

I didn't want to cry.

I didn't want to hurt.

I didn't want to bleed.

The thoughts dampened my response, calmed me down some, but I retained enough control to reply, "If you can show me pleasure, I would like to know it."

His brows rose, and as I took him in, I accepted that he was beautiful, that he reminded me a little of Giulia, and that for all he was a biker, he had clean fingernails, his boots weren't dirty, the cross suspended from the chain hanging around his neck gleamed from being polished, and he smelled of apples.

No.

Not *just* apples. My *babusya's* apple pie.

I swallowed when he queried, "You sure you know what you're asking?"

"I speak English. I thought already we'd established that."

His lips curved at my reply, but I didn't know why. I wasn't being funny. Did he mistake my words for a joke?

I thought about them, how I'd formulated the sentence and spying a potential grammatical error, carefully repeated, "I thought we'd established that already." I blinked. "I thought we'd already established that."

He snickered. "English is hard."

I frowned. "Which is right?"

"The last two are fine."

I hated these words.

Fine. Nice. *Well.* Get.

They were used so much, but their meaning was vague.

I hated vague.

Sarah had said to me once upon a time, "Vague is good. It means that you can fake it, ride it out, and if you're confident, no one will know you made a mistake."

That was back when we'd had hopes of escaping our fate.

Before she'd died.

In a cage.

Before her putrefying flesh had been gnawed on by rats, and I'd had no alternative but to lie there, watching it happen, just wondering when it would be my turn—

"Little bird?"

I jerked back when I realized how close Hawk was now, but I regretted it when he froze.

Having watched him for the last few months, having watched them all, North, Giulia—the whole family, Dog, their father included

—I'd grown accustomed to their manner and knew that the kindness he'd shown me over the past week was unusual.

Dog was cruel, careless. He was quick to hit, to lash out with his fists and his temper, and I'd seen him hurt the clubwhores too many times for me not to celebrate that he was dead.

It came as no surprise that his children were aggressive, but each in their own way. None of them were bullies like their father though.

Giulia's assertive nature was overlaid with a caring side she didn't want anyone to see.

North, the twin who'd disappeared with his father's wife, was happy-go-lucky, playful, but I'd read the writing on the wall long before anyone else had. Not only because I'd seen him sneaking around with his stepmother, but because, deep in his eyes, I'd seen an inherently weak man who relied on his brother too much, and who used charm and charisma to get him through life.

I knew what a man with no strength of will looked like.

Dog.

He was just like his father, even if North treated women better than him.

Hawk, on the other hand, was the opposite. He was grouchy. Grumpy. Quick to temper, but quicker to let that temper fade. He was hard-working, unafraid of getting his hands dirty, and respected the MC like it was the law.

The MC represented anything *but* the law, but that didn't mean I couldn't appreciate his honor was intact. Even if it was in the wrong place.

Hawk didn't hurt women.

He used the whores as did all the bikers, but he didn't cause them pain.

I knew—I'd watched.

That was why I was mad at myself for flinching. He hadn't hurt me. He hadn't hurt anyone I'd ever seen him with. If anything, what I'd seen shored up my determination for him to follow through with his offer.

"I apologize," I said stiffly, relenting with a weak smile. "My mind drifted..." I winced, tacked on, "...somewhere else."

He hummed as he took a seat again. The porch swing sagged under his not insubstantial weight.

I tried to imagine that weight on top of me, but I couldn't.

Just the prospect made sweat bead on my upper lip, but he'd said, hadn't he? He wouldn't put his *khuy* in me.

"I get that. My mind's been drifting recently too. Can't stop thinking of all the shit that's been going on."

"I'm sorry about your father," I told him softly, sort of meaning it. I was sorry for Hawk, but not for Dog. I was glad he was dead. Men who hurt women deserved to die.

"Thanks." His smile was rueful. "He wasn't the best man. Wasn't the best father either." He heaved a sigh. "He treated Mom like shit, hurt Giulia... I'm not sure why I even care that he's dead."

Anger lit up inside me at that—Dog had hurt Giulia? I sincerely hoped his death had been painful then.

It was difficult to answer, but I managed to modulate my tone, "I suppose it's because you wish for what might have been."

He grunted. "You're probably right." His gaze turned from the view to me, before he said, "I know you have issues. It's natural. But I think you should think about what you're signing up for."

"I thought I was signing up for an orgasm," I told him blankly, even though I knew what he meant.

I imagined him heaving on top of me again, but whenever that made the cold sweat appear, I overlaid it with Giulia's growl.

I wanted to feel that.

And if it couldn't be with Giulia, then Giulia's brother was a good substitute.

"Are you sure?"

No. I wasn't. But I knew I wanted to growl, and I also knew that today was the day, all those years ago, I'd left my family home for the final time.

Had they looked for me?

The question plagued me.

I hoped they did, but was scared they hadn't. We'd argued. Most families did, but not mine. I was my family's future. I was going to take them away from poverty with my skills, and then I'd broken my ankle. Everything had changed. They wanted me to dance through the pain, and I couldn't.

Not *wouldn't*, just was physically incapable of continuing the aggressive training a ballerina required.

I could still feel the sting on my cheek where Father had slapped me. He'd never done that before, and despite all the other things that I'd endured since, I still remembered that burning sensation, the way his wedding ring had cut into my flesh like it was yesterday, not years ago.

"Amara?"

Blinking at his gruff tone, I shot him a look. "I'm not sure, no. But I would like to experience pleasure. At least once before I die."

His brow furrowed. "You planning on dying soon?"

I shook my head.

"Then why you thinking about death, little bird?"

"Because death has chased me for a long time." I hitched a shoulder. "It is only natural that, at some point, it will catch up with me."

"Fuck's sake, this ain't *Final Destination*, babe," he grunted under his breath, but though it came with a growl that reminded me of Giulia's, and which sent shivers down my spine, and while it was nasty and violent, I wasn't scared.

I was in the MC's lawyer's home. There were always people around, be it Rachel who worked on the property, or her brother, Rain. Nyx, Giulia, Rex, Cyan, and Keira were also living here until the clubhouse was constructed. If I shouted, someone would come running.

Though there was security in that, I also knew I didn't need it.

"Isn't it, 'for fuck's sake?'"

He cut me a glance. "You really want an English lesson?"

"Every opportunity to learn should be taken advantage of," I parroted, which made him frown.

"It is 'for fuck's sake' but I'm pissed."

"At me." I nodded. "I tend to pissed a lot of people."

A sheepish smile curved his lips. "You tend to piss off a lot of people," he corrected.

Piss. Off.

I heaved a sigh. "I hate these little words." What was it Sarah had called them? "Prepositions."

He smirked at me. "You'd know, Amara. I wasn't that great in school. Never learned the fancy names for things like that."

"I didn't mean to piss you off."

"You didn't. Your mindset did." He grunted—I noticed he did that a lot. "I should have kept my mouth shut."

"Why? I liked your offer. I want you to do it."

"I was thinking with my dick. You deserve better than that."

"I thought you said you weren't going to use it." My heart skipped a beat at the prospect—and not in a good way.

"I wouldn't use it," he clarified. "Doesn't mean I won't get a boner eating you out." His eyes narrowed on me. "I bet you taste of cherry blossom."

My nose crinkled. "Is that good?"

"The best," he confirmed with a grin which slowly started to die.

I knew why too.

"If I gave you pleasure, would you give me it?" I didn't want to, but I wanted to growl enough that I'd switch my mind off to experience that.

He shook his head. "I'm not reneging on the deal, little bird. I'm just not sure if you have the right frame of mind for it."

"For an orgasm?" I scowled. "Is there a left frame of mind?"

His lips twitched. "You need to stop making me smile, Amara."

I hadn't intended on making him smile, and I told him as much, "It was unintentional."

"I know. That's why it's funnier. And I'm not mocking your English, it's just cute."

Cute.

Another of those strange words that meant everything and nothing.

"I would like pleasure. I want to growl."

He blinked. "You want to growl? Like a dog?" He shrugged. "Everyone's got their kinks."

I *loathed* that term.

Kinks.

I'd heard that so many times. So many had used it as an excuse to abuse me. To hurt me.

My pain was *their* kink.

Swallowing down memories of the past, I rasped, "It isn't a kink."

"What is it then?"

"It's a sound of pleasure."

His expression was, to put it mildly, unconvinced. "You don't have the nature to be a growler. I bet you're a squeaker."

My scowl made an appearance. "A squeaker?"

He nodded, but his grin peeped into being. "Yeah." Then, in a tone that was somehow mocking but not cruel, he moaned at a pitch a few octaves higher than his regular baritone, and whimpered, "More, Hawk. More."

Cheeks flushing, I replied, "I might not sound like that."

"I think you will."

Will. Not would.

His tenses were changing.

That was a good sign.

I wasn't sure why I was having to renegotiate with him when he was the one who'd come up with the offer, but that whimper of his cemented things. I wanted to squeak too.

"I want to growl," I repeated.

"You're not aggressive enough."

"How do you know that?"

"You're sneaky. Aggressive people don't lurk around corners, listening in to shit. They storm into a room and get in people's faces." His grin turned cocky. "They don't perv on a couple having sex."

"If you know I did that, then that's because you were perving on me. But you just growled."

His cockiness morphed, shifting into something else. For a second, it blinded me. His dark brown eyes were the color of rich coffee, but the way the lids flared, and the creases either side of his mouth deepened, I'd say he looked delighted.

"So, she has claws." He nodded. "Any self-respecting bird, little or not, has claws." Then, he winked at me. "I was using the bathroom. You, on the other hand, *weren't*."

"You can't use the bathroom in the hallway. That would be disgusting."

He snorted. "Yeah, it would. Moving swiftly on, if you want to growl, then I'll do my best. If you're sure."

"I am." I hadn't been. When he'd made the offer, I'd been speechless, until the desires and the fears had bombarded me to the point where speaking English had been beyond me.

"You should tell me your triggers."

I plucked my bottom lip before I asked, "Triggers?"

"They're the things that turn any pleasure you might experience into pain or fear. You'll have many," he said with ease. "That's okay. I won't try to push your boundaries."

His words *triggered* a visceral reaction in me. My skin turned clammy, and my heart started pounding. I could hear my pulse in my ears, and felt a little shaky as a result. My body was telling me this was stupid, but my mind disagreed.

My mind knew Hawk's intentions were good.

My mind knew that no other man might ever make such an offer.

My mind knew that, for me to heal, for me to move on, I needed to experience the opposite of what I'd endured. Even if it was only once. Then I could carry on with my life, for however short a time that might be.

It took me a while, long enough for me to think he'd walk off, but he didn't. He sat there, taking over the swinging of the porch swing by propping those semi-polished boots on the side of it and rocking us. He was everything I wasn't—calm and relaxed.

"I don't like weight on top of me." My words were stiff. My voice wooden. Though Giulia had growled because of this, I knew it would take me back into the past, when I was aiming for a glimpse of the future. "I don't like my hair being pulled. No knives, no cutting. No blood."

"Jesus," he muttered under his breath.

My brow puckered. "You want these things?"

"No. I'm just fucking pissed that you had to clarify those were triggers. Little bird, I want to give you pleasure, not go Dracula on you." He raised a hand. "I wasn't bitching at you, I'm just pissed at the necessity is all."

I understood.

He was angry on my behalf.

His anger shouldn't have meant anything to me, but it did. It meant everything. Someone was angry for me. He couldn't know how much that was like a warm hug.

(Also—pissed *at*. Mental note recorded.)

"What else aside from the weight on top of you and the hair-pulling, the knives, cutting, and blood would turn you off?" he rumbled.

The trouble was, I knew how dark someone's pleasure could be. What it necessitated. As a result, it meant it was hard to clarify without annoying him.

Hesitantly, I said, "These things cause me no pleasure."

"Okay."

"Shit. Urine. Whips. Cages."

He was still for a second, so still that I peeped a glance at him and knew he was trying to contain his wrath for my benefit.

I wanted to tell him that he didn't have to. I'd have liked to see the fireworks, but his tone was measured, *calm*, as he murmured, "Of the things you mentioned, I'd only be likely to rest my weight on you and to tug on your hair, but you have my promise I'll do neither. Do you understand?"

"I do." I hummed under my breath. "Do you have triggers?"

"Not like yours," he rumbled, his hands finding the side of the porch swing and squeezing down. I noticed his fingers turned white under the pressure, and the woven strips of cane groaned too.

"What like?"

His nose wrinkled. "I mean, I don't get off on that stuff, but it's not a trigger because, to be fair, most people don't fuck like that, little bird."

"Most people I knew did."

He grunted. "That's because you knew some fucking weirdos. Sick bastards who had to pay to use a slave to get off because only someone without a choice would permit that." He shook his head. "I'm firmly of the mindset that my kink don't gotta be your kink, and yours don't have to be mine, but when you have to own a person to use them for that, then it turns into something else."

"Like what?"

"Well, little bird, it's not a kink anymore—it's a fucking crime."

"You're a criminal," I pointed out.

"Did I say I liked philosophy?"

Despite our conversation and its seriousness, I grinned. "You did."

"Shit," he grumbled sheepishly. "I'm a regular criminal. There's a difference."

"Not according to the law."

"Well, that's where you're wrong," he retorted. "If all crimes were equal, we'd all go to jail for thirty years."

He had me there.

I smiled a little. "You're right."

"To a degree. I know what you mean. But there's a difference between what the club does and what those sick fucks did. I can't give you details, but trust me on this, I'm not lying."

Crazily enough, I believed him. I had no reason to. No need to. But I did. His disgust, his irritation, his *agi*tation, all of it resonated with the truth.

It gave me the confidence to state, "You made the offer, Hawk, not me..."

"My dick gets me into trouble sometimes, but yeah, I made the offer, and if you're sure you're okay with it, then it stands."

Dipping my chin, I got to my feet and said, "I'd like to feel pleasure now."

THREE

HAWK

I WONDERED if she knew how regal she sounded as she made what might as well have been a royal decree.

Even as I grinned to myself over her imperious tone, a part of me was nervous. I'd made the offer on a whim, thinking that she'd never say yes. Yet, here she was, saying exactly that.

What the fuck had she seen when she was perving over Nyx and Giulia?

I sure as shit didn't want to know, not the details, I mean, she was my fucking sister, for Christ's sake. Only the fact that Nyx was a crazy cunt made it so that I never bitched at him or sniped over the noises that filtered out of their goddamn bedroom.

I'd heard mating cats sound less frenzied than those two, which was already a level of TMI I didn't even want to go into.

But whatever it was she'd seen, they were definitely the reason behind Amara saying yes.

I wasn't exactly a manwhore, but I didn't think much about random hook ups, and was more than willing to pull my dick out to any chick who asked for it. This, unfortunately, wasn't like that. Amara wasn't a random hook up. She was damaged. Not that that took away from how beautiful or sexy she was to me, it just meant that this had the possibility of going downhill fast.

I was either going to end up being bitten and slapped, kneed in the balls, or getting the shit kicked out of me by Nyx because if Amara was upset, even though things were strained between her and Giulia now my sis was aware of her crush, Giulia would sic her Old Man on me in a heartbeat.

Fun stuff.

Hiding a grimace in case she thought it was aimed at what I was about to do, I got to my feet and asked, "Your room or mine?"

She tilted her head to the side as she contemplated the answer to that question. "When was the last time you changed your sheets?"

My lips twitched. "Good question."

"Does that mean you do not know the answer."

"It does," I confirmed dryly.

Her nose crinkled. "That's disgusting."

It was, I agreed, but to be honest, I'd been in a funk of late. The only thing that had broken me out of it was seeing Giulia's Posse hovering around Amara like they were vultures and she was fresh roadkill.

I didn't want to question *why* that was. How she could make me forget that North had, effectively, abandoned me.

After thirty years glued to each other's sides, he'd just gone. Left me like I was so much trash. Never thinking to tell me about his affair with our stepmother, never thinking to tell me that he was leaving for good. I got *why* he hadn't, because I'd have slapped him upside the head and asked him what the fuck he was thinking. But still, we were twins.

Wombmates.

That went deeper than any other fucking bond—just not to North.

And that betrayal stung.

It stung hard.

Then there was Dad's death.

The mystery around it.

I was pretty sure the council knew who was behind his murder, and that it wasn't North like some in the MC were whispering, because otherwise, they'd have triggered a war over it, or at least got up in the sheriff's face. But they'd done neither.

That meant they knew who the real culprit was, and they didn't think to tell me, his son. His fucking son.

Giulia had always hated Dad, so I couldn't even put pressure on her to find out from the council who was behind his death, but still, the double hit to the gut was difficult to get over.

The pain of loss, even if one was far less permanent than the other, had seen me getting drunk a lot, becoming a bar fly when, before, though I'd always enjoyed drinking with my brothers, it had never been at the top of my daily agenda.

Until now.

Working a few random shifts at the MC's bar on top of my regular job at the strip joint as a bouncer wasn't helping either.

Amara pulled a face. "If you haven't changed the sheets, then we can use mine. At least my bed is clean." She flicked her wrist, and that was when I saw the brand there.

The fuckers had marked her.

It shouldn't have come as a surprise, but it did.

I didn't excuse myself for being gross, because seeing that robbed me of my thoughts, I just let her lead the way as we left the porch and headed into the house itself.

Whatever the MC was paying Rachel, it was evidently big bucks. Why she'd chosen to live so close to the compound was a mystery, because having seen her and Rex interact now that he was back from the hospital, at least, some of the time, it was clear they didn't get along. That she stuck close by was confusing, but women often were, weren't they?

Look at Amara. I'd been chivalrous, never thinking she'd take me up on the offer, but look at her go. One growl coming up...

The hall contained an antique grandfather clock that drove me insane because it chimed every fucking fifteen minutes, and donged at the top of the hour. If I could have driven a sledgehammer through it, I would have, but as it stood, we were here by invitation only—I wasn't that bad a guest where I was going to destroy something that made me want to deafen myself every time its bells rang throughout the house.

There were some other antique pieces, a few that reminded me of a grandmother's house, when Rachel was anything but—GILFs were one thing, but Rachel was hot as fuck with that uptight way she had about her. You just knew a chick like that was going to be nasty in the sack.

Because the holiday season was in full swing, Rachel had put up decs too.

From the front door, the staircase was straight up ahead, and each newel post had carvings on it as well as festive wreaths looped around them. Ivy and birds entwined each stand, making me think she'd had them imported from England or someplace, because it reminded me of something you'd see in one of those Jane Austen movies.

Mom had always loved that shit, so much so she knew all the words to *Emma* and *Pride and Prejudice*, which meant I knew a lot more about antique architecture than I wanted to. Well, as period as the TV ever got.

My lips quirked up a little with the memories of her being glued to the TV like each time she watched it was the first.

Grief had etched its path on my heart when she died, but the etchings had turned into engravings when Dad had passed on as well.

I thought we were all way too young to have lost both of our folks, but that was life, wasn't it? Had a way of kicking you in the balls when you were already on your knees.

Passing a Christmas tree that was lit up even though it was early in the day, I trudged after Amara, eyes on my boots, trying to think about how I'd approach this. Would she let me kiss her? I had to finger her, or lick her pussy—I mean, I was a magician in the sack, but getting her off without touching her was impossible. She had to recognize that some touch was necessary, right?

Mind whirring with thoughts I didn't figure I'd need to think today after a long night at work, I followed her to her room. The second we made it inside, I cast a glance around and found the connecting bath.

Going in there without asking, I shucked out of my boots and socks, proceeded to wash up, before I headed back to the door with a towel in hand, only to find Amara standing there, looking at me with big doe eyes that made me think she was regretting this.

Then, of course, she decided to stun the shit out of me by reaching for the hem of her baggy sweater and throwing it overhead. Underneath, she wore a lacy camisole that showed off her tits. They were already on the generous side but when she gained some more weight, they'd be Sports' Illustrated-worthy.

About ten more pounds, and she'd be there, so that told me that for all she was melancholic by nature—understandable—she wasn't suicidal. Not like her earlier statement had led me to believe.

Relieved because she was clearly eating, I watched as she stripped out of the cami as well, then unfastened the button on her fly and that was when I asked, "You okay with me kissing you? Touching you with my fingers?"

She stilled, her head tipping to the side. "I have had sex before. I know some touch is required."

That was a kind of non-answer. "What about kissing?"

Her shrug told me she'd never had a really great kiss before. "If you must."

If I must...

My mouth quirked into a smile which died a death when she shoved down her pants and panties at the same time, revealing a bare pussy that I was about to have access to. Not full access, granted, but some of it was better than nothing.

"I am clean," she said woodenly. "In case you were worried about me being diseased. Stone tested us before. I—" She cleared her throat.

"I know we aren't... I mean, I know we're not going to sleep together, but I'm also on the pill."

The way she talked about herself worried me more than her being 'diseased' did.

"I'm clean too. I never fuck without a rubber." Her words made me curious—as well as annoyed on her behalf. *Diseased.* Jesus. "Are you taking the pill because you want to have sex eventually?"

Her cheeks turned pink. "That time when..." She frowned. "There is blood?"

"A period," I said.

She nodded. "It is painful. Stone gave me the pill and said it would ease the pain and stop me getting pregnant."

"Good to know," I murmured. "Does it?"

"Does it what?"

"Stop the pain?"

"Yes."

"Then, I'm glad." She didn't deserve to suffer a moment more for the rest of her goddamn life.

My reply surprised her into biting her lip again, and I tossed the towel in my hands over my shoulder because they were dry now as I moved deeper into the room. She tensed with every step I took, so I veered toward the bed, even as I was wondering if both of us were insane to think about doing anything like this.

Talk about a time bomb waiting to explode...

Mom always said I was reckless by nature. I'd just never thought I had a death wish too.

Aware I had a beating from Nyx in my future, and fully embracing it, I clambered onto the bed, and lay flat out on it.

She eyed me with confusion, but it didn't stop her from tilting toward me, her tension draining out of her now that I didn't present a threat.

Of course, she wasn't to know that any man could be as threatening on his feet as he was on his back... Although, I guessed, if any woman *was* aware of that, it'd be her.

She hadn't needed to strip off, could have stayed in her sweater, and that she hadn't, told me a lot about her. Amara had an ease with her body that spoke of her being more accustomed to nudity than being clothed, which made any potential erection that may or may not have been in the making now that I'd seen her pussy, wither away like a cucumber shoved into a jar of vinegar.

I'd expected her to be shy and fumbling, but she wasn't. This was normal for her. Uncomfortable sexual scenarios were her norm, and she was only doing this because of whatever she'd seen Giulia experience.

Knowing this chick needed a shrink made me regret the offer again, but now I was here, and she was undressed for the task, I rasped, "Climb on my face."

She blinked at me, but stepped nearer to the bed, then placed one knee at my shoulder, before cocking her leg and pinning me there too.

"I'm gonna touch your ass," I warned her, grabbing her butt and moving her so that she was closer and I didn't have to strain my neck. The tension in her legs told me that she was holding herself off, so I informed her, "Little bird, the most honorable way for a man to die would be via suffocation in a woman's cunt. News of that kind of death would travel far and wide." I grinned at her, hoping it would lighten the severity of her expression.

It didn't work.

If anything, she frowned harder.

But her concession was to relax, to do as I asked—shove her pussy right into my face.

Not messing around, I sucked her off, plying her clit with my tongue. Mostly, I wanted to grab her tits, play with her nipples, but I was making a point here, even if she wasn't to know that yet.

I figured if we got the most invasive part out of the way, she'd get frustrated when it didn't work. Chicks weren't like dicks, were they? Took a lot more to get them off than just sucking them down and swallowing them whole.

I kept my tongue stiff enough that as I slipped it through the folds of her sex, I knew she'd get whispers of pleasure. I focused on her clit mostly, sometimes circling her hole and letting it dart inside. As I thought, every time I did that, she tensed up, and I needed her not to be like that. I needed her to be pliant in my arms or we'd never get anywhere.

When she let her hips rock that first time, I wanted to howl with relief because, shit, my tongue was not only aching, it meant my doofus plan had worked.

If I was gonna get my ass handed to me by the psychotic VP of the club, then it had better be worth it in the end.

A grunt escaped her as she finally touched me—her hands coming to press against my stomach as she leaned back and started to squirm. When she rocked against my face, I tasted the real her, not just the slickness from my tongue, and felt even more triumph whirl through me.

As she got hotter, she got a little less inhibited, and her fingers started to press into my abs, each tip depressing slightly harder than the others as she kneaded me there, her fingers acting of their own volition as the need to touch and be touched worked against her.

I didn't need her to touch me, but I needed her to be into it, because otherwise, the pleasure she eventually received would be skim milk. It wouldn't be delicious fucking cream.

When she started to grind into me, I knew I was almost there, and a scant few minutes later, she groaned, "Hawk, help me."

I smirked and gave her clit a final kiss before I let my fingers grip her hips and urge her higher so I could talk without a mouthful of her pussy lips in my way. "You relaxed some?"

She tensed. "What?"

"I said, are you relaxed some?"

"Some what?"

Grinning, I shook my head as I leaned up and sucked on her clit. She yelped. So far I'd been ungenerous with the sucking action. "You want an English lesson or an orgasm?"

"A-An orgasm," she whispered.

I hummed in satisfaction, then said, "Lie on the bed." I slapped her ass lightly when she stayed in place, murmuring, "I won't hurt you."

"N-No, I know you won't." Though she'd stuttered at the start, I didn't take any offense because I heard the truth in her voice—she really wasn't scared of me.

Good. Fear and orgasms didn't go hand in hand. Not in my experience, at any rate.

When she slowly clambered off me, her movements weren't as edgy as before. When I rolled up on my hands so I could peer down at her, spying her naked form against the turquoise sheets with silver detailing around a bunch of flowers, a stupid thought occurred to me.

I'd like to see her in a field of wildflowers.

I'd like to see her naked, her legs spread, her face flushed with pleasure, no nerves, no tension, just a need for me etched into her features.

See? Stupid.

My imagination, goddamn its hide, running away with me.

But she looked beautiful. The rich turquoise seemed to make her pale olive skin all the more golden, and it highlighted her coloring, making her seem as much of a jewel against the sheets as the hue that brought her alive with its vibrancy.

Spying those flushed cheeks, her dazed eyes, the little quiver to her tits as they wobbled when she breathed, I reached down and circled a finger around the tip of one. They were big enough to sag into her armpits and curiosity had me asking, "Must have been hard dancing with these titties."

She blinked. "I bound—" she gasped when I rubbed one of the nips between my forefinger and thumb. "—them," she ended on a sigh.

Wincing, I mumbled, "Fucking tragedy."

"Why?"

"Binding tits like these. Crime," I grunted, before I dropped my head and let my mouth circle the tip I'd been teasing.

"That's why I don't wear bras now," she said on a sigh as her fingers came up to my hair, her nails dragging over my skull, sending a lot of my personal pleasure hotspots zinging to life.

With a groan that I knew would vibrate around her nipple, I raked the tip between my teeth, sucking hard on it before I bit it. She whimpered in surprise, not in fear, so I did it again.

Because of her triggers, it didn't take a fucking rocket scientist to figure out that her pain threshold would be higher than most, so I kept it light. No way did I want her to associate this with those other times.

If this was going to be her one good memory of sex, it had to be phenomenal. No bad, only pleasure.

Releasing her nipple, I started to mouth my way up over to her chest, nuzzling my face in her throat, sucking and nipping there too. When she shivered beneath me, her body wriggling against the sheets, I smiled to myself, satisfied that she was all-in by this point. I lashed at the place where neck met shoulder, bit her earlobe which made her jerk like I'd spanked her, then moved along her jaw so that our mouths could finally meet.

When they did, I supped from her.

Carefully.

Gently.

I'd never been a careful or gentle person before. Especially not in the sack. But if this was going to be her first decent kiss after the nightmare she'd gone through, I wanted it to be memorable too.

I kissed her like I'd seen that Darcy dude kiss Lizzie Bennett in *Pride and Prejudice*, I was careful and gentle, until her nails dug into my skull and she urged me into more.

Whether she knew it or not, I was listening to her body, to her reactions, because she was a 'no entry' zone just waiting to happen, and I didn't want to do anything that would upset her. That was the opposite of my intentions.

When she dug her claws into me though, I slipped my tongue against hers, and wished like fuck I could roll between her legs and rock my dick against her cunt, but that wasn't to be. Instead, I slipped my hand there, letting my fingertips find her clit.

It was only then that I saw the tragedy for what it was—she'd been unschooled in the art of kissing. Not only a virgin, but unkissed too before she'd been taken.

God.

If I could kill the Sparrow bastards who were behind this global ring of sex traffickers, I would have done it.

More attentive than I'd ever been to a lesson in my life, I taught her what to do, how to kiss, how to savor, how to enjoy.

As I rubbed her clit, she got deeper into it, her pleasure starting to crest as her movements grew sloppy, and she began writhing against the sheets. I moved my hand, letting my thumb graze her clit instead so I could thrust two fingers into her. She wasn't tight, because even though she felt like a virgin, she wasn't, so I slipped another one inside to give her the fullness she'd need, and hooked my fingers against the front wall of her cunt.

When she gasped into my mouth, her head fell back, our lips breaking apart as she gulped down air and started to ride my hand like it was my dick, her hips bucking, her legs spreading wider as she sought her pleasure.

A shriek escaped her, followed by some of the sexiest fucking moans I'd ever heard in my life as she came. She was noisy. Noisier than I'd have imagined. The guttural sounds went straight to my dick and I buried my face in her throat, sucking hard on her there, hard enough to leave a hickey as she rode her way through her first orgasm.

When she sagged into the bed, her arms spent, I rumbled, "I told you you wouldn't be a growler."

For a second, she tensed, and then she giggled.

It was the most light-hearted sound I'd ever heard her make. So loaded down with her youth that, for a second, I was reminded of the fact she was young. So fucking young.

"How old are you, Amara?" I asked softly, curious and wanting to know more about her.

"Twenty-one," she answered on a sigh, one that was loaded with redolence, like a cat who was purring now it had knocked over a carton of milk and had lapped it all up.

Twenty-one? I hadn't realized she was that young. Fuck, when had they taken her? Before she was legal? Those sick cunts would have probably earned a better price out of her that way.

Sadness filled me, enough for me to utter the unthinkable, "You want another orgasm, you come to me, okay? I got your back."

She stilled, not like before, not with fear or tension, but with surprise. I knew the difference—that was how much I'd been watching her recently. "I thought this was a one-time thing?"

So had I.

I replied with a non-committal grunt, before I told her, "It's an 'as many times as you want' kind of thing."

Amara went quiet, then after a few minutes, whispered, "Thank you, Hawk."

"You're welcome," I said gruffly, pressing a kiss to her shoulder and savoring her taste before I had to walk away so I could go jack off in my bathroom to thoughts of what I'd just done.

My dick wasn't happy about the offer, wasn't happy that my fist was going to provide me with relief from enjoying her orgasm, but hell, what was I supposed to do other than eradicate every goddamn memory she had by replacing the shitty experiences with pleasurable ones?

And they said chivalry was fucking dead.

FOUR

AMARA

TWO DAYS LATER

I SQUINTED at the sun that speared its way through the drapes, landing right on my face as if it were insistent I wake up.

Considering I'd closed them last night, fully, I wasn't sure how any light was getting in at all, but with a groan, I opened my eyes, and stared at the two-inch gap that was the reason I was awake.

Letting my forearm fall over my face, my mind drifted, unerringly finding and digging into my actions this morning.

Hawk's shifts were late. He either rolled in smelling of perfume from his job as a bouncer at the MC's strip joint, or beer and cigarettes from his time at the bar. I'd been awake at the time, mostly because I didn't sleep much, but also because I'd been waiting up for him. That had nothing to do with what he'd done for me, just a force of habit that wasn't going anywhere fast.

When I heard the gates open, I'd tucked myself in the corner of the porch, knowing he wouldn't see me, and I'd watched him climb up the stairs, stretching and yawning as he moved, before he headed inside.

A part of me had wanted to call out to him. Another part had wanted to stay silent.

That final part had won.

I'd stayed tucked in my corner, the chilly night air making me shiver as I stared out into the nothingness of the dark. Though cold, as winter was approaching, I'd felt somewhat at ease once he was back. With Hawk home, that meant everyone was tucked up in their beds, and that gave me a semblance of peace, enough that I could finally get to sleep.

I always knew where most people in the house were or were supposed to be. It was a trait I'd formed with my second-to-last owners. For a year, I'd been locked in their house. I'd slept in the basement where they'd visit me, but I was allowed out to clean the rest of the place. Knowing who was at home meant that I could prepare myself for whatever they'd put me through next.

Mrs. Sandra had been more aggressive than Mr. Jason, so I'd always been more on edge with her at the house. Knowing who was lurking around the next corner had been a case of forewarned being forearmed.

Not that I'd been able to defend myself when I was wearing shackles, but still, it had helped stop the panic attacks they'd beaten me over.

As a result, I knew that today was a Friday, and I'd heard Rachel and Keira talking about how, today, the teachers were having something they called a 'staff development' day, which meant Rain and Cyan would be at home as school wasn't on, Keira would be working a shift at the diner, Rex would likely be at the hospital, and Rachel would be in her office as she worked every day, not just weekdays.

Giulia and Nyx were harder to keep track of, but with the sun as high as it was, I'd hazard a guess and say she might be at the tattoo parlor where she'd recently gotten a job. As for Nyx, I had no way of knowing his location for sure.

Hawk, I imagined, would be in his bed.

Had he changed his sheets yet?

I was used to sweat-stained, urine-soaked bed linen, but ever since the Sinners had saved us, I'd grown accustomed to being clean.

I liked the soft sheets, the gently perfumed scents that permeated every breath I took when I rolled onto my side as I tried to get to sleep. It wasn't anything special to most, but a small luxury to me.

Did he sleep naked?

Wear boxer briefs to cover himself up?

Was he a bed hog? Did he sleep light or heavy?

I had a million questions that I knew he'd answer, but I didn't dare ask them. I didn't want to want to know, but equally, I did.

It was confusing.

Hawk was confusing.

Months of watching him around the compound, of seeing his gruff resolve as he waded through the shitty jobs the MC had for him as a Prospect, watching that bullheadedness as he broke the rules by fucking any and every clubwhore who came onto him even though they were supposed to be for the brothers only, seeing him interact with his family… I wasn't sure if he knew how much I'd learned about him over my time at the Sinners' clubhouse.

Hawk was reliable.

Fierce.

Unafraid to stand his ground.

Loyal to the Sinners.

Still, when he'd stormed into the kitchen to find Alessa holding my hair in her fist as she slammed me into the tabletop, I'd been surprised by his defense of me. Surprised and warmed.

No one ever defended me.

Not once in my whole life.

It was… different.

Pleasant.

A change of pace.

Rubbing the love bite he'd left me, I thought about what he'd done to me two days ago. What he'd said. What he'd offered, and I knew that one of the main reasons I'd stayed outside instead of waiting for him inside, was because I'd wanted to take him up on his promise. Freezing myself in the cold had been the only way to keep my new desires at bay.

A sigh escaped me at the thought of what he'd made me feel, and when I experienced no revulsion or lingering disgust, I sighed again.

It was nice not to hate myself so soon after waking up.

A vibration buzzed from the yard, and a clicking sound promptly followed. I recognized both sounds as coming from the automatic gates. Curious as to who had opened them, I clambered off the bed and onto my feet. Squinting through the gap in the drapes, I frowned when I saw a vehicle I didn't recognize pulling into the driveway.

A few seconds later, Keira and Storm's daughter, Cyan, darted out, a bag on her back as she ran toward the car. It was heavy, whatever it was she carried, because she grunted and pulled a face when she let it fall from her shoulders and after she opened the door, hefted it into the backseat.

I stared at the man behind the wheel, well, the little I could see, and didn't recognize him. His jaw and mouth were visible, but they only told me that he wasn't young. His chin was drooping a little, the fleshy parts sagging, which told me he was maybe in his fifties. There weren't many brothers around that age, a couple in their sixties, but they had big, bushy beards like *Svyatyy Mykolay*, St. Nicholas. This one was clean shaven.

Once the bag was deposited safely, she dragged open the passenger door, jumped in, and the car took off.

Strange.

As I watched the dust plume and surge, rising in a wave once the wheels hit the sandy road, a few seconds later, I heard the rumbling of a bike as it was kicked into gear, and then I saw the thin shoulders of someone who could only be Rain, Rachel's brother.

What the hell was happening?

An uneasy feeling filled me as I stepped away from the window, one that had me ignoring my semi-urgent need to use the bathroom, and twisting around to grab the burner cell that Giulia had given me a couple of weeks ago. I palmed it for a moment, wondering if there was someone I should tell about what I'd seen.

I started to second-guess myself. Was what I'd seen that unusual?

For Cyan to be picked up? She had extra-curricular activities, so maybe it was her coach?

But... I'd know if she had a coach. I listened in to most conversations in the house. Knew a lot about Rachel's work for the MC as a result, was aware of the arguments Keira and Storm were having as they tried to steer their new normal, and knew that one of the clubwhores who'd helped betray the Sinners was being hunted down by the council.

What I also knew was something the MC wasn't broadcasting—Cyan was being groomed.

I gnawed on my bottom lip as I thought about the discussion I'd heard as the brothers attended what they called 'church.' They'd discussed things I shouldn't know about, things that I could go to the police over, but the police weren't my friends. The Sinners weren't either, not really, but they hadn't hurt me like the law had.

The law, after all, had owned me.

In church, the men had spoken of Nyx's haunted path as he destroyed pedophiles.

They'd spoken of Cyan and her being targeted by one such monster.

They'd spoken of many other things too where my English had failed me, but as I watched the car and Rain's bike in the distance down the drive, I had the nastiest feeling that the council's discussion and what I'd just witnessed were linked.

And I listened to those feelings.

My instinct, my gut, had saved me far too many times to count.

Because I had no idea where they were going, I rushed to the bathroom and quickly used it. Dragging on a hoodie that I'd left on the chair in my room, I pushed my feet into the slip-on sandals I wore around the house, uncaring that I'd be cold as I raced out of the room, down the stairs, and into the hall where I rummaged through the small unit that Rachel had beside the front door where she hung her keys.

It was wrong to steal a set, but the urgency in my being wouldn't be denied. Promising myself that I'd apologize later if I'd made a mistake about Cyan, I grabbed the fob to the SUV I knew she drove, hurried outside, hit the button, and practically leapt behind the wheel.

With the gates still open, I could speed down the drive, and I hit the accelerator, traveling far too fast because I was very much aware that I might already have lost them. That my prevaricating had done nothing other than waste time.

The road was bendy and dusty, making visibility low and danger high especially as it was a one-way track. If another car came up this way, I could crash into them, but fortune was on my side. In more ways than one.

There was a slight incline as I approached the clubhouse, which let me see down the way, and even though the car was out of sight, Rain's bike wasn't.

Pressing my foot to the floor, I sped down the road, and as I made it to the turn-off, I found Rain in the distance again.

With him tailing Cyan and whoever the hell was driving, I knew that as long as he didn't lose her, I was good.

I had no idea where we were going, no idea why, but I knew one thing only—the sun had woken me up this morning for a reason. The drapes, which had been closed last night, had been open for a purpose. Both of which, I had the feeling, was so that I could share this journey with the MC's youngsters.

FIVE

QUIN

I STARED at the ceiling overhead as it rushed past me. It was like those time-lapse sequences you saw on the TV. Where the camera stood still and life went on around it.

That was me.

Except, I wasn't sure if I was dead or not.

Would I hurt if I was dead?

I could feel where the bastard had shivved me. Could feel it, and it hurt.

Badly.

So badly in fact that I gasped, and began writhing around on the gurney I was on. When a hand clamped down on my arm, I heard a slight rattle, and was reminded that I wasn't a free man yet.

My brother, Nyx, had come through for me.

He'd managed to get me out of Rikers ahead of schedule with a pardon from the governor scheduled to be announced within the week, but apparently, that schedule didn't match up with someone else's.

Someone who wanted me dead.

Someone who didn't want me on the outside.

What did I know that was worth killing over?

In all honesty, I wasn't sure.

Truly.

I was only twenty-two, and the last time I'd seen the outside world, I hadn't been able to legally drink. I literally knew nothing, so what could be worth killing me over?

That rattle of the handcuffs cemented the fact that I wasn't a free man, and that, if this wound had its way, I never would be either.

Tears leaked from the corners of my eyes as I thought about all the things I'd wanted to do, all the shit I'd wanted to achieve, but as powerful a motivator as the loss of those dreams was, I couldn't will my heart to stop pumping blood out of an open wound.

Dreams weren't Gorilla glue.

They would only keep you going for so long.

"*She's coming.*"

The voice sent a shiver down my spine.

"*Your sky girl needs you. Hold on for her. She needs you.*"

The lights began to blur overhead and I felt the pressure on my wound change, lessening some as I heard the buzzers sounding when the endless reel of locks were activated.

Sky girl.

My dream girl.

The only person who'd never left me.

Memories of her hand on my cheek, a hand that was connected to a body I never saw, lips that kissed my temple, connected to a face I didn't know, bombarded me but I felt myself drifting even as the fresh air hit my cheeks, scalding me awake with all the bitterness of a New York day in the fall that was edging toward winter.

I shuddered as the gurney connected with something, sending pain spiraling through me, hands shifted, shuffling along the railings, moving all around me. The sky appeared, bright blue with little dots of birds as they soared and swirled around in mid-flight, possessing a freedom that no human would ever know. Two loud squawks snagged my attention, and I frowned, seeing big bewinged blots tumbling around in the sky...

What did that remind me of?

My eyelashes fluttered.

My vision quest.

The buzzard and the hawk.

A blur of faces took over from the lights and the sky, shielding the birds from my sight, and I recognized the furrowed brows of people who were going to work hard to heal me.

"Take those fucking cuffs off," someone growled, and, magically, someone else obeyed.

I felt my arms being freed and moved to lie at my sides, but the rest of the words that spun into being might as well have been *Omàmiwininimowin*, the native tongue of my people and a language I'd never really managed to learn, for all I recognized.

I could feel myself fading as the gurney collided with an ambulance, so much so that when the vehicle surged into action, and the lights and sirens stirred into being, I didn't hear it, didn't see it, and didn't sense it either.

Blackness overtook me, and I didn't even have the strength to care whether that was for the best or not.

SIX

REX

"WHERE THE FUCK IS HE?"

At my side, Sin growled out the question, his hands furling into tight fists as he watched me ringing Storm's phone number—yet again.

The bastard was glued to his cellphone, so where the fuck he was, I didn't know. I'd been ringing him non-stop ever since Rain had called me, telling me Cyan, Storm's kid, had gotten into some strange fucker's car back at Rachel's house.

This was not the moment for Storm to be MIA.

"I don't know," I rumbled under my breath, but a few seconds later, I got another message from Rain. Seeing he'd sent his live location, I shared that text with the rest of the council, and told Sin, "Instead of bitching about this, go after them. You have to haul ass. They're making good time."

"Got it," Sin rumbled, pounding his fist into his palm with relief now that I'd let him loose.

"Watch your temper, Sin," I drawled as he started to stride off.

He twisted around. "Why? Fucker deserves a beating."

"Don't want you in jail. Not now that they've crossed over the state line."

His mouth twisted into a sneer, but he dipped his chin in agreement as he started to run across the road to the parking lot where our temporary bikes were parked.

Fuck, why was nothing easy in this life?

My dad was in the hospital, and I'd stopped off at the MC-owned diner for some fucking eggs over easy with sausage links and hot cakes. I'd wanted some calm before the storm of sitting with my father, watching him fade away before my fucking eyes.

Instead, we had chaos.

As per fucking usual.

Rubbing a hand over my face, I eyed the little marker on the map while my cell was trying to call Storm, wincing at how long it had taken Rain to ring us, even as I was grateful he'd managed to get the message out, period.

I knew for a fact he was new to riding on the back of a hog, and was well aware Rachel wasn't happy about it because she'd bitched at me for being a bad influence. He'd saved up his own money for a long ass time to get the damn thing, so she couldn't gripe at him too hard, and moaned at me instead.

Still, riding one-handed wasn't easy at first, not with a bike that size, and he'd taken a risk to send out the SOS so I couldn't be ungrateful. And I wasn't. I was just nervous.

They were over an hour away, and while Sin would break the speed limits to follow the fucker who thought he could take one of our own, it wasn't like he could travel faster than the speed of fucking sound.

By the time Sin caught up with the cunt, they might already have stopped and he could *already* have done a million horrendous things to Storm's baby girl.

Jaw tense, I carried on watching the dots, and knew that I couldn't keep this much longer from Keira, Cyan's mom. She was working a shift in the diner, and the only reason she wasn't in the loop already was because, as luck would have it, Rain had called as I was making my way out.

What with Maverick and Alessa on their knees on the sidewalk still, her cradling him as he got over another attack with his CTE, I hadn't needed to add to the drama of the moment by getting her involved.

I'd hoped that her fucking husband could be the one to break this shit to her, but it looked like it would be on me seeing as he'd ignored thirteen of my calls.

Sucking in a breath, I muttered, "Mav, you need to get off the sidewalk, buddy."

He shot me a look so redolent with feeling that it was a kick to the gut. I wasn't used to him emoting as much as he had done ever since shit had gone to shit and he'd been diagnosed with brain trauma so grave it could and would affect his memory at any time. Meeting, falling for, and marrying Alessa had changed him, but the chaos in his eyes reflected the havoc in my soul.

Maverick always had felt too much, which was why he'd worked hard to clamp down on all his emotions when he'd joined the army. The CTE, his new wife, and the craziness of our world right now were tearing down his walls.

Mine too if I was being honest.

Mine, fucking, too.

Blowing out a breath, I raised the phone to my mouth, deciding to leave a message now I knew Storm really wasn't going to answer.

"Get your ass to Rachel's place. Cyan's been kidnapped. I thought you'd want to know—maybe I was wrong. What the fuck, man? Answer your phone the next time I goddamn ring you."

Everyone knew to answer when I called. It was a fucking law in the MC's handbook. Along with bang as many chicks as you want once you're a brother, and if you get caught by the cops, keep your fucking mouth shut.

As I disconnected the call, I dug my thumbs into my eyes,

rubbing hard as I tried to prepare myself for the shitstorm that was about to hit.

Of course, life could never be that simple.

One hand on the diner's door as I prepared for the fallout of sharing the news with Keira, my cellphone buzzed again.

Scowling, I stared down at it, and caught a glimpse of a name on the Caller ID that I rarely saw.

Brows high, I lifted my cell to my ear because this was not a conversation I needed to have in public, and asked, "Is everything okay, Mr. O'Donnelly?"

SEVEN

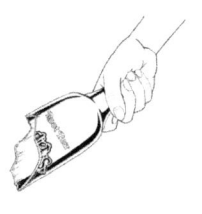

AMARA

I'D NEVER UNDERSTAND these roads.

Highways, and interstates, and beltways.

I'd seen a ton of names but didn't really know where I was going, was just following Rain, grateful for his direction.

I even went so far as to monitor when he turned his flashers on because it had been a very long time since I'd driven. Too long. And it felt good to be back behind the wheel, good to know that I could go anywhere, had the freedom of time on my hands and no one who gave a damn about me to hold me back, to keep me in one place.

Of course, that didn't explain why I was haring off after a little girl who meant nothing to me in the grand scheme of things.

She was a stranger to me, as was I to her. I just lived under the same roof as her, we shared a kitchen, and my bedroom and hers backed onto one another.

The MC meant nothing to me either. I was grateful for what they'd done for me, for us, and I was relieved to be free of the nightmare of my history, but I didn't feel beholden to them. At least, I didn't think I felt that way. I wasn't even sure why I was still hanging around, why I hadn't taken off in the middle of the night to make my own path.

They owed me nothing, but I... well, maybe I did. They'd never asked me for anything, didn't even ask me to help clean up around the place. I was a little like a lost pair of socks that were forgotten, but remained drifting under the bed until someone found them.

Not many people even spoke to me all that much. Even before she'd found out I had feelings for her, Giulia was busy with her life, so she didn't have time for me anymore, and now she did know about my crush, she avoided me like the plague.

When the compound had burned down and Tatána had perished in its flames, Alessa had moved to Lily's home, and I'd gone to Rachel's. Ever since then, the group therapy sessions with Tiffany had been canceled, and I hadn't spoken to anyone in-depth apart from Rachel, regarding my immigration status, and Hawk.

What a time to realize how lonely I was.

What a time to realize that, for all I wanted to be out on this open road, for all that I wished for the freedom to do as I wanted, to be me with no expectations, with no one knowing about my past, judging me and pitying me with every glance, *I wanted to belong.*

The ache was strong, and it wasn't just in my heart, but in my stomach and in my head too.

I wanted what Alessa had found with Maverick, even if their path was bound to be difficult thanks to his condition.

Tak, I wanted to belong.

Throat thick with tears, my eyes blurred, and I quickly swiped at them, not needing my attention to shift when I had to concentrate on not crashing. Rain was a child, still. Cyan was practically a baby. They needed my help. They needed me not to smash the damn car before I got anywhere near them.

I sucked in a breath as Rain started to slow down, his brake lights flashing on. The other car was too far in the distance for me to see, but I followed Rain's directions, and began reducing my speed as well.

We'd crossed state lines and were deeper into Pennsylvania than I'd like. There'd been signs for a place called Allentown for the past ten minutes, and it looked as if that was where we were pulling off.

As I followed Rain, I saw his driving change, turn erratic as he started to sway on the road. It wasn't difficult to figure out why—he was looking for the car.

He'd lost them.

"*Pizda rulu!*" I snarled under my breath.

It wasn't like I could fault him, though. *Bozhe moy*, he was a kid, and I wasn't much better at trailing people. Neither of us were trained for this kind of thing. That we'd managed to make it this far was a miracle.

Praying that he'd taken this turn off for a reason, I hoped it wasn't wishful thinking on his part that Cyan's kidnapper had come here. Although, what there was about Allentown, PA, that represented wishful thinking to an eighteen-year-old, I had no idea.

Hands tightening about the wheel, I watched his head whip from side to side, wincing as the bike moved with him. He was going to end up crashing if he wasn't careful. Didn't he realize that he was putting himself in danger?

I bit my bottom lip, gnawing hard on it as I stopped watching him because he was making me nervous. Instead, as I rode into the city limits, I started scanning for places that might appeal to whoever it was that had taken Cyan.

A motel?

We hadn't been driving for that long, so it wasn't like they'd need a break, but I knew men like this *pederasti*. They were impatient. Volatile. Quick to temper when they couldn't get their own way.

This *suka* had snatched Cyan, and he'd be riding the high of that. He'd be loaded down with triumph that was soaked in adrenaline, and he'd want to take immediate advantage of his situation and play with his new toy.

My stomach churned at the thought, everything inside me

praying that we weren't too late, that Rain hadn't made a mistake by taking this turn off.

It was by accident that I saw the small sign for the motel that led off the main drag. It was broken, which was why I thought Rain hadn't seen it in his panic, and half of it was hanging on by a thread that flapped in the wind. Fate had let it rise up under a gust of air, just long enough for me to get a glimpse at the sign.

It was bright yellow with green lettering and declared to the world—Dun Roamin' Motel.

Nerves hit me again as I hoped I wasn't making a massive mistake by letting my link with Rain die, and I turned off, heading down some bendy roads that were sign-posted too.

It felt like a lifetime until I reached the building itself, and when I saw it, the grimy walls, the Christmas lights which looked as if they had been there for the last thirty years, the dirty parking lot which had trash everywhere, a low, distressed wail escaped me when I didn't see any cars.

Then I turned around another bend.

And it was there.

The strange hybrid of truck and SUV.

A silvery blue color.

Old, definitely not new, but not a clunker either.

I gulped when I realized I'd found them, but it was nausea that had me almost crashing into the posts that stood either side of the driveway entrance when I took the turning into the lot.

The motel was a lurid pink that had faded in parts so it looked more like blotchy skin with a tendency for acne, and around each window, of which there were many, there was a square block of bright yellow paint. Whoever had painted this place either had no eye for color or these had been the cheapest options from the store.

Pulling up, I raced out of the car, leaving the engine running and not even bothering to close the door behind me. Tilting my head back, I let my gaze scan the row of windows as I tried to find where Cyan might be being kept.

Parked vehicles didn't correspond to a certain room, unfortunately, because where the truck was parked, the door was open and there was a cleaning cart outside. I could even hear the housekeeper humming as she worked.

There were three floors, each with an open walkway so you could see the doors and the windows from the road. All of the curtains were open—except for one set.

My heart quickened at the sight. It might be nothing, could mean that a weary traveler was taking some time to sleep before they took off again on the road, but it was nearly three PM by this point. Did people sleep during the day when they were driving? Wasn't it more common to try to travel with the light?

Deciding that instinct and my gut had gotten me this far, I rushed over toward the staircase just as the housekeeper started singing, and darted up the steps toward the second-floor room I hoped Cyan was in.

About twenty feet from the door, relief and dread filled me as a cry seemed to pierce my very soul.

It came from the room.

It sounded young. More of a warble than a full-throated scream, and I knew, like always where my instincts were concerned, I'd been right.

I nearly collided with the door in my haste to reach it, and when I did, I slammed my fists into the cheap plywood. The noise I made was such that I almost didn't hear Cyan crying, "Please! Help me! Help me!" But when I did, I twisted to the side and began ramming my shoulder into the door like they did in the movies. Though it felt flimsy, my joints didn't agree. The first time, the agony that slalomed along my nerve endings was enough to steal the very breath from my lungs. But I'd been stabbed, whipped, raped, sexually tortured, had almost starved to death and had watched someone I'd come to care for die and decompose in front of me.

I knew what pain was.

I knew how it weakened someone. I knew how it could drain you of your life while your heart still beat.

So, no. I had to stand corrected. *This* was not pain. This was a setback.

With a roar, I shoved my way against the door once more, and this time, there was even less bounce than before. Knowing I wasn't strong enough was going to haunt me for the rest of my life, and then, like a song from God himself, I heard it.

"Ma'am? You can't be doing that!"

The outraged voice came from the housekeeper on the first floor. I recognized it from the Southern lilt to the way she'd been singing as I climbed the steps.

I rushed over to the railing and called out, "I need to get into this room. My daughter's in there. H-He stole her from me."

The woman's eyes flashed with distress. "She's been kidnapped?"

Frantically, I nodded, and cried, "Please, hurry! He's hurting her."

She bit her lip but did the kindest thing—she took a step back as she reached down and detached something from the belt around her waist. She wore a tabard, a pair of jeans, and a baggy tee that declared '*I voted for Davidson, did you?*' When I heard the rattle of the keys, I sucked in a breath as she circled her arm and tossed the bunch high.

For a second, my heart froze. Time stilled. I watched the keys, knowing I needed to catch them if I wasn't about to waste a second with Cyan being in that predator's clutches. The throw fell short, and I rested my stomach against the railing to reach out further, but as I did so, my concentration broke as the low throb of a bike echoed around the lot.

I didn't dare look, if I did, I'd never catch the bunch, but as I reached over the railing, I nearly tipped forward, my center of balance shifting. Shrieking, sure I was about to fall, my fingers snagged on the bunch of keys. Problem was, I was nearly two thirds of the way over the side.

Grunting, my face red with sweat and exertion, a soft whimper filtered into my awareness.

It spurred me on like nothing else could.

"Amara?"

I ignored Rain's confused call, and instead, heaved my way back over the edge of the railing, well aware that my stomach was going to be loaded down with bruises for a while.

Keys in hand, triumph surging in my veins that I hadn't fallen over the side, I ran over to the door, twisted open the lock after wasting precious seconds figuring out which fit, and barged my way inside. As I did, the keys tangled with my hand, and I pulled them out for ease even as I was sweeping my glance around the room.

It was basic, ugly, but clean. There were two twin beds on the back wall, a TV stand opposite it, to the right was a door that led to the bathroom, and partway between there, a table loaded down with what appeared to be snacks and drinks.

"I'm calling the police," I heard the housekeeper holler, and though the police would be no friend of mine, I didn't stop her. Didn't stop her because this *zhopa* needed to be taken in.

A second was all it took for me to read the situation, and for me to discern that Cyan was going to die if I didn't act.

The *suka* was dressed only in his boxers. His chest was surprisingly muscled, his entire body actually, making a liar out of my guesstimate on his age because, from the head up, he looked to be in his fifties. It was clear that he worked out. His fitness levels didn't bode well for me somehow managing to incapacitate him but I had to.

He held a gun to Cyan's temple.

It was burrowing into the flesh, digging deep, and she was terrified—who'd blame her? Her sobbing resonated with me on a soul deep level. I knew what it was to be this scared. Knew how it felt, and wished it on no one. Neither friend nor foe.

Bulbous tears fell from her eyes, dripping from her lashes, splashing against her cheeks and rolling down to the arm he had around her throat to immobilize her. Her mouth quivered, her body shook like she was a sapling trying to face down a hurricane on her own, but she wasn't alone.

Not anymore.

I whispered, "Let her go. The police are on their way."

"Fuck off," the *suka* spat at me.

I swallowed. "I-I can't do that."

"And I can't let her go." He sneered at me, but he shifted his hold. The muscles in his forearm bunched as he tightened it around her throat while he turned the weapon on me. "You want me to let her live, you're going to walk out of that fucking door—"

"What was the game plan here?" I demanded, my voice shakier than I'd have liked, but I tipped my chin up, refusing to let him scare me with a gun.

Worse things had been done to me with a man's hands than a weapon. Death wasn't something I wanted, otherwise I'd have chosen to end it all months ago, but I wasn't about to let another person hold my life in the palms of their hands.

"Don't question me, bitch—"

"Was this a quick pit stop so you could rape her? Before you carried on your way?" My top lip curled into a sneer. "You're all the same. *Animals*," I rumbled. "No better than a wild beast in the forest."

"Shut the fuck up, bitch," the *zalupa* snarled.

"What leverage do you think you have over me? A gun?" I arched a brow at him. "Shoot me. Waste all your bullets on me so that when you step outside and there's an army of bikers out there, you won't be able to defend yourself."

He blinked. "I didn't hear—"

"No, you wouldn't have over her screams."

I took a step closer to him, maintaining eye contact even though I knew it was useless to try to negotiate with him. He was a pro at this. Whether those skills were honed in the military or as practice in abducting little girls, I wasn't sure, just knew he was stone cold. Unmoved by my presence, but wary about there being bikers outside.

That was my in.

"If they're here, then why did they send you in?"

"Because I arrived first. They'll kill you like the *korva* you are."

"Who the fuck are you, anyway?"

"I'm nobody," I told him honestly. "You can kill me and no one would care—" My words waned as he tipped his head to the side. It was the smallest of gestures.

The *smallest*.

But I recognized it.

Where did I recognize it from, though?

The distraction was costly, because he shoved the gun against Cyan's temple once more.

"You're not going to kill her," I said calmly, knowing that I spoke the truth. "She's far too valuable to you."

His jaw tensed, revealing that I was one-hundred percent correct. I was taking a step closer, when he snarled, "She isn't going to do me much good if I'm in a box though, is she?"

"M-Martin, please, you're frightening me," Cyan whimpered.

Martin.

I'd known many male names in my time, many female names too, and though the females were the ones I'd grown to be more scared of, I remembered them all. Every single one of the *zalupa* and *blyat*'s who'd hurt me. I made sure to catalogue them away, made sure that I'd never forget them because if God did exist, and St. Peter was waiting on me at the gates to heaven when I died, I hoped he'd scan my mind and see every single atrocity that had been done to me.

Perhaps that would make up for however it was I died.

With my soul on the line, I scanned every face in my memory banks for his, but this one I didn't recognize. Yet, somehow I did. It was strange. I never forgot a face, but I knew of no Martin, and the gesture was one I—

Could he have had surgery?

If he was a pedophile, then that would fit. As a *pederasti*, it would be smart for him to have changed his identity, I supposed. Was that why that slight tip to the head had triggered a memory in me?

Though confused about his identity, I didn't allow it to distract me. I took a step closer, saying, "There are many ways to die, aren't there?"

He scowled, and his voice was sharper as he asked, "You think you're being funny or something?"

And that, right there, was where I recognized him.

His voice had been modulated before. Softer, somehow. More gentle. That wasn't the man I'd known.

My mouth tightened with the sudden onset of memories as I recalled this bastard hurting me when I was fifteen. He hadn't been called Martin back then, though. His name had been Jeremiah Berlin.

A strange welter of emotions filled me, almost like I'd been hurtled into the middle of a tidal wave that was about to collide with the shore.

I felt like I was both choking and hyperventilating which, let me tell you, was a curious feeling.

No wonder my mind felt like it was spinning, churning, round and round. Him plaguing me, hurting me, raping me, taking everything from me. Proving that I was nothing. No one. To anyone.

He'd been the one who'd broken me in.

He'd been the one who held me down when I was being branded.

Vomit curdled in my belly, surging up to my throat, but for all that I wanted to be sick, mostly I just wanted to make him feel what I had. I wanted him to feel the agony I'd endured.

I'd come up here unarmed. Stupid, stupid. I should have—

The keys rattled in the palm of my hand.

I tightened my grip around them, slotting the longest shaft between my pointer and middle fingers, tangling another by my thumb and, uncaring if I died, if he shot me, I took another step closer, and closer.

He watched me, wary like he'd never been before when I'd been shackled to the bed, uncertain as to my next move because he sure as hell hadn't expected me to walk toward him like I was doing.

For Cyan, I'd have stopped him.

For me, I'd kill him.

I had one chance.

One shot.

If he moved when I did, I could miss my target.

Cyan whimpered, and that sound snapped something inside of me that had been broken for a long time. The ragged edges of the wound never coming together to form a healed expanse.

My heart was no longer racing.

My lungs were no longer burning.

And my eyes saw with a clarity that I'd never had before.

Time itself seemed to slow down, ticking by like a metronome, letting me hear the tempo of life. The natural rhythm of the world.

I hadn't danced in six years, even though I probably could now that my ankle was fully healed, but it was like I heard the piano setting up for Swan Lake's *pas de deux*. My body knew the moves better than my mind did, as if I was, at that moment, able to sweep into the backbends, arms outstretched as I pleaded with the heavens, legs twirling in traveling arabesques as I was lifted overhead, the corps echoing my movements.

There was only one similarity at that moment—my plea to the heavens.

That they'd guide me.

That they wouldn't forsake me.

"What the fuck are you doing, crazy bitch," Jeremiah muttered under his breath as I raised my arm.

Rain, at that moment, came to my aid. "Cyan," he called out, his tone desperate, his relief real, but that was all I needed. That split-second break in Jeremiah's composure, in his focus, and I struck.

For a second, I thought he was going to move, I thought my aim wouldn't be true, but I wasn't forsaken.

With a quick jab, and God on my side, I sank the key into his eye as deep as the shaft and my knuckles would allow.

His scream of agony combined with a spurt of blood that geysered out of the wound. He released Cyan to clap a hand over his eye, roaring, "BITCH!" as he aimed the gun at me.

A swift flick of my hand and I ground the key into his flesh, dragging it down his cheek as, with the fingers of my other hand, I quickly aimed at his remaining eye. This time, I wasn't so fortunate. A part of me longed to feel that squelch again, the spurt of soft tissues giving way to my penetration, but the gun went off, making me jump and shift my target.

Because time still felt like it was frozen, I could feel the rush of energy, violent and black, powerful and heinous as the weapon discharged the bullet, but I twisted to the side, surging onto my weak ankle as I twirled into an arabesque that hadn't served me in years.

I felt that powerful heat, so angry, throbbing with energy burst past me, and as the shot went wide, I turned to Cyan, saw her horror, her fear, but more importantly, I saw her relief too. She knew she was safe and she jumped out of the way, leaping across the space to where I knew Rain was waiting.

With Jeremiah snarling, one hand clapped over his eye, the other on his gun as he shot off more bullets that went wide—I assumed because of his depth perception—I shouted, "Get out of here," to the kids. Whether they listened or not, I had no idea, whether I spoke in English or Ukrainian, I didn't know, my mind was elsewhere as I rushed behind my rapist, using his blinded side to my advantage, shadowing his movements even as I was looking for a weapon. Something, *anything* that would let me end this *suka*.

When I glanced at the table, my gaze drifting over the snacks and discarded trash there, I saw a glass bottle.

I had no idea what root beer was, had no desire to know either, but I dropped the keys, snatched the bottle, then smashed it against the side of the table, uncaring that sticky soda exploded everywhere, dripping in dirty great globules to the already murky carpet.

With the neck in my grip, I lifted the ragged edge of the now-broken bottle to his throat and I jabbed forward.

Hard.

I sliced across, and down, diagonally, and every other which way I could, hitting his face and his throat, damaging every piece of skin I could to cause the maximum devastation, doing what it took so long as it ended this *musor*, so long as he was the one who suffered today and not Cyan.

Blood gushed out of him in a wave that was almost majestic. The spatter, as I'd hit his carotid, spurted far and wide. By some miracle, I avoided the majority of the spray, but it decorated the room with his malevolent essence.

It should have been black, should have been as poisonous as he was, but that wasn't to be.

Even the lifeblood of the world's evil was bright red.

Heart pounding, lungs burning, strength failing, I gave it one last burst of energy and stabbed the ragged edge of the crumbling glass bottle into his throat, twisting it so that it stuck out obscenely.

As he staggered to his knees, dropping down with a heavy thunk, I moved around him, keeping to the side and away from the blood spray, wanting to be there as I looked into his one remaining eye while his life drained from him.

He started to sink forward, gravity and momentum urging him into face-planting the carpeted floor, but I grabbed him by the hair, and with a strength I didn't know I possessed, I not only kept his dead weight from heaving forward but I twisted his head so that he was looking at me, the slit in his throat obscenely beautiful because *I'd* done that to him.

With his focus on me, I rasped, "That's for all the little girls you broke, Jeremiah."

His eyelashes fluttered at the name, recognition finally hitting him as I watched him bleed out, satisfaction filling me, a sense of wellness too.

That had felt good.

Better than good, in fact.

It had felt right.

True.

Purposeful.

He knew a victim of his had done this to him.

The violence he'd reaped in me was what I'd sown in him.

When someone died, it was said that their life flashed before their eyes. I had no way of quantifying how much misery Jeremiah had left in his wake, but though I wasn't the one dying, my life flashed before *my* eyes.

Not for the first time, I saw the faces of every man and woman who'd hurt me.

Who'd raped me.

Who'd caged me.

Who'd flayed me.

I saw them all as clear as glass, as if they were standing in front of me.

Only, on this occasion, I didn't see them as the victim of their crimes, but as someone who had it in them to kill. To do what had to be done.

And I knew, at that moment, *I knew.*

They all had to pay.

Just like Jeremiah had.

I needed to make them pay because, when my time was up, I didn't want to see their faces smirking at me as they tortured me.

I wanted to see their faces as *I* tortured *them.*

That would be my legacy.

My purpose.

And as that settled inside me, relief and a sense of righteousness did too.

I knew the path I was taking was just.

Now I needed to figure out how to make it happen.

EIGHT

AMARA

"WHAT DID YOU DO?"

The words were frightened, *young*.

I cast Cyan a glance, rasping, "Do you know what he was going to do to you?" I grabbed an empty 7-11 bag from the table and shoved the bottle that was dripping blood into it.

She blinked, bit on her lip and huddled into Rain's protective embrace. They were both so young, so *khuy* young, that it seemed impossible to me that there were only a few years between us.

Rain, I knew, was eighteen. He'd just celebrated it recently because, in the fridge when we'd started staying at Rachel's place, there'd been the remnants of a birthday cake.

Three years between him and me, but it felt like thirty.

At eighteen, I'd seen and done a lot worse than what he had, but that wasn't his fault.

If anything, his innocence should be protected, *kovna*, not just his, but hers too.

They deserved to be shielded.

That was what I'd done today—shielded them. Taken the stain on my soul to keep theirs clean.

Still, when Rain snapped, "Are you trying to make her upset?" my top lip quirked up into a snarl.

"She needs to know what she just escaped so that it doesn't happen again. You let him into your life, Cyan. You. No one else—"

"That isn't fair!" Rain growled, his arm tightening around her as she turned her face into his chest, her hands sliding around his waist as they deepened their embrace. I didn't realize they knew one another, because they never did anything more than grunt at each other in the morning when they were going to school, but from the comfort she found in him, I thought I was wrong.

"Isn't it?" I asked coolly, before repeating the truth, "You welcomed the parasite into your world, Cyan. You're just lucky that someone else was around to stop it before things went too far."

I knew she hid her face from me because she was well aware I was right.

"You're victim shaming her—"

I raised a hand to stop him from uttering another word. Imagine my surprise when he actually complied.

"She isn't a victim. Thanks to you and me. She got into that car by herself, Rain. She wasn't at gun point. She knew what she was doing, she just didn't know how it was going to work out." I jerked my chin up, aware that I sounded cold and hard but the adrenaline from taking Jeremiah's life was starting to fade. "Be grateful, Cyan. Be grateful that we got here in time. Not every little girl is so fortunate." I cast a look at Jeremiah's corpse, earning myself a delicious zing of pleasure as I beheld my handiwork, and murmured, "We need to get out of here. The housekeeper said she was calling the police."

Rain licked his lips. "The MC is on its way."

"On a rescue mission," I retorted, "not to clean up a dead body."

My words triggered a wave of sobs from Cyan, and though that did make me feel guilty, there was no time for guilt.

"We need to hurry," I said coldly.

The *musor*—the cops—had never served me well before, had

never been around to protect me in the past, but I had a feeling that luck wouldn't be on my side where this was concerned.

The bag in my hand, I rushed over to them, grabbing Cyan's arm as I started to drag her toward the door, knowing that was the way to get Rain to move, and it worked. As we headed into the outer corridor, over the railing I saw that the housekeeper was staring up at us, her eyes big and wide as we came running down the stairs.

"This your baby?" she barked at me as I made it to the parking lot.

I nodded. "She needed me to protect her." To Rain, I spat, "Get on your bike. Go. I'll drive Cyan."

I felt his hesitation like it was a living, breathing thing, but in all honesty, I didn't have time for him.

I turned back to the housekeeper and said, "He was going to rape her."

Her nostrils flared. "She's only a girl."

"I know."

Her gaze darted to the room and its open door. "Ain't gonna be a pretty sight up there, is it?"

I shook my head. "No," I concurred, my grip on the bag tightening at her comment. "But he tried to shoot us first."

"I heard the shots." Her words were punctuated by the roar of Rain's bike as he seemed to come to his senses, and did as I asked—left.

"It was in self-defense."

Her jaw clamped down as she rasped, "There's no security footage in the lot or around the building—the owners are too cheap for that. I-I'll tell the cops that I found him that way. When I called 911, I just said there was some commotion going on, so it shouldn't seem out of place for them to find a dead body up there." She cringed. "Lord knows, there's been worse found up in these rooms."

The woman's generosity was more than I could stand at that moment, and a curious cocktail of emotions bubbled up inside me. For the first time today, I felt tears prick my eyes and I reached up to dash them away.

My hand was shaking though as I whispered, "Thank you."

She dipped her chin, then, reaching for something in her tabard, pulled out a pack of wipes. Shoving them at me, she muttered, "Here, clean your hands up. There are some dots of blood on your cheeks too." She swallowed. "You need to go. They said they'd be twenty minutes and that was five minutes ago."

I bit my lip. "Truly, he was a bad man."

"Ain't they all?" was her skeptical retort.

"Some are worse than others." Strange how my mind shifted to Hawk at that very moment, but I shoved thoughts of him aside and mumbled, "I can't thank you enough."

"Sure you can. Get gone."

She turned away from me then, seeming to suck in a sharp breath as her shoulders straightened which made me think she was girding her loins for what she was about to see.

For her sake, I wished it wasn't so gory, even as I wished I'd been able to eke out Jeremiah's suffering for far longer. I could only hope she wouldn't be the one who'd have to clean it up.

The thought had me grimacing, and I turned to Cyan to ask, "Do you have any money?"

Without Rain propping her up, Keira and Storm's daughter stood there, shivering at my side.

"I-I have about two hundred."

I held out my hand. "Give it to me."

She pouted a little, and though I saw a protest forming, I flapped my fingers, not letting her argue as she reached into her pocket and pulled out some notes.

Before the housekeeper could go too far, I rushed over to her and said, "Here. For the mess. My apologies."

Her brows rose high, then she smiled a little. "Not to keep me quiet, huh?"

"No," I said calmly, well aware that the next words I was about to utter were true, "I don't need to do that, do I?"

She pursed her lips. "No."

"Your keys..." I winced. "I'm sorry. They're up there. I dropped them."

Her grimace made me feel worse, but she just grumbled, "What did I tell you? Get gone."

I obeyed, at long last, and hurried over to the driver's side, barking, "Get in the car, Cyan."

She jerked into action, her movements wooden, and while I knew she was in shock, I didn't have time to deal with that right now. Nor was I the person who she'd need comfort from. I was a stranger to her. Just because I'd saved her didn't make us friends or me the person she'd turn to.

Having been in her shoes, I'd know. Opening up to the various people in the MC who'd tried to help us had been next to impossible, enough that I'd hidden how well I could speak English.

By the time the door closed behind her, I'd shoved the bag containing the bottle with my fingerprints on, behind the driver's seat and had fired up the SUV. Once she had her belt on, we raced out of the lot. I didn't go the way I'd come, just to be on the safe side, and though I knew it was likely there'd be cameras in the vicinity, I had to hope that they wouldn't pick up on Rachel's vehicle and the times it arrived and departed the motel's parking lot.

Biting my lip, my heart in my ears, I didn't relax until I was away from the motel, deep in Allentown, with no cops at my back and no sirens blaring nearby.

When I could, I found the Interstate, and managed to get back onto the road with a lot of help from Cyan and Google Maps.

When we were back on track, the route to West Orange set in her GPS, I whispered, "You're safe, Cyan."

It was the softest tone I'd used with her all day. I wasn't sure if it helped or not, because a few seconds later, she burst into tears.

My throat grew choked with emotion as I felt her relief and fear like they were tangible things, but I said nothing, and neither did she.

About twenty minutes into the journey, I saw three bikers in the distance, heard the roar of their engines as they rolled toward us like they were flying and had wings, and though it took me a good three attempts at figuring out how to flash them down, as I turned on the windshield wipers instead and then, the one in the back, finally, I figured out where the damn lights were.

A shocked gurgle of laughter escaped Cyan at my ineptitude, and I turned to grin at her, admitting, "I haven't driven in a long time." Even then, it hadn't been legal, just driving around my parents' meager plot of land.

"I can tell," she whispered sarcastically, her eyes still bloodshot, her face bright pink with the tears she'd shed.

My lips twisted, and I turned back to the road, flashed the lights —after knocking on the *khuy* windshield wipers *again*—then, finally, I saw Sin register who I was, saw him take Cyan's presence in the car into consideration, and I hit the turn signal to pull over onto the nearest exit.

Knowing they were watching, I parked, then I used the wipes the housekeeper had given me to clean up with as I waited for them to arrive.

It didn't take long, only ten minutes at the most, and in that time, any amusement Cyan had felt at my fumbling disappeared, as she cried, and I let her. It wasn't in my nature to be affectionate, to hold her and comfort her, but I could be a safe space and let her express her emotions.

I peered down at us both, relieved that there wasn't much blood on us—she'd had a few stray droplets on her cheeks, and considering I'd gotten in Jeremiah's face, I only had it on my sandals. Some of that was even root beer, not blood.

Thankful that the spray had hit most of the furniture and not us, which made this all seem even more fateful, my hands curved around the steering wheel and I squeezed it tightly as, finally, the brothers showed up.

Toeing out of my slip-ons to be on the safe side—spreading

evidence about the state wasn't high on my to-do list—I opened the door, and strode over to them barefoot, rasping, "The cops are at the motel where he took her."

Sin grunted, "Shit," under his breath, whereas Link and Steel just shared a glance before Steel headed around the SUV's fender and moved over to speak with Cyan, at least, that was what I assumed.

"What happened?" Link demanded in a tone I'd never heard him use before.

He was, or so I'd thought, one of the most laidback brothers in the club, but at that moment, I understood why he was on the council, why he was one of the leaders.

Just because someone was playful didn't mean that when *korva* went to *korva*, he couldn't toughen up.

Knowing Lily, his Old Lady, knowing what she'd been through, I figured she needed both sides of him. One to feel safe, the other to feel comfortable enough to open up.

"I made it there, just in time," I replied, my tone free from emotion. "He was partially undressed, and she was screaming. I managed to get into the motel room thanks to a housekeeper who gave me her set of keys, and he had Cyan at gunpoint."

Link pursed his lips. "Would have been useful to know that you spoke English so well when I was talking to you about Tatána, Amara."

I shrugged. "I told you the truth. The truth needs no translation."

He shook his head though I saw a glimmer of something in his eyes which looked like respect, but who knew where these strange men were concerned? They were two parts noble, two parts outlaw, and one part sinner.

Sin ruptured that by muttering, "You involved the housekeeper?"

"I had no choice. I couldn't open the door."

I felt no need to defend myself. I'd done what I could at the time, and I truly believed the housekeeper would keep to her word and tell the police that she found Jeremiah that way.

"Why was Rain heading back to West Orange? He should have

stayed with you," Link said gruffly, his arms coming up to cross against his chest.

"You saw him?"

"Yeah, and he didn't pick up his phone when I tried calling."

"I made him leave. I didn't want any of us there when the police arrived."

Sin pulled a face. "The housekeeper was the one who called the cops?"

"When I asked for her keys. She only gave them to me because I told her he'd kidnapped my daughter."

"Loose ends," Link muttered.

"Goddammit."

"No," I disregarded sternly, because loose ends, I knew, had a way of being tightened up. "She means us no harm. She thinks Cyan is my daughter. She said she'd tell the cops she found Jeremiah that way."

Sin's cheeks puffed up with air as he studied my expression, then he turned to Link and asked, "Who do we know in the Allentown PD?"

I reached out and grabbed his wrist. "Do not hurt her," I warned grimly, fingers flexing. "She helped Cyan too. Without her, I'd never have been able to do what I did. The MC owes her gratitude. She doesn't deserve to be in danger for helping me help one of your own."

His jaw clenched but he dipped his chin in begrudging agreement.

"We know a couple of beat cops," Link answered him, his tone pensive. "No detectives. Not as far as I know. Never needed anyone other than uniforms to help us out as we ride through their district."

Sin winced. "Shit."

Link, evidently in agreement, nodded. "He's definitely dead? There's none of this coming back on us?"

Before I could reply, Sin's cell buzzed. I watched him read the Caller ID, and knew he was going to take it so I just shook my head, and curious, listened in as Sin demanded, "Rex? We got Cyan." He blinked, then, mumbled, "Fuck. You're kidding me?"

"What is it?" Link rasped.

I knew it was bad because neither of them seemed to remember I was there, as Sin replied, "Quin got shivved in jail."

"Motherfuckers," Link snapped, his hand bunching into a fist as he slapped one into his palm. "Those goddamn Sparrows!"

His snarl, as well as the expletive—sparrows wasn't a word I'd have thought a biker would use—had my brows lifting high, but Sin just continued, "He's in a clinic in Flushing. Nyx is on his way there." He scrubbed his hand over his jaw. "Rex, we might have a problem here. Cyan's abductor is dead."

I didn't have to have super-hearing to know that Rex was pissed because Sin grimaced, and pulled his cellphone away from his ear.

I knew it wasn't my place, but I held out my hand for the cell, and murmured, "I will explain it to him."

Sin shook his head, then groused, "I'm gonna stick around here. Make sure shit's on the up and up. I don't think there are any ties to us, but I want to make sure before I head out." He nodded at whatever his Prez said, then cut the call.

Link questioned, "How's Quin?"

Sin winced. "Not doing well, but the Pointers got him out of the joint and into a decent clinic, so that's something."

"Yeah, he's out of the butcher's shop at least," Link said gruffly.

"Who is Quin?" I asked, curious.

"Nyx's baby brother."

Tipping up my chin in understanding, I said, "The weapon I used... it's in Rachel's car."

Sin's brows rose. "What is it?"

"A bottle."

Link laughed. "Color me impressed." He raised a hand to his throat and sliced his finger along it. "Like that?"

"Yes."

Sin whistled. "Leave the bag in the SUV. I'll deal with it when I get back." He groused, "You killed for the MC, Amara. You know what that means, don't you?"

Warily, I pulled back. "What?"

"It means we owe you."

He didn't sound happy about that, and neither did Sin appear to appreciate it either.

"I don't want anything." And I meant it. The MC had already done enough for me. I didn't feel indebted to them, but that didn't take away from how much they'd done for all of Lancaster's victims.

"No?"

"Lily is giving me more than I need," I told him softly, aware that he knew she'd given Alessa and I access to some of her fortune as an apology for what her family had put us through.

Some might consider it blood money, but I wasn't above accepting that.

After a lifetime of poverty, of being a small ant in a big, big world, when her millions transferred into the account Lily's broker was setting up for us, I'd be a very happy woman.

Of course, that meant I had to look into exactly what being happy meant.

I doubted it would make me smile more, doubted it would do anything other than help me feel secure, but that was one definite plus to being rich. No one, and I meant, *no one* would own me again.

Resolve filled me as I admitted, "I knew Cyan's abductor."

Whatever they'd expected me to say, it certainly wasn't that. Link's mouth gaped, and Sin's eyes flared wide before they narrowed into thin slivers.

"Who was he?"

"One of the men who bought me."

They both winced at that, and I knew Hawk was right—there were some crimes that were permissible. That were forgivable. That one could atone for. But buying another human being wasn't one of them.

These men in front of me might be criminals, but I'd prefer their company to the upstanding citizens who'd owned me along the way. And they *had* been upstanding, as well. Mr. Jason, one of my owners, had been a politician. He'd had one of those photos on his desk, where he stood in front of a US flag, smiling into the cameras like he wasn't a snake.

I'd polished that photo frame so many times, wondering if the general public could begin to imagine what their representative did to me, things that belonged in nightmares.

"That can't be a coincidence," Sin rumbled.

"The *suka* had had surgery. His face was different, but I recognized his voice. His eyes."

For the first time, my voice sounded choked, and I knew my features were creased into an expression I couldn't hide. I'd worked long and hard to make people think the mask I wore was a permanent fixture, but my memories wrecked that mask, making a liar out of me.

Link reached out, his hand hovering at my shoulder like he wanted to touch me but was afraid to hurt me. "It's okay, Amara. You're safe now."

Because I believed him, I closed my eyes, released a shaky exhalation and murmured, "I protected us. It was self-defense."

Sin nodded. "I'll sort it out. You don't have to worry about the cops."

I didn't think there'd be anything that needed to be sorted out, in all honesty, but I was grateful nonetheless.

"We still owe you," Link rasped. "The MC always pays its debts."

I frowned. "I told you that isn't necessary."

He just shrugged. "It's how it works."

Sin nodded like he was in full agreement, but simply said, "You need to leave now. Go straight to Rachel's place. Keira is waiting on her there."

"What about Storm?"

"We don't know where he's at."

Uneasy, I just nodded, but then that sliver of information I'd stored, the mention of that word resonated with me again. Ringing as loudly in my ears as a bell.

"You called the men who hurt Quin 'fucking sparrows.'"

Link shrugged. "Just a turn of phrase."

I didn't believe him, but I appreciated him trying to roll things back. I was many things, however, and a fool wasn't one of them.

So I shook my head. "No. I thought that at first, but then—" I tapped my forehead. "No. It's a name."

The men shared a look, and I heard heavy footsteps as Steel rounded the vehicle, obviously leaving Cyan to her tears, asking, "What's going on? Cyan says you killed Martin London?"

I turned to him with a frown. "I knew him as Jeremiah Berlin."

As one, they all seemed to clench their jaws, but I ignored that, instead, demanding, "You called them sparrows. This is not a regular English insult." I'd know. I'd heard most of them along the way. I'd also heard a lot more than my captors could possibly realize. "I have heard of these sparrows."

"They're just birds, honey," Link placated.

I didn't know that, but that only confirmed what I thought.

Men did not insult other men by calling them birds' names.

I tipped my chin up, insisting, "I heard Lancaster speak of them."

The men grew still, but it was Sin who rasped, "You need to talk to Rex, Amara."

I blinked. "Why?"

"Because he's the Prez. Whatever you know, he needs to know too."

"I will tell him when we return," I said softly, but from the glances they shared, I got the feeling my information wouldn't be worthless to them.

Link murmured, "Go on, Amara. Get Cyan home."

Nodding, I turned around and jumped back into the SUV. Something stuck in my heel, a stone, I thought, but I ignored it, not even limping as I rubbed my foot against the carpet to let the pebble loose, then I took off.

I didn't have a home, but Cyan did.

Unlike me, she wasn't lost.

Without meaning to, however, today, I knew I'd discovered a way to be found...

Maybe finding a place within the MC wasn't as out of reach as I'd feared.

NINE

STORM

THE NA MEETING hadn't provided its regular comfort, but nothing was regular anymore.

Recovering addicts needed monotony, repetition. Calm. We needed routine, too. Everything about the past couple of months had ruptured that. Life had a habit of working out that way, though, didn't it? Just because you needed something, didn't mean the universe would grant it to you.

I was pretty sure the homeless on the streets didn't need to be sleeping in the corners of store fronts, but that didn't mean the benevolent Oz granted them a Brownstone each.

Life sucked sometimes.

The strength of an addict's mettle was revealed during times of crisis.

Would they fall off the bandwagon? Would they stick fast to the promises they made to themselves?

Moving to Coshocton had already broken the habit I had of attending an NA meeting once a week. I didn't do well with strangers, anyway, and the joy of Manhattan was its anonymity.

Here, I was just another recovering addict, one among millions. In Coshocton, that anonymity wasn't as pervasive.

Not only was I a newcomer to the town, but I was the new Prez at the Satan's Sinners' MC chapter, which meant I'd had all the old bats' eyebrows surging high and doing a wave whenever I showed my face.

Nothing about the NA meeting I attended in town would be anonymous. *Nada.*

So it was comforting to be back, but I already knew that I needed to find comfort from somewhere else. My regular place, headed by a guy called Christopher, who was one of the least judgmental people I'd ever met, just didn't fit me anymore. I felt like I was wearing a favorite sweater that had shrunk in the dryer.

I wriggled my shoulders at the thought as, before I left St. Barnabus' community hall, I wandered over to grab a donut. This was a ritual too. Confess my sins before I ate a donut as a reward, then punished myself with some of their horrendous coffee.

But even that tasted different.

The coffee wasn't that bad and the donuts were stale.

I winced as I finished off my drink and tossed the donut aside.

"Haven't seen you in a long time, Asher," Christopher murmured, appearing out of nowhere like he usually did.

It was always weird hearing my birth name. Not even Keira used it.

I turned around to stare at him. "Yeah, I moved away."

His brows rose. "How's that going?"

My mouth tightened.

Badly.

Of all the shit that was going on though, there were two things that were messing with me.

Scarlet.

My baby sister.

The nightmare Tasmanian devil who'd always managed to leave chaos in her wake.

Dead.

Not missing. Not ignoring me like I thought. Just dead.

Murdered.

And then, my family. Not the Sinners, Cyan and Keira.

I felt like a real fuck up when my family situation filled me with more regret than Scarlet's death. She'd been gone a long time, though, and she'd cut herself off before she'd died, so it wasn't like I had much to regret. Feel angry about? Sure. That was another matter. But regret? Not so much.

I'd made so many mistakes with Cyan and Keira though. So fucking many. Any regrets belonged with them.

I closed my eyes at the thought, just as Christopher asked, "Asher? How's the move going? During the meeting, you said you were clean still—"

"I wasn't lying," I rasped, reaching up to scrub a hand over my face. "It's just, Keira and me broke up."

"I remember," Christopher murmured, his tone soothing. "You weren't dealing well with the transition."

That was an understatement.

I'd fucked my way through so many of the clubwhores it was a wonder my dick still didn't have friction burns on it.

"No," I muttered. "I wasn't."

"Has the move helped? Did they go with you?"

"They stayed here," I said.

My mouth twisted as I thought about how Keira had fought me on this. I'd wanted her and Cyan to move to Ohio with me, but she'd refused. The bitch of it was, I couldn't blame her.

"That must be hard," he said softly. "I know how much you love them."

"I do. More than I know how to handle," I admitted gruffly, turning my face away so I could look down at the array of donuts and coffee in front of me rather than have him bear witness to the obsession I lived with on a daily basis. This wasn't an obsession he'd be able to understand, however. It had nothing to do with crack or heroin, alcohol or even sex.

"You can handle it, Asher. You just need to have faith in yourself."

"It fucks with my head when I make so many mistakes with them. Why am I so weak?"

"You're not," Christopher countered.

"I don't deserve them."

"You do. You just have to work harder to make sure you're worthy of them."

I gritted my teeth. "It's not that simple."

"Nothing that's good in life ever is."

"How many times a day do you say this stuff?" I groused, peering over at him.

His lips twisted into a genuine smile. In all honesty, he was the most earnest guy I'd ever met. I'd thought he was too good to be true the first time I'd attended a meeting here, but he'd been this way, consistently, for nearly fourteen years.

That was way too long to be wearing a fucking mask.

"Not as often as you think."

"No? I thought this was all addicts could do. Regret. Whine about the shit they'd done—"

"You're not whining," he countered, as calm as ever. "You think because you're a recovering addict, you're not worthy of a decent life? You think that's it now? You should just end it all because of what you did wrong in the past?"

I shook my head. "I'm too selfish to end it all." And my brothers needed me. Just like I needed them.

"Well, then. You can drown in that cup of mud or you can come out fighting, which is what you're good at, Asher."

I *was* a good fighter. In more ways than he knew, too.

"I want my family back, Christopher."

He shrugged. "Then fight for them."

"I've tried. She doesn't want me back. The shit I did—" I swallowed. "I'm not sure it's possible to get over."

"Have you apologized?"

My brow puckered. "Takes more than a fucking 'sorry' to rectify what I did."

He shook his head though. "I didn't say that it would. But it's a start. Maybe you'll never get back together, but that doesn't mean you can't be friends for the sake of your daughter. What's her name? Cyan?"

I nodded, always surprised at the information he retained. "That's her."

"If the split isn't amicable, then who knows how it's affecting her. You both need to think of her, not yourselves. Not the things you did wrong, or the things she can't forgive, but just focus on Cyan. There's a freedom in that, Asher. Working toward a common cause, doing what's right for a person that you both made together."

His words resonated in a way I wasn't sure anyone else's ever had—not even Rex, who was probably the wisest motherfucker I knew.

I thought about all the arguments, all the bitter words spewed, all the anger and the hatred she'd lobbed at me, and I knew it was justified, I also recognized the unthinkable—I hadn't said sorry.

Sucking in a sharp breath as I wondered how much of a dumb fuck I was that I hadn't even apologized, I admitted to Christopher, "When she found out I'd cheated on her, I just admitted to it. I never said sorry. I don't think I ever have."

Christopher sighed. "'Sorry' isn't a Band-Aid, but it's certainly a start."

I nodded. "You're right."

"The cheating... were you clean at the time?"

My mouth tightened. "No. But that's no excuse."

"No, it isn't," he agreed, before he reached over and clapped a hand to my shoulder. "If this is the last time I see you, Asher, maybe it's wise if you take my card. You always refused to get a sponsor, and even though the distance isn't helpful, I have a feeling that you'll avoid NA meetings for a long time until you're settled.

"I remember when you first got here, you didn't say anything for months. I don't want that to inhibit your recovery."

Shaking my head, I told him, "That isn't necessary."

His brows rose. "Why do you turn away from help when that is what will let you become the man your family needs? They don't need you to relapse because you wouldn't accept a helping hand, one that's freely offered."

I blew out another breath. "Okay."

He smiled, and dryly admitted, "I should bring them into it more often, they make you much more compliant." He squeezed my shoulder, then dipped that same hand into his jacket. Pulling out a card that he handed to me, he said, "You're past the first steps of recovery, Asher. Even with the other addiction you have. But that doesn't mean there still isn't a lot to learn. Call me when you're back in Ohio. Call me at three AM or four in the afternoon. I'll be there."

My throat felt thick at the unexpected generosity. "You don't have to—"

"It's what a sponsor does."

Jaw working, I accepted that I'd be beholden to him in a way he'd never understand. That sensation of being indebted was one of the reasons why I'd always shied away from getting a sponsor, but he was right.

I needed help.

There were no guarantees in this life.

Once Rex was back in charge of the gavel, when Bear was out of the hospital, I'd be returning to Coshocton, and I'd be leaving my family behind again.

I needed all the help I could get, because even though they were hundreds of miles away, I'd still be fighting for them. Every fucking day I didn't jack off, didn't get high, it was for them.

I'd always been weak, but Christopher was right—they needed me to be strong. The strongest I'd ever been.

At that moment, I accepted what I never had before.

I might not get back together with Keira.

This might be permanent.

But that didn't mean I had to stop trying.

From the moment I met her, I'd known she was it for me.

Club life, my family background, my history, the shit I'd done in the Sinners' name, it had warped my soul. But through it all, Keira had been there, as pure as the driven snow. So fucking clean that I always felt so dirty.

Throat still thick, I managed to grate out, "Thank you, Christopher."

"You're welcome, Asher. Stay safe out there."

As he walked off, I turned back to the refreshment table and even though it was out of my routine, I poured myself another coffee. Anything to take away the stone that felt like it was lodged in my throat.

After I sank it back, I plucked up another donut, surprised when that one tasted better.

Feeling a little more settled, I reached into my back pocket and dragged out my cell.

Thirteen missed calls from Rex.

Ten from Nyx.

Dozens from the rest of my brothers on the council.

My nostrils flared as concern hit me when I connected with the voicemail alert, and Rex's words were enough to have me dropping to my knees before I registered I didn't have time for that.

My family needed me.

"Get your ass to Rachel's place. Cyan's been kidnapped. I thought you'd want to know—maybe I was wrong. What the fuck, man? Answer your phone the next time I goddamn ring you."

TEN

HAWK

"WHO IS HE?"

Curious as well, I turned my attention from the corridor outside of Quin's room in the clinic to Indy and Giulia who, begrudgingly, had left the waiting room when two guys in suits had showed up.

At first, I'd thought they were cops, but then I'd realized that no cop wore three-grand suits on the job.

Even the guy who wasn't in charge, the one who'd lagged a few steps behind, wore expensive clothes, and though I assumed they were the Irish Mob who were our allies in this city, I'd like it confirmed.

Giulia shrugged at Indy. "Irish Mob. Don't know who, though."

Indy frowned. "Tiffany said that Sin was the liaison, and that he speaks with a guy called Declan?"

"Maybe that's him."

"Neither of you should know that information," I said sardonically, folding my arms across my chest as I leaned back against the wall.

Giulia's look could have felled a lesser man, but I'd grown up with the bitch. None of the stunts she pulled or the shit she threw would ever surprise me.

Of course, I'd thought the same about North, had never imagined he'd be able to shock the crap outta me, but there he went—overachieving for the first time in his life.

Still, Giulia wasn't like North. If anything, she was fiercer. A hundred times more ferocious than our brother.

I'd come across psychotic bitches like her when I was working as a bounty hunter, but truthfully, I knew Giulia was too smart, and Nyx was too obsessed with her ass, to ever let this crazy cunt find its way to death row—probably where she belonged.

"Why shouldn't we know that information?" Giulia rumbled, her voice low, threaded with a warning I'd always ignore because that was the perk of being her brother. Her older brother at that. "Because we have pussies?"

"Yeah, because you have pussies," I retorted, "and because none of the brothers want your asses hauled into interrogation rooms so the cops and the Feds can scare you straight."

She sneered at me. "You think I'd break for a Fed?"

"Nah, but I don't know about the rest of this Posse of yours. You might be a head case, baby sis, but that don't mean the others are as fucked in the cerebellum as you."

Though she sniffed, something shifted in her gaze, something that told me she heard my words at long last and understood what I was saying.

Some people could survive an interrogation, some people couldn't.

I wasn't saying those who couldn't all possessed vaginas, because I had a healthy respect for vaginas and the poundings they took, but I just knew that I wouldn't want any of the women to land in jail for the crap we were involved in.

Maybe that was chauvinism, maybe it was fucking chivalry, I didn't know.

"Tiffany wouldn't stand up to an interrogation," Indy commented, almost making me snort.

If Tiff could handle Sin, the guy whose rep was forged on his ability to beat grown men to death, then I figured she could handle an interrogation. Not that I was about to say that. If I spread doubts amid the Posse, maybe they'd calm the fuck down and would stop lynching innocent people. Like Amara.

Although, there was no denying their tactics had worked where finding Tink was concerned... that didn't mean we needed to encourage them. You didn't give LSD to already insane people—that was just asking for trouble.

Giulia frowned at Indy, evidently contemplating whether her sister-in-law was right on the money where Tiff's capacity for interrogation was concerned. "I dunno. She's gone through some rough shit this year and she stayed strong."

"True." Indy rubbed her pointer finger over her lip. "Alessa... I would never want her to be interrogated. I don't think she'd crack, but she's been through enough."

My sister scowled at me. "You're a prick for making us doubt my bitches."

I shrugged. "Just keeping your asses safe. If that's a crime, then I'm fucking guilty."

When she snarled at me, I just smirked back, but I'd admit I was curious about the conversation going down in the waiting room too. If Psycho Susan, AKA Giulia, had answers, I'd have totally squirreled them out of her, but as it stood, we were all in the dark.

About most things to be fair.

We'd arrived here ninety minutes ago to the news that Quin had died once before being resuscitated. He'd lost a lot of blood but the doctors were comfortable in saying that they thought he'd recover. Ever since, we'd been waiting around for news, Nyx's temper throbbing through the room like a hurricane was brewing.

Then, two guys in sharp suits had turned up, and Nyx had kicked out Indy and Giulia, asking me to guard them, so they could talk.

I wasn't on the council so I didn't know as much as the guys in the waiting room, but the whispers around Rachel's house were that Quin was getting out of jail soon. There'd been no official date mentioned, at least not to me, but I knew the intention hadn't been for him to come home in a goddamn body bag.

Reaching up to scratch my jaw, I kept an ear tuned into my sister's conversation with her sister-in-law, because if anyone needed watching, or *listening to*, it was Giulia, while I tried to eavesdrop what they were talking about in the waiting room.

No dice though.

There were too many beeps, too much static noise that kept the discussion private.

Resigned, I gave Indy and Giulia's conversation my full attention, but as I did, I heard an alarm blaring, and I knew what it meant.

Panic lit up my sister's eyes, but I knew it was for Nyx, not Quin.

Who the fuck could imagine how that nutcase would react if his baby brother died?

"I thought he was coming out of it," Indy cried, her terror for her brother so tangible I almost choked on it.

The women scrambled into action, running into the waiting room as I twisted my head to see a bunch of doctors and nurses barreling toward us, their destination Quin's bedside.

Sucking in a breath, I did what I hadn't done in a long time—I prayed. For Quin's safety, for his health, because even though I wasn't religious, and hadn't gone to church since Ma had dragged us there a few token times when we were kids, I prayed because we needed it.

Not just as an MC, but as a family.

If Nyx's brother died thanks to whatever the club was embroiled in, there'd be no holding him back.

My sister was pregnant. My niece or nephew needed a dad, not a lunatic monster who sent hellfire through the tri-state area to avenge his lost kin...

So, yeah, I prayed.

I prayed hard.

And I just hoped that God was receptive to a man who proudly wore the label of Satan's Sinner.

ELEVEN

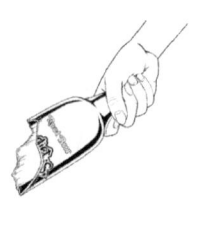

KEIRA

HAVE YOU EVER SWITCHED OFF?

Literally, shut down. Like a computer. Like a machine.

That was me right now.

I wasn't catatonic because I could hear and process and understand and sadly, *feel*, but I knew that if I didn't switch off at least some of my functions, then I'd go insane.

That I'd lose it.

My baby girl... *taken*.

I'd known we had issues. Known it, and we'd been working toward coming back from that, but somehow, he'd gotten to her.

I'd taken away all of her electronic devices, had made sure that I spent as much time as I physically could with her when I wasn't working, saving up for us to have a better future, one that didn't rely on the Satan's Sinners, but it wasn't enough.

I had to accept that.

I had to accept that I wasn't what she needed.

Her daddy was.

Cyan had always been Daddy's little princess. They'd always been so close, two peas in a goddamn pod.

At first, she hadn't been happy with our separating, but things had worsened when the brats at school had started calling her names, started saying things they had to have heard fall from their parents' lips because there was no way children would know that kind of stuff.

I'd tried to make things better, and though I knew nothing would take those cutting words away—the cruelty of children never failed to astound me—everything had devolved when Storm had to leave and move to Ohio.

I'd refused to go, had wanted to stay here, in my home town where I was an outsider thanks to my affiliation with the Sinners, close to parents who had spurned me a long time ago, and this was how my stupid loyalty to West Orange repaid me.

I should never have torn daughter and father apart.

My phone buzzed, the vibrations shooting through my hand with how tightly I was clutching it.

Desperation had me praying it was about Cyan, and when I saw Link's name flash up on the Caller ID, hope and worry flooded me.

Link and I had always been close. Shit had changed since Lily had come into his life, but I wasn't upset. For the first time, he was in love, and she was his priority. Not only that, but I'd been working so much and he had a lot on with the Sinners.

I knew he'd gone to get my baby though.

Was there a reason why he was the one who called me? Had they made him ring me to soften the blow?

"You not going to answer that?" Rachel's voice was surprisingly soft. I wasn't used to that from her. I didn't know her that well, but she was always cold. Had been even at school, and her rep had preceded her from the halls of high school to the lofty heights she'd reached as a lawyer.

"I-I am," I whispered, pressing connect.

Instantly, I heard the road whizzing by, and it made it hard for me to hear what Link hollered at me. "You okay, Keira?"

"I will be when you get my girl." I knew from that greeting alone he didn't have news, was just calling to check in.

Christ, why couldn't I have fallen for Link?

He was a good man, *loyal*. He wouldn't have decimated my heart.

"We're almost there," Link assured me, and as he was Road Captain, I knew that he'd be in the lead, charging the way into hell itself to get my daughter back.

She was, whether I liked it or not, Sinner spawn.

That meant she was protected.

That meant, whoever took her, wouldn't be coming home in handcuffs and in the back of a police car. His destination was the morgue.

"I-I can't breathe, Link," I gasped. "What if she's—" Rachel squeezed me. "He might have done anything to her by now. This is all my fault."

"No, it ain't," Link barked, and Rachel compounded that by hissing, "No, it isn't. Shit like this happens all the time."

"Storm would have made sure this never happened."

"Then it's his fucking fault he wasn't around to stop it," Rachel muttered.

Link heaved a sigh that was so loud, I heard it over the oncoming traffic. "Keira, babe, you know what he's like. Has he called you yet? Rex couldn't get in touch with him."

"I think he's on his way." Tears burned like acid along my lash line. "Why's he got to be like this? Why can't he just be—"

I didn't finish the sentence.

Why couldn't I be his everything like he was mine?

Once upon a time, I'd decided I was too fucking pathetic to live, but that was when I'd grown some balls and had kicked him out.

This was how that had turned out.

Cyan would be here, safe and sound if I hadn't cut him loose. Even though he hadn't been around as much as he should, there'd always been a tight bond between them.

He'd have seen the signs.

Would have stopped them in their tracks.

Instead, I'd put space between them, both figuratively and literally. She'd overheard my conversation with him, had learned things from our shouting match on the phone that no daughter should ever know, and that had to have messed with her head.

Guilt and shame and fear coalesced inside me, turning the anxiety in my stomach into a knot that made me wonder if I was going to be sick.

This was why I'd shut down.

Why I'd switched off, just waiting on news from the MC about Cyan, but Link's call wasn't the news I needed.

"Honey, I gotta go," he hollered in my ear. "I swear, we're almost there and the second we have her, she'll call you."

"Thank you, Link," I whispered, unsure if he heard me before I cut the call.

"She'll be okay," Rachel told me, and because she wasn't the kind of person to be trite, I almost had faith.

Minutes passed but they felt like weeks, and my mind whirred with the horror of what she could be enduring at that very moment.

It was only by luck that Rain had even seen her getting into that fucker's car.

Willingly.

Jesus help me.

The emotions wouldn't remain locked down as I pressed a closed fist to my mouth. Rachel curved an arm around my shoulder, and I tried to take comfort from her, but she was the Ice Queen. That she was trying at all made me realize just how bad the situation was, which didn't help.

Insanity beckoned, so I turned my phone around again, hoping for more news even though Link had practically promised she'd be the next voice I heard on the other end of the line, which was when I saw Dane's name.

Dane: *Last night was great. Hope we can do it again sometime?*

Was this my punishment? For trying to have something more? Something else? Some*one* else?

My daughter needed me, but she needed her daddy too, and

there I was, hooking up with one of the customers at the diner. A nice guy, all round.

But even though he was pleasant to look at, handsome, even, he hadn't made me feel the way Storm did.

I'd have taken it though. Would have accepted second best, because Storm was a no-good cheater, but as Dane was trying to get me off, my daughter had been making plans to run away from me.

To leave me.

To go be with some old stranger.

A stranger who was going to hurt her.

I bit my lip as I turned my phone upside down.

"This isn't your fault."

Rachel's words were kind, but her tone, as usual, was hard. For all that, I knew her well enough to recognize that she meant every word she said.

She believed what she was telling me.

"Isn't it? Who else's fault is it?"

"Shit like this happens every day, Keira."

I cut her a glance. "You've been hanging with the MC too long. You don't swear that much."

"Wouldn't you swear when your home was like a halfway house for stray bikers?" she asked wryly.

Though I pulled a face, I was in agreement.

"Why did you let them stay here?"

"Because they're my best clients?"

I snorted. "You and I both know they're the kind of bastards who will always land on their feet. They're like cats."

"True enough."

"They've bought that motel now. You could kick them out, make them stay there."

"I could, yes," she agreed.

"But you won't." I arched a brow at her. "Why not?"

"I have room." She laughed a little. "Plus, for all their sins and mine, they're family."

"Yeah," I whispered softly. "They are. I never felt that way before."

"Before what? Today?"

"No," I countered. "Just recently. Since Storm left, they've come around me and Cyan in a way they never did before."

"Probably because you let them in," she replied. "Trust me, I don't keep up with the various BS from the clubhouse, but even I know that you were distant. You didn't go to the parties or take part in any of the ceremonies. You didn't even go to Rex's mom's funeral."

I winced. "I didn't think I was welcome."

She shrugged. "Maybe they felt the same way about you."

"Storm never really asked me to come. I guess I know why now."

"Because he wanted to cheat on you?"

I shrugged, misery swirling inside me as it always would—everyone, to my shame and humiliation, knew why we'd broken up.

"We've always been toxic together," I rasped.

"I don't think that's fair. You were very good for him. Cyan was too. Storm's always been—"

I turned to her when she pulled a face. "Always been what?"

"Well, he was tamer than Scarlet, but he's always been wild."

There was no denying that.

"God, I hated Scarlet," I whispered, feeling bad for saying it out loud but meaning every word. "I was glad when she ran away."

Rachel hummed in agreement. "She wasn't the type of woman who needed to be liked by her fellow sex, was she?"

"She was cruel and heartless." I shook my head. "I hated when I had to invite her into my home. It was like bringing a viper into the place and hoping it wouldn't bite. I never packed enough antivenom."

"They had it rough growing up, but—"

"That doesn't excuse them," I retorted. "We all have it rough growing up in our own way."

"True," she agreed, "and I was just about to say that that gives neither of them any excuse." She squeezed me. "You should know, though... Scarlet's dead."

My eyes flared wide. "What?"

"We only found out recently."

Brow puckering, I put one and one together. "When Rex rode to the Summit?" That was all Giulia and the rest of the girls had been talking about recently. What Rex had learned, what he'd done...

I'd never even heard of a Summit before, but it was a bigass meeting. Really important. When New York's major crime families got together for a meeting to discuss mutual enemies—at least, that was the assumption.

As out of it as I tried to be where the Sinners were concerned, even I knew there was a war going on with the Italians. Even *I* knew to be wary of threats... I just never imagined this would be how my family was torn apart.

By a fucking pedophile.

"Yes. Rex found out then." She cleared her throat. "Keira, this might seem like a strange question, but... you know Scarlet and Storm were born addicted to crack, don't you?"

For a second, the world seemed to stop spinning, and trust me, I was pretty sure that was how it felt before, as I waited, in this endless stasis for my daughter to be returned to me.

"What?" I breathed, not only twisting in her arms, but turning fully around so I could stare at her. "His mother was a crack addict?"

She nodded. "I'm disappointed he didn't tell you, but it doesn't come as a surprise. They struggled all their lives with addiction."

My mouth worked. "Are you being serious?"

"Why would I lie?"

I licked my lips when gaping at her for endless seconds made them dry out. "I've been married to him for thirteen years, Rachel. Are you seriously trying to tell me that he was lying about that as well?"

"Is it a lie? Or just an omission?"

I snapped, "Now isn't the time to turn into a lawyer, Rachel. For God's sake, this is about my husband."

"Soon-to-be ex-husband," she pointed out. "If you still want me to go through with the divorce."

"My *ex* who managed to hide a massive chunk of his past from me." I reached up and rubbed a hand over my face. "Why are you telling me this now?" My jaw worked. "You saw the message from Dane, didn't you? What is this? You're trying to push me back into a relationship with Storm?"

She snorted. "Keira, credit me with some respect, please. I'm thirty-five years' old and I've spent most of my life single—for a reason. A woman doesn't need a man for anything." Her brows surged. "*Anything*, do you hear me? If you want to get back together with him, do or don't, I don't care. I'm just telling you that maybe he isn't the man you think you know because he never let you in."

"And is that my fault?"

She hitched a shoulder. "I don't think fault or blame are appropriate words for this conversation. Storm evidently didn't want you to know. Maybe you should ask why he didn't.

"If you two are going to move past this, if you're going to work together as a unit to help Cyan, because let's face it, she needs all the help she can get, well, maybe you need to look into your own relationship and heal that first."

My mouth trembled at the candor in her words, because I recognized the truth of them.

Storm and I had a strange relationship.

I'd been an obsession at first.

Then, as I'd always feared, that obsession had died a death, and he'd been stuck with me. A pregnant teen wife that he didn't know what to do with.

But, I had to give him credit—he'd stood by us. He'd never let us down. We'd had a nice house, a lovely yard for Cyan to play in, toys aplenty, good, quality clothes, a packed fridge, and I never had to worry about bills or anything like that. It was only when I'd kicked him out that I'd taken a stand and gotten myself a job.

Even then, money had gone into our shared bank account. He'd never tried to punish me by withholding it from us.

In his own way, Storm was honorable.

Just not how I needed him to be.

Rachel, unaware of the pit of my thoughts, muttered, "Let me repeat, I'm not saying you should get back together with him. I'd castrate the fucker first. But I'm saying that Cyan is more important right now, and if you two are bickering, well, it's only going to make things worse. A united front is what you have to work toward.

"I've seen enough horror stories in family court to write a book. Don't be one of those families, Keira. Fix shit now before things derail even more. Whatever's happened to her, she needs you both. She's what matters most. Don't you think?"

I agreed.

Wholeheartedly.

But I gnawed on my bottom lip as I thought about what else he'd hidden from me. Even though I recognized that what he'd done was inexcusable, was I partly to blame?

I'd done stupid stuff over the years. When I thought he was away from home too much, I'd withheld sex, even though I knew there were clubwhores on tap... and truthfully, Storm's sex drive was immense.

He was a bastard for cheating on me, but I'd never thought he was a saint. Had never wanted him to be one, either. After a childhood of having the church forced down my gullet, he'd been a breath of fresh air.

A sinner.

Out and proud.

It was one of the things I'd fallen for all those years ago.

Instead of staying at home when there were parties, why hadn't I joined in? At first, he hadn't wanted me to come, but I knew if I'd taken a stand, he'd have had no choice...

I knew, deep down, I'd never truly forgive him for cheating on me when I was pregnant, for all the other countless times he'd done it, but could I move on? For Cyan's sake?

The bitch of it was, Rachel was right. I had to. *Forgive, but never forget...*

I had to let go of the bitterness, of the regrets, because they'd helped forge *this*.

Had helped create a situation where Cyan's vulnerability had been used against her.

She'd been crying out for her father, and I'd permitted the distance between them to not only span emotional miles but hundreds of physical miles too.

No, this wasn't my fault.

No, this wasn't Cyan or Storm's fault, but Rachel was right. I had to do something, I had to make this better, because I was her mommy, and that's what mommies did.

I swallowed at the thought, just praying I had a chance to make this better before it was too late.

With Rain on her tail, surely the bastard couldn't have had the time to hurt her? Would he have had the chance—

My cell phone buzzed.

I saw Steel's name on the Caller ID, and I almost sobbed when I connected the call and heard my daughter's wobbly, shaken voice, "Mommy?"

I closed my eyes, the terror and the fear and the relief merging into one ardent desire—a need to puke. But I held it back. Had to. She needed me.

"Baby," I whispered, and I let Rachel's arm creep around my shoulders again, and let her support me until Storm made it back to his rightful place.

At my side.

Rachel was right—we didn't need to be together as a couple to present a strong force as we meandered this path as a family, on a journey that would heal our daughter and what was broken between us that made her think she needed to run away like she had.

And maybe it was fitting that, at that moment, I heard the straight pipes roaring down the driveway and I knew, somehow, that it was Storm.

He might never be my Old Man again, but he was Cyan's father. That was what mattered now.

She was all that mattered.

TWELVE

AMARA

WHEN MOTHER AND DAUGHTER REUNITED, I watched from behind the wheel.

I'd never have that.

Ever.

I didn't know if my mother was dead, and even if she wasn't, I'd never go back. I wasn't the Amara they'd raised, and I didn't want them to come to learn *this* child. The one who had been treated like a dog by the rich. The one who'd been pissed on and starved. The one who could kill.

I wasn't ashamed because I thought that was a waste of time, energy and emotion, but that didn't take away from the throbbing ball of *something* that pulsed in time to my heart as it cemented a place in my chest.

I watched their reunion with a weathered eye, but even my cynicism was no match for a mother's love.

At least, this mother's.

Storm hovered on the porch, watching his wife and child, and it was then that I recognized something only a kindred spirit would sense—he was an outsider. Or, at least, he felt that way.

If he didn't, then he'd have rushed into the fray, hugging them both while sheltering them in his arms.

Instead, he hovered, watching, his eyes drifting over his woman and child before they collided with mine. His gaze flared wide, but then, jaw clenched, he dipped his chin before mouthing, "Thank you," at me.

Not needing his gratitude, I just blinked at him, and he shifted his focus back to where it mattered.

He remained on the outside looking in until Keira turned around, blindly seeking him out. She lifted her arm, beckoning him forward, but only Cyan crying out, "Daddy," made him move.

Despite myself, I felt the prick of tears start at the sight, and I recognized that I'd cried more today than I had in a long while. I'd cried after Sarah died, and I'd cried throughout the healing process as Stone and Giulia worked hard to bring us back together again, to heal what others had broken, but ever since then, tears hadn't been necessary.

Until today.

Kindness and love had triggered them, two things I hadn't felt in a long time until the Sinners had come back into my life.

The small family unit went inside, taking with them the emotional storm-cloud that was engulfing them.

This, here, was the first step toward healing, but they had a long journey ahead of them, one I didn't envy.

As they left, I saw Rachel and Rain watching them too. He had his arm loosely wrapped around her waist, and she hugged him tight to her.

Had he told her what I'd done?

When Rachel's eyes met mine, I knew he had. I knew he'd shared the truth with her.

I saw neither anger nor acceptance, just felt the weight of her cool regard, and that was more of a relief than anything.

She was an oddly cold person, and her temperament suited her job to perfection.

Because I sensed we were at a standoff, I dipped my chin at her, and finally climbed out of the car. My bare feet touched the pebbles on the driveway though, and while the pain wasn't there, I leaned back to grab my sandals. When I bent down to toe into them, I saw the blood stains on the clean stones, and remembered that, when I'd climbed back into the car after speaking with Sin, Steel, and Link, something had got stuck in my heel.

Twisting my foot around, I saw a large, bleeding gash, and grunted, knowing I needed to clean it. I'd long since lost much feeling in my feet, and that had nothing to do with my owners, and everything to do with my ballet training. We did worse things to our feet than get something stuck in the heel. Still, I didn't need it getting infected, so I'd have to clean it straight off.

Shoes on, a foot bath in my future, and doing as Sin had asked and leaving the bottle in the car, I crossed the yard, and after moving over to the porch, said, "I apologize for stealing the SUV."

She shook her head, a frown puckering her brow. "There's no need for apologies. You saved Cyan."

Rain pulled a face, but I knew that was more to do with what he'd seen, rather than a reaction to her words.

Rain had watched me take a life today, and that was something few should ever witness.

"I'll clean it later. There may be some blood—"

She raised a hand. "Cruz will see to it."

I blinked, but content to change the subject as I came face to face with her resolve—Rachel was nothing if not a woman who knew exactly what she wanted—I asked, "Where is Rex?"

"I don't know. He'll be home—" She winced, then corrected, "I mean, he'll be back soon I'm sure."

I nodded. "I'll be in my room. Would you tell him that I need to speak with him? Sin, Link, and Steel seemed to think it was important that we talked."

She blinked, but shrugged. "Sure."

I made to move past her, and her hand came out to my shoulder.

She clasped me there, squeezed softly, and said, "The club owes you, Amara. Don't forget that."

"You're bleeding."

Rain's blunt comment had me staring down at the floor, and seeing that blood had indeed begun seeping over the sides of my sandal.

Pizda rulu.

Sighing, I just muttered, "I cut my foot."

His brow furrowed. "How?"

"Do you really want to know?" I snapped.

When he blanched, Rachel laughed. "Rain's stomach isn't forged of iron yet."

He sniffed. "Yeah, I'm not as hardcore as my ancient sister."

She surprised me by grinning, because she wasn't the type of woman to smile freely, and ruffling his hair. "You really wanna be in my bad books today, huh?"

"I'm eighteen, Rach. You can stop with the older sister outrage now, seeing as you can't ground me for leaving the house without telling you first. Especially not when I did what I did. I think you'll find I saved the day." He cut me a look then, awkwardly, shifted in her hold. "I mean, until, well..."

I shrugged. "I'd never have found her if it wasn't for you, Rain."

"I lost her," he said flatly.

"Only at the last hurdle."

He shook his head. "I had a feeling they were heading to Allentown because his turn signal flashed whenever there was a sign for it. I lost him about twenty minutes before we hit the town. I don't know how, but he slipped my net."

That probably explained how Jeremiah had felt comfortable enough to start stripping down.

Had he known he was being followed? Rain's bike wasn't exactly anonymous, not with all the racket it made.

"How did you find us?"

"I searched for nearby motels on the off chance he'd decided to stop. I saw you hanging over the side of the wall as I rode by." His Adam's apple bobbed. "Lucky break, I guess."

I pursed my lips at that, because nothing about today was *lucky*, not in the conventional sense of the word, but I was just grateful the day was over and that Cyan was back home, safe. *Korva*, that Rain was too.

Jeremiah had been armed with a gun. God only knew what he could have done to both children if I hadn't been around. And yes, I considered Rain a child as well. To me, at least, he was.

They both had a lot of growing up to do, something that years wouldn't help them with.

Because I could tell he was a cocktail of humiliated, wary, scared and uncertain, I shot him a calm smile and said, "She's safe, Rain, because of us. That's something to be proud of, and that's all that matters."

I caught Rachel's gaze, watched as her own rare smile made an appearance, and knew she was grateful for my appeasing Rain.

Or, at least, trying to.

I dipped my chin, then, limping, I headed inside. The pain didn't affect me, but the blood made each step slippery.

From somewhere on this level, I could hear Cyan and her mom crying, the low, husky tone of Storm speaking with them, hopefully manning up to the job of being the husband and father they needed, and I sighed, relief filling me as I trudged toward the staircase.

A few steps up, my cell buzzed.

No one really knew this number, so I almost ignored it, but I peered at the screen, saw 'Unknown Number' as the ID.

Curious, I opened it.

Unknown Number: *Heard about your heroics, little birdie. Hawk.*

My heart both calmed and fluttered at his endearment.

Unknown Number: *You'll have to tell me all about it when I get back. You did good, Amara. I'm proud of you.*

It was pathetic to straighten my shoulders a little tighter at his words, but I couldn't stop the smile from dancing on my lips as I took another step toward the upper floor.

On my way, a voice I'd always recognize called out, "Amara? Rain says you're bleeding. Want me to check it out?"

I turned back to look at the woman who'd brought me back from the brink of death all those months ago, and I shook my head. "No, it's okay, Stone. I can deal with it myself."

She scowled. "Well, sure you could, but why would you? I'm a doctor."

"It's only a cut."

She sniffed. "One that's bad enough to have you staining the carpets."

Peering down at my feet, I winced at the bloody footsteps I'd left behind. "I'll clean them," I offered quickly.

I knew how to get blood out of most things. Staring down at the tread, though, I recognized it as being wool, not polyester or viscose. Would my peroxide solution still work on natural fibers?

"Amara, Rachel isn't worried about her carpets, honey," she said drolly. "I'm just making the point that you might need stitches. And how you're not in agony, I don't know."

My nose crinkled, but I hitched a shoulder. "Okay, thank you."

She hummed with satisfaction, and I watched as she moved over to the staircase, her bag of medical magic tricks in one hand, the other going to the rail as she helped haul herself up the first step.

I knew she was still weak from her own brush with death, knew she might always have health issues, and as I looked at her, remembering the woman who'd saved me, who'd been stocky and strong, bristling with volatile energy, I saw that this one was the same, just a little diluted. A lot tired.

"I'll come to the kitchen."

She heaved a sigh, stared up at the stairs, then cast me a glance. "Thanks. It's been a rough couple of weeks and I haven't been sticking to my PT."

"No need to thank me," I retorted, meaning it.

She took each of the three steps she'd taken one at a time, muttering, "I'm not sure why stairs are so damn hard."

"If you take the elevator at work, then you don't get to use them much, do you? Your place on the compound is flat."

"There's a step in it."

Despite myself, I had to laugh at her indignant tone. "A single one?"

"Look, Amara, if you were in all the positions under the sun with Steel, you'd think you could handle a puny staircase." She grumbled under her breath, "Don't tell him. If you do, he'll make me go on the elliptical or something. I hate that fucker."

My lips twisted into a smile, but I just said, "I won't say anything."

I rarely spoke to the bikers. In truth, I'd spoken with them more these past three days than I had in three months.

Even when Link was interrogating me about my affiliations, about Tatána and Tink, I'd kept it to one-word answers.

Conversing when you were pretending not to speak the same language was not only boring but hard work because it took an intense amount of concentration not to reveal the truth.

As we moved into the kitchen, I heard Cyan wail in that gibberish that only kids in deep distress—and at risk of the worst punishments—ever used.

Hunching my shoulders, I cast Stone a look, saw she was already watching me as she said, "She wouldn't let me check her over. That's why I'm here. They're trying to convince her to let me but she says he didn't hurt her. The way she freaked out when she saw me hasn't eased their concerns any."

"He was semi-dressed when I got there. I think he scared her, but he didn't have the chance for anything else."

"That's a relief to know. But the brothers won't be happy until she's checked out." Storm's voice filtered from the other room, louder and sterner than before. "She'll be grounded until she's forty, I'm sure."

I grimaced. "Is that the best way to deal with that?"

She shrugged. "Not our place to question. Seems to me they've had a lot going on for a long time. Maybe that's exactly what they all need. To be grounded together."

"Isn't Storm the Prez down in that other chapter he moved to?"

Stone nodded, then laughed. "That would be amusing for sure. Shame we wouldn't be around for the entertainment of seeing Storm actually being stuck somewhere." Her lips twitched. "He's got the worst itchy feet that I've ever seen. Always got to be on the move."

"Why?"

She shrugged. "They all do. Guess it's the bikes. Motor oil in their veins instead of blood."

"Sounds unhealthy," I said crookedly.

Her grin said she didn't disagree. "I never really got it until Steel let me onto the back of his hog again. When I was younger, I always kept my eyes closed, scared of crashing. Now," her words waned, before she gave me a tight smile, "I know there are worse things out there than the open road."

"I can't imagine you being scared of anything."

A brisk laugh escaped her. "You'd be surprised." She grabbed a chair, dragged it out from the kitchen table, and said, "Right, let's get this foot checked out."

"I really can do it myself," I told her softly.

She shook her head. "There's no need though. You need stitches."

"I could probably handle that too."

"But it would be damn awkward, wouldn't it?" she pointed out. "Let me see the damage."

Grunting under my breath, I shucked the sandal off, and walked on tiptoes to her side.

I'd always been careful to hide my feet when I could, and in all honesty, the last time Stone had checked me over, she'd been too focused on the rest of me to worry about my misshapen toes. This time, however, her focus was on that particular area, so I didn't think there was much hope of avoiding her questions.

Her brows rose when I turned my back to her, put my knee on

the seat, and stared away from her so she could easily tend to the wound without me having to twist into a pretzel. I mean, I could do that too, but this was more comfortable.

"Christ, Amara," she hissed under her breath at the sight of my foot. "Why weren't you limping?"

Did I tell her the truth?

That a high tolerance for pain was a ballerina's stock in trade? That my owners had always enjoyed playing with that tolerance? Trying to make me hurt, trying their hardest to make me cry out?

My mouth worked at the memory, not in sadness or even regret, just with resolve.

Like with Jeremiah, the face of every man and woman who'd tried to break me flashed before my eyes again, and I was left seeing a botched moving picture of people who'd make the Inquisitors look friendly.

Anger whispered inside me as Stone murmured, "I didn't realize you were a ballet dancer."

Pride filled me as I said, "I should have gone to the Kyiv Choreographic College. I earned my place there."

She cleared her throat. "Is that good? I'm sorry, I have no idea about ballet."

"It's the best ballet school in Ukraine. My parents had high hopes for me."

"Oh."

There was a welter of emotion hidden away in that small, soft sound. A conversation neither of us wanted to have, one that dealt with the regrets and sorrow that we each felt for what might have been but never would be.

I was content to remain silent while she tended to my stupid wound, leaving me to think about the past and how I wanted it to dominate my future—on my terms, and no one else's.

THIRTEEN

QUIN

THE LAST TIME I'd taken a beating, it had been in the yard.

Two white supremacists had come at me, calling me shit about not being a *real* American even though my fucking ancestors had been here for millennia before theirs, and they'd whupped my ass.

After being raped and that attack, I'd had no alternative but to bulk up.

Those bastards had broken so many goddamn bones that I could still feel the lingering aches in my being, and that was nothing to those other cunts who'd hurt me worse than with their fists.

The damage to my soul triggered a weird flush of pain that wasn't physical, like with bruises or busted noses and broken bones. It was inside. Like I was exhausted and hangry. Like migraines were going to be my friend for a long time. I was also thirsty and really in need of a fucking shower.

Those were my first thoughts as I let myself register where I was.

Beeping.

The stench of disinfectant.

Was that blood? Or was that just me?

A clinic, then.

I let my eyes drift open, winced at the bright light, then heard a soft, husky, "So, he wakes."

Expecting to see either Nyx or Indy, I was shocked to find a stranger there.

Tension hit me as I remembered exactly what had brought me here—some fucker shivving me in a cell. Some faceless cunt working for more faceless cunts.

"It's okay," the guy rasped. "I'm..." He frowned. "Your brother-in-law?" His hand came up to rub his chin. "My sister and your brother. Does that mean we're tied?"

I shook my head, then regretted it when my brain felt like it was rattling in my skull. "No." It took way too long to be able to rasp out, "Not with a title, other than family."

His lips twisted into a grin. "Family it is." He sank back into his seat, his legs encased in thick jeans that were crossed at the ankle, a taut stomach that was covered in a navy wifebeater, revealing thick arms that were bunched as he curved his hands around the armrests, and what should have instantly told me I was safe—a cut.

Only the sight of that really eased me, because anyone could have claimed they were family.

I was out of practice.

We wore our affiliations proudly in the outside world—I had to remember that.

Not hidden on our skin, tucked beneath brown DOC jumpsuits.

"You kept on dying but apparently, you're a tougher motherfucker than you look."

I squinted at him. "I died?"

"Yeah. Didn't see the light, huh? That's a shame. That sounds cool."

"Does it?" I asked warily.

"Well, better than there just being a black hole at the end of it, right?" He heaved a sigh. "I'm Hawk, by the way."

"Cool road name," I told him.

"Thanks, but it actually ain't one," he said with a smirk. "Dad said he gave me and my brother road names from birth, and apparently I ain't done anything interesting enough to get called by something else yet so I'm more than happy to stick with the one I've got."

"Nyx picked mine."

He arched a brow. "Thought yours was your real name until I heard the doctors call you Caleb."

I raised my chin. "Quin's short for Algonquin. My tribe. Nyx ain't got much of a soul, but he said he had to honor the people who saved his baby brother," I said dryly.

"Saved you?"

"Yeah. Was always sick as a kid, anyway—" I really didn't want to talk about any of that right now. "—do you know where Nyx and Indy are?"

"Outside in the waiting room, but they're sleeping. They've been in here all day and most of the night, so I said I'd take this shift to sit with you while they got some rest."

"That doesn't sound like them."

"You haven't met Giulia, have you?" was his wry retort. "Little Mussolini usually gets her way."

Still drowsy, I blinked. "Is she a fascist?"

"No," he said with a snort. "But she's a dictator and she's Italian. If the name fits, then I'll use it."

That took me a while to process before I tiredly mumbled, "It doesn't fit though. Nyx is Algonquin. Mussolini wouldn't fuck a dude, first off, and wouldn't bone someone who wasn't Italian or white."

Hawk rolled his eyes. "Save the political correctness for when you've met her, and you'll see exactly what I'm talking about."

My lips curved. "Nyx seems really taken with her. When he talked about her, I could see she helped him."

Hawk shrugged. "Takes one fucking headcase to fall for another I guess. She's no angel, so you'll be disappointed if you're hoping she's tempered him."

Did I want that?

Or did I just want him to have some peace?

For over two decades, my brother had been at war. With himself, with the world, with predators... If peace came with a dose of dictatorship from a woman who loved him, was that so bad?

"I hope I like her." I yawned.

Hawk blinked. "I'm not sure Giulia is likable. She just is."

Despite myself, I had to grin. "You really paint a nice picture of her."

He grinned back. "I do, huh? She'd slap me upside the head if she heard me, but she shouldn't have gone to sleep, should she? They'll all be pissed that you woke up on my watch. You really scared them."

I winced. "I didn't mean to."

My gaze darted around the clinic, before it settled on a pitcher of water and a few cups of Jell-O. When I reached out, two things struck me.

I wasn't chained to the bed.

I was in a nice hospital room, not the dump Rikers called a clinic. There was such a difference that it was jarring. It took me a few seconds to register just what it was like in the outside world, and to process the sheer joy I felt at not being caged in any longer.

My lack of cuffs confirmed that I'd been released, and I didn't know how many strings had been pulled for that to happen, but it made me grateful that I'd been stabbed.

Insane, I knew, but truly, another day spent in the joint was a day too many.

There was even a strand of tinsel on the back wall, taped in place, with a few gold baubles dangling from it to make it 'festive.'

I used the word lightly, but it was more than I'd have gotten back in Rikers.

"I guess it will take a while for you to get used to this," Hawk remarked softly, waving a hand to encompass the clinic I was in, picking up on something I hadn't expected—my joy. And let's face it, anyone who'd be joyful in my position had to have been fucking desperate before. But that was Rikers for you. A pit of hell within NYC itself.

I was only supposed to be there thirteen months, but my case had dragged on, and with no other Sinners in there, I'd had no real gang affiliation so I'd been a weak link. A target. Every fight I'd gotten into to defend myself added months to the final sentence, until years passed and I was no longer a kid, but a fucking man, one who was forged in a purgatory that made this stabbing seem heaven-sent.

I knew Hawk recognized my joy because his voice was softer, his eyes kind. I hadn't seen anything like that, anything that might even resemble sympathy or empathy from someone who wasn't family in way too goddamn long.

This, I told myself, *was my path back to humanity.*

To being treated like I was human again, and not just another number to the guards and an enemy to the inmates.

"It's probably going to take longer than that," I agreed, voice husky, watching as he got to his feet, his destination my bedside.

Even though he'd been nothing but kind, it was difficult not to tense up, to fear what he was about to do. When you were inside, life was a game. A push-and-pull tug of war that came without rules, that was lawless, and most often, involved violence.

Right this second, I wasn't capable of any of that, of playing that game, just sitting here, talking, breathing, *feeling* was all I could manage. So, warily, I monitored him and found myself releasing a relieved breath as he reached for the pitcher of water and poured some of the liquid into a plastic cup. When he handed it to me, I raised a shaking arm and winced at the sight of the tremor in my fingers.

"You're going to be weak for a bit," Hawk intoned softly. "No point in rushing it. You're not inside anymore. You can take each day as it comes."

It was rough bringing the tumbler to my lips but I was grateful that he didn't try to help me, because that would have been embarrassing, but also, hard to accept.

I could see that I didn't need to act as if I was untouchable here, but that was a habit that was going to be impossible to break.

What I'd gone through, the injustice of it, didn't take away from what I'd had to endure. My time inside had changed me forever, but even that wasn't what had skewed me. Nyx's revelation during his one and only visit did that. Had twisted what was straight. Broken what was bent.

Even the water tasted better out here. The chilled liquid felt good against my tongue, enough to make me sigh out of sheer enjoyment. I spilled a lot of it down myself, but the cold silk felt good against my skin which seemed as parched as the rest of me.

Hawk took a seat again and I eyed him with caution as I lowered the cup, then, all my barriers soared high when he said, "Aside from the wound, you're in good health."

My jaw clenched as I thought about my time inside. "Any STDs?"

Hawk's eyes flared wide as he shook his head. "No."

My nostrils flared. "Good. I wasn't—"

He raised a hand. "No judgment here."

"Fuck that. No judgment? I didn't ask for..." My words waned. "They vaccinated me against Hep B before I went in. Those fuckers knew I'd be a soft target."

Hawk flinched. "Well, they screened you for everything. You ain't got any STDs or Hep B or whatever."

I just grunted.

"It's a good thing you didn't die."

I snorted. "Well, it is for me."

He shook his head. "Nah, it's good for a lot of people. Word's going around that Nyx is putting down his creaky armor—"

"What's that supposed to mean?" Interest had me forgetting myself, had me sitting up and releasing a pained cry before I plunked back down against the pillows, gasping for breath.

He didn't say anything, just watched me get myself together

again before he eventually murmured, "Can't exactly say it out loud here, can I? Only fuck knows who's listening in."

Still panting hard, I rasped, "Creaky armor? You mean... he told me he won't do *that* anymore, or are we talking about something else here?" I had no idea what Nyx had managed to get himself into since I'd been sent up.

Hawk shrugged. "No. We're on the same page. You know Giulia's pregnant, don't you?"

Despite the pain I was in, my lips curved at the thought of Nyx as a daddy. "Yeah. He told me during his last visit."

"Well, that's why."

"How do you know? Are you on the council?"

"No."

"Did Giulia tell you?"

He sighed. "Giulia and me don't talk. We usually argue, and she wouldn't tell me something like that. It's just gossip is all. Shit's changing around here, Quin. It's a good thing you're out, even better that you're alive because Nyx would have dived face-first into hell to make sure he avenged you."

My throat almost closed at his sincere words, which was really bad timing considering it was hard to breathe.

I'd never told the truth about why I was inside, had never uttered a word about being fitted up for a crime I hadn't committed because I'd never wanted to drag the MC into this, so I'd been dealing with Nyx's disappointment for years.

As I looked back, I realized how stupid I'd been. How idealistic. I'd thought jail would toughen me up, that I'd get out after a year, gain a rep for having served time, and that was it. I never imagined how it would destroy me.

I never imagined that I'd have to kill someone within the prison system, risking more years in a place that was ravaging me from the inside out.

So much had happened, so much had changed, but through it all, Nyx's disgust at my being caught had never wavered.

To hear Hawk say all this confirmed what I'd seen in my brother when he'd come to meet me at Rikers— I wasn't a no hope.

I was his brother.

I was blood.

I was worth avenging.

Stupid how that made me want to cry, but I closed my eyes to shield the tears that burned and prickled along my lash-line, muttering instead, "Yeah, we need Nyx to stick around for his kid. Guess I fought to live so my niece or nephew would have a daddy."

Hawk snorted. "And a mommy. Wherever Nyx goes, Giulia follows."

Despite their wateriness, my eyes popped open. "Huh?"

Hawk hitched a shoulder. "I told you, she's a headcase. I guess we're destined to save our siblings from themselves."

When I thought about the rage burning inside me, a rage that, even in my state, wasn't dampened, just waiting for it to suffocate me once more, I thought Hawk was wrong.

But I didn't say that.

I just rasped, "She'd really go to war with him?"

"She already has. In her own way." He pursed his lips. "Anyway, you get some sleep. You need as much rest as you can get. The plan is to get you home as soon as we can."

"'There is no home anymore," I pointed out gruffly.

"Well, the clubhouse is being rebuilt. It's a slow process but the foundations are already complete, and construction is underway. It's going to be bigger, hopefully better."

"It won't be the same," I countered.

"Nah, decades' worth of DNA makes a house a home, I know." His lips twitched as he got to his feet. "You'll be staying at Rachel's place though."

"Rachel Laker?" My brows rose. "The club lawyer?"

Hawk nodded. "Yeah, a bunch of us are staying there, some are at Link's Old Lady's, and then the MC bought the old motel just off the highway. Most of the single brothers are there, lot of the clubwhores too." He pulled a face. "Not that there are as many as there were."

My brain scuttled to a halt though as I asked, "Why is Rachel letting Sinners stay at her place?"

"No idea, but I'd prefer to stay there than at that skeevy motel." He shuddered. "It's a gnarly dump, man. That needs demolishing too."

The only motel in West Orange had needed tearing down twenty years ago, so I didn't think he was wrong, but my mind was elsewhere.

Rex and Rachel.

They fought like a cat and a dog had been shoved into a bag and kicked.

That she'd invited Sinners under her roof not only astonished me, but worried me.

It was a sign of how much had fucking changed since I'd gone.

What else had I missed?

I stared worriedly up ahead, looking at nothing, focusing on my time inside.

It was hard to process that while I'd been stuck, the hours and days passing on the outside world had evolved at a faster rate than mine had.

As Hawk settled in the chair opposite the bed once more, I whispered, "I need you to catch me up, Hawk."

"You need to sleep," he countered.

But I shook my head—sure, I needed to rest, but I needed information more. I needed to understand exactly what had happened while I was gone.

"Seriously, Quin. You ain't ready for what's going down."

My mouth tightened. "Tell me."

He huffed out a breath. "Well, first things first, Storm's girl was just kidnapped—"

"Cyan? What the fuck?" I almost sat up again, jerking into an upright position before I remembered. And the warning look he sent my way told me that if I hurt myself again, he wouldn't say another fucking word.

Goddammit.

Huskily, voice hoarse with pain and distress, I demanded, "Is she okay?"

"Yeah, she's fine. We got another little helper..."

"Explain," I growled when his words waned.

A gruff breath whistled from between his lips. "Well, it all started when..."

FOURTEEN

HAWK

RELIVING the past year for Quin's benefit wasn't pleasant. The shit that had gone down, the blood that had been spilled, the devastation and the despair—the betrayals, the losses...

In all honesty, it made me relieved to get the hell out of the clinic, to be on the road—even if it wasn't open and was in congested NYC—and to be on my way back to the club's territory.

Having stuck around for when Nyx and Giulia woke up, just because I'd wanted to see Quin's reaction to my sister, I'd slipped out as Indy came barreling in, wild-eyed, crazy-haired, and desperate to see her baby bro.

They had a #lifegoal relationship, IMO. Like, seeing them together made me wish Giulia and I were closer. It had always been me and North against the fucking world, though, and what with the age gap, I guessed we'd always pushed her out.

Guilt twisted inside me, a dash of shame too, because maybe she wouldn't be this much of a fucking nutcase if we'd had a calming influence on her. Maybe she wouldn't be content to live with a guy whose brain was full of clusterfucks and would have done as she dreamed—gone to NYC and...

My nose crinkled.

And done what?

At least she'd found her place here, and now she had her tribe—excuse me, *Posse*—whereas in New York, she'd have worked a dead-end job and lived in a rat-infested apartment.

As it stood, I had no idea how much Nyx was worth, but I knew he, like the rest of the council, was minted. Now she was claimed, bagged and tagged as his Old Lady, she was untouchable, and what else would I want for my baby sister if not that?

My thoughts weren't pleasant, twisted and snarling, the past and the present seeming to be biting us all in the asses, making me wonder what was coming up ahead. The only release I had was once I made it out of the Lincoln Tunnel, and finally hit a stretch of open road where I revved my engine and raced down the highway toward home.

Even as I thought that, I wondered to myself what was going on there. Amara had gotten involved somehow, all Nyx had said once he'd gotten the call from Sin, was that she'd taken out the threat.

I was sick of talking in doublespeak. All throughout my recounting of the past, I'd had to be cautious about the words I used, so it would be a relief to be home.

Taking out a threat meant killing someone, so Amara had killed for the MC?

I wondered if she knew what that meant. If she was aware of how big a deal that was to the club.

My jaw worked as I thought about the other day. Her riding my face like she should have ridden my cock, like she should have felt *free* to do so, and even though I wanted to say that I didn't see it in her, didn't see that kind of violence, I knew it would be a lie.

It was there.

Hatred and bitterness bubbling away like her soul was a cauldron, acid tearing at the walls, destroying it and strengthening it all at the same time.

Just like Quin.

Something was riding him as well, more than the shitty hand he'd been dealt.

Something like Amara's but unlike it too.

Amara's was personal. Like a shield.

Quin's smacked of regret. I'd only registered that once I'd seen his face light up when Indy had made an appearance earlier, then dim with a smack of something I couldn't translate as he buried his face in her hair, shoving aside the pain he was in to hug her like there was no tomorrow.

Well, for him, there almost hadn't been so I guessed that could explain the regret I saw... I doubted it.

Instinct told me there was a deeper story at play.

When I finally turned into West Orange and took the long, privately-owned road past the clubhouse and toward her property, the gates to Rachel's house were open. That rarely happened, but was indicative of the fact that people would be coming and going for the next few days.

I didn't worry because I knew Lodestar would have this place tucked up safe and sound. With Mav back in hospital again, the club's security was down to Lodestar, whose abilities more than preceded her.

I'd gone slower on the road so as not to wake anyone up as it was only five AM, but when I got there, I saw there were lights here and there dotted in each bedroom, and after what had gone down today, hell, this past month, maybe it made sense that not everyone would be able to sleep.

As I pulled up in front of the six-piece garage, I stretched and yawned, feeling exhaustion tugging at me as my boots crunched against the pebbled-driveway while I walked to the front of the house.

It was probably only because I'd approached from the side, Rachel having bitched at me about parking in front, that I saw her. Or, maybe it was because I was aware of her like I'd never been before. I always managed to find her, even when she thought she was hiding from me.

Tonight, though, she was on the porch swing again, out in the open, her eyes on me, glittering in a way that was positively supernatural.

There wasn't that much of a moon tonight, and the lights were all in the upper story, but I felt her attention like a brand and my heart quickened.

I had no idea why.

None whatsoever.

But that wasn't the only thing that had 'quickened.'

My dick started to get hard as I clomped up the first few steps to the porch, and without saying a word, I took a seat at the other end of the porch swing.

Hand shifting to the armrest, my fingers clenched around it as I set the swing into motion.

A breath whistled from her lips.

I stared straight ahead, trying not to think about why my heart was pounding.

"I killed a man today."

Five words.

They weren't what music was made of, weren't even heaven sent to make my cock hard, and yet, I had to accept that I was probably as fucked up as Giulia because my dick stopped twitching and finally went to full mast.

Of course, it had been that way ever since I'd gotten a taste of her sweet cunt.

"How does it feel?"

"*It?*" she whispered. "Don't you mean, how do I feel?"

"I can already tell," I told her calmly, maintaining my position by not looking at her. "You're fine."

"You're right. I am." She clucked her tongue.

"How does it feel knowing you've taken a life?" There was no judgment to my tone, just interest.

Amara hesitated, before eventually asking, "Have you killed someone before?"

I cleared my throat. "Twice."

She stilled. "Really?"

"Yes." At that, I turned my head to the side. I couldn't see her, not much more than a shadowy specter of her shape, but I wanted her to know she had my focus as I told her, "I'll never lie to you, Amara."

"People always lie."

It was funny how she did that. Her hatred wasn't aimed solely at men, but at people in general.

That told me women had hurt her too, and why that infuriated me more I had no idea.

Anger filled me to the point where I felt like I was choking on my words as I managed to grate out, "People lie, but I ain't just anyone."

She hummed. "Only time will tell."

I dipped my chin. "True." My hand tightened around the armrest. "I used to be a bounty hunter."

"What is that?"

"When you make bail..." I winced, knowing she wouldn't understand that either. "Okay, so when you've been arrested and charged for a crime, you go up before a judge who sets bail. You can pay it and be let out until your court date is set, or you can stay in jail until that date. You with me?"

"Yes, I am with you. I am here."

My lips twitched, flushing some of the anger I felt on her behalf away. "I meant, do you understand?"

"Oh, yes."

"A bounty is triggered when someone cuts and runs before their court date. I mean, when they run away so they don't go through the process of a trial.

"Bounties are like a cash prize. If I caught the escapee, then I got the prize."

"And you hunted them?"

"Depending on your definition of literally, yes. I didn't shoot them." Not all of them. "I just had to snatch them and haul them in to the cops. I got paid their bounty when I did. There are a bunch of shows about this shit. You might like them." In fact... "You should watch reality TV, it'll get you up-to-date with informal phrases and stuff."

Amara, not unsurprisingly, ignored that, and asked, "You killed one of the people you were hunting?"

"Yes."

"On purpose?"

"One, yes. The other..." I hesitated. "No."

"What happened?" she asked softly, twisting slightly in her seat.

It was strange to know I had all her attention. She had a way of looking at me as if she was aware I was there, but wasn't interested.

I'd say she was apathetic but I thought it went deeper than that.

Heaving a sigh, I admitted something that could get me arrested, but Christ, I knew shit about her that could get her arrested too. A secret for a secret? Was that what our friendship, our *relationship*, would be forged on?

"The first guy, it was purely accidental. I chased him down this alley, and the dumb fuck decided to go headfirst through this window into a warehouse. He landed on some railings that were being stored there. Went straight through his gut." I pulled a face. "That was fucking nasty, let me tell you." The tears in his abdomen had been so extensive, I'd seen his intestines.

It wasn't technically murder, but the reason he'd been running away from me had nothing to do with my hauling his ass back to jail, but because of what I'd been about to do to him... The fucker had beaten his wife to death. I figured he deserved some of that love too.

Up to that point, I'd been a model employee, so my bosses had chosen to believe me when I'd told them I'd come across him being beaten by a mugger, and when he'd seen me, he'd taken off running.

"And the second?"

My mouth tightened as the memories of those case notes flooded my mind. "You know what a foster parent is?"

"Someone who is paid by the state to care for children who have no parents? Like Lodestar with Kati?"

"Pretty much. Well, they get a subsidy from the state. Don't get me wrong, lot of good people out there who are doing that, but there are some bad weeds among the flowers."

"Aren't there always?" she rasped.

I couldn't deny she was right.

"This one had four. Not sure how the system failed those kids, but I picked up the slack."

"He hurt them?"

"Yes. Boys, the lot of them." I cleared my throat. "One of them had issues—" The thought still had the power to make me feel physically sick. "Rectal issues from what the bastard did to him."

The swing creaked as she turned to me. "What did you do to him?"

"You really want to know?" I asked cautiously. "It isn't a pretty story."

"I sliced Cyan's groomer's throat with a broken bottle of soda and stabbed him in the eye with a key," she said flatly. "If I could have sawn his penis off, I would have done but there was no time. He had a gun and Rain and Cyan were in danger."

"He'd have deserved that," I concurred, almost wishing she'd managed to achieve that with the cunt who thought he could take a Sinner's flesh and blood and mold her into his sex toy.

"Then we're on the same page," she whispered. "Tell me what you did."

Jesus.

That whole shit about 'people in glasshouses shouldn't throw stones' rang loud and long in my ears as I thought about how often I gave Giulia and Nyx crap about being fucked in the head.

This was the reason I'd stopped being a bounty hunter, though, because the second I'd acted, I'd gone from being an upholder of the law to a vigilante, and the worst thing was, I didn't, *couldn't* regret it.

Scraping a hand over my jaw, I admitted, "I fixed a knife to a chair and made the guy sit on it."

"That's it?"

For a second, I just blinked, then I rumbled, "Not sure which part of that you didn't understand, little bird, but trust me, that's no way to die."

"Wait, he died?" she queried, and the porch swing squeaked again as she turned to me fully. "I don't understand."

With a sigh, I muttered, "It was point up, Amara."

"Point. Up," she repeated, then mumbled something in Ukrainian to herself. I waited for her to get the picture, not really feeling like painting the scene for her when it still played on repeat in my dreams some nights. "He had rectal problems after, *tak*?"

I snorted at her matter-of-fact tone, one that told me she was still figuring out the dynamics.

I wasn't sure how this had gotten lost in translation, but I figured this wasn't the topic of most people's conversations.

"If he hadn't bled out first, yeah, he'd have had rectal problems."

She waited a beat, then asked, "Hawk?"

"Yes?" If I sounded wary, then so be it. I was almost surprised she hadn't gotten to her feet and stormed off.

"I am ready for another orgasm."

I blinked. "Huh?"

"You said you'd give me another orgasm when I wanted. I want. Very much."

My brow puckered. "Now?"

"*Tak*."

"*Tak* means 'yes,' right?"

"It does." She got to her feet, then she swept down and her hand unerringly found its way atop mine. Her nails dug into my wrist as she slipped her fingers around it, and she pulsed that grip, punctuating the urgency of the situation as she snarled, "Now."

FIFTEEN

AMARA

I'D BEEN in a strange state all day.

Edgy, wary, waiting for the other shoe to drop. Waiting for the axe to fall.

It hadn't.

It never would, either.

Whatever Sin was doing in Allentown, he'd yet to return, but I knew if there'd been a problem, someone would have come to me.

Instead, I hadn't seen anyone since Stone had tended to my foot. After, I'd retreated to my room until I heard the bedroom doors of everyone in the house close, then I'd come outside.

Rex hadn't returned from wherever he was, Nyx and Giulia were probably with Nyx's brother, the bubble around Storm, Keira, and Cyan had yet to be popped but every now and then, a sad, soft wailing could be heard, and as for Rachel and Rain, well, I had no idea what they were doing.

The one who'd interested me the most was Hawk. I hadn't seen him all day, most of the night, and I didn't like that.

I was used to him coming in late. Used to him appearing with his hair stinking of smoke and his clothes rumpled. But not *this* late, after a day away from the house—a day with little to no sleep.

I didn't want to say I was concerned, but it was a definite relief to have him back here. To know he was safe. Something had happened today, something I hadn't been privy to, but that was okay. One thing I was learning about the MC was that a lot of things I'd never be privy to. It was how they worked. I knew, for example, that if Hawk hadn't been involved in whatever was happening, he'd never know about what was going down either.

Everything worked on a strictly need-to-know basis.

I was more than fine with that.

Even as he sat there beside me, even as I felt his confession in my soul, even as his words sent aftershocks through my body, I recognized that he hadn't said a word about where he'd been, and I didn't expect him to.

I was used to being kept in the dark.

At least, this time, I wasn't being caged too.

I'd been gripping his wrist, but he tugged his hand away and slid our fingers through each other's, making a bridge with them as we walked silently into the house and along the hall, up the stairs and toward my bedroom.

When we made it there, I pushed open the door, switched on the light, and squeezed his hand before I moved deeper into the room and went to close the curtains so I didn't have another rude awakening like... yesterday. God, that was yesterday now.

Time... it had a habit of slipping through one's fingers, but never more so than during a crisis.

As I dragged the drapes closed, the metal eyelets rattling against the rail, he moved into the bathroom. I didn't turn around, but I heard the thud of his boots falling to the floor, the rustling sounds of clothes being removed, of his metal belt buckle clipping the tiles, and something else—maybe his wallet?—thudding as it hit the ground.

When I heard the shower turn on, I twisted around to look at him, and caught a glimpse of his backside as well as the lean length of his hip and thigh, the muscles that bulged in his back.

A man should look defenseless naked.

He should look vulnerable.

Hawk didn't.

He looked magnificent.

And the shower, thanks to its glass doors, revealed everything to me.

He had a mop of hair that was a strange length to me. Neither long nor short, but faintly curly, and beneath the water, it turned into ropes of silk. He closed his eyes as he tipped his head back under the fall, and I bit my lip as I watched the sinews in his throat come into play.

I wasn't sure why, tonight of all nights, I was seeing something I hadn't noticed before, but I wasn't going to complain, not when I registered his purely masculine beauty and recognized that he was going to let me have a part of that.

The water made every inch of him gleam, and in the overhead light, his skin seemed like rippling gold beneath hard muscles that I knew, if I wanted, I could touch.

Feel.

My fingers curled in on themselves—I wanted to touch him.

Unlike the other day, I hadn't wanted to. But tonight, I did.

He'd harnessed that strength for me, and I wanted it again. I wanted to experience that soaring rush of pleasure and ecstasy and triumph once more, because, I'd realized earlier, what I'd felt seeing Jeremiah die could only be likened to the orgasm I'd felt the other day.

And I wanted it.

More of it.

I was greedy for it.

Greedy for the man who'd given me that, who'd given me pleasure with no pain. Who'd given me acceptance with no expectations of more.

Even now, after a long day, after something that had made his voice heavy and husky with fatigue, here he was, cleaning himself up, with the intention of giving me pleasure.

Hawk twisted around and reached for a bottle of soap from the shelf in the stall, then after rubbing it between his palms, he started smoothing it over his chest, under his arms, along the lengths of his biceps. I focused on the singular tattoo on his chest; the compass was large, black and negative space made up the points, and I knew what it represented—*North*.

Did North have a Hawk tattoo?

I'd seen and done and been a part of much worse, but heat made my cheeks turn pink as I watched him, in a matter-of-fact way, reach down, grab his cock and clean it, before he smoothed more soap down the length of his muscled thighs, and up again.

He turned around, presenting me with his ass that was so peachy, I wasn't even sure what to do with it—I knew women would say it was bitable, but I didn't want to bite or be bitten. That round curve would show the depressions of my nails to perfection, but I'd experienced that and knew it could hurt.

As I looked at a man who I recognized I was attracted to, I also came to terms with how fucked up I was.

Arousal—I felt it, so that was a relief—but worse, I didn't know what to do that wouldn't remind me of what I'd done and experienced.

Any other woman would want him on top of her, rutting on her with a wildness that I knew existed in him, those eyes of his were kind, but I saw the glint of steel. I knew he was known for being gruff, taciturn, even grumpy, but with me, he hadn't been. That just meant that other side hadn't come out to party yet, but I knew it had to at some point.

I'd bet that when he was between a woman's thighs, he turned darker. Not mean, just more domineering.

Could I cope with that?

Him telling me what to do?

Or would it be guidance?

Deep inside my stomach, I felt the sweet ache of a feeling I'd only ever felt when I was younger, when I'd realized what sex was for. Back then, I'd dampened it down because I didn't have time for boys, but a few stolen kisses at school dances and birthday parties had been enough to show me what innocent desire and sweet passion was.

This was like that, but there was fear and regret and resentment all whirring together like the smoothies Rain made in the morning and that I watched him prepare in the massive Vitamix they had on the counter.

I wanted so much.

I knew I couldn't have it.

And that was a sweet torture of its own.

My hands started to ache, and I realized that I'd been gripping down on the windowsill to the point where my knuckles looked like they could burst through the skin.

Wincing, I released my grip, saw how white the skin was, and I shook them out. Pink flooded the yellow as I stretched them back a little, and by that point, the water had cut off and Hawk was drying himself down.

Did he know I was watching him?

I made no bones about it, didn't try to hide that I was looking at him, but he hadn't cast a single glance my way.

The towel went over his head and he scrubbed at his hair then his face, and when the terry cloth sagged, falling over his shoulders instead, his gaze pinned me in place at long last.

With our eyes connected, he tossed the towel over the stall so it hooked over the door, then he pulled them open and stepped out.

He was magnificent.

There was no taking away from it.

Beautiful, graceful, elegant, even.

But he was a man.

Eventually he'd hurt me.

Something flickered in his eyes, those glorious kind eyes that saw so much while he said so little, and silently, he trudged over to the bed, lifted the covers, and lay down beneath them.

I watched him with a frown, taking note of the slick strands of hair that would make my pillow damp, the way his muscles shifted as he leaned back with a deep, tired sigh, and murmured, "Come to bed, little bird. There's no need to fly away tonight."

My throat closed at his words, but that was nothing to the prickle of tears that made my eyes burn.

His words were an order, a soft one, but a command nonetheless, and it didn't irk me or pain me to comply. If anything, I slipped out of my shoes, the jacket I'd been wearing, and moved over to the bed in my jeans and camisole.

When I got under the covers, his presence was solid at the other end of the bed, and I turned my face to stare overhead at the ceiling when I realized that looking at him would be far more interesting.

Pivoting to the side, I saw he was watching me watch him, and I pointed out, when I knew I shouldn't, "You were gone a long time today. You must be tired."

"I am," he said with a sigh. "Nyx's kid brother got hurt. He almost died." Concern for Giulia flared in me, but it was tempered by the weariness in Hawk's face.

"I heard about him." I should have realized Hawk would be with his family after something like that happened.

"It sucks. Poor bastard was only just about to get out." He clarified, "Quin's been inside a couple years."

"Inside where?"

"Prison."

"How badly was he hurt?"

"He almost died."

I frowned. "It was a bad fight."

"Yes."

"What is 'shivved?'" This was the word I hadn't understood from the brothers' conversation earlier.

"It's when someone is stabbed but with a makeshift weapon. In jail, they sharpen plastic spoons into knives, things like that." He pursed his lips as his eyes fluttered to a close. "I won't hurt you, Amara."

Swallowing, I rasped, "They all say that."

"I'm not 'they,'" he murmured, and that he'd taken no offense at my statement soothed something inside me. "You'll learn. I don't lie."

"Why don't you? Everyone lies."

I saw a sliver of his chestnut brown eyes in the light and noticed the gleam of amusement as he explained, "I'll lie about whether something tastes good if Giulia made it and I hate it because I value my dick being attached to my body, and if a woman asked me if her ass looks big in a pair of pants, I ain't about to be a dumb fuck. But some shit you can't lie about. That's why folk think I'm mean. I ain't. I just don't like bullshit."

"Bullshit makes the world go around."

"It does, just not my world. White lies exist for a reason. They do no harm. But the truth..." He heaved a soft laugh. "Well, it'll set you free, won't it?"

I wasn't sure why that was funny, but I asked, "Does the truth set you free?"

"Maybe. Maybe not. Didn't help Quin. That's Nyx's brother," he explained. "He got sent up because of a racist fuck of a judge, and maybe something else... *someone* else helped him on his way."

I didn't understand every word he said, but I got the gist of it, and I hurt for this unknown brother-in-law of Giulia's. To be imprisoned through no fault of your own—that was something I understood.

"I want to—" My words waned. "Hawk...I..."

"Not like you to be hesitant, little bird," he muttered softly, his eyes catching mine again. "This is a safe space. Ain't gonna do nothing that hurts you, ain't gonna judge you."

He said that now.

"Cyan's... the man. I knew him. He was the first person..." Why was this so hard to say? I'd already spoken of this once with his brothers, but Hawk wasn't his brothers. Hawk was, well, I didn't know what Hawk was exactly.

I just knew he didn't make me feel like I was in danger, and that was infinitely precious.

"It's okay," he said softly. "You can tell me tomorrow."

Gulping, I reached out a hand and pressed it to his chest. "No, I-I want to tell you." He didn't reply, but his tired gaze remained firm on mine, making it both harder and easier to get this out, to confess to the truth. I sucked in a sharp breath, then whispered, "When I was first sold, there was a man who broke me in. Cyan's groomer was that man."

His nostrils flared. "I really wish you had sliced off his dick now."

A shocked laugh escaped me, one that sounded far more like a sob than anything else. Slowly, a grin appeared as I felt the weight of his acceptance as if God himself was applying a soothing balm to my soul, and I huskily agreed, "It would have felt good."

"I'll bet." He placed his hand on mine, tangling our fingers together once more, before he closed his eyes again.

I bit my lip, aware that I should let him sleep, so I twisted slightly and reached above the nightstand where there was a wall switch for the overhead light. Once I was shrouded in darkness, my eyes darted about the room, seeking the darkest shadows, the pitchest black of them. As a child, I'd thought those were the scariest parts, but now, I knew that there was nothing scary about the dark.

In fact, the dark was a blanket. It hid sins. It sheltered secrets.

The light was dangerous.

The light was where you saw malice in someone's eyes, in their heart.

Biting my lip was no longer enough, I started to gnaw on it as my mind began racing.

All day, I'd been thinking, trying to process what had happened, trying to accept it, and trying to dissuade myself from where my brain had gone during my fight with Jeremiah, but there was no avoiding the truth—I'd enjoyed it. I wanted to do it again. I *needed* to do it again.

I was lying in bed with one of the most beautiful men I'd ever come across and instead of him being on top of me, instead of his dick plowing into me, making me come, instead of my hands dragging over the muscles in his back, nails digging into his ass to encourage him to pump into me harder, I was chasing shadows in the dark.

Exhaling through my nose, I whispered, "Hawk?"

He hummed. "Uhhuh?"

"I liked it."

I felt him shift from drowsiness into awareness. It happened slowly, over the course of a few moments as he registered exactly what I was saying. What I was admitting.

"You liked killing him? That's understandable," he rumbled. "He hurt you."

Hurt was an understatement.

He'd destroyed me.

My innocence.

My hopes, my dreams.

He'd ruptured them like he'd ruptured *me*.

Clenching my eyes closed at the memories, wishing they were a black hole too, I whispered, "I want to do it again."

"To anyone in particular?"

"Everyone who hurt me. Who hurt Sarah, Alessa, and Tatána."

The bedding shifted as he rolled onto his side. "Is that possible?" he asked.

"Is what possible?" I replied. "Hurting them?"

"No, hurting them is the easy part. But you were in their keep for a long time, little bird. Do you even know who hurt you?"

Mimicking him, I rolled onto my side so I faced him. In the dark, it was easy to admit, "I remember every single face I've ever seen since I was three. I can tell you them detail for detail."

He snorted in disbelief. "You're kidding, right?"

His lack of faith didn't offend me.

No one had ever believed me on the rare occasions I shared my gift with anyone, but it was true. Even though I hadn't been 'diagnosed,' and only knew it had an official name because a teacher had once discussed it at school, I'd come to learn I was something called a super recognizer—such a simple name for something as powerful as the ability to never forget a face.

"I wish I was."

His hesitation told me he had questions, and I didn't mind answering them. I just hoped he could help me.

"How does it work?"

I shrugged. "It's not magic. I just remember a face and it never disappears."

"So, what you're saying is that you'd be able to remember the face of every person who'd ever hurt you? You'd be able to describe them to ID them?"

That he sounded bewildered was a given. I was used to that. Not even my mother had believed me, and when she'd told Papa, and he'd chided me for lying and making things up, I'd never shared the truth with anyone again.

It wasn't much of a talent, just required a good memory, and in my life, a good memory was the last thing I needed. If anything, I wished I could scrub it clean, erase all those laughing, cheering, mocking, sadistic faces that haunted me.

"Yes," I whispered. "But I'm no one to the MC, Hawk. I'm a burden. They have no reason to help me—"

"You killed someone to protect a brother's daughter, Amara," he countered instantly, brushing my words away. "You don't realize how indebted the MC is to you. But... what is it you want?"

I hesitated over how to describe it, but my thoughts were in tune with my needs as I eventually rasped, "I want to erase them."

"Erase the faces? Or their lives?"

"Both?" I shrugged. "Either? I don't care. I just, well, today, I knew that the feeling of eradicating him from this planet, stopping him from hurting someone else, it was the right thing to do, Hawk."

I licked my lips. "If I have to, I'll use the money Lily gives me to do it.

"I only accepted her offer because I wanted the security—I wanted to know that, no matter what, I'd be financially safe, but I'm not safe when I close my eyes." Distress had me hiccupping as I felt the edges of my control begin to shrivel and shrink, growing smaller and smaller until I felt certain the yawning pit in my soul was going to overtake everything else. "They're there. They haunt me. I see them when I go to sleep. I see them in my nightmares. I can't deal with seeing them anymore."

He was silent for so long that I was sure he was either going to tell me I needed a psychologist—which was true, and which Tiffany had been helping with—or that I was a sick bitch and he wanted nothing to do with me.

"May I hug you?"

I tensed. "Why?"

I felt him tense up too. "Because I'd very much like to hold you?" He sighed. "No expectations. No pain. Just holding you, giving you the comfort I can."

It shouldn't have sounded tempting, but I was coming to realize that Hawk, and his unusual manner, was disarming. Enough that he made me want to try the things he suggested.

I'd come to bed wanting an orgasm, his tale of doing as I wanted to do—eradicating evil—reminding me of the euphoria I'd experienced when I'd climaxed and when I'd killed Jeremiah, but now?

Things were different.

I wanted a hug.

We'd had group hugs during the sessions where Tiffany gathered us together and we talked about our pasts, about our trauma, but we hadn't had that since the clubhouse had been destroyed.

I missed those meetings, I realized.

I missed them more than I might have imagined.

Because I wanted to feel his arms around me, because I wanted to feel safe and Hawk had yet to hurt me, and would, I knew, protect me if anyone tried to come into my room and force me to do things I didn't want, I edged nearer to him.

Inch by inch, I approached him and he didn't move.

Then, when his breath brushed my forehead, his heat like a wall against my side, his arms slipped around me. One hand sliding under my neck, one resting over my waist. He curled me into him, pulling me tighter until we were tucked together, huddled as a unit, and the solid feel of him, even the pressure of his dick against my legs, it felt good.

Surprisingly so.

A shaky exhalation rushed from my lips as I turned my face into his chest, and with my expression hid from him, I whispered, "Thank you."

"You don't have to thank me." His touch was hesitant but I appreciated it nonetheless as he started to stroke his hand over my hair. He was gentle, soft, and the motion was enough to make me sag into him. I'd always loved having my hair played with when I was a girl, and this reminded me of that. Of Mama braiding my hair for ballet class. Not the hard tugs of men and women as they raped me, not the locks that fell free as they pulled it from the roots.

This was everything my past wasn't.

"You need to speak with Rex," he murmured softly. "And if he says no, then Lodestar. She's the one to go to. She's the one who'll help, but you need to at least try to get an okay from Rex first."

"Why? I'm not a brother."

"No. But I am. You're not doing this alone, little bird, and I can't be with you if it isn't sanctioned by the Prez first." He hesitated. "If he says no, Lodestar will help, but I'll have to figure something out."

My brow puckered. "I can do this alone, Hawk. You don't need to get involved."

He squeezed me, hauling me tighter into him in a way that didn't feel aggressive, but more like he needed to hold me rather than vice versa. Like he needed the comfort too. "Yes, I do," he stated grimly.

Then, his lips moved to my temple and he pressed a kiss there. "Tomorrow will come soon enough, Amara. Let's get some sleep."

I didn't argue because I was also tired, but his words, that he'd want to take this journey to redemption with me, filled me with something I hadn't experienced in too many years—warmth.

Not just the physical kind, even if that had been scarred over the past few years.

The emotional.

That yawning pit of despair and grief and loss and rage felt farther away, like I wasn't about to tip headfirst into it, which, for tonight, was enough.

If anything, it was a luxury.

SIXTEEN

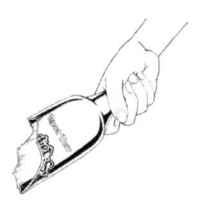

HAWK

I WOKE up to soft lips brushing against mine, gentle hands smoothing over my chest. They were tender touches, reverent almost, and that was why I woke up with a smile on my face, my sleepy eyes drifting open as I sighed into each caress.

A slap to the face would have had me jerking into an upright position. This? Christ, a man could get used to being awoken like this.

My body responded before my mind came online, and when it did, that was only because my eyes caught on the mussed up silk that was Amara's short but shaggy hair.

She was beautiful.

Early in the morning, late in the afternoon, or in the depth of night, it didn't matter when. But, all told, it wasn't her beauty that drew me. I couldn't even say she got my dick hard. When I looked at her, I didn't think only about sex—I thought about a lot of stuff. Most of it crazy.

As I stared at her, watching her lips press soft kisses to my cheek, appreciating this tenderness more than I really knew how to articulate, I reached over and carefully slipped my hand over her head, moving it around so that I could cup the back of her neck.

The second I did, she tensed, and her eyes darted to mine.

"I won't hurt you," I reassured her, my voice husky from sleep.

I felt like I hadn't slept enough but from the light in the room which illuminated the pinpricks of her pupils, I knew it was well past midday. If I hadn't seen her visceral reaction to our conversation, I'd have known she was scared simply by how still she was.

A cornered rabbit.

Though the last thing I wanted to do was move, I murmured, "Stay here."

I didn't think it was asking much because she was frozen solid, but I untangled myself from her and padded over to the clothes I'd left on the bathroom floor before my shower early this morning.

Bending over, I reached for the knife I always carried. A soft intake of breath had me casting a glance at her, and hiding a smile because she was totally checking out my ass.

Despite the seriousness of the situation, for her at any rate, I strutted my way back to the bed, aware she was watching me like I was the prey this time, and she wanted me. *I could see it.* Those pupils of hers had dilated, and her body was no longer so tense, her focus intent on me.

I knew where as well, because she didn't even notice the dagger until I slapped it on the side of the bed and took a step back from it so she knew I wasn't going to pick it up and use it against her.

I'd seen her scars. I knew someone had cut her along the way.

Her gaze drifted to the bed, her interest limited, then she saw the weapon and stiffened up again.

"My dad gave me that," I told her softly, folding my arms against my chest as I leaned against the wall at the side of the bed.

"Why? This is an odd gift, isn't it?"

My lips twisted. "Maybe. Not for a brother in an MC. He gave it to me when I was nine, that's probably the oddest thing about the gift." I tugged on the chain around my neck, the one with the cross on it that Mom had given me and North when we were kids.

"He gave a nine-year-old a dagger?" She frowned. "I thought children here were protected. Sheltered."

"Some are. Not in an MC." I shrugged. "It was the last birthday present he gave me."

"He stopped giving you presents at nine?"

I shrugged at her deepening scowl. "He wasn't a very generous, gift-giving kind of guy."

Now he was gone, it was easier to accept how much of a jackass he'd been.

"It is precious to you?"

I nodded, because I couldn't really explain why it was. The man had been a shitty father, so why should his last birthday gift to me matter worth a damn?

I had no reasoning as to why it did. It was just how it was.

"Then why do you give it to me?"

I could have told her that it was just for the moment, just until I left the room, but I couldn't. The words wouldn't fall from my lips. "Because I want you to have it."

Her frown deepened. "I could just use one from the kitchen."

"You could," I agreed. "But that one has meaning. It's been with me since I was a kid, and it's protected me from a lot of shit—"

"Then you need it more than me."

"Not if you go ahead with your plan."

Her mouth flattened as she looked down at the blade, and the way she held it felt familiar. Not like someone who was handed a knife to cut a fucking onion, but who'd used one before—on another living thing.

I'd guess she'd butchered animals before, which told me that her father had either been a hunter or a farmer.

Storing that away, because getting information out of her made pumping Giulia for details look easy, I murmured, "If I ever hurt you, you can stab me with it."

Her eyes darted to mine, shifting away from the scuffed handle that I'd clutched so many times when I was in a dangerous situation. Even when you knew you were safe, it felt good to be armed. To know you could defend yourself. Maybe not against a gun, but guns weren't always an option.

"I-I don't think you'll hurt me."

The declaration spilled from her like a confession, and I wouldn't lie that it made me feel good. Being treated like a potential rapist wasn't great for anyone's ego. While she clearly recognized the truth, her body didn't.

"You helped me with the others," she whispered. "You're..."

When her voice waned, I said, "Your body doesn't register that yet. It might never do. I touched your neck, little bird, and you tensed up like I was pulling your hair out by the roots. Maybe knowing you're armed will make you feel better?"

She blinked up at me, but there was an abyss in her eyes this time that hadn't been there before. I couldn't even describe what made me think that way. The irises hadn't changed color, and it wasn't like black had splintered through, but they were so loaded with desperation and despair that I felt my breath being stolen from me like she was the Angel of Death on earth.

"What if I can never have my neck touched? Or my hair? What if I can never enjoy another person?"

Oxygen rushed into my lungs to the point where I felt woozy as I finally took a breath. Gulping, I rasped, "Do you want that? To touch and be touched? Or do you just want to be left alone?"

"I look at you and know that I want you," she admitted, and her gaze danced over me again.

"Maybe attraction isn't enough," I murmured, even though it definitely felt good to know that she wanted me.

There was something about her... something that clicked.

It hadn't before. I'd seen her around the compound. Hunched shoulders and a serious case of resting bitch face. I'd been more interested in the club snatch, especially when they were *verboten*—Prospects weren't supposed to fuck clubwhores until after they were patched in. But now, after becoming a full on member of the MC the very night the clubhouse had been bombed, after the shit my family, both by blood and the MC, had gone through, it was like my eyes were open.

I saw her.

I'd seen her when Alessa's hands were deep in her hair and Amara had allowed her to shove her face into the table like she was a bag of groceries, and I'd seen how much of a lost soul she was when I'd stopped Giulia and her fucked up Posse from going after her some more.

I saw her.

Now I couldn't stop.

My jaw tensed at the thought because I didn't like the ramifications of all that, especially not when she was admitting shit to me that no red-blooded man needed to hear.

I sucked in a breath, though, and rasped, "You want me, maybe that's enough for the moment."

Like it protested, my dick got hard when she palmed the knife, her hand tightening about it as she eyed the blade rather than look at me some more.

The way she handled it, fuck, my dick wanted some of that handling.

Gritting my teeth because we might never have that kind of relationship between us, might only ever be friends—friends who'd seen each other naked—I edged away from the wall and moved over to my dirty clothes once more.

When I scooped up my jeans and started to dress, she whispered, "It isn't fair."

I turned back to look at her. "No," I agreed. "It isn't."

She clenched her hand around the handle once more. "May I try something?"

I arched a brow at her, aware of what she was asking by the way she was staring at the knife. "Another man might be fearing for his balls the way you're eye-fucking that blade, little bird."

She cast me a glance. "You're not just any man, though, are you, Hawk?"

My lips twitched into a smirk. "I'd say I was one of a kind but that's a lie."

She blinked. "Why?"

"Because I'm a twin," I teased.

A breath sifted from her lips. "Oh, yes, I forgot."

"Wish I could," I muttered on a sigh.

"You miss him?"

"Very much," I told her simply.

"Even though he betrayed your father?"

"Didn't betray me, and he wouldn't have. North always was a romantic." I pulled a face. "Dog didn't treat women right. Not my ma, probably not his Old Lady, and probably not Giulia at one point or another." I hitched my shoulder but conceded, "You grow up with abuse, you get used to seeing it, you start accepting it... If Katy twisted and tugged at his heart strings, I'm not surprised North did what he did. He always did see himself as a white knight."

"What is a white knight?"

"A woman's savior. It's a weird thing from, like, romance movies and shit." I crinkled my nose as I moved back to the bathroom door and raised one arm high so that I could lean against the jamb. If I was playing into her attraction for me, then so be it. I'd be a saint for her, to help her, but that didn't mean I wasn't all sinner too.

Maybe she'd never be able to touch me back, maybe she'd only ever be able to take, but I wasn't going to keep shit free from temptation. In my opinion, temptation made the world go round.

Amara was stronger than she knew. If she had the brass knuckles to kill a cunt, she had the brass balls to control her sexuality.

I watched her, aware her gaze was hot, loving how she licked her lips, how she swallowed when her eyes found my cock. I wasn't ashamed that I had another boner. I'd have been dead from the waist down if I didn't respond to her but there was something about her that made me see past getting off.

That made it okay that I didn't.

Probably helped that she was A-okay with killing the dudes that had hurt her.

To be a man was to hurt a woman, what with the whole Venus and Mars shit, so this was not the kind of chick that you got on the bad side of.

Right, this was getting fucked up.

Why did my boner ache even more at the thought of that than anything else?

The words drifted from my lips before I could stop them—the curse of being a man whose not-so-little head was doing the thinking for him—and I told her, "Amara, you're not a victim anymore. You can do whatever the fuck you want and when." As if the world was in agreement with me, a burst of sunlight warmed the room, making shit brighter than ever, before it turned darker. Like a cloud had passed over the sun. "You're rich, you're about to get a green card because Rachel won't stop until you're legal here, and you know what you want to do with your life. That seem like the mentality of a victim to you?"

Her brow puckered, but the shadows from the murkily-lit room cast her eyes into darkness. Kinda fitting considering the topic at hand, no?

"There is a difference between acting and between accepting what happened to me and moving on from it."

I shrugged, not about to let that wooden tone or those defensive words of hers stop me from making my point. "You need to ask yourself if killing the fuckers who did shit to you will solve anything then. You have the chance for a normal life, Amara. You can be legal and go traveling, find your-fucking-self in the wilds of Alaska or party away in Key West. But nothing's gonna change how you feel about yourself on the inside."

"And fucking you would solve that, would it?" she sneered.

My lips curved into a grin. Her question stung, but I was a big boy. I could take any shit she threw down.

"Don't see me offering myself on a platter to you, do you?"

Her gaze dropped to my dick again. "That says different."

"It does, but dicks have a habit of getting hard around hot chicks," I told her flatly. "Dunno if you looked in the mirror lately, but you're hot as hell."

That, for whatever reason, had her licking her lips. "I'm ugly."

The flat tone had me arching a brow. "Ugly?"

She scowled. "This is the word, no?"

"I don't know what you're trying to say, because you might be many things, little bird, but ugly ain't fucking one of them."

Out of nowhere, rage floored me. *This* was the mindset I had to break. Fucking wouldn't do shit, but making her see herself for what she was might help, and I wanted to.

In any way she'd let me.

I had no idea why when she was a stranger to me, no idea whatsoever, but those fucking eyes of hers, they'd ensnared me in a trap I didn't want to get free of.

I stormed forward, watching as she tensed up on herself. She knew I wouldn't hurt her though, she fucking knew it, so I felt no guilt as I leaned down and hauled her into the air.

"Let me down, you bastard! *Poshel na huy!*" she snarled, her hands forming fists that hammered against my legs, thighs and butt. "*Khuy tebe v zhopu!*" She almost took me down with a well-aimed punch to the back of my knee, but I righted myself by latching onto the door and straightening up fast. "*Idi v zhopu!*"

"You take me down, we both go down," I snapped. "Why the fuck would I rape you in the bathroom when I have a nice bed there?"

My words seemed to get through to her, and though I understood the instinctual response, and was pleased that she'd chosen to fight instead of curl up into a ball like she'd effectively done with Giulia's pussy Posse, I was also pissed.

Not enough to add to her fear by being a douche and almost

dropping her on purpose, but enough that I could have handled her more gently when I hauled her back over my shoulder and forcibly twisted her around to stare at herself in the mirror.

My hand was under her chin, forcing her to look at herself as she fought me, nails digging into my wrist, the tips dragging against my flesh, hard enough to mark as she wriggled and writhed against me.

My boner was RIP so the wriggles did nothing for me aside from confirm that I wasn't a rapist piece of shit, because why would you wanna fuck a chick who was struggling this hard when you could screw them senseless by treating them right?

She twisted around to try to bite my throat, and I spread my fingers out wide, letting them net around her jaw so that I could better control her.

"Look at your-fucking-self," I growled. "See what I see. A fucking fighter. A goddamn warrior queen. You're a pain in the ass, Amara, you're bloodthirsty and angry, but fuck, you're hotter than hell."

She tensed up as I carried on, "Look at that fucking face. See what I see. You're beautiful. So fucking beautiful. And those goddamn eyes of yours, you trapped me with them that day in the kitchen. Ever since, I can't get them out of my mind. You looked at me like you were lost, but you're not lost. You're anything but.

"You need to stop treating yourself like you're the victim you were, because you survived that shit to do better, to be better, little bird.

"You want to take those fuckers out, and I get it. I'll even goddamn help where and when you'll let me, but if you want to get back at them, you live your best fucking life, do you hear me?

"Get a sick kick out of taking 'em down, but enjoy your life in between—"

"It isn't as easy as that! They haunt me. I remember everything, I can see their faces, their enjoyment, I remember it—"

"So? Don't let that take away from what *you* did. Don't let that stop you from looking in the mirror and seeing you for what you are. A fucking survivor.

"I ain't been through the shit you have, I know that, but I know what you are, and I know that every time you don't do something *you* want, you're the only person who's suffering.

"Those cunts couldn't give a fuck about what they did. They're probably tormenting some other poor bitch as we speak. They moved on—it's time you did too. You're the one who decides how.

"You, not them. *You*, little bird."

I sounded like I'd been running for a couple of hours when I finished, my breathing was coming in harsh inhalations and rough exhalations, but that was just how impassioned I felt.

"Fuck me or don't," I ended hoarsely, "but see yourself how I do, little bird, and that's half the battle won."

Her cheeks were pink from exertion and from the blood having rushed to her head when I'd hauled her across the room. Her tits bounced with her own panting breaths, and even from this angle, her reflection was stunning. She was like a beautiful doll, well, if Barbie got killah with it, and I refused to leave this goddamn bathroom until she accepted what she was.

Gorgeous.

Her flared nostrils quivered once as I stared down at her, willing her to look, but she rasped, "I haven't looked at my reflection in years."

"Why not?" I rasped.

"Because I see myself in front of the barre. I see myself en pointe, hair slicked back in a tight bun, my skirt dancing around my thighs as I move into position. I see myself as a ballerina, how I was, not how I am." Her accent grew thicker the longer she spoke, the words deeper and more passionate.

"Your present has changed," I informed her softly, like she didn't already know that, but I got it. For someone who said she never forgot a face, for someone who remembered everyone she'd ever seen, looking at herself in the mirror back *then*, would have been like signing a death warrant, I guessed. "You're with me now," I whispered, and even though I had no right, I dipped my chin and pressed my lips to her temple.

I figured it was rejection that had her head whipping away from my caress, her face finally angled toward the mirror and not twisted away from it, but when the reflection of our gazes entangled, I whispered, "See yourself how I do, Amara. You're almost there, little bird."

She swallowed, and all the goddamn while, those eyes of hers slayed me.

I felt as if each individual striation in her irises was a strand of light that was heaven-sent to blind me. To steal the breath from my lungs, to rob the words from my lips.

I'd never known a power like it, something that was close to fucking magic as it ensnared me in a way no other woman ever had or probably ever would.

I felt as if we stared at each other for a lifetime, then her lashes fluttered; once, twice, and she stopped looking at me and finally looked at herself.

When her bottom lip quivered, I slipped my hands around her, changing my hold, moving my fingers from her jaw, and instead, curving it around her waist, hugging her, supporting her, gifting her with my strength.

She sagged into me, accepting what I offered as she looked at herself.

And though neither of us said a word, I knew we were both thinking the same thing.

That she was, as I'd told her, *beautiful.*

While I didn't have a mental checklist of things that I needed to do today, I knew I could scratch item one off it even as I approached the next issue—confronting Rex and getting his help.

Amara had a bucket list of motherfuckers to kill, and I wasn't about to let her do that on her own.

SEVENTEEN

STORM

WHEN MY CELL buzzed with an incoming message, I yawned and blinked bleary eyes as I turned away from the bed where Keira was sleeping and where I'd been watching over her all night.

We'd almost lost our daughter.

Neither of us could get over that.

I wasn't sure if we ever would, or if we ever should.

I was well aware that it was all my fault.

That the mistakes I'd made over the course of our marriage had led to this moment, and that I didn't deserve for her to even look at me, never mind talk to me, but yesterday, when Cyan was sobbing and raging and hurting, Keira had looked at me, and I'd seen her ask me for help.

Silently.

Not a word uttered.

Not a single request whispered.

Just like before. Just like when we'd made sense.

I'd known then that she'd let me in for Cyan's sake. I'd known that she could hate me and loathe me and detest me all she wanted, but for our baby, she was going to stop pushing me out.

That was why I was here tonight.

I'd been sleeping in the motel the Sinners had bought for the guys who'd been made homeless in the blast to live in, but she'd let me sleep on the strange sofa that was in her room. It was old and long, thin, too. Like the L-part of the sectional without the other seats attached to it.

It hadn't been the most comfortable night's rest but it was definitely better than the bed at the motel.

She was here.

My wife.

My woman.

My obsession.

A never-ending infatuation that ate away at me, gnawing at my bones worse than any cancer ever could.

Some days, she was all I saw. Even when I was in fucking Ohio.

She was all I breathed and ate and drank and felt.

I'd never admitted it in AA or NA or any of the many fucking support groups I'd attended over the years, but she was worse than heroin. She was a cocktail of crack and Big H and LSD all wrapped up in one.

A shaky breath whispered from my lips as I reached down for my cell. The battery was close to dead but Rex had messaged me, and even though I was a Prez now, on the same standing as him, he was not only the leader of all the Sinners, I'd always be his *numero dos*.

I was happy with that. Even though I hated Coshocton, the best part was being the Prez, but Rex was always the ultimate.

The guy I'd aspire to be, and the guy I'd never live up to.

Rex: *You awake? We need to talk.*

I rubbed my eyes and tapped out:

Me: *I'm awake. Give me twenty.*

Last night, I'd made a decision that wasn't going to be popular as I tried to get to sleep. Listening to Keira cry into her pillow, and knowing that she didn't want me to hold her, had been a kind of purgatory in and of itself. She was one of the strongest women I knew, but she was forged in her upbringing—men made the hard choices, women went along for the ride.

That was the only reason she'd stuck around for as long as she had anyway. Because her momma had done the same and so had she. Until she'd snapped.

The day she'd tossed me out was a day I was the proudest I'd ever been of her.

Even if it had destroyed me—I deserved that and worse.

Yesterday's crisis had her falling back on old habits, and while I shouldn't encourage that, I was going to take advantage.

That made me even more of a bastard than I already was, but I knew what Cyan needed.

Me.

Her Mom.

Together.

She needed for me to be the father she deserved, and I could only do that when we were in the same goddamn town.

I'd fucked up, screwed my baby girl over so that she'd gone looking for what I freely offered as her daddy in the arms of a man who'd taken her need for paternal love and had twisted it into a sick game where she'd almost been raped and God only knew what else.

So, no, I had to pay for my mistakes. I had to rectify them. And we needed to do that as a family.

Rex: *Okay. We need to talk about yesterday.*

Me: *Yeah, we do.*

I clambered to my feet, trying to be quiet because Keira needed the rest but when I stretched, trying to wake myself up for the shitty day ahead, I saw she was watching me.

It was past twelve, so even with the curtains closed, the light illuminated her in a way that just reminded me of what a fuck up I was.

Paul Newman had once said, 'Why go out for a burger when there's a steak at home.' Well, Keira was more than a fucking steak. She was an All-You-Can-Eat buffet that served prime Wagyu goddamn beef.

I'd always known that.

Just like I'd known I wasn't worthy of her.

Never would be either.

Throughout my stretch, I felt her gaze dip over my bare chest, and when her eyes locked on my new ink that peeked out from under my jeans' waistline, she tensed up.

I knew why, too.

Couldn't blame her for her surprise, not when I'd shafted her the way I had.

Even Indy had mocked me when she'd done the job, because everyone was aware of how much of a screw up I was.

"You had no right to do that," she rasped, her cheeks pink, even as the rest of her was a curiously pinched white. Her eyes were bright and wide, but I saw the way her breath skipped from her lungs.

She was a good girl.

We'd never fucked nasty.

I'd always made love to her. Treated her like she deserved.

She'd never think about the shit I imagined when I used to jack off to thoughts of her.

I wasn't sure if fate was cruel or not to pair me—a hardened sinner—with a woman who'd been spoon-fed the Bible along with mushed up carrots as a baby.

"I was just stating a fact."

"A fact?" She blew out a breath. "Some fact when that dick's seen more action than a Terminator movie."

"Want to see the rest of it?"

Her gulp was audible. "No," she said immediately, but her gaze belied the truth.

She did want to see it.

Even if it was only to satisfy her curiosity.

Even if it was only to know that I was forever marked this way while she'd never let me into heaven's gates again.

I didn't exactly ignore her, but she'd seen all this before and I had to shower, so I slipped down the zipper, enjoying the way her breath caught as I shucked my jeans down my hips and kicked out of them.

"What have you done to yourself?" she whispered, her eyes wide with distress.

"What I should have done a long time ago."

She licked her lips at the resolve in my tone. "Does it hurt?"

"Not really. It just means—" I shrugged, then I strode over to the dresser where her purse sat. I grabbed it and tossed it on the bed, murmuring, "Check your keys."

She frowned. "Huh?" Her gaze was still connected to my cock.

"Check your keys," I told her softly.

She scowled as she snatched up her purse, and blindly did as I asked.

Keira was the kind of woman who never took the keys off her ring, and I was well aware she still had some from the first house we'd lived in together. It wasn't that she was being lazy either, just a nostalgia thing, which was how I knew I could do this without her ever spotting what I'd hidden on there.

As her hand drifted through the crap she kept in her purse, she whispered, "How long did it take to heal?"

"Couple months."

She tensed. "You did this before you left for Ohio?"

I dipped my chin. "I did."

"What? Why?"

"Why do you think, Keira? The tattoo says it all, don't it?" Without looking, because I knew where each fucking letter rested on my groin, I traced the words that Indy had shaken her head over:

Property of Keira.

Of course, that declaration was only cemented by the heavy-duty padlock I had threaded through the Prince Albert piercing at the tip of my shaft.

When her hand collided with her keyring, she tugged them out and I said, "The key's been on there for a while now. It'll always be there too. There's only one, there'll only ever be one. You own this. You own me. You always have."

She snapped, "Bullshit."

I shook my head. "Not bullshit. The truth." I wasn't upset by her disbelief or her anger. I'd earned it. "I fucked up, Keira. I always fuck up.

"Do you know what it's like to be sent to hell, to sit among the shitpile with other lost souls, and to look up, and to see an angel flying overhead, one that let herself be snagged by a dirty fucking cunt like me?" As her breath caught at my words, I shook my head. "I never should have touched you. You should have had better. I know that. I also know you'll never touch me again, and I'm okay with that too." Just the thought of her fucking finger on my body, a single goddamn fingertip, was enough to give me a boner. She saw it and gulped. "This is my penance. This is my truth." Done with the conversation, I twisted around, telling her, "I need to speak with Rex."

"Y-You can't just leave—"

"Nothing has changed for you, Keira. Just because I went ahead and did this, doesn't mean you'll ever forgive me. I'm not asking you to." I stared at her over my shoulder, caught her checking out my ass, and whispered, "You deserve the best, and I'm so far down the ladder that I'm worse than the worst." Licking my dry lips, words that choked me spilled free, "I know about Dane, and I give you my blessing with—"

"What? How could you know about him?" she snapped, her eyes flaring wide as she jerked upright into a seated position.

"I followed you," I told her simply. "And if I can't follow you, I pay a brother to follow you."

"What?" she rasped, wide-eyed as I turned back around.

"You heard me."

If I was going to confess to my sins, I'd go all out. The weight off my chest was surprisingly liberating. But it was a day for being honest. In the face of yesterday's nightmare, after a situation that could have been a thousand times worse than the hell it already was, honesty was required from here on out.

So, I released a breath, one so deep that it almost felt cleansing, and admitted, "You always have eyes on you, Keira. Always. You always will as well, no matter where you live or what you do. But I'm going to ask you that, even if this guy makes you happy like I never could, that you don't stop me from what needs to be done."

"What are you talking about?"

"The three of us are going to Coshocton today. We're leaving, and we're not coming back. This place isn't good for me, or for you or Cyan. It's loaded with memories. We need to be free from them.

"I ain't ever fucked a clubwhore there, not since I was Prez or before when I stayed at the compound on a run. No one really knows me because a lot of the old guard did a runner when I took over.

"It's a fresh start. I'll set you up in town, fix you up in a nice place, and you can do whatever you want. Get a job and save for school or you can just go straight to school—I'll pay."

Her mouth gaped as I admitted I knew about her dreams of being a nurse.

I was ashamed that I'd been holding that goal over her. Praying she'd come to me for the money for school when, instead, she'd worked herself to the bone to attain it for herself. Which, of course, had helped lead to the situation with Cyan.

All my fucking fault as usual.

"It's your life, and you can do what you want, and I'll pay for that, but I just ask that you let me eat dinner with you every night. We need to present a strong front for her sake."

She blinked at me. "You know about school?"

I heard the dazed tone, recognized it.

"I know everything where you're concerned, Keira. But I was a dumb fuck and never acted on it." It choked me to ask because she could say no, just like she had when I'd left for Ohio the first time. "Will you come with me, Keira? It's the only way to right the wrongs we made, to ensure Cyan doesn't suffer for the shit I've done, and for the path it took us down." While I'd presented it as an order before, I knew I couldn't make her do shit.

Her bottom lip trembled and when her gaze caught on my padlocked dick once more, she whispered, "We can never be, Storm."

"I know that. I'm not asking for us to get together, just for you to let me be the father I should always have been."

She sucked her bottom lip between her teeth but, after what felt like a lifetime, finally nodded.

And the relief that filled me was immense. Like a burden off my soul.

"Thank you."

I made to head for the shower again, but she whispered, "Why did you have me followed? Didn't you trust me? Did you think I'd cheat on you or something?"

I frowned at that, and spun to face her. "You're too good for this world, Keira. I wasn't about to let anyone taint you."

Her mouth worked, and I saw the confusion in her eyes, confusion I couldn't alleviate. "I don't understand you," she whispered miserably, her hands clutching at her purse, raising it to her chest like it was the teddy bear—George—she'd had since she was a little girl and which she had kept in our bedroom since we'd moved in together.

My smile was sad. "'You and me both, Keira." I heaved a sigh. "You and me both."

The anger would come later for the years of breaching her privacy, for the moment, she was shell-shocked, not just from yesterday but from what we'd discussed this far.

But I'd take it.

So long as she came with me, so long as she let Cyan be with her dad again, I'd take everything she had to give.

For decades, I'd lived up to the image I'd forged for myself. A man who was intent on leading a 1%-er MC, who accepted no shit, who took no prisoners. It had ruined my life, wrecked the only woman I'd ever love, and had nearly destroyed my beautiful baby girl.

It was time to change.

Time to be whatever they needed.

The buck stopped here, with me, which meant I'd be spending the rest of my life in atonement, and I was more than okay with that.

EIGHTEEN

REX

WHEN A KNOCK SOUNDED at the door to the dining room, I peered over at it, and debated over whether I could pretend about being in.

Rachel wasn't happy about my taking over the space as an office, but she was being accommodating which was weird. I wasn't used to her not riding my ass over petty bullshit.

I'd have missed that side of her if I didn't also appreciate what she was doing for me, for my brothers. For the MC. For Dad, too.

Bear was the real reason she was cutting me some slack. Our mutual love for him was the only thing we had in common anymore. I wasn't in denial, but that she was tiptoeing around me rather than slamming my face into brick walls was a change and I needed that change.

For so long, we'd been fighting. So much wasted time...

It was everywhere at the moment.

Wasted, precious time.

More valuable than money.

The most priceless commodity in the world.

I gritted my teeth as I thought about Dad leaving me behind soon.

It would never have been easy, but in all honesty, the way he'd been hurt made it a thousand times harder.

The need to avenge him was real, but so was the need to right the wrong that had been done to Mom, to Scarlet, Storm's sister, too.

So many fucking wrongs right now.

I reached up and pinched the bridge of my nose, and guilt hit me at letting whoever was out there hover.

Being Prez wasn't just a case of being the leader of a bunch of motherfuckers who ran drugs across the borders, guns and other contraband too. It wasn't about keeping them out of gang wars or keeping them safe. It was about keeping the MC together. About making sure nothing tore us apart.

For that reason alone, I grumbled, "Come in."

The door edged open and I saw Amara's face peering through it.

"Go on in, little bird," someone muttered, and I saw Hawk next as he shoved the door wide. "He won't bite."

That she might be scared of me made sense. It was unnecessary but I'd already noticed that Ghost—I meant Alessa—Amara, and that bitch Tatána had always had a problem looking at me in the face. Meeting my eyes. Normally, that'd make me distrust a person, but after what they'd been through, it wasn't like their submissiveness should come as a surprise.

What did?

That endearment—*little bird*.

Hawk was sniffing around Amara?

One of the grumpiest bastards I'd ever come across was calling chicks 'little bird?'

Had I entered the *Twilight Zone*?

Brow furrowed, I watched as he strode in, while she hovered at the door.

Considering I'd been given updates by Sin on what she'd done to the bastard who'd, potentially, murdered my mom, and might have sexually abused Cyan—Storm and Keira couldn't get a yes or a no out of her as to whether the cunt had touched her, and she started screaming whenever Stone tried to give her a checkup—her wariness was dichotomous to the killer of yesterday.

When Hawk realized she was still hovering, he grumbled under his breath, trudged back to the doorway then curved his arm around her and jimmied her into moving.

I'd set up the dining room table like it was a desk. The long side was where I sat, in the middle, and I had all my shit, the new computers I'd had to buy since the blast, and a bunch of records that, thank fuck, we kept in a secure vault at a warehouse we owned in East Orange, scattered on the surface in front of me.

The other dining room chairs had been moved around the other side, neatly distributed so it didn't fuck with my OCD. I waved a hand at them and said, "Take a seat."

Watching as Hawk pulled out a chair for her, then prodded her into sitting down, I cast him a curious glance as he stood at her back, one hand on her shoulder.

I'd have bet a hundred grand that, until the blast, he'd never uttered a single fucking word to her, and considering how traumatized she was, I didn't know what the fuck he'd done since to make her trust him, or, at least, to get her to open up to him, but something had definitely happened.

Something I wasn't sure I was happy about.

Hawk worked for the MC, wasn't on the council, but he was Giulia's brother, my VP's brother-in-law. That put him in a position where he could overhear shit, and Tatána's treachery still stung.

I'd always prided myself on having a tight knit circle, but somewhere along the line, shit had started to fall apart. I didn't even know why or where it had begun, just knew that it had.

The rot had set in years before my reign, though. It had happened on Dad's watch, and I'd just inherited the subsidence, but I was still left to handle the structural repairs, repairs I didn't know how to make.

I'd had confirmation today that the bastard Amara had killed yesterday, that London fucker, had gotten onto our compound and he was the one who'd set the bomb which had essentially murdered my father and destroyed our home. But that destruction came in more waves than just the physical—it hurt our rep, and in this world, that was everything.

Tink, an ex-clubwhore I'd tossed out after she'd started beating on Stone, had helped that fucker gain access to the compound, and she was roaming NYC while my men hunted her down like the vermin she was.

Tatána, one of the women we'd spared from a certain death alongside Amara and Alessa, had screwed us over to help some stalker cunt who was obsessed with Indy, get more information on her. Tatána's corpse had been found in the burning wreckage of my office of all places...

So, no, trust was an issue at the moment. Especially when it involved a woman who'd been close to Tatána, and who, potentially, had access to Giulia and Nyx through Hawk.

Either way, there was no denying what she'd done yesterday. For the MC, for Storm and Keira, but most importantly, for Cyan.

My voice was husky as I told Amara calmly, "The MC owes you a debt."

She licked her lips. "I knew him. I did it for me and for everyone he's ever hurt. You don't owe me anything."

I arched a brow at that, especially when Hawk grunted, "Amara."

She frowned, but didn't look up at him. "I-I'm here because I'd like to ask you something."

"Ask away," I rumbled, taking note of her English level—she'd really pulled the wool over our eyes which didn't inspire that much confidence in me.

"I'm not requesting this as a favor. I truly mean it when I said there is no debt owed."

Waving a hand as I slouched back against my chair, I murmured, "Go on."

"I-I have an ability to recognize every single face I've seen."

Well, that had my attention.

Sitting up, I leaned forward, elbows on the table as I asked, "I've heard about that before. They use people like that in the intelligence community. I know Britain has a whole squad of them."

She blinked. "I-I didn't think you'd believe me."

I shrugged. "No reason to think you'd be lying when you want something from me. Especially when it's something that could be easily disproven." I smirked at her. "I don't take being fooled lightly, Amara. You should have figured that out by now."

Slowly, she nodded. "No one has ever accepted it without question before is all."

"Understandable. But I take an interest in a lot of things. Most of them varied." Especially when it came down to evading law enforcement.

In the UK, the cops there used people like her to trawl through closed circuit footage, watching hundreds and thousands of hours of recordings to pinpoint faces in crowds. These squads were more accurate than fucking computers.

Pursing my lips, I asked, "How accurate are you?"

"I have no way of knowing."

"True." Damn, I was curious now. "Who was the first face you saw who wasn't family?"

"I don't know her name, but I can draw her face. She was a nurse."

"Who was sick?"

She shrugged. "I don't know. I just remember her face."

"How do you know she's a nurse?"

"She wore a uniform."

Humming under my breath, I plucked a pen off the table and grabbed a sheet of paper from the printer and passed both over to her. "Draw her."

Though she complied, as she started sketching, she murmured, "I'm not the best, but I can usually make someone easy to recognize."

I didn't say anything, just cast a look at Hawk and saw he was peering down at the sheet of paper with interest. It didn't take a genius to see he wanted to believe her but wasn't sure if she was bullshitting him or not.

Because I was willing to give her the benefit of the doubt, I explained, "You ever heard of face blindness, Hawk?"

He kept his eyes trained on her drawing. "Yes."

"This is the opposite of that. Both have been documented for a while."

"I'd never heard of anything like this before," he admitted.

"The human brain can pull off a lot of weird shit."

"I guess."

Amara stayed silent throughout the short conversation, but when she was done, she winced as she peered down at it, muttering, "My skills haven't improved over time without practice."

Intrigued, I watched as she turned the paper around, revealing the picture she'd drafted.

In all honesty, it reminded me of the illustrations in those Dr. Seuss books Rain had loved as a kid and which I'd read to him some nights when Rachel and me had been friends.

With no point of reference, I couldn't calculate her accuracy, so switching my attention to my computer, I pulled up the footage of London infiltrating the compound.

I wasn't sure how Lodestar had done it, but she'd managed to get a close up of his reflection in the windshield of the truck, and she'd matched that to the fucker who'd come to the house yesterday. Both shots were stitched side by side on my screen, and I murmured, "Draw me the guy you killed."

She dragged the sheet of paper back toward her and got sketching.

I couldn't help but notice that she didn't flinch at all at my words.

Not that she should, considering who the bastard had been to her, but still... Her lack of guilt or remorse or fear was interesting.

A few minutes later, I was looking at London in three separate images.

Scraping a hand over my chin, I contemplated her a second

before asking, "What do you want, Amara? Why are you telling me this?"

"I remember every single man and woman who abused me." Her voice broke a second, and I noticed Hawk's hand squeeze her shoulder in comfort. "I see them like ghosts that haunt me."

I pursed my lips. "You want to take them out?"

She didn't answer that, just gushed, "I'm willing to spend the money Lily gave me to find them. I'll give it to you—"

"That's your money," I said gruffly. "And it's between you and Lily, anyway. She'd be pissed if you gave that away. She wants you to feel safe."

"I'll never feel that while these people plague me."

Rapping my fingertips against the table, I mused, "Link mentioned something you said yesterday. About the Sparrows." Those fucking bastards. We were going in blind with these cunts. We had no solid leads as to who was a Sparrow and who wasn't. No names, no faces.

Amara dipped her chin. "The people w-who we serviced..." She gulped. "...they were Sparrows."

I froze at her words, a welter of excitement filling me until I saw her nervousness, the little flutter of her pulse at her throat.

Was she lying?

"All of them?" I rasped.

"M-Most of them." Here was the catch... "Some were married to them."

I shot a look at the pictures of the Sparrow-sent assassin Lodestar had emailed over, then glanced at her drawing...

Bullseye.

NINETEEN

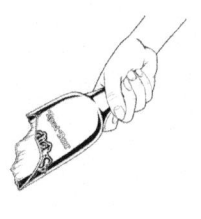

QUIN

I WOKE up with Indy curled beside me on the bed, and Nyx and Giulia hissing at each other on the other side of the room.

Aside from the sister-in-law who I was pretty certain was certifiable—just like her brother had said—it was business as usual.

I'd spent way too much time in one clinic or another over my lifetime, more than I'd been in jail, in fact, and I'd often woken up like this—Indy beside me, sleeping, Nyx pacing like he could walk off his demons.

It never worked.

I always felt like death warmed over, while he just looked like walking death.

Bleary-eyed, I rubbed at them, yawning, "What's wrong?"

My words had Indy stirring, but she'd...

God.

She'd always slept like a log when I was in the hospital and she napped with me, but I remembered how she was a light sleeper as a kid.

Was that because of that cunt uncle of ours?

Did she feel safe with me, with Nyx, because she knew we'd die first before we let him get his hands on her?

Even as Giulia was twisting around to stare at me, Nyx too, I felt as if my body was in the grip of Satan himself, and that he was shaking me to the point where my brain rattled, memories overwhelming me in a rolling reel as my sister-in-law growled, "Your brother's being insane."

Indy huffed out a sleepy laugh, telling me she was half-awake. "Isn't that what Nyx does?"

"Yes, it is," Giulia concurred, but her voice was tight. "But that was before he made promises." She jabbed her finger into Nyx's cut. "I refuse to raise this kid on my own. Can you imagine me as a mother?"

"Can you imagine Nyx as a father?" Indy muttered with a laugh, but she was grinning as she sat up, yawning as Giulia glowered at her. "The pair of you will both be crazy parents, but together, you'll make some semblance of normal. Anyway, he made *me* that promise, Giulia." She arched a brow at Nyx. "If you're thinking about going on some other kind of spree, then think again, Nyx."

Our elder brother's jaw grew tense as he scanned me with a look that, I was sure, was more penetrating than a fucking X-ray. "You think I can just let this go?"

"You have other responsibilities, Nyx," I told him, knowing he was talking about my attack. "You can't take everyone else's troubles on your shoulders."

"You're not everyone else. This is blood, Quin. Blood. You were nearly taken from us. I lost Carly, but I'm not about to lose either of you."

Giulia snapped, "And what am I? And what's this kid? Chopped liver? What the hell are we supposed to do if you end up in jail, huh?"

Nyx gritted his teeth. "I don't get caught."

"Bet your ass you'll get caught now you just said that. It's Murphy's fucking law," she snarled, her arms coming up high against her chest in a move that was both ballsy and impatient but also, self-comforting.

As much as I recognized the madness in this woman, a madness Hawk had described pretty aptly, I also saw the way she looked at Nyx.

Exactly the same way he looked at her.

Their two types of crazy gelled perfectly.

I'd seen Nyx with a lot of women, but never had I seen him like this. It'd be borderline whipped if, ya know, he wasn't willing to go on a murder spree to avenge me.

The only way to keep him here, however, was to guilt trip him and a little like Indy and Giulia, I was fine with that. Nyx had spent over two decades killing, butchering, and torturing his demons, all without ever being caught.

Giulia was right—a run of good luck had to end at some point.

"I can avenge myself," I said softly, before Nyx could argue or say anything else that would piss off his half-crazy Old Lady.

Nyx scowled. "That ain't how it works. You want to end up back in jail?"

I shrugged. "I won't ever go back inside."

Indy tensed and turned to frown down at me. "That had better not mean what I think it does."

"Means whatever you want it to," I disregarded. "Just saying, I'm never going to let myself be caught. Anyway, there's no one to avenge," I rumbled. "Never caught a sight of the fucker who shivved me, all I know was that the officers were in on it because they kept the coast clear.

"What are you going to do, Nyx? Go and slay all the guards who were on duty at the time of my stabbing?"

His mouth tightened. "It's a start."

"A messy one."

He dipped his chin in begrudging agreement. "Do you know why they got to you?" he asked softly, stepping forward so he could grip the foot-rail.

His knuckles held on so ferociously that they bled white, and I could practically hear his bones grinding as I murmured, "I ain't got a clue why they'd shiv me. I know fuck all."

Nyx shook his head. "That can't be true. You must know something but you just don't realize it."

"Same difference, isn't it?" Indy groused, slumping back against the headboard after she snagged one of the Jell-O cups on the rolling table I'd shoved aside before my nap and started spooning some into her mouth. "Whether he knows what he knows or not, he ain't got any answers for you, Nyx."

"We gotta work it out because whatever it is, it's worth killing for." Nyx's mouth tightened. "I can't do shit without Rex's say so anyway. I ain't the Enforcer anymore. My responsibilities lay elsewhere."

"Yeah, like you'd wait on Rex's word," Giulia scoffed. "You got a twisted sense of right and wrong, baby. I know you too well, you forget that."

His jaw clamped down but when she tucked her arm through his and leaned into him, I saw the tension in him ease some.

It was weird—Nyx being comforted by a woman. A little like learning the Great Wall of China had been built by Martians. It made sense, but was still mind-blowing to accept.

In all honesty, it was a relief. Watching Nyx suffer through the torments of our family's past wasn't something I needed to behold.

Knowing he might possibly be moving on, that he might have a future was enough to make me want to drop to my knees and pray to a god that I didn't even believe in.

Because if someone had found a soul mate for Nyx, then it had to be some kind of deal made by divine or enlightened beings.

Men like Nyx didn't get happily-ever-afters. They were left to become alcoholics or drug addicts, seeking escape in substances that would eventually kill them.

Nyx wasn't a good man, he'd done shit that was wrong on so many levels, but he was my brother, and I loved him. I wanted the best for him, and if that came in the form of a spitfire who hissed venom worse than a rattlesnake, well, I was all for it.

Especially since Indy seemed to like her, and I wasn't sure Indy liked anyone.

Yeah, my family was weird.

Isolated, insular, all the 'i' words that spoke of kids who'd been raised to be scared of people, of kids who'd endured what no other child ever should.

Though it hurt like fuck, I raised my arm and tucked it around Indy's shoulder, enjoying the way she snuggled close to me.

I'd missed this shit.

She was the only person I could ever really be affectionate with, and I knew that went vice versa. None of us were particularly tactile, but we'd always been huggers among ourselves.

Nyx released the handhold he had on the foot-rail and reached up to rub his eyes. "I can't let this go. It's an affront to the family, worse, to the MC as well. We've already been disrespected in the eyes of the fucking underworld thanks to the blast, this is just the rotten cherry on the cake."

"It's an affront to me. I'm the one in the hospital, and in all honesty, I'm fucking glad because it meant I got out early. You know that place was killing me slowly."

Giulia slipped her arm around his waist and hugged him. "Listen to Quin, Nyx." The glance she cast me was grateful and, if I wasn't mistaken, pleading.

She wanted me to fight for this.

And because she was carrying my niece or my nephew, I did.

"Bigger fish to fry," I told him. "I heard about this shit with the birds."

Nyx heaved a sigh. "Sparrows, not birds."

"What a stupid fucking name."

"Agreed," Indy muttered with a grumble. "Fucking cunts."

"If they're behind my stabbing, then going after them will sort shit out, won't it? Think of the bigger picture—"

Nyx snarled, "You are the bigger fucking picture. The only people who fucking matter to me are in this goddamn room."

"I'm offended on Cruz's behalf," Indy drawled wryly, but even though I knew she'd said it to lessen the tension, I was also aware that she meant it.

Nyx grunted. "He can look after himself."

"He's family now," she retorted, sitting up again and dislodging my arm.

"He's a fucking chemist," Nyx rumbled, but I knew what he wasn't actually saying—dude melted corpses for the MC for a living.

Indy growled. "Like that doesn't come in useful sometimes."

Giulia tugged on Nyx's arm. "Don't be a dick. He makes her happy."

"I love him, Nyx. Don't be giving him shit."

"It's my job to give him shit," he countered. "Someone has to make sure the bastard treats you like the princess you are."

Indy snorted. "I never wanted to be a princess."

Giulia chuckled a little. "Biker princesses aren't like the regular kind, Nyx." Her eyes were twinkling as she reached up, smoothing her hand over his jaw to make sure he was looking at her. "We don't need tiaras, just pearl necklaces."

I groaned. "I'm too sick for sexual innuendo."

Giulia's chuckle deepened, but I saw a flash of something on Nyx's face, a raw and brutal hunger that seemed to make Giulia's smile turn incandescent—like they were the perfect amount of fucked up for each other.

I mean, I knew that already, just from the limited interactions I'd seen between them. I knew how Nyx was with bitches. They weren't there. They might as well have been holograms. Nyx *saw* Giulia.

In fact, now that I thought about it, it was like when she was in the room, she was all he saw.

A fierce desire hit me—to have something like that. To share that. To be a part of something bigger, better than just me on my own, going after the cunts who hurt kids who were incapable of protecting themselves.

I wanted what Nyx had, I wanted to feel that hunger, but I also wanted to feel that protectiveness that Nyx had triggered in Indy over Cruz.

I understood why he wasn't happy about her being with Cruz, but I'd never seen her melt into a guy like she did when he was around. It made me hungrier to feel the same.

I was a lot younger than both of them, and I'd been raised differently too. Spending years in the hospital on dialysis, in and out of treatment centers the way I'd been, I'd been coddled like they hadn't.

It made me both more mature and more immature than them, because I'd hung out with older people a lot, but had been raised within the safe walls of a hospital.

I knew I had time to find what they had, if I didn't have to end it all before I got caught, but the craving went deep.

Soul goddamn deep.

Uneasy and wistful, I tuned back into the conversation, aware that Giulia had turned a corner somehow in the discussion because Nyx was pressing a kiss to her temple, muttering, "Don't encourage her, Indy."

"Me?" my sister groused. "I ain't done shit."

Nyx just snorted, then the audible buzz of his phone rang, and I watched him pull it out of his jeans, and scowl down at the screen.

"Church in ninety minutes." He pursed his lips and shot me a look. "Rex is sending Hawk over."

"I don't need a babysitter—"

"Take the fucking babysitter," Indy and Giulia sang at the same time. "You can't protect yourself from any threat right now," Indy tacked on after the women smirked at each other.

"Thought you liked him. You said he got you all up to date with shit, no?" Nyx rumbled.

"I did like Hawk, don't mean that I want him being a bodyguard."

Nyx just shrugged. "Tough." I scowled at him, watching as he smirked. "This comes from way up high, baby bro. Ain't jack shit I can do about it."

"Bullshit. Like Giulia said, we both know you move to your own beat."

"Not where club business is concerned," he intoned, his pious tenor pissing me off.

I flipped him the bird and grumbled, "Pass me a Jell-O cup, Indy, unless you've eaten all of them."

She laughed. "Big baby." And when I flipped her the bird too, she grabbed it, twisted my hand around and bent it backward. "Play nice."

My nose crinkled even as I yelped in pain. "Bitch."

She winked. "You know it, bro."

TWENTY

LODESTAR

"WHAT DO YOU WANT, D? Unless, is that really you? Maybe you're just spoof calling me again? Ya know, because that's your idea of a fucking joke, Conor."

There was a hesitation on the other end of the line, before a soft feminine voice that definitely wasn't Conor O'Donnelly pretending to be a high falsetto, sounded in my ear, "Who's Conor?"

My brow puckered. "Shit, that really is you, D."

"Why would someone pretend to be me?"

"It's this stupid game I have going on with a—" Hell, what was Conor? Shit had changed between us since we'd shared our real names with each other, so even though he wasn't a rival anymore, I called him that because D was used to me having nemeses. "He's just a rival."

She chuckled. "Only you think it's fashionable to collect enemies like they're shoes, Star."

My lips twisted as I pressed my back into my chair. "I know what to do with enemies, you can attest to the fact that I'm a shitty friend."

"Not so shitty. Wouldn't be calling otherwise, would I?"

I just hummed. "Depends. What do you want? You calling in a favor?"

"Maybe."

Grunting, I muttered, "See? Confirmation I'm a shitty friend."

"Actually, no, confirmation you're the best hacker I know."

Considering we'd both come up together at Langley, that was high praise. Neither was D the kind of woman who blew smoke up someone's ass. She had enough on me to force me to comply with her wishes, but she wasn't like that.

Never had been, even if the Agency had tried to make her that way.

"Haven't heard from you since you set up shop, Cin," I said huskily, using her real name too. She'd gone from Lucinda to Cin to Dead to Me to D—names were confusing in my line of work.

"I've been busy. It's not easy gaining a reputation in all the wrong places, Star, you should know that."

I grinned at my screen. "True dat. What do you need a hacker for?"

She hesitated. "I'm in Jersey, Star. Can we meet? This isn't the kind of thing we can talk about over the phone."

My brows rose, curiosity striking me as I stated, "You know where I am... this is serious."

"Maybe, maybe not. Just heard some whispers is all. Whispers I'd like to share with you."

"You're not trying to get me out in the open, are you?"

She snorted. "Have you had a gift from me today?"

"No, but you haven't said when you want to meet."

"In an hour would be perfect. I know you're in West Orange. Heard on the grapevine you got tangled up with some MC?"

I grunted. "That's some fucking grapevine." My brow furrowed. "You know you're going to have to tell me who told you that."

I heard the shrug in her voice. "I still have friends at Langley."

"You always made more than me." Which wasn't saying much.

"I'm not sure how they still will help you after that little contretemps you had with upper management."

"People don't like Reinier. You know that."

That was a given. The Agency Director was an asshole. The one good thing President Davidson had done was get the Feds to investigate his ass. Of course, they were as fucking corrupt as the Agency. Naturally, even though Reinier was as sickening as Lyme disease, they'd found bupkis.

Fuckers.

Tracing my finger over the natural grain of wood on the kitchen table in Lily Lancaster's kitchen where I'd established my home office, I asked, "That's interesting the Agency's keeping tabs on me when they couldn't help me out when I was a sex slave in the Middle East."

One thing I liked about Cin—she wasn't a bullshitter. She never pitied me for what I'd gone through, which I was grateful for. I didn't need pity.

I needed revenge.

"That's because they wanted you there, Star."

Her words had me tensing. "You know that for a fact, huh?"

I heard the sound of bikes in the driveway, and as I peered over my shoulder to see who was on their way, she distracted me by murmuring, "That's why I need to speak with you."

"Someone just pulled into my driveway. You sure you haven't sent me a gift?" Cin's street name was Dead To Me. She had the nasty habit of sending gifts to her targets. One of the most capable snipers of our year, she had one twisted sense of humor. Her gift bags were always labeled, 'Sucks To Be You.'

Apparently, I was twisted as well because I always smirked at the thought of some poor bastard ending his life with a smile on his face as he thought he was about to get a gift.

Or she, I guessed.

Cin always was into equal opportunities.

"Look, if I wanted you dead, I wouldn't be calling you," she said bitingly. "I just happened to come across some information that might help you is all."

I pursed my lips. "I've got a situation on my hands."

"What situation is that?"

"I'm in a wheelchair right now."

"Jesus. Why?" she sputtered, her shock clear.

The Agency weren't keeping that close a tab on me then—that was something, at least.

"Got caught up in a blast."

"A bomb?"

"Well, kind of."

"What do you mean? Kind of?"

"We had the Feds sniffing all over the place, but I managed to cook the books."

She snorted. "A little gas explosion, huh? Like that place in Beirut in '09?"

I grinned. "Yeah. Like that."

"You haven't changed, have you, Star?"

"Not really. Don't think you have either. Anyway, if you want to come to where I'm staying, you're welcome. But I can't leave. My mobility is limited right now, especially without getting someone else involved."

"Can we speak freely there?"

"Of course. Wouldn't be staying here if I couldn't."

"Okay. Send me your address. I don't think I'll be long. I'm in West Orange now."

I hummed. "See you soon, then."

She cut the call just as the front door opened. The mansion was so big that the kitchen was on the other end of the house, but it was a massive megalith that, no matter how gently you closed it, a boom of sound always echoed around the entire property.

Heels sounded down the hall, not just a pair, but a few pairs. I recognized one set—Tiffany's Mom, whom Lily was letting live here like a human-shaped tapeworm. The other two pairs I didn't register.

Curious now, I kept my attention on the door. Dismissing the tapeworm, I saw Hawk and Amara, just before a boom sounded again, and I heard the heavy thuds of Rex's boots as he clomped down the hall.

My gaze drifted over Amara who looked a mixture of scared, exhilarated and comforted—which, trust me, was a weird combination—then Hawk, who I felt was here in a supportive role more than anything else.

As for Rex, when he showed up, I saw the excitement in his eyes, and because he possessed one of the best poker faces I'd ever come across, I had to admit, it made me straighten up in my chair some.

Which, of course, made me wince because, ya know, broken bones.

Ouchie.

Tapeworm peered at us all like we were the scum, seeming to forget she was a parasite who had a Prime addiction Lily was funding, but when she caught sight of Rex, her cheeks blanched and she scuttled away.

I'd heard her rip into Tiffany and Lily about their men, but whenever the men in question were there, she usually disappeared. Even tapeworms had some brain function, it seemed.

Rex and his ilk were not the kind of fuckers you made enemies of. The guys would take some dissing from a relative of their Old Lady but outright insults? Nah. Not for long, at least.

"What's going on?" I asked when the parasite had done a disappearing act with a bottle of water and a diet bar in her hand.

Rex, who'd clomped over to the fridge upon entering the kitchen, retreated with the makings of a sandwich, some water bottles, and a banana.

He set up a place by the chopping board, and pulled out some bread. As he cut slices, he said, "This ain't my story to tell but I'm here to make sure you act on what Amara shares."

I cocked a brow at him. "You boss Maverick around, Rex, not me."

He sniffed. "You'll like what she has to say."

"Just so we remember that I ain't a brother, and you ain't my Prez." I was aware that I had him pinned with a gimlet glance because he just rolled his eyes.

I wasn't sure why but Rex had a lot of patience for me, which meant I got my own way a lot. Exactly how I liked it.

"Understood," he grumbled as he slapped PB onto the bread and began smushing the banana onto it.

Turning my attention back to Amara and Hawk, I saw that she'd slipped into the seat opposite me, while Hawk had her back.

"You together now?" I queried, wondering what was happening in the MC as nearly all the council had cozied up to a chick.

Most of them had gone nearly twenty years without getting entangled, and in barely no time at all, they were all branding their bitches.

It was weird.

Like a fucking pandemic or something.

Amara licked her lips. "Hawk is helping me."

The man in question didn't give me an answer either way, just stared at Amara like she'd set the moon in the goddamn sky or something.

Seriously, puppy eyes on a biker was the most messed up shit I'd seen in a long while.

And I'd seen a lot of messed up shit.

"What do you need help with?" I tipped my head to the side, studying the woman who was a lot more fascinating than I'd pegged her for.

That she hadn't just managed to return Cyan, Storm's kid, back to the fold but kill the fucker who'd been instrumental in some of the club's recent downfalls made her worthy of study.

I'd thought she was a dullard.

I liked it when I was proven wrong.

Of course, she didn't do much to prove her case because she fell silent, her gaze on her lap or on the table until Rex grunted out, "You know what a super recognizer is?"

I cast him a dismissive look. "Of course. They're very rare—" My words waned as I figured out where he was going with this. "You're one?"

Amara dipped her chin, her gaze still on the table. I'd thought that was a sign of her nerves but maybe it wasn't.

Maybe it was a force of habit, and not just submissiveness.

We'd shared a similar life path, unfortunately for us, but I wasn't made for submission so I wasn't particularly sympathetic to those who'd allowed themselves to be broken.

If that made me a bitch, then so be it.

"She says that some of the people who owned her were Sparrows."

Now I understood Rex's eagerness.

I leaned forward. "You telling the truth?"

"Why would she lie?" Hawk snarled, his hand coming up to cup her shoulder.

"Why wouldn't she?" I asked simply. "That's a big claim to make."

"What has she to gain? She's already going to be rich once Lily gives her that money."

I conceded that with a dip of my shoulder. "So, what gives? What do you want, Amara? You tell me, as well, not these guys. You got a mouth on you, don't you?"

Her gaze darted to mine, and her eyes were loaded with a wildness I didn't necessarily understand but could empathize with.

She was on a bridge to something better—she knew it, too. She just had to reach out and grab it for herself.

"I can describe them in great detail," she whispered.

"I figured you could put them through a facial recognition program, Lodestar."

I didn't bother looking at Rex, just kept my eyes trained on her. "And what's in it for you?"

Her smile, when it came, was soft. So soft that it made me think she was going to say something completely different to what she actually uttered:

"I get to kill them."

Her words didn't shock me, nothing really did, but I still mocked, "One death and you think you're Freddy Krueger, huh?"

"Everyone knows you're hunting for vengeance, Lodestar," Hawk reasoned. "Why shouldn't Amara be on the hunt for the same thing?"

Because I didn't have an answer for that, and I didn't like engaging in arguments I couldn't win, I kept my mouth shut.

"Indy can draw them," Rex inserted. "She has the talent."

"It takes a particular skillset to recreate portraits," I said softly. "As far as I know, she doesn't do portraits, does she? Isn't it line art she's famous for?" I clicked my fingers. "Mandalas. Those circle things." I actually liked them, and was contemplating getting her to give me one before I left West Orange.

Rex muttered, "We can give it a shot before we get people involved in our business."

"True." I pursed my lips. "I want a test run first."

Amara shrugged. "Go for it."

"Is it just faces? Or do you remember other things too?"

"In detail, it's faces."

That was a real shame.

"You were kept in that cabin in the woods. Do you know why?"

She stiffened up, and I knew that no one had ever asked her these questions because she'd been lying about being able to speak English.

Untrustworthy cunt.

Well, *okay*, that was semi-mean.

We'd all been tiptoeing around the women until now. Alessa had been honest from the start, and we hadn't interrogated her. But now Amara wanted this, she had to pay the fucking piper.

Her chin trembled a second before she firmed it, her gaze fixed squarely on mine better than Gorilla Glue could do, as she rasped, "We were being punished."

"What for?" I asked softly.

"Sometimes it was just for misbehaving, sometimes it was for disobedience. That was why Alessa and Tatána were there."

Hawk squeezed her shoulder. "You mean, you weren't kept there all the time?"

"No. Just for punishments. Sarah was sick, and they weren't doing anything to help her. We agreed to try to run away to see if we could find help. It didn't work."

I knew Hawk wanted to explode at the words that were uttered in such a flat tone it belied the trauma of what she'd gone through. A woman didn't try to escape that kind of place to help a friend without crying over how she'd had to watch that friend die in front of her.

"Whose idea was it to run away?"

"Mine. Sarah was getting sicker. I had to do something."

"Who was she to you?"

"Nobody." Her jaw tensed, before she released a shaky sigh. "We traveled over from Ukraine together."

"Christ!" Hawk boomed, before he managed to compose himself—barely. With a soft grip of callused fingers, he cupped her shoulders with a tenderness that few bikers were known for, and in a husky voice that throbbed with emotions he was trying to contain, asked, "You were together from the beginning?"

"As much as was possible. We were sold to separate owners along the way."

"And it's the owners who were Sparrows?" I queried.

"Some of them. The last place where we were was a kind of—" She muttered a Ukrainian word. "You can buy women for sex there."

Her English definitely wasn't perfect, but it was a damn sight better than my Ukrainian.

"A brothel?" Rex questioned.

"Yes. It was a brothel. We saw many men but I know they were Sparrows."

"How?"

"The same people transported me around from the beginning. It makes no sense for them not to be linked. The men who drove us were friendly with the clients."

"Who transported you?"

"I don't know their names. Just their faces." Her jaw clenched. "I can recreate them all if you would like me to."

"That's a lot to ask for," Hawk argued. "Shit, Amara. That's going to be hell on you."

"Rex said I can kill them, and if Lodestar can give me an identity, then that takes me one step closer to that goal." Those changeable eyes of hers, the hazel irises flaring from light to dark brown, seemed to freeze over. "For that, I will recreate them all. The suffering would be worth it."

"What makes you think you can kill them?" I asked her, even as a part of me wanted to dive on her for more information about the brothel's location as well as details on who she'd serviced along the way. "One guy, in the heat of a messed up situation, is one thing. Cold murder is another."

"I see their faces when I close my eyes before I sleep. Maybe I'll rest easier if I see their deaths instead."

Huh. "I can't fault that logic." I shrugged at Rex when he cleared his throat to draw my attention—she made complete sense to me, no matter what his scowl said.

"Hawk, I need you to head to Quin's ward, and take over for Nyx for a short while. I've called church to keep everyone up-to-date on the situation. Indy is there, too." To Amara, he said, "I'm sure you had ways of knowing who was important and who wasn't. Types of suits, the jewelry they wore—I need the most powerful, the richest men first. You can understand why."

"I can." Her head bobbed. "I'll do whatever I can to help."

I reached out and grabbed her hand. "Do you know where the brothel was? I've been trying to find it but it's hidden too well."

"It was just a regular house in a regular street. Like something from the movies."

"There must have been a lot of traffic," Rex countered. "Wouldn't that have stood out on a cul-de-sac?"

"I do not know, I just know there were other houses in the neighborhood, but either side were businesses." She pursed her lips. "Where cars go to get fixed, *tak*?"

"Odd question but do you know how long it took you to get from the house to the dungeon you were kept in?"

She looked down at the table. "Maybe twenty minutes? The time passes strangely when you are traveling blindly." Her forehead puckered in thought, her eyes narrowing as she finally tilted her head back so our eyes could meet. "There was a lot of noise... I think we must have driven on a highway or a busy road or something. I don't know if that helps."

It was more than I'd had before—fuck all.

My stomach churned at the thought of that kind of crazy shit going down in the heart of suburbia, but if I recalibrated the location of the cabin they'd been stored in, and tied it into the nearest subdivisions, maybe I'd get a hit.

It wasn't much more to go on, but I had to try.

As disturbing as it was to know they'd been whored out, it was almost a relief because it meant that there were probably staff there, tending to any women who remained at the property.

That they were slowly starving or dehydrating to death wasn't going to be on my conscience as I tried to figure out where the hell they were.

When a ping sounded from my security program, I averted my attention to that, monitoring the goings on in the vicinity as I went through all the new cameras I'd installed since Lily had permitted me to take over the service rather than remain with the company she'd hired after her father's death.

As I scanned the footage, Amara and Hawk disappeared, doing as Rex bid, leaving us alone.

When he plunked his ass down at the table beside me, I cast him a quick glance, grousing at his intent stare, "What?"

"You were harder on her than I was, and I have more reason than you to dislike her for lying. I heard about what Giulia and the others put her through—why is everyone nice to Alessa and not to Amara? Because Mav claimed her? That's hardly fair, is it?"

"She lied about speaking English."

He snorted. "Pull the other one. That shit with Alessa beating on her happened before any of us knew she could utter more than three words in English."

I shrugged. "Can't speak for the others. I neither like nor dislike her, but I ain't about to cut her slack when we went through the same shit.

"Just because she says she can do something doesn't mean I believe it. Not until she's proven herself.

"As for the others, the assumption was that she and Tatána were friends. That Amara would know more about what Tatána was doing. Alessa had to prove herself, prove that she was reliable. That's what started that particular witch hunt."

Rex scowled as he took a large bite of his sandwich. "Link had already spoken with her. On my orders."

I snorted. "Yeah, you might be God to the guys, but bitches work differently. We have a whole other scale of trust. Plus, that doesn't take away from the fact that Alessa felt like she had to clear her name, prove to the club that she wasn't affiliated with Tatána."

Rex pulled a face, but stopped asking stupid bullshit questions and filled his face instead.

"You sure you managed to delete all the feeds that were routed out of the clubhouse?" he questioned after a couple of minutes of blissful peace—why did that never last long around this place?

Scornfully, I glowered at him. "I'm a pro, Rex. Of course I did. That cunt David had all his video footage uploading to the same server. A master coder he wasn't. Just a creepy fucking stalker."

Indy's receptionist had been hunting her like she was a wild ring-necked pheasant, pinning down her movements at her apartment, at the clubhouse once he'd learned she was dating Cruz. Talk about a bastard.

Rex hummed under his breath. "I still don't understand how Tatána and he met."

"Not sure we will ever know. We didn't keep an eye on them 24/7, did we? Plus, if David knew she was from the compound, then it would have been in his best interests to cozy up to her to gain access to the clubhouse, wouldn't it?"

"True." He drummed his fingers against the table. "Amara's scared of men. I can't see her letting someone like David into her life."

"We each have different coping mechanisms. Tatána wanted security, the kind that Alessa had. Married, she'd be able to get a green card, wouldn't she? Instead of just hoping that Rachel would be able to sort one out for her."

"Have you looked into the visas that sex trafficking victims can get?"

He shrugged. "I glanced over the files Rachel sent me."

"Hundreds of thousands of known cases, and only a couple grand are entitled to a visa. It's like the lottery, except you need an expensive therapist to help you get over what you've been through."

"Funny how if Tatána had waited some, Lily would have set her up for life."

"That's the rub, isn't it?" My lips twisted. "Satisfying as fuck though."

He snickered. "Maybe. A little."

"There's always one bad egg, but in Tatána's case, you can't fault her. She was doing what she'd been bred to—surviving the only way she knew how."

"Spreading her legs," he muttered grimly, dumping the last few bites of his sandwich on the table.

"Don't pin your hopes on this shit with Amara, Rex. I saw how giddy you were when you walked in."

"You didn't see what I did," he argued, but he didn't deny that he was excited. A part of me was too, but I was more accustomed to disappointment than anything else.

The prospect of having an eye-witness who could describe Sparrows to us, who could finally help us label the cunts and let us find our feet so we could take them down was intoxicating. You couldn't take down ghosts. If Amara could do what she claimed, a nice chunk of the NWS wouldn't be ghosts for much longer.

"What do you mean?"

"I had her recreate London's face. She did it. The drawing was crude, but I knew who it was."

"She only saw him yesterday. The last time she was with a Sparrow was months ago. Plus, a 'crude' drawing might be enough for the human eye but not for a facial recognition program," I warned. "Better to err on the side of caution and not put your eggs in one basket."

"Stop mixing metaphors," he chided, the furrow between his brows and the thoughtful way he was shredding the remainder of the crust on his sandwich into a million pieces telling me that all was not right in his world.

See, it was thinking like that that made me a perfect candidate for Mensa.

"I feel as if you were looking forward to eating a jar of cookies, but someone finished them off before you could get there." I studied him warily, unsure if I wanted to get involved or not. "Problems at Rachel's place?"

"Not really. Just…" He rubbed his eyes. "I was hoping for more time."

Christ. *Time?* That was something we all wanted more of. "What would you do with it?"

He shrugged. "Sit with Dad some more. I'm going to have to get back into the swing of running things, because Storm just told me he's heading back to Coshocton sooner than I'd have liked."

"Dumbfuck," I muttered.

Because Rex evidently figured out where my mind had gone, he shook his head. "He's taking them with him." He grimaced. "He's making the right choice, it just means… Never mind."

I rarely felt bad for people, but I felt bad for Rex. Bear wasn't going to get better. Call me callous—many, many, *many* people had called me much worse—but I knew a dead man when I saw one. What was left of Bear wasn't looking good.

"Keira was trying to be independent," was all I said, because pointing out that his father was about to die wouldn't make shit better for him, pointing out that his ex-VP was a fuckface who didn't deserve his wife or child didn't either but it made me feel fucking brighter.

"She's making a sacrifice for Cyan's sake."

"Being a mom sucks," I commented.

"You make sacrifices for Kat all the time," he pointed out. "You don't act like it sucks."

"Well, it does and it doesn't," I agreed. "Some shit's fun, some shit's hard. Most of the time, it's just hard." Especially when it meant you had to leave your home, the people you knew, people who cared for you, and traipse over to Buttfuck, Ohio, to live it up in a new MC so that you and your daughter's father could try to fix what was broken.

"Poor Keira," I mumbled softly.

"Not poor Storm?" He arched a brow. "You'd be surprised what a good man Storm actually is if you knew him."

"Don't need to know him. He's a cheater, that's a synonym for lying cunt."

He snorted. "Everything's black and white for you, isn't it?"

"I think you'll find that I live in the gray." When he rolled his eyes, I grumbled, "Okay, then, so what could possibly justify him cheating on his wife?"

"You ever put someone on a pedestal before?"

"Figuratively or literally?" I asked dryly. His scowl warned me not to fuck around so I grunted, "My dad."

He dipped his chin. "Okay, the example isn't as easy, but—"

"Let me stop you there. I put him on a pedestal but I always realized what a fuck up he was. I was perfectly positioned to see it firsthand."

"Storm put Keira on a pedestal, to the point where she was like some kind of idol to him." He shook his head. "He and Scarlet weren't raised the best way. Mom tried but it never really helped. How could it? He was a crackhead from birth—"

I scowled. "His mom was a junkie?"

"Yeah. She was." He winced. "Anyway, that ain't my story to tell, none of this is, and it's not like Storm can't defend himself but I'm just saying, they were never going to work out. Not with him thinking he was a piece of trash and she was the Queen of fucking Sheba."

Shaking my head at him, I retorted, "If you think that excuses what he did—"

"Ain't saying it does, ain't saying it doesn't. Just saying you can't expect something to work out when two people are broken."

His mouth turned down at the corners, in a way that made me think he wasn't just talking about Storm and Keira.

Another ping sounded on my computer, snatching my attention, and I cast a look at the screen, aware that was a security breach.

When I saw Cin stepping onto the side of the property, just by the pool and the poolhouse, I had to shake my head.

Trust her to breach my perimeter.

I'd be offended but she was one of the best, and it took someone like her, who I trusted—as much as I trusted anyone—to help me level up my security game.

Breaches were impossible to control, as Conor O'Donnelly knew firsthand...

"We have a visitor," I told Rex calmly.

His brows rose. "Who?"

"She's a friend of mine. You might have heard of her."

"I doubt it. We don't exactly run in the same circles."

"You'd be surprised," I muttered drolly. "You come across the name 'Dead To Me.'"

He paused. "You're friends with her?"

"We came up through the CIA together." I winked. "Stick with me, Rex, I'll introduce you to the cool crowd."

TWENTY-ONE

QUIN

HAWK'S SHOULDERS were rounded slightly thanks to his hands being dipped deep into his jeans' pockets as he entered my hospital room, his attention more on the person who'd come with him than anyone else. I watched as Nyx strode over to him, pulling him aside, and still, Hawk's attention never veered off course.

I'd have eavesdropped into their conversation, but my gaze was focused on the woman that Giulia was eying up with a wariness that put me on edge. Even Indy was tense at the woman's presence, and she reacted as if she was a frightened mouse, her head bowed as she scurried over to the window, not a greeting on her lips for any of us.

"You're kidding?"

I knew Nyx hadn't meant to boom that out, but he failed. His question drew all our attention, and he grimaced when he caught sight of Giulia's raised brow and Indy's scowl.

"What's going on?" Indy demanded.

Hawk cleared his throat. "Indy, the MC needs your help with something."

"With what?" she queried, frowning at Hawk.

"We need your drawing talents."

Indy's frown deepened. "What the hell for? I'm not sizing you up for a tattoo now, Hawk, Jesus."

Nyx grunted. "It's club business, Indy."

"Meaning, what? You won't share it with me because I have a pussy?"

Nyx snorted. "Meaning it ain't got jack to do with tattoos." He cut me a look. "You might be better for the task at hand though, Quin. You up to drawing?"

"Indy's better—"

Nyx shook his head. "Nah. Not with faces."

Indy ceased bristling, then turned to me. "Don't diss your portrait skills or I'll have to stick my finger in your knife wound."

The stranger gasped, spinning around, cheeks a pale white as she rasped, "You wouldn't!"

Her voice hit me like a foot to the belly, but I forced out a grin. "She would."

The woman's eyes were round with distress. "That's horrible."

"That's how you control two *horrible* brothers, Amara," Indy said dismissively. "If you ever want to have any say in anything you do, that's how you do it."

Ignoring Indy's BS, I focused on the woman.

Amara.

Christ, that was a pretty name.

I wondered what it meant.

Nyx just scoffed, "Keep on telling yourself that, Indy."

"Oh, I will," was her retort.

"What kind of portraits?" I queried, pushing the button on my bed that saw the incline on the backrest surging upward. It triggered a myriad of aches but I was mostly used to them now.

Pain wasn't always a curse, sometimes it grounded you in the best kind of way. Our grandmother had taught me that.

"Amara needs to describe some people to you. We need an accurate drawing so that we can scan the faces through software."

"To ID them?" I questioned.

Nyx nodded. "You think you can do that?"

I shot Indy a look. "Can I borrow your iPad?"

She shrugged. "Sure."

"Rex said to have you draw the faces," the woman, Amara, pointed out uneasily.

Her arms came up to wrap around her stomach, much as Giulia's had earlier, but it was then that I realized how, by comparison, Giulia was incapable of looking insecure. This woman embodied it.

Her shoulders were hunched, making the stark lines of her collarbones protrude that much more. The way her posture curved her back made her tits seem even bigger.

It took a little while for both of my brains to connect the dots, especially because she was the most beautiful woman I'd ever fucking seen, but Hawk had mentioned an Amara the other day. She was like Mav's Old Lady—one of the women who the MC had saved from Link's father-in-law.

As I looked at her, I could see that she'd been hurt in the past. She was vulnerable in a way that tugged at my heart strings. In a way that Indy, though she'd been through hell too, had never let me see before.

Amara wore her feelings in her expression—whether she knew it or not—and for that reason, it made the combination of pensive fragility and wishful concern all the more interesting.

What fascinated me the most was her voice.

I knew it.

I'd heard it before.

But... *when?*

Where?

I'd never met her, that I knew for sure.

Reaching up to rub my forehead where an ache had started to gather, I barely managed to tune into the rest of the conversation.

"Rex would have passed down that decree," Indy said snootily. "He doesn't know Quin is even better than me at drawing."

Her pride had me shooting her a sheepish smile, but my gaze quickly averted to collide with Amara's.

When our eyes tangled, her cheeks turned a hot pink for a scant second before she dipped her chin and broke the link between us.

Shooting Hawk a look, I saw that he'd witnessed all of that and more, but I couldn't make out whether he was annoyed about it or not.

They hadn't come in together and, the other night, he hadn't mentioned he had an Old Lady... Had I been eye-fucking his woman without even knowing it?

Nyx muttered, "Quin, if you think you're strong enough—"

"Nyx, I already told you, I'm fine." Well, I had been. Something about Amara put me on edge as I tried to figure things out that were impossible to figure out.

"Have faith, child. Aashaa will guide you." Like it was only yesterday, I heard *Nòkomis,* my grandmother, speaking into my ear, giving me strength as she did what modern Western medicine had never been able to achieve.

"The doctors don't agree," Indy said wryly, rupturing my thoughts.

With more of a snap than she deserved, I groused, "What the fuck do they know? Stone looked over my charts, didn't she? She knows what I'm like."

"The Energizer bunny?" Indy drawled, shaking her head.

To make up for being a grouch, I almost joked that I could go all night long but with Amara in the room, suddenly, it didn't feel right to make those kinds of jokes.

I just had no idea why it didn't feel right.

After thinking about every word that left my lips for the longest time, it was easier than before to control my tongue though. For the first time, I was glad. This frightened rabbit didn't need a reason to hop away, especially if Rex really wanted some portraits drawn up of whoever it was Amara had seen.

Curious now, I asked, "You on your way out?"

Nyx cocked a brow at me, but I saw a glimmer of amusement in his eyes as he glanced between Amara and me, murmuring, "Yeah. Giulia, babe, you coming with?"

She nodded. "I'll be back, Quin, with some decent food."

Having heard about how good she was in the kitchen, I wasn't about to protest that fast food would be more than adequate after the swill I'd eaten in jail, instead I shot her a grin. "Chicken Parm?"

Her lips twisted. "If that's what you want, that's what you'll get."

"Good choice." Nyx hauled his arm around his Old Lady's shoulders then tossed at Indy, "You staying?"

She bit her lip as she looked at me. "I should open the shop."

"Then, go. It's okay. I told you, I'm fine." I shoved her a little. "Anyway, how am I going to check out your browsing history if you're watching me use your iPad?"

Nyx laughed as she scowled at me. "Come on, you two. Let's break shit up. I have to go and your brawling is only going to cause me more shit with the nurses than I'm already in."

"What did you do?"

Nyx cleared his throat but Giulia murmured, "He can tell you another time when he isn't in a rush."

"Fucking cavemen," Indy muttered under her breath as she shifted off the bed, shoved her toes into her Converse, then straightened up.

"See you at the ink parlor, Indy," Giulia called out. "I might be a while but I'll work late."

Indy waved a hand. "Don't worry about it. I can manage. It's more important that you get this runt fed."

"You're mean because you love me so much," I teased, casting a look at Amara and seeing that she was watching us both like we were a new flick she'd paid thirty dollars to see at the movie theater.

Indy's lips twisted but she bent over and pressed a kiss to my cheeks, before she whispered in my ear, "Behave. I can see you eying her like she's a crawfish boil—"

"You're the one obsessed with New Orleans, not me," was all I said, neither confirming or denying that Amara interested me.

She just arched a brow as she grabbed her purse, dug around in it and handed me her tablet and the charger.

"No passcode?"

"What can I say? I don't have trust issues." She tweaked my toes on the way out then followed Giulia and Nyx into the outer hall, leaving me alone with Hawk and Amara.

While Hawk and I had shared some shit the other night, that didn't take away from the fact that I barely knew him. Amara was a stranger too.

For all that, though, I cast a look at them both and asked, "We at a wake or something? You both look miserable as fuck."

Amara cleared her throat. "It's been a stressful day."

"A stressful couple of days," Hawk corrected.

"Yeah, well done for killing that rodent. I fucking hate rats, don't you?" I told her cheerfully, even though I wasn't feeling at all cheerful. The need to make her feel better was what drove me though. It was strong, an instinctual urge that came from nowhere.

I was the one in the hospital bed, after all.

I was the one who was fresh from a prison where the guards had allowed me to be shivved.

If anyone needed a little cheering up, it was me, but *I* didn't matter at that moment.

She did.

And she wouldn't even look at me.

"Amara's on edge," Hawk excused, like he had the right to excuse her.

I tipped my head to the side at him, and even though it wasn't my place, asked, "Is she yours?"

A gasp escaped Amara, who whipped away from the less than stellar view outside my room window to gape at me. "I am no one's," she hissed.

I shrugged. "Just wanting to make sure I'm not stepping on another brother's territory."

Her eyes rounded. "I am not a new country and you are not Christopher Columbus."

I sniffed. "No, I goddamn ain't. That cunt pretty much destroyed my people."

She blinked. "Your people?"

Hawk cleared his throat. "Quin and his family are Native American."

"Algonquin," I corrected, trying not to smile when she mouthed the name then struggled to pronounce it. I wasn't being a jerk, it was just cute. Everything about her fucking was.

"I should read more about this," she murmured. "School wasn't a priority when I was younger, dance classes were, and then, after... I haven't read a book in nearly eight years."

It was my turn for my eyes to round in horror. "You haven't read in eight years?"

She shrugged. "No."

"Christ." I hadn't been a bookaholic prior to being sent up, but in the interim, my time in the classroom and the shitty selection of books in the prison library was the only thing that had gotten me through the days.

Especially after I'd been given my real welcome to Rikers.

Mouth tightening at that particular nightmare, something that had happened only the one time before I'd proven that no fucker could make me their bitch, I murmured, "We need to rectify that. You speak good English but it'd be better to get you Ukrainian books for stuff like history." I pursed my lips. "I wonder if Amazon stocks that kind of thing?"

When I brought up the site on my iPad, Amara muttered, "You don't have to—"

"Of course I do. You need to read about how Columbus raped my ancestor's fucking country."

When she tensed, Hawk sighed. "Good going, Quin."

I shrugged, but told her gently, "It's only a word, Amara. It's only got as much power as you let it have." At Hawk's disbelieving glance, I murmured, "I've been raped—" I'd never know why the next words slipped from my lips, but it was so seamless, so perfect, that I didn't even register I'd used them as an endearment until much later, "—sky girl. I've had my choices taken away from me. Don't let them have power over your vocabulary too."

I was aware that I'd caught their attention, but I didn't look at Hawk, because he already knew about this. I'd never intended on saying a damn thing about what had gone down while I was inside, but in the face of her suffering, how couldn't I?

We all had coping mechanisms. There was a massive reason I'd trained like I'd just been given a leading role in a Marvel movie. Making myself look hotter hadn't been the aim of that particular game. But being frightened of words wasn't the way forward, simply a step back.

"You were forced?" Amara choked out.

"Some guys tried to make me their bitch." My top lip curled. "It didn't work."

"Does Nyx know?" Hawk questioned softly, drawing my attention.

His hands remained stuffed in his pockets, his fists bunching, but I could tell he was uneasy. That he'd immediately thought of Nyx told me he was still worrying about Giulia's man going off the rails.

"No, he doesn't, and won't ever either," I warned briskly, watching him dip his chin in silent agreement.

"Why did you tell me? *Us?*" Amara whispered, finally taking a step closer to the bed, inadvertently answering her own question with her actions—to make her approach me.

"Does it matter?" I replied softly. The truth was out there now. It needed to be.

I looked into her eyes, changeable eyes, hazel but not. Grandmother would have had a weird name for them, some kind of magical word that made no sense to me even though she tried to teach me the way.

Not for the first time, I regretted not listening as well as I should.

When I'd been a kid, our ancestry had fascinated me. Then, when she'd cured me, afterward, I'd been a teenager and I'd been more interested in tits and ass than the correct pronunciation of words and whether or not some plant was poisonous.

God, I hadn't thought about *Nòkomis* in way too long. Not since the early days in county jail, before I'd been transferred to Rikers, and I'd prayed for her guidance at night.

She hadn't spoken to me.

She never did.

If ever there was a grandmother who'd haunt their grandchild, it was her.

I bowed my head a little to hide my expression, and instead, murmured, "What kind of books would you like?"

Her hand moved over to the blanket. She had plain, unadorned nails, none of the crazily colored tips that I knew a lot of chicks liked, and the skin on her knuckles was a little worn, like they'd been put to hard work over time.

"You don't have to—"

I ignored the awkward mutter, and repeated, "What would you like to read?"

"Amara's going to be a millionaire soon enough," Hawk said sarcastically. "She can buy her own books then."

Hitching a shoulder, I merely told her, "They wouldn't be a gift then, would they?"

Her brow puckered but she whispered, "I'd like to read a romance novel."

My eyes widened, before I grinned. "You would, huh?" She could have slapped me with a fucking sea bass and I'd have been less surprised.

She scowled. "Are you mocking me?"

"Amara doesn't like being mocked," Hawk said flatly, but when I cast him a look, I saw a bubble of humor in his eyes.

"Mockery is cruel. There's nothing cruel about me finding it cute you want a romance novel," I corrected, even as I handed her the iPad. "You're not going to learn about Christopher Columbus in those kinds of books though."

She accepted the tablet with care, her big eyes on the screen.

"My mom used to read historical romances," Hawk joked. "I'm sure she learned something other than how to make Mr. Darcy fall in love with her."

I snickered. "I'll bet."

When Amara started tapping on the screen, my attention veered to her, and for a little while, there was silence in the room but Hawk and I watched her like she was a flight risk. A quick glance at him confirmed she fascinated him as much as she did me.

Of the three of us, she was the most timid, the least boisterous. Yet, somehow, she captivated both our attention. A beautiful woman could do that to a man, especially one who hadn't had sex in way too goddamn long, but this was different.

This felt...

I sighed.

Decided I was doped up on whatever the nurses had given me a little while ago.

"This one, please," she said, passing me the tablet back.

Hoping Indy was signed in, I went through the checkout process.

"It'll be delivered to Indy's ink studio. I'll tell her to watch out for it when I give her the money."

She bit her lip. "You really don't have to do that."

"I really do," I told her quietly, but I thought she heard the steel behind the words because she huffed out a soft breath. "You want to get started?"

I didn't, and I didn't think she did either to be honest, but she nodded, then twisted around to grab the armchair that Nyx had fallen asleep in earlier.

As she began to drag it against the floor, Hawk made an appearance and lifted it to where she wanted it.

She thanked him with a smile, but her eyes were big and somber in her pale face as she took a seat.

Hawk bustled around the bed. There were two cups on the table, one I used for water, and one that I'd had coffee in earlier. He filled both with water, passed one to Amara and the other to me.

I watched her take a sip, and once again decided that not having had sex in way too long was making me weird, because the thought of us sharing a cup was a fucked-up turn on.

"Do you want some Jell-O?" I asked her as I switched onto a drawing app.

"I'm not hungry."

Hawk sighed. "You haven't eaten today."

"Neither have you," she pointed out.

His nose crinkled. "I'm gonna get some take-out. What do you want to eat?"

She frowned. "What do you mean?"

Hawk frowned back. "What do you mean what do I mean? What do you want to eat?"

"I'll have what you're having."

I tensed, and suddenly got it. Choices... to people who were imprisoned, we had way too few of them.

I licked my lips, murmuring, "Amara, is there something in particular you'd like to eat? You can have whatever you want."

Her head jerked back like I'd slapped her, and a part of me wondered if the MC had been keeping her prisoner too. She'd looked at Amazon like it was Ali Baba's cave and take-out was new to her? I guessed she wouldn't have access to her own money, which also sucked and made it harder for her to have choices.

Hawk grimaced like he was picking up on this too, then said, "You want pizza? Curry? Thai, Indian, Japanese? A burger?"

She blinked, mouth working as she eventually gulped. "I've seen them on TV—they're like potato chips but with cheese in them."

Hawk mused, "Checkers' Monsterella Stix?"

"Sounds like it," I agreed. "You want a chicken burger with it? It's fried chicken. Has like this crispy shell on it." I shuddered. "It's epic."

Hawk grinned. "I know what I'm ordering you, then, huh?"

I hadn't expected him to get me anything, not when Giulia had left, declaring she'd be bringing back food, but I grinned at him, pleased to be included.

Jesus, my time inside really *had* made me weird.

Sheepishly, I murmured, "I'll just have a meal deal. Whatever's cheap, you know?"

Hawk frowned again, but drew out his phone, then shoved it at me. "Pick your own."

God, it had been way too long since I'd had my hands on a phone that wasn't ancient. The iPad was nice, but this beat that.

Almost drooling at the new iPhone in my paws, I scrolled through the selections and made my choice. Then, I showed it to her. "See? There are lots of options."

"Are they good?" she asked, peering at the screen.

"They're the best." My mouth was already watering. "At least, they used to be."

"They ain't changed," Hawk reassured me.

"Good," I muttered with relief, which made him chuckle.

To her, he said, "The fries are the best."

She pointed to one. "I'll take that."

I shook my head. "No, you need to scroll through the options. Pick a drink too. I bet you'd like the blue raspberry slushie." It couldn't be as sweet as her, but it might be close.

Her brow puckered, but she nodded, and returned her attention to the phone. She stared at each item for a long while, making me wonder if the translation was hard or something, then I watched as she stroked the image, and a bizarre kind of sorrow filled me.

I'd been sent to jail after being framed for a crime I didn't commit. I'd had my choices torn from me, my future too in some sense because anyone with a record always found the most basic shit impossible, I'd been abused and hurt, but what she'd gone through couldn't compare.

Human rights didn't matter to sex traffickers. I'd at least gotten some mediocre healthcare if I'd been sick. What did she get? Fuck all.

My throat definitely felt choked as I watched her deliberate over a fucking chicken sandwich menu, and when she finally said, "This one. Please." Her smile was like the sun peeking out of a fluffy blanket of gray clouds. "And the slushie you said."

The way she pronounced slushie made me wonder if she didn't know what that was, but I watched as Hawk moved over to her side, bent down and tapped away, showing her how to make the selections she needed.

After he'd inputted the order, he murmured to her, "I'm just over there. If you—" He heaved a sigh. "You're not doing this alone, is all I mean."

I was, by no one's calculations, a rocket scientist, but I knew the guys we were about to recreate together were the ones who'd abused her.

Just thinking about the fuckers who'd gotten to me was enough to make my blood pressure surge—a fact that the monitors made clear—so to get myself back under control before the nurses made an appearance and bitched at me for overexciting myself, I stated, "They can't hurt you, Amara."

When her smile made another reappearance, this time, it didn't belong to a woman who was finally being given options after too fucking long as a prisoner, but of someone who knew what it felt like to be a predator—as well as prey.

"I know." She sucked in a breath, then leaned into the armchair, closed her eyes and said, "This one had brown hair that—"

TWENTY-TWO

AMARA

BY THE TIME the order came, my hunger had gone. Vanished. Especially when I knew that the man I was describing was actually one of my nicer owners. It was his wife who'd been cruel.

Still, I knew he was important. I could see the photo of him in front of a US flag like the frame was in my hand and I was dusting it as I'd done so many times before.

Describing him was difficult in English, and sometimes, I had to use my phone to translate a word, but I managed. Barely.

Quin was good. Better than I could have imagined. He seemed to go with my descriptions, then add a dash of flair that somehow brought them to life.

By the time he was finished with the first drawing and was willing to show me, his skill stole my breath.

The guy didn't look like my captor, but how he'd managed to achieve that drawing from my ramblings felt like magic.

"It's okay if it's not accurate," he told me softly, his gaze just as soft as his voice. "We needed somewhere to start and now I can adjust."

I nodded, keeping my face tilted down so that I wasn't looking him in the eye. Not out of shyness, but because I liked how he and Hawk looked at me, and that way lay danger.

Neither saw me as a victim, even though they were well aware of my past.

They looked at me as if I was just a woman.

A woman they wanted to do things to.

Things that I wasn't sure I'd ever be able to manage.

Quin was Hawk's opposite. He was bulky, a little like Nyx, to be honest. His skin was almost bronze it was so dark, and his hair was pitch black. It was oddly cut, like he'd hacked it off with a knife that wasn't sharp or something, but the shaggy locks fell in lines so straight they were like rulers.

He had shadows under his dark brown eyes, and his cheekbones were high enough to make his cheeks look concave, as if he was sucking them in, when he wasn't. His lips were a dusky brown, but the heart of them was a tender pink.

He looked like a much younger version of Nyx, but darker. As if he'd been in the sun longer, which I doubted as he'd been in jail.

Now that I thought about it though, Indy was darker than Nyx. Did they have the same father?

Considering the MC lifestyle, I wouldn't have been surprised to learn they didn't, but their bone structure was too alike for the familial resemblance to be muddied too much.

I'd closed my eyes at first as I recreated my tormentors, but watching him was a pleasure.

As was watching Hawk.

I knew he was playing around on his phone, and it made it easier for me to describe the person who'd bought me like I was a chicken from the market.

When I leaned over to tell him, "He had gaunter cheeks," Quin murmured, "It'd probably be easier if you sit on the side of the bed. There'll be a lot of alterations."

"You've done this before?" Hawk questioned, his interest clear.

"Not really, but it's common sense."

A ping sounded from Hawk's phone and he said, "I'll just be outside. Our order's here."

"Should you leave us?" I asked warily. "Is Quin in danger?"

"I'm tipping extra to get the guy to come to the waiting room," he soothed as he pulled open the door and stepped outside.

"You like him."

The question was flat, no tinge to the tone that gave me an insight into why Quin had asked me that.

"I like how he treats me."

"And how is that?"

I stared down at him. "Like I'm normal." I refrained from telling him it was none of his business if I did like Hawk. But why I held my tongue was something I couldn't answer.

Resting my butt on the side of the bed, I twisted a little, until Quin heaved a sigh and muttered, "Just sit next to me."

He shuffled to the side, making room for me, and though it wasn't at all intimate, not really, it felt like it.

My cheeks burned as I muttered, "I-I don't think I should."

"Why? I don't have head-lice."

Eyes flaring wide, I sputtered, "I never thought you did."

He grinned. "You should see your face."

"Why is everyone trying to make me see my face today?" I grumbled with a huff.

"There's a story there," he pointed out softly, his smile fading a little.

I shook my head. "It doesn't matter."

He hummed disbelievingly, then patted the space he'd made beside him. "It's okay. I'm not going to hurt you."

That was the rub.

Just like with Hawk, I knew he wouldn't.

How? I had no idea, just had to trust that my gut wouldn't see me wrong.

Warily, I settled beside him. I didn't push back into the pillows like I'd seen Indy do earlier, I just pointed to the man's brows and said, "They were sharp."

He frowned. "Sharp?"

"Yes, with points." I mimicked the shape with my finger.

"Like a triangle?"

I nodded. "A triangle, *tak*."

He hummed under his breath as he erased what he'd done and made adjustments to the drawing, but even though he was patient and tried, I grew impatient.

I needed to figure out a way to make this easier because if Rex had me doing this for every single man who'd ever hurt me, we'd be a long time waiting for answers.

I'd never actually counted the faces, but I knew it was in the hundreds. It would have been more if I hadn't been sold to this particular man I was describing.

I felt dirty. Every day of my life, I felt unclean. But as I sat here, aware that I'd have to describe each and every single one of my abusers, I realized that Hawk would know just how many I'd been with.

Nausea started to tear at my insides, and when Hawk came in a few seconds later, I jerked upright, shifting over to the window once more. A flurry of pigeons were on the sill, and I twisted around, facing away from them even though I didn't want to look at either of the room's occupants because I hated birds. Always had and always would.

Hawk frowned at me, then looked at Quin whose gaze was on the iPad. Whether he was inspired to draw or if he was just being kind and giving me some privacy, I didn't know, but I tensed up with each and every step Hawk took toward me.

These men weren't innocent. They had clubwhores who they slept with indiscriminately. They weren't virgins, so I had nothing to be ashamed of when they were just as promiscuous, but I did feel ashamed.

I felt dirty. Every day of my life, I felt unclean.

When Hawk dragged the table on wheels over to me, I just whispered, "Thank you," as he set up the order I'd made.

I had no desire to eat any of the food I'd taken such pleasure in ordering, but Hawk unwrapped it all for me as if I was a child, even popping the lids on the little cartons of sauce.

When he drew his own out, and did the same, he gestured at his, saying, "Try mine, you might like it."

The prospect of eating made me want to vomit, but when Quin called out, "Let her try some of mine as well. We need to open up her palate to the wonders of fast food," guilt wracked me.

Here they were, trying to be nice, and here I was, spurning their kindness because of those bastards who'd hurt me.

Again and again, they managed to score soul-deep wounds on my being, even though they were nowhere near me and I was safe.

Because I was.

I knew the MC would keep me safe so long as I was under their protection, but more than that, I knew Hawk would protect me too.

I knew that because, even though he didn't say all that much, I'd seen him with other women and knew this wasn't how he treated them.

He wasn't careful with them.

He used them.

Not like I'd been used, not in a harmful or damaging way, just in a disinterested one.

The clubwhores knew what they were getting when they became the brothers' sex dolls. I hadn't signed up for that, yet Hawk treated me differently even though the clubwhores were like virgins in comparison to me.

Because they were both looking at me expectantly, I wanted the floor to open up and swallow me whole.

Hawk prodded, "Little bird, it's going to get cold."

I gulped, reached for the sandwich he'd set out for me first, and noticed my hand was shaking. Some lettuce fell from the bread as a result, but I managed to raise it to my mouth without spilling it everywhere.

The scent of oil and chicken and seasoning and mayonnaise was pleasant, but it could have been ashes as my senses explored the new flavor profile. I took a bite and was pretty sure I'd never be able to swallow it when the tang of the spices and the clean taste of the lettuce made saliva burst in my mouth, letting me chew without discomfort.

It tasted... good.

I bit my lip as I finished that bite, then shot them both a look and found them grinning.

"What?" I queried warily.

"You like it. I knew you had good taste," Quin teased.

"How did you know that?" I questioned—he didn't know me. We'd only just met.

He shrugged. "Instinct." The bright white stylus in his hand was held aloft as he prodded the air. "Try the others."

He was very bossy.

I bit my lip because my hunger hadn't returned, but theirs did look nice. I tried Quin's first because his didn't have cheese with flecks on it, and found that was even nicer than mine. A final bite of Hawk's had me moaning as my tongue tingled thanks to those spicy flecks in the slice of cheese.

My mind averted, memories gone, I focused on the here and now —*food*.

Hawk chuckled as I pressed a hand to my mouth to hide my moan, then he winked and said, "You can have mine."

"Do you mind?"

He grinned, shook his head then snagged the one I'd ordered and took a big bite as he grabbed Quin's and moved over to hand it to him.

In the carrier bag, I found some drinks too. One contained a light brown liquid, the other two were sweating. The drink I assumed was the blue raspberry had lumps of ice in it.

Knowing they wouldn't mind, I tried them all and groaned at the blue one.

"It tastes good. I didn't know blue raspberries existed. America is amazing."

Quin chuckled. "It's all chemicals, baby. Good though, right?"

I almost drooled as I took a deeper slurp.

"This is root beer," Hawk said, wiggling one at me after he peeled back the lid and sniffed.

Root beer?

I'd killed Jeremiah with the glass bottle of root beer.

After a bite of my sandwich to cleanse my palate, I tasted the drink. My nose wrinkled, which had them both laughing, before he handed me the next one.

"Sweet tea."

"Wow, that is very good," I said with a small moan, sucking down some more.

"I can't believe we never ordered take-out for you guys," Hawk rumbled, shaking his head as he snagged one of the odd fried things that they'd called Monsterella stix.

"Giulia's a good cook."

Hawk shrugged. "So? Can't replace shit like this sometimes. Ya need the bad stuff every now and then."

"This is America's heritage," Quin joked. "Carbs, sugar, and fried foods."

"Well, it is very tasty," I replied, not even minding that they both laughed at my fervent tone of voice.

The stix were a little much for me, but the fries were delicious.

I devoured the meal, not even grateful for the reprieve because it was so good that I forgot everything else but what I was eating.

The two men started talking, but I tuned out, taking a break from English as I stared out the window and looked onto the little I could see of New York.

It was very bleak.

Not much of a view, but it was beautiful because I knew that, if I wanted, I could head outside and go left or right, get lost in the streets, and was free to do what I wanted and when.

Freedom tasted better than this sandwich, but I'd definitely have to try other things once Lily transferred the money over to me.

For the first time, thoughts of the trust she was setting up for Alessa and me didn't bring on a feeling of bitterness, more excitement.

It was covered in blood, but I'd be able to buy as many fried chicken sandwiches as I wanted. I'd be able to go and do and be what I needed.

The thought was intoxicating enough to spur me on.

For whatever reason, I was finding the politician harder to recreate than I should, so, once he'd finished his meal, I asked Quin, "Do you mind if I try another one?"

"My drink?"

I smiled a little, surprised but pleased by his generosity. They both were like that. It was oddly comforting.

"No, another drawing?"

He shrugged. "Sure."

"This man used to drive us," I whispered.

"To and from the cabin if you misbehaved?" Hawk asked softly.

"Yes, but also, long distances. The first man, he lived far away from the place where we were found. It took a long time to get there.

"He is how I know the Sparrows are the men I served. He was important, and the one who transported me from the beginning until the end was friends with him."

"He crossed borders?"

I shrugged. "Yes."

"Do you know where the first one lived?"

"I think it was Washington DC."

Hawk and Quin shared a glance, but Quin just said, "Go ahead, sky girl, describe the cunt."

The endearment was a strange one. Much like Hawk who called

me little bird. Why did both of them associate me with the sky? With a creature who could fly?

If anything, I'd been tethered my whole life...

Did they think I was free now?

Should I tell them that I hated birds? That the idea of flying made me break out in a cold sweat?

"He had round cheeks and they turned red easily. When he got out of the car, the wind would make them burn like apples." My mind drifted. "I remember one time, he used the bathroom then dragged me out of the truck and made me suck him because, 'Why should I waste paper when I have you to clean me up?'"

My gaze turned distant as I remembered the way he'd pulled on my hair to the point where I was sure some would tug free of the roots. The sticks and stones beneath my knees, the harsh wind that cut through the skimpy dress I wore.

I was used to worse treatment than a dick that tasted of piss, or cleaning an ass speckled with shit, but the memory of looking up at him, of scanning his features, of hating him, was stark.

"He had blond hair, cut like he was a soldier." I gestured at my head. "Shaved here, and to the back. It was flat on top, but a little longer. He used a lot of gel. His eyes were blue, inset, the brow hooded." The description flooded the room, and I suddenly knew why.

I couldn't just remember the man, I had to remember what he'd done, and I had to remember that I hated them.

Instead of blocking out the memory, I had to embrace it.

Fully.

I had to become the memory so I had the energy and patience to endure describing the bastards who'd hurt me.

"Fuck."

Quin's outburst had me returning to the present, and when he showed me the driver, it wasn't perfect, but it almost was. His cheeks were thinner, his forehead longer, and his hair wasn't right, but Quin still said, "I know this bastard."

Hawk leaned forward, the armchair cushion creaking as he did so. "Who is it?"

"The detective who helped set me up." His hand drifted over the iPad and when he turned it back to me, the adjustments I'd thought about, but hadn't said out loud, had been made.

"Who is it?" I asked.

"His name is Craig Lacey." Quin's jaw appeared to be set in stone.

"I'll tell Rex," Hawk intoned grimly.

Quin nodded, but his gaze was on the tablet. "I hated this bastard before, but now I hate him even more." He shot me a dark look. "Amara, I know you must be tired—"

I shook my head. "No. I'm not." If anything, his identifying one of the men who'd taxied me around the country and along the different coasts, filled me with relief.

I could do this.

We could do this.

It wasn't a pie in the sky dream.

We'd identified one, now we just had to identify the others, until they could all be taken out like the *musor*—the trash—they were.

TWENTY-THREE

HAWK

I COULD HAVE CALLED Rex from the hospital room. I could have even called from the armchair beside Quin's bed.

There was a lot of shit I *could* have done, but I was incapable of it.

Absolutely fucking incapable of it.

Just sitting there, listening to her describe the cunt who'd shoved a piss-covered cock into her mouth like she was a piece of toilet paper, who'd abused her and transported her like she was a cow for market, filled me with such rage that, for the first time in my life, I understood what fueled Giulia.

I'd always considered her a Little Napoleon. Small woman syndrome and all that shit. Scrappy Doo because she had to make her voice heard.

But at that moment, even though I'd wanted to help Amara without hearing the details of what she'd endured, I knew I'd stand at her side, no matter what she did, and feel no shame or fear.

As a society, we put bad dogs down all the time. One bite, and that was it.

Well, these motherfuckers had done more than just bite Amara.

They didn't deserve a gunshot to the head.

They deserved castration. They deserved to dine on their balls, served to them after they'd been fucking flambéed.

So, with a righteous wrath swirling around my insides like a tropical storm that was brewing, I stepped out of the hospital room and stomped into the waiting room for some privacy.

The urge to put my fist through the wall, to release some of this fury onto some unsuspecting inanimate object was tempting. I could have picked up a couple of chairs and hurled them across the room, smashing everything and anything in The Who-style, but knowing I wouldn't be allowed back in, would be detained in a cell, would be kept out of this process, made me refrain.

Amara had endured this. She deserved for someone to stand by her as she purged herself of the past.

My lips twisted into a snarl as I kicked the door shut once I spotted that the place was clear.

I knew I couldn't speak as freely here as I could outside in the street, but it wasn't like I could go far when I needed to watch over Quin. Even the waiting room was too far away, yet I had no alternative, simply because discussing this shit in front of Amara was beyond me right now.

If I let my temper loose, then only God knew how she'd react. Any steps forward I might have made with her in the past couple of days would be ruined for good.

With that in mind, aware that I needed to keep the council in the loop, I called Rex.

"Quin sent the drawing over," was his greeting. "That came fast."

"They work well together," I gritted out, my voice raw as I struggled to contain my temper.

"Quin's sure it's Craig Lacey?"

"He's positive."

Rex blew out a breath, then cut the call. I half expected for that to be it—I was only a brother, after all, not on the council—but a second later, the FaceTime app popped up and when I hit connect, a video shot up of my brothers around the makeshift office Rex had made his own. I'd have laughed if the situation wasn't so infuriating. The lot of them were shuffled together at one end of the table with the phone at the bottom so they were all visible.

"You got earphones?" Sin queried gruffly.

I reached into my pocket for my AirPods and shoved them in. When the Bluetooth pinged in my ear, I nodded. "Go ahead."

"You wouldn't ordinarily hear any of this shit," Rex stated calmly, "but it's clear that Amara's grown attached to you—"

It was?

I frowned. "I don't think so—"

"You looked like you were the only thing keeping her from folding in on herself this morning," Rex pointed out, his tone dry but not amused.

I shrugged because that I couldn't deny. The early morning bravado had been chased away by the prospect of having to speak with Rex. I wasn't sure why he scared her, but he did.

"You really think she's got the chestnuts to kill the fuckers who hurt her?"

I focused on Link. "Chestnuts?"

He shrugged. "Seemed better to give you code words so if you repeat them, anyone listening in won't understand."

My lips twitched. "I can hold my tongue," was all I said before wryly telling him, "Just use big words then I won't repeat them for being too weird."

"Fucking chestnuts," Nyx grumbled under his breath. "Dumbass."

Link flipped him the bird but kept his focus on me. "Well, *do* you think she can do it?"

"We know she can do some of it," I pointed out. "She enjoyed yesterday's day trip."

"Who the fuck could blame her?" Rex heaved a sigh and ran a hand through his hair. "That bastard was the first person to break her in."

Just the words had rage filling me. I wasn't used to feeling this much, wasn't used to being this angry, but it was like losing North and Dad so shortly after Mom had opened up a geyser in my fucking soul.

Now I'd let feelings in, I couldn't stop them, and around Amara, shit grew even more muddled.

She was nothing to me.

So why did that feel like one big fat lie?

"As glad as I am that she..." I struggled with my words, trying to keep them PC because of my location. "...found some peace, I wish I'd been there to help her draw it out." I shook my head. "Fuck."

"Agreed," Rex muttered. "And she ain't even my woman."

Those words... did that mean he thought she was mine?

I didn't argue, didn't make him walk back the statement, which was probably telling in itself.

Just watching Quin check her out earlier had made me realize how possessive I felt of her. Had made me recognize how my view of her had changed.

What had begun as me wanting to give her pleasure a couple days ago, what had started out as something freely offered and selfless, had twisted into something else entirely.

Knowing she had the 'chestnuts' to do what needed to be done was both a relief and a curse.

I was accustomed to women who took the bull by the balls and got shit done.

My mom had been like that—whenever Dad had hit her, she'd hit back twice as hard.

After an argument, if he did something that put her in the ER, he'd be the one walking out of the hospital a few days later because she got him back.

One time, during one of their many arguments, I remembered her tearing the sink from the wall—the fucking wall—and throwing it at him. Actually throwing the fucker at him. She wasn't the Hulk, but Christ, in a temper, Lizzie Fontaine was one nasty bitch—Giulia came by it honestly. That was for fucking sure.

Whether it was by good aim or good eye, Mom had managed to clip Dad on the side of the head. If the sink hadn't just clipped him, he'd have died.

As it was, that had been the reason she'd taken us away.

That level of rage burned inside us all, I knew.

Giulia was the only one who frequently let it out. Me, I preferred to control it.

If I didn't, well, that's when I did stupid stuff.

I'd had a good career as a bounty hunter, but the day I'd started seeking vengeance instead of justice was the day I'd known I had to turn my back on the life. I'd known that once wouldn't be enough, but it hadn't stopped me from trying... The second time it happened was when I'd handed in my resignation.

Funny how, even though I'd stepped away from that career, vengeance had sought me out anyway, wasn't it?

Proof enough, I guessed, that our fates were written in the stars long before we were born.

The thoughts racing through my mind made it hard to tune into the council meeting, which was dumb because, one day, I fully intended on sitting there, on being a part of church, and this was a glimpse into my future.

Nyx barreled into the soft shit between my ears by growling, "Brennan O'Donnelly and his man warned me about Craig Lacey yesterday."

"When they came to visit with Quin?"

"More like make sure things were copacetic between us, Sin. They'd have preferred to talk to you for sure."

Sin shrugged. "They don't like change."

"Considering I was the one who dealt with them before—"

Sin snorted. "As insane as I am, that's nothing to you, bro. I guess they like a dash of sanity with their updates."

Nyx pulled a face. "I'm on a promise now. No more insanity."

I arched a brow, but the rest of the council just shook their heads, and I got it. Took more than a promise, and a baby on the way, to make a man change. Especially when he had a woman like Giulia—she wasn't exactly the kind of gal who kept a guy on the straight and narrow.

"They said that Lacey hired a car to cross into Jersey. Even though he has an SUV of his own. They think he's transporting something—"

"Yeah. Women," I grated out, lowering my voice just to be safe. It wouldn't stop any bugs from picking up on the conversation, but we weren't the ones trafficking people across state lines—nah, that job was up to the good old 'boy' in blue.

Fucking typical.

"Women?" Nyx shook his head. "Is that likely?"

"According to Amara, he transported the girls across the country sometimes."

"Maybe there are brothels in Manhattan or NYC and he's taking them to wherever Lancaster kept them?" Link suggested.

"Seems likely. O'Donnelly never said anything about him going on long distance journeys—"

"Nah, but we've only known about Lacey being dirty for, what, a week? Max? At least, as far as we know. They'll have only just established stake-out crews on him. I told Finn O'Grady at the Summit about Lacey's involvement, so they haven't had much time to build a bigger picture."

"True," Nyx conceded. "They hadn't seen him cross state lines, just picked up the details from his bank records. At least, I think. They're not exactly open with us, are they?"

"Not like we are either," Rex pointed out. "Sharing is caring but this isn't a fucking prayer circle." A knock sounded at the door, and Rex tipped his chin to the side, hollering, "That you, Lodestar? Come on in."

"This had better be fucking worth it," the hacker rasped as she wheeled herself into the room and in front of the camera. When she peered at the screen, saw me, she dismissed me by focusing on Rex. "What did you want?"

"Why should I share what Cin had to say when she's your friend?"

"Who's Cin?" Sin questioned, brow puckered. "I assume you're not talking about me," he said wryly.

"Not unless you got two DDs, brother," Rex half-joked. "Cin is... drum roll, please, Dead To Me."

A snicker escaped me. "No fucking way. That's like an urban legend or something."

Rex's brow surged. "I wouldn't have said urban legend, but I know what you mean. She's certainly made a name for herself pretty fucking fast."

I tried to think about what I knew of the legend, but in all honesty, it seemed insane to me.

A sniper did not announce a murder by sending a gift bag of all fucking things.

If she really did exist, then it wasn't just rumor when they said she delivered a gift to her target, tied with balloons.

Although it would be typical if that kind of person was friendly with Lodestar.

"What's with the messed up message she sends first off?" I rumbled at Lodestar.

She sniffed. "I ain't her, so I don't know why she does what she does."

"Your attitude always this shitty?" I countered, glad that I hadn't had many dealings with the bitch if she was this dismissive of non-councilors all the fucking time.

"I make a habit out of being a cunt," she retorted sweetly, her eyes narrowed on me as she silently told me to go fuck myself.

"Who the hell is Dead To Me?" Steel groused, scraping his hand over his head. "I ain't heard of her."

"You been living under a rock?" Nyx complained, slouching back in his seat. "That sniper who sends gifts to the targets before they kill 'em."

Steel's brow furrowed. "I really need to get out of Stone's pussy 'cause fuck, I don't remember hearing about that shit."

Link snorted. "Time stops for the best pussy."

Steel and him shared a grin, and though it was ridiculous to feel envy considering what they'd both gone through to get their women, I kind of was.

They didn't look like men who were suffering much now that they had a ball and chain. If anything, they looked happy.

Happy.

Christ, it felt like a long time since I'd been that way.

Long before Dad's death and North's disappearance. Shit, longer even than before Mom's passing.

Had I lost any right to happiness when I'd killed that cunt?

Maybe.

I thought about this morning, waking up to the feel of Amara's hands on me, the tender strokes, the gentle exploration, and I recognized I'd been happy then.

A kind of happy that was priceless because she hadn't been trying to do anything to please me, and I'd been mostly asleep at that point so it wasn't like I'd had a say in my emotions.

Didn't that make what I'd felt more powerful though?

"What did this Dead To Me dude have to say?"

"Ain't a dude," Lodestar retorted. "It's a chick."

"Only a chick would figure out a way to spend money while making it."

She flipped the bird at Sin, who just grinned at her. "She told us about some shit that's on the brink of going down."

"That's the reason for the emergency church," Rex concurred.

"Tell us more," Nyx ground out impatiently.

"Antoni Vasov died the other day."

My brows surged high at that. "The Bratva Pakhan's dead?"

Lodestar nodded. "Yep. Cin said the Bratva were trying to make out it was an accidental death or something, but she said her mole talked about him having his skull caved in. That sound accidental to you?"

Steel snorted. "Not unless he put his head through a meat grinder by accident."

She smirked a little. "Not likely. Anyway, the reason she was telling me was because of something that's cropping up in the city."

"Lemme guess," Link rumbled as he rolled his eyes. "Bratva factions are at war?"

"Yep," she said cheerfully.

"So, now, we've got two out of four of the city's major players at war with themselves, Christ," Sin muttered, scrubbing a hand over his face. "The O'Donnellys should have kept us in the loop about this."

"They should, but you know we ain't sharing everything," Rex pointed out again. "We only share what we want them to know so it's a given that they'd do the same with us."

Before any of us could reply, what seemed like a dozen pings went off, as I got a message from a number in a group chat that, I assumed, Quin had shot off to me, as well as the council.

As I tapped on the screen to see the new picture, my brothers around the dining room table pulled out their devices, but I hissed under my breath the second I saw the face.

"Jesus Christ," I rasped.

Rex hissed. "Isn't that Jason fucking Young?"

"My phone ain't loading," Sin grumbled. "Jason Young, as in, that cunt Hewett's running mate in the last presidential election?"

"Yeah," I whispered, and for the first time, it occurred to me exactly how high up this shit went.

Hewett had lost to the now-President Davidson by the skin of his teeth, and if Amara was certain the people who'd owned her were Sparrows, and Young was a Sparrow, that meant we'd almost had one of those bastards in the Oval Office.

I felt like I was in some kind of thriller drama on Netflix as hard home truths resonated with me in a way that I couldn't begin to process without feeling like a conspiracy theorist.

It was one thing to believe that all politicians were corrupt fuckers, but to see it?

To know it?

To come face to fucking face with it?

I gulped, a peculiar kind of anxiety rumbling to life inside me like a fire that was sputtering into being as I whispered, "This is so much bigger than we could have known."

Link bowed his head. "No fucking joke."

Rex blew out a breath. "Hawk, you're gonna have to tell her that what she wants ain't possible."

My mouth firmed and while I knew he was right, she deserved for me to argue on her behalf. "She deserves closure."

"There's closure and there's killing a high profile politician."

I winced, because he wasn't wrong.

"What's more important," Rex pointed out softly, "her getting closure or her staying out of jail or not serving time on death row for fucking treason?"

"I heard from aCooooig," Lodestar remarked softly, breaking into the dead stare me and Rex were engaged in.

"Who's he?" I questioned with a frown.

"None of your business," she said with a sniff.

I growled. "I'm a fucking brother in the MC. Who the fuck are you?"

"She's entitled to be here," Rex said calmly. "I told her she had a right to any information about the *Famiglia* so long as she works with us and not against us, and ever since we learned they were just a front for the Sparrows, well, this falls under that."

She shot me a triumphant smirk, which Rex crumpled by explaining, "aCooooig is one of the Five Points. He and Lodestar—" He hesitated. 'I don't fucking know. Break firewalls or some shit."

Lodestar snorted. "Yeah, that's it. I'm just a human-shaped sledgehammer." She cast me a dirty look but begrudgingly remarked, "We have an opportunity to help the Bratva and the Irish. *If* we want to..."

"How?" Sin demanded, his interest clear.

"From what Cin says, the Bratva's split two ways. The old Sovietnik and the Obschak are wanting to consolidate power to remain in charge. Not sure who'd be promoted to Pakhan but they have worse problems at hand than just duking it out over who'd take the spot of top dog."

"They're concerned about the other faction?" Sin queried. "Who is it?"

"It's headed by Maxim Lyanov. Vasov's bodyguard."

Silence strummed around the council table at that, before Nyx eventually murmured, "Pakhans are usually selected by Moscow, ain't they?"

"Fortune favors the brave," Lodestar replied. "Lyanov's trying to tip their hand and get himself to the top of the ladder, and to be frank, I'm giving you the option but I'm telling you now, whether you decide you're on Lyanov or the old council's side, I ain't letting those dirty fuckers go through with their plan without getting involved."

Rex raised a hand. "What are you talking about, Lodestar? Give us all the facts before you start making threats that'll make me forget you're more of a man than you are a chick."

She squinted at him. "I got tits, don't I?"

"Yeah, but if a brother had talked that kind of shit to me I'd have smacked them down for it..."

She hissed at the warning like a rattled cat, but mumbled, "I could take you. Even in a fucking wheelchair."

"I'll bet," was all Rex rumbled.

"Weren't you in on this conversation?" Link demanded. "How don't you know what she's about to say?"

"Apparently they were talking in some kind of code." Rex sheepishly rubbed his chin. "Went over my head."

"That's what it's like dealing with the CIA," Lodestar retorted smugly. "But in this instance, she texted me the details. She got an update."

"Which is? Don't keep us in fucking suspense."

"The Sovietnik and Obschak, Abramovicz and Lukov, are on the losing side. Dissent is rife and they're not gaining ground, so they've taken over a factory in their territory. That's their base. Cin says they're making moves to snatch someone high profile—"

"Who?"

"If you'd let me speak, Nyx," she snapped, "I'd fucking tell you. Cin says it's the new O'Donnelly brides."

"Brides? Plural?" Sin rasped. "I know Eoghan got married and Declan got back with his woman but they ain't married—"

"Cin says the second eldest son, Brennan, just got wed. To Vasov's eldest girl."

She held up her phone and showed it to the table.

"My eyes fucking deceiving me?" Nyx rasped.

Sin's own eyes were wide. "No, brother. They ain't."

"How the fuck did we have a Bratva bitch in our midst for years and didn't fucking know it?" Steel growled as he slammed his hand down against the table.

Nyx swallowed. "Shit."

"Cammie was the daughter of a Pakhan?" Link whispered to himself. "Good God." He reached up and started fiddling with the rosary beads he wore. "We're lucky Vasov didn't come at us with fucking Molotovs."

Steel muttered, "Maverick has a lot to answer for. Talk about dropping the fucking ball."

"Remind me to ream him another asshole when he's better." Rex ground his teeth. "These clubwhores are becoming more trouble than they're fucking worth." He shook his head. "Might be time to start going to the source and heading to our titty bar for a show instead. Less fucking hassle, and less expensive in the long goddamn run."

"Speaking of club snatch," Link rasped, cracking his knuckles, "I have news on Tink's location."

Interest had me leaning forward at that, because we'd been hunting for Tink ever since we'd realized she'd been an integral cog in the wheel that had decimated the clubhouse.

TMI tended to be about information that was skeevy or gross.

This was TMI because of how many torrents of information were flooding the conversation. Much more, and we'd be drowning.

Swallowing, I listened as Rex demanded, "Where is she?"

"In the Fridge," Link replied. "Me and James Dean snagged her this morning. She was staying low in Brownville."

Nyx, still looking shellshocked at the fact he'd been boning a daughter of the Bratva, rumbled, "Don't tell Giulia. She and her bitches will be there, beating the crap out of her before we get the chance to question her."

"Look, this is very interesting," Lodestar growled, "*not*, but we got bigger fish to fry. I mean you've had treacherous cunt around before and you ain't done shit—"

Link grimaced. "We shoulda axed Kendra a while back for what she did to Keira."

Rex muttered, "She begged to stay."

"So? She wrecked Storm's marriage."

"Storm did that," was Rex's retort.

"What kind of benchmark is that? The crime was committed so the accomplice can split the deets to the cops?" Link snapped. "That's some bullshit."

"He's not wrong, Rex," Steel agreed. "Was a shitty thing she did."

"You know as well as I do she don't have anywhere to go."

It was easy to see the Prez did not appreciate this topic of conversation.

"She's the one who jeopardized her position here," Link rumbled. "Ain't our problem if she was in love with Storm and has been since fucking high school. She should never have said shit to Keira. Look at the fallout—"

"As fascinating as this is," Lodestar groused, "I ain't showing you pictures because this is 'Show and fucking Tell.' Vasov's daughters are being targeted—Lukov and Abramovicz are going to kidnap them."

Rex shook his head. "Until it happens, we can't do shit, Lodestar. I'm sure you want to get your nosey ass involved, but if we approach either the O'Donnellys or this Maxim fucker with this news, they'll want to know how we came by the info—the source of which I'm assuming Cin won't want to give us—"

"She won't," Lodestar confirmed. "I already tried to get it out of her."

He sighed, then reached up to pinch the bridge of his nose. "Okay, then, we can't get involved until the women are taken."

"Fuck that," Nyx snarled. "We can't just let them be snatched—" His head whipped to the side in outright rejection. "I treated her like shit, I know that, and I know I have no fucking right to make out like she meant something to me because she didn't, but she was one of us, Rex. If she was still fucking me, still a clubwhore, we'd go after her."

Rex straightened up, evidently surprised by Nyx's defense. "Christ, Nyx, I think I actually just saw you grow some morals."

The VP's mouth tightened. "It's Giulia's fault."

I snorted. "How? She's the most immoral person I know."

Nyx wriggled his shoulders. "She's the one with my kid in her belly, ain't she? I got to be a better man for them both."

Even though I'd admit to being surprised, I was mostly relieved. If Nyx was head over fucking heels for Giulia, that was nothing to what she was for him.

If anything happened to him, I didn't even want to know what kind of destruction Giulia would cause. It would be worse than Pandora opening that goddamn box.

A shudder whispered down my spine, like I knew what I'd just thought was a premonition. Like it could happen if Nyx was ever lost to his Old Lady.

Nyx would go to war for Giulia, he'd ride into hell itself to keep her safe. But Giulia, like any woman, had Satan on speed dial.

Shivering again at the thought, I tuned back into the conversation.

"You and I both know that if we get involved before there's an attack, they won't believe us. They'll think we're pulling shady moves."

Nyx's grimace spoke loud and clear—he agreed.

"We wait," Rex rasped. "I don't like it either. Cammie was good people. Wasn't her fault she wanted more from you—"

Link snorted. "A lot more. Christ, Nyx, you'd better hope that Brennan O'Donnelly never finds out you were the one she was hooked on. Ain't he their Fixer?"

Sin shook his head. "No one really knows what he does. He's a scary motherfucker though. Rumor had it, when he was a kid, that he came up with that nasty shit for the Aryans."

Steel gagged. "The concrete boots before they were dumped in the car crusher?"

"They say he laughed when he hit the button."

Rex sniffed. "People and rumor and 'they' say a lot of useless shit." To Lodestar, he stated firmly, "You got a way of keeping tabs on the women?"

"Cin's already back in Manhattan. Keeping an eye on the situation. I ain't got a clue how she knows, but she says the girls are going to Vespers—"

"Cammie's religious?" Nyx boomed out, his eyes bugging wide. "What the actual fuck?"

Lodestar ignored him to say, "I'd like to think they'd be safe at church, but who the fuck knows?"

"Why are they targeting the O'Donnelly brides?" Link argued. "That makes no sense. They're married. There's no power moves—"

Lodestar raised a hand. "Look, I don't know why, but what I do know is that Cin's intel is top class. She rarely gets shit wrong. If she says they're going to be kidnapped, then that's what's going to happen."

"She's got ears in the Bratva?"

Lodestar shrugged. "Probably eyes too. Does it matter? Trust me, she's good. World class. She caused a lot of shit over her time in the CIA before she mapped out her own path."

"Is she trustworthy?" Sin queried.

"I'd trust her with my life, and let me tell you, it ain't often I utter those words."

"Why's she getting involved? Why tell you?"

Lodestar shrugged. "We've all got our fingers in a lot of pies."

"Bullshit. She must want something out of this," Sin retorted.

"You'll owe her. In our world, favors are a commodity."

Rex pursed his lips. "Either way, I don't want Cammie getting hurt, so we have to get involved.

"Tell Cin to keep her eyes on the situation, then let us know when we can get involved.

"If we know their location, and can confirm the site they'll take the women to is this factory, we can get in touch with this Lyanov."

"Not the O'Donnellys?" Lodestar asked with a frown.

For a few seconds, Rex stared blindly ahead, before slowly replying, "No. Like you said, a favor means a lot."

"The ex-Pakhan's daughters might not mean anything to Lyanov."

"He can leverage their safety to gain alliance with the Irish." Rex pursed his lips. "This gives us an in with the new faction. It's always good to keep in with fresh blood, and either way, the women are safe."

"You don't know that for sure," Sin pointed out.

Rex tapped his fingers against the table. "No, not for sure but a feeling. There was no love lost around the Summit table for Vasov. I doubt the Irish and Chinese will respect his top ranking men." Rex shrugged. "Going with my gut here and it rarely lets me down."

"You want us to head back into the city?" Sin asked.

"No. We can help from afar. You can get a number for Maxim Lyanov, Lodestar?"

"Of course."

Rex hummed. "If Cin does have eyes and ears on the place, maybe she's in a similar predicament—if she gets involved, she'll leave her source wide open." He scratched his chin. "Anyway, there's nothing we can do until—"

A sharp scream jerked my focus from the screen and I darted to my feet.

Shoving the door open, I heard my brothers demanding news on where the scream came from, but even though I didn't have any answers, even though there were a dozen other private rooms on this ward, I knew.

I knew in my fucking gut.

Rushing into Quin's room, I came across a scene I'd never forget.

Ever.

Quin was passed out, bleeding from a wound on his head—the way he was slouched had my heart sinking. Was he—?

No.

He couldn't be.

I switched focus onto the real threat at the moment, and even as I rushed forward, even as I helped her, I had to shake my head.

This woman.

It was hard to believe that she'd been held captive.

As I watched her strangle the intruder with the call button cord, pride swelled inside me.

She hadn't come to the realization yet that she was too strong now to be prey but she would soon.

And with me by her side? She was untouchable.

I'd make fucking sure of that.

Even Batman had needed Robin...

TWENTY-FOUR

GIULIA

I WASN'T SUPPOSED to listen in to church meetings.

I knew for a fact that if the brothers ever found out about me eavesdropping, I'd get my ass handed to me. But there was a vent in the dining room that let me hear what was being said in the kitchen, and I was far too weak not to bow down to temptation.

Their voices were muffled, but I could make out almost everything, and even though I knew there was big shit going on for Lodestar to have been called in, the second those bitches' names were mentioned, it was like a light bulb going off in my head.

Kendra.

Tink.

The cunts.

One had destroyed a family.

The other had destroyed my home.

Tink had wrecked the one place my Nyx was at peace.

She'd killed brothers and clubwhores.

She'd ruined lives.

And Bear was a tangled mess of amputations because of her.

Because.

Of.

Her.

She needed to pay.

She had to pay.

I was under no illusions about the Sinners. They'd torture a woman if she betrayed the club, and I wasn't even sure if they'd be all that squeamish about it.

Whether you were in possession of a pussy or a cock, if you let the club down, you were fucked.

But I knew, point blank, they wouldn't do as good a job as me or my girls.

That was why, the second I learned she was in the Fridge, I hightailed it outta the kitchen. I had to be sneaky because Nyx was preternaturally aware of me and my shenanigans so I tiptoed past the dining room door and made my way to the front veranda.

Once there, I snatched my cell, opened up the group chat, and tapped:

Me: *Link confirmed Tink is in the Fridge.*

It didn't surprise me that messages rolled in almost immediately.

Lily: *Is that place still operational?*

Me: *Why wouldn't it be?*

Stone: *We had Feds crawling all over the place.*

Me: *So? Cruz will have cleaned it down. We'd have heard something about it by now if the Feds had found anything.*

Lily: *True. Plus I heard Link say that Lodestar fixed it so the blast looked like it was started by a gas leak.*

Indy: *How the fuck do you fix that?*

Lily: *No idea. Maybe we should be thankful for small mercies though, hmm?*

Tiffany: *You really think Tink is at the Fridge?*

Me: *Heard it from his lips. I'm driving over there now. Join me?*

I got a flurry of messages telling me they were on their way, but I detoured to the side of the property where the garages were, and looked at the wall of tools and garden implements Rachel stored here.

The woman was anal in a strange way. Lots of shelves, so many of them that they took up the entire back wall of the massive garage. Each one was full of shit, it was just organized shit.

I made my way to the tools, well aware that what I was looking for might not even be here.

Having been raised around an MC, and then moving into the home of a guy who sold used cars, I was well acquainted with tools, but this one was a certain kind of hammer.

I remembered it from shop class. The ball-peen hammer.

It had a flat side and a rounded edge, with that edge being hemispherical it was so perfectly round—perfect for what I had in mind.

My gaze scanned the shelves until I found one of four tool boxes. I pulled them down, finding screwdrivers in one, all flatheads, and another containing pozidrivs. Shaking my head, I pulled out another and hit the jackpot.

Hammers.

And there it was, the one I wanted for the bitch who'd been tossed out for beating up Stone and trying to fuck with her Old Man.

Literally.

I hefted the weight in my hand, tightened my grip around it, then curiosity had me peering into the fourth tool box where I found something that was outside of the plan but I figured would come in handy.

Pocketing the pliers, I moved everything back, just in case their presence on the floor raised suspicion, and headed toward one of the cages that had survived the blast and which were parked up here for the moment.

In the ignition, as usual with cages, there was a set of keys swinging, so I twisted it, wincing at the noise it made, then carefully reversed and backed out onto the drive.

With one eye on the house, making sure that no one was looking out of the windows and watching who was driving off, I didn't gun the engine until I was through the gates and a few minutes down the road.

The next problem was getting past the construction site which was manned with brothers, who'd see me driving up the driveway.

They'd also see a bunch of other cars if my friends all decided to come in single vehicles.

Deciding that I just had to be fast and that I wouldn't wait for them in case brothers tried to drag me away, I was careful as I pulled into the compound, traveling sedately as I made it onto the driveway. When it came to the part where we off-roaded across the plains to reach the Fridge, I kept glancing at the rear-view mirror to make sure no one was following me.

The ride was bumpy, but the truck was used to worse terrain, and I didn't bother gunning it because I didn't want to raise eyebrows.

Tire tracks had already scored their way into the earth, confirming someone had traveled down this path earlier, so I was hoping the construction workers would think I was just a brother, heading out to the Fridge to chat with our prisoner.

An unholy grin lit my lips as I made it to the bunkhouse without any hassle, and when I jumped out, I reached for the hammer that I'd placed on the passenger seat.

Holding the grip firmly in hand, I walked over to the building.

It was pretty rough around the edges, beaten up in more ways than one. There'd always been rumors about this place, but I'd never been here before. It had a couple of steps up to the door, there was a kind of lean-to, and then just a general air of disuse.

If Cruz was as good as they said, then the FBI wouldn't have been interested in the Fridge anyway because it looked like someplace that had been abandoned years ago.

Hell, maybe we were lucky urban explorers hadn't come a-calling.

Grinning at the thought, I rushed up the stairs to the door. It was, unsurprisingly, locked with a heavy-duty padlock.

Hefting the hammer, I shattered through the padlock's arm after a good dozen blows, rupturing it before opening the lock up. Security once we left would be diminished and that concerned me, but I figured brothers would be riding my ass soon enough. I needed to get a couple of licks in with my tools before that happened and they could lock this shit back up again for me.

For a second, my heart sank when the door wouldn't budge, as I thought maybe they had a secondary lock on it, but after I shoved it a couple times with my shoulder, it caved in.

Relief whistled through me, until I heard the sounds of an engine in the distance.

Twisting around, I caught sight of Indy's Camaro, and smirked, content that the others felt my urgency too.

I'd admit, when I looked inside the Fridge, my stomach did a bellyflop. I knew what the brothers were capable of, knew what *I* was capable of, but it was hard to see a woman chained to the wall. Hard to see her collared and pinned in place with a metal leash.

She'd killed people, she'd betrayed the club, she was scum, but it was still hard to swallow.

That didn't take away from what I was about to do, which would be a thousand times worse than what the brothers would, but I didn't like the wobble—it made me feel weak.

She was, as far as I could see, injury-free. No signs of being beaten, no black eyes. If anything, she looked her usual self, just scared.

When our gazes connected, her vision adjusting to the light after the solid dark of the Fridge, there was a sneer on her lips but I saw, deep in her eyes, she knew what was coming.

"What did he pay you to help bomb my home?" I asked softly, emphasizing 'my' because she'd lost her right to having the clubhouse as her home way before the blast had even happened. "Or didn't he give you anything? Just satisfaction at fucking us over?"

Tink turned her face away, but I didn't give her shit because I heard footsteps. When I turned to see who'd arrived, I was shocked but pleased to see that almost all the bitches had showed up—Lily, Tiff, Stone and Indy were here.

"No Alessa?"

"She and Maverick are at the hospital still," Stone reasoned softly. "She's in there?"

I nodded. "Probably for the best. Alessa doesn't need to see this."

Indy peered over my shoulder. "Creepy," was all she said.

Tiff frowned. "They collared her to the wall?"

Stone shrugged. "What else were they supposed to do?"

She bit her lip. "I guess."

"If you're too chicken shit, Tiff, back off," Lily rasped, surprising me with the zeal in her voice.

But then, of course, I knew she'd helped erase her dad from the earth here.

I wasn't supposed to know that, but I'd gotten good at blowing Nyx and could usually worm most info out of him if I tried.

He forgot about plausible deniability when I was tonguing his balls.

Of course, he got his own back when he went down on me. I didn't remember my own fucking name when his turbo tongue got to work, never mind shit the club was involved in.

Considering the government couldn't force a wife to testify against their husband, I was really surprised Nyx hadn't hauled me over his shoulder and made me his ball and chain. That the rest of the men hadn't either, to be fair.

Was that their version of commitment?

'Death do us part' wasn't enough of a vow, but 'I love you enough to trust that you won't rat me out to the FBI' was?

Tiff's shoulders hunched. "It's normal to be freaked out by this," she argued.

"Ain't no time for freaking out," I rumbled even though I definitely had a couple minutes ago. "Only time for action. They'll come soon enough."

"She's right," Stone agreed. "They'll want to deal with her too."

"They have bigger fish to fry right now," I stated, "but Nyx'll see I'm not cooking for Quin like I said I would. He'll figure it out soon enough."

"Best get to it then," Indy stated calmly, and she was the first of us to step into the building.

A few seconds later, a light switched on, a bare, naked bulb that made the place even creepier. It looked like it belonged in a horror movie—it'd look even more fitting once I was done.

"Why did you do it?" Indy demanded, as usual not taking any shit or pissing around.

"Fuck you," Tink hissed, turning her face away which made her chains rattle. The sound sent shivers down my spine. "I ain't gonna say shit."

"You're going to whistle like a birdie," I countered instead, hefting the hammer again. "Indy asked you a question. So did I for that matter."

Tink hacked up some saliva and spat it on the floor.

"That ain't an answer," I told her calmly. Casting Indy a look, I saw she was watching me. I nodded at her as I stepped forward, murmuring, "You get one arm, Lily, get the other."

As a unit, we approached her, and she leaped to her feet, hands raised in front of her like this was a boxing match. I swung the hammer, evading the way she tried to grab it, and as Lily and Indy reached for her, I aimed at her left shoulder.

The second the hammer made impact, her howl ricocheted around the Fridge as she crumpled to the floor like a fallen house of cards.

Indy and Lily didn't even have the chance to hold her down, she just sank to the ground for us.

"Make sure she can't hit me," I told Indy as I moved over to the shoulder I'd hit.

She cradled it to her side, but I punched her in the head and snatched her arm. As I straightened it, she screamed, then I directed, "Lily, put your foot on her wrist."

When a daintily shod toe made an appearance in my line of sight, I smirked. 'You're gonna ruin those Louboutins, Lily."

"Worth it," she rumbled, sounding as bloodthirsty as I felt.

Never let it be said that Ms. Society Princess was a pussy.

She went one step further, digging the heel into the soft flesh of Tink's wrist, which had her whimpering, legs kicking out and flaying like a dying octopus but, without asking, Tiff and Stone were there. We kept her pinned down as I got to work.

"I'm gonna bust a knuckle for every time you don't say a word, Tink," I informed her, my tone conversational. "It's gonna hurt, and it's gonna suck, but I want answers."

Even though her face was a mottled combo of bright red and white, tears and snot making her flesh shiny, even though her eyes were wild, and the flesh around the band on her throat was starting to bleed now she'd agitated it, she still hacked up a loogie and spat it at me.

When it landed on my cheek, I wiped it off, and said, "So be it."

The wrist immobilized, I grabbed her little finger and, sticking my tongue between my teeth as I concentrated, I hurled the hammer down against the upper knuckle on her pinkie—just below her nail.

Her howl was almost satisfying it was so agonized. She wriggled, writhed, body twisting and turning as she screamed out her pain.

Dispassionately, I watched it all, uncaring that she was suffering when she'd caused so much of that with her actions.

This was simply an eye for an eye.

Posse-style.

"Did he pay you to help?" Indy intoned, her voice cool.

I cut her a look, surprised by how at ease she was, but I guessed I shouldn't be. Not really. We were all violent. Reared by it, with it soaked into our DNA, this was our way. We weren't modern women, we belonged in another time, another place.

"F-F-F-F-F-F-Fuck you."

"It kind of loses the effect when you stutter," Lily pointed out, tone conversational, not like we were about to torture someone.

Which, of course, was when I'd realized for the gazillionth time I'd found my people.

My lips twitched, and I shrugged. "Have it your way."

I hefted the hammer, noting how she was struggling hard enough to buck the Posse off her, but my aim was true.

Righteous.

I hammered her straight in the central knuckle on her pinkie.

She blacked out.

Tiff blew out a breath. "Who knew torture was a better workout than yoga?"

I snorted, twisting around to face her so I could mutter, "Three times a day will get you fit as fuck."

She shot me a sheepish grin, then stared down at Tink. "What do we do if she won't speak?"

"She will," I told her calmly.

"How do you know?"

"Because she has twenty-eight other knuckles to destroy. Might take a while but we'll get there."

And I'd enjoy every fucking break.

TWENTY-FIVE

AMARA

THE CORD WAS SLIPPING in my hands.

That was when fear hit me.

Fear that I'd let go of the cord, fear that I'd lose the momentum I'd gained in controlling the intruder. Fear that he'd keep on striking Quin with his baton, hurting him, *killing* him.

I regretted, wholeheartedly, leaving the knife Hawk had gifted me behind. But this morning, I'd simply forgotten about it as the prospect of speaking with Rex triggered a mushroom cloud of anxiety inside me. How I wished I'd been braver. How I wished I had that knife in my hand now.

I needed it here.

Needed to eliminate another threat.

My throat felt tight, and I knew I wasn't breathing enough, but I couldn't. Exertion had my heart pounding and my lungs burning, making breathing simply not an option right now.

I just had to get through this.

Hawk would be here soon.

He'd come for me.

I knew that.

I knew it like I knew I was called Amara.

I knew it like the sun surged into the sky in the morning and the moon drifted into being in the night.

"Where are you, Hawk?" I groaned in Ukrainian.

In those moments, where time seemed to be sped up, where it blurred it moved so quickly, I came to some realizations that I would only be able to process later.

I trusted Hawk.

I trusted him to keep me safe.

I trusted him to protect me.

Even more, I trusted him to never hurt me, and to stand by my side.

How he'd managed to make me believe that in such a short time was ludicrous but the belief was so strong that it felt resolute, like it was cemented into my soul, and it was enough to make me feel like I'd overdosed on caffeine. It made my tiring biceps, and my weakening grip cease their faltering, and instead, I tightened up my hold on the bastard who thought he could come in here and—

Later.

I'd think of that later.

Hands reached for the man who I'd thought we could trust because he wore a security guard uniform, and I finally heard Hawk whispering, "It's okay, Amara, you're safe now. He can't hurt you."

He was dead?

I let go of my hold on the cord, the call button the only thing I'd been able to see that I could use in our defense because my knife was back in my nightstand at Rachel's place, and I staggered back, my spine colliding with the wall as I stared at the scene ahead of me.

Only, I blinked and realized the man's chest was still lifting up and down. He was alive, but unconscious.

I'd done that.

Me.

The sense of empowerment was even more beguiling than the wonder of knowing I trusted Hawk.

Though there'd been a strange rivalry among the slaves, with Sarah, I'd known her the longest. While I hadn't trusted her implicitly, there'd been some, enough for me to help her out when she was sick, but she was lost to me now. Gone forever. As was the trust between us.

Yet, Hawk had done as I knew he would—he'd come.

He'd proven I was right to believe in him.

I watched him as he turned the *suka* on his face, and grabbed his wrists, tugging them behind his back.

"Go and get security," Hawk told me softly, his gaze on the man. "The real kind."

For a second, I hesitated, not sure if my legs would keep me up, but they did, and though I staggered a bit at first, I managed to get to the door, bypassing the unconscious man and the one who'd done the impossible—wormed his way into my trust—and made it into the hallway.

I didn't have to look far.

Two guards were running my way, batons in their hands, aggression in their face as they prepared for whatever was up ahead.

I scanned their uniforms, trying to see if they were like the imposter in Quin's room, but I noticed differences—a bleating two way radio attached to their waistband. A jacket with more patches on it, badges too. These men were armed with stocky guns but the intruder had only been armed with a baton.

Not a quick and pleasant death for us—someone wanted our ends to be from a brutal beating.

"Someone tried to kill me!" I told them, and because I knew they wouldn't react well to a woman who didn't seem emotional after an attack like that, and because my lack of visible response might cause us problems in the long run, I burst into crocodile tears.

One of them veered toward me, a hand coming up to my shoulder before he shoved me behind him and entered the room.

"It's okay, officers, I have him contained."

I peered around the door, and whispered again, "He tried to kill me."

One guard dropped to his knees after pulling out a set of handcuffs. He cuffed the man while the other triggered a security alert.

It took me a minute to realize that Hawk had removed his leather vest, the one they called a cut. It made sense that that wouldn't look good with the police, especially knowing what the Sinners did for a living. I had none of the details, but it didn't take a mind reader to figure it out.

I cast a glance at the iPad that had been tossed to the floor in the struggle, and edged my way into the room. While the guards' focus was turned onto Hawk and the attacker, I slipped to my knees and, spying his cut under the bed, I carefully picked up the tablet and held it close to my chest.

A few minutes later, the guard spoke into his radio, and within seconds, Quin's bedside was flooded with staff.

Hawk and I were shuffled out into the waiting room, but over the next couple hours, most of the Sinners' leaders showed up too, as did Rachel.

When the cops came, she dealt with them, and I pretended to speak only broken English, saying enough to give them the answers they needed, but not explaining what had really happened.

It was clear that the Sinners believed whoever had attacked Quin in prison had come for him in the outside world.

But they hadn't.

They'd come for me.

The attacker had dealt with Quin because he was a threat, a *man*, where I was just a *pizda* apparently incapable of defending myself, but his intention had been to deal with me.

The problem that was a bunch of sex slaves on the loose.

As I sat, huddled on a waiting room chair, Hawk at my side, his hand clamped to mine as he dealt with the rowdy chaos of a bunch of outraged bikers, I felt the walls closing in on me in a way that reminded me of being locked in the underground cell of that dump in the woods.

I remembered the scents of Sarah's putrefying flesh.

I remembered Tatána's cries and Alessa's whimpers.

I remembered the way the cold metal cage had fused to my skin, the way my legs had felt endlessly cramped and, in a way that had nothing to do with the cold, had been numb.

So numb.

Dead.

I remembered the agony of when Link, Steel, and Nyx had carried us out into the forest, of the atrophied muscles that had made even standing up painful.

I remembered Giulia trying to clean us up with baby wipes and bottled water, my fragile skin tearing under even the gentlest ministrations.

I remembered Tatána almost killing herself with a piece of cutlery, and I remembered eying the vials that Stone had used to medicate us, wishing I had the strength to pick up a random bottle of pills and swallow them all down.

To take away the misery of what I was enduring.

I remembered clinging to Giulia, thinking myself in love with her because she was kind. She fed us, she cared, and no one had cared in so long. However I realized that what Hawk saw in me was true—I was a survivor.

That was why I hadn't killed myself.

Why I hadn't taken the easy way out or come to rely so early on a man like Alessa had and Tatána had tried to.

I was strong.

Stronger than anyone, even myself knew.

Twice now I'd defended people who were weaker than me.

I wasn't just a cum slut.

A human toilet.

A breathing set of holes for others to fill with whatever their sick minds wanted.

I was powerful.

"We owe you."

The soft words penetrated the dazed fog in my ears, the whirlwind of memories, and I blinked, dazed, and found the entire room focused on me.

Hawk sat on one side, but I realized Nyx had taken a seat to my left. Giulia and the other women had finally shown up, and she was perched on his knee, looking at me with concern etched into her features, Rex was opposite me, and all around, in a loose circle, there were the brothers. The men they called their council.

I stared up at them, and was about to correct them, but Rex murmured, "Amara, once Quin is better, we need you to carry on with your work IDing the men. Can you do that?"

"Of course." I frowned, confused. Why would they think I'd stop?

He sent Hawk a look but he merely said, "I didn't have time to tell her, Rex. Not in the aftermath. How could I?"

Rex pulled a face, then he scratched his beard. The rasping sound was quite pleasant, like one of those ASMR videos Rain played in the kitchen while he was working on his studies at the table.

"What did you need Hawk to tell me?"

"I know you want vengeance, Amara, but—"

I tensed at the word 'but.' No matter if a sentence started out positive, once that word made an appearance, the rest was negative and nothing about Rex's sentence could be that. Not if I wasn't going to lose my chance at finding sanity.

"The first man you identified," Rex continued, "he's a congressman, and he was the running mate in the last presidential election. If he'd won, he'd have been the VP."

"The Vice President," Giulia explained softly.

My throat clamped at that, as recognition hit me that this was why they'd tried to come for me.

This.

They didn't know I had the ability to never forget a face, but when a man had the ambition to seek the White House when they had a past as murky as my old owner, what wouldn't they be capable of?

With their connections, they had to know Alessa and I were free women now, so what wouldn't they do to hide the stains of their past and to clean them up?

My brain whirred once more with a multitude of thoughts, but Rex hadn't stopped talking just yet.

"If you keep on identifying such high-ranking men, Amara, you can't just go and... Well, you know. One is different, five? Ten?"

My jaw tensed. "Hundreds?"

He blew out a breath that whistled from between his teeth. "The men who used you deserve to pay, but we have to do this differently. You can see that, right?"

My teeth ached from how hard I clamped down on my jaw.

The rational part of me did understand.

Of course it made sense.

I couldn't kill every single man who'd used and abused me.

Neither could I target every woman.

I'd been raped by a small army, one that was manned by both sexes.

I was sullied in ways that these people here, looked down upon by regular society, would never be able to comprehend.

My stomach started to churn as my brain wiped away all those empowered thoughts I'd had mere moments ago.

The rational part of my brain wouldn't kick in—something held it back. Maybe that part that had seen the threat and had acted. That had taken a simple piece of hospital room furniture, and had made it into a deadly weapon. That had been able to strangle a grown man with her bare hands and an electric cord.

That part of me definitely wasn't rational.

It was triggered by instinct.

It was no longer on my tongue to tell them that the attacker had come for me.

Rex was in a reasonable frame of mind—I could see that. He felt bad for taking this away from me when he was going to find such use from my ability to recognize any and every face from my past.

This was a negotiation.

Because I'd done them another favor.

In their eyes, I'd saved Quin.

Slowly, I asked, "Quin will live?"

"Head wounds bleed like crazy," Giulia said softly.

I nodded, aware of that. He'd used the baton in his hand to strike Quin so hard that I was sure he'd caved his skull in. That he'd been injured because of me was another knife to the heart.

His smile was so pure, his desire to let me try new things so genuine, and his need to help me recreate the monsters so earnest that the idea of him dying, of that smile dying because of me, made pain splinter my soul.

"You want to bring them down as much if not more than we do, don't you, Amara?" Giulia asked calmly, and a part of me hated them for doing this.

For taking the one person who'd seen me through the early days and using her against me.

Hawk's hand tightened on mine, and just when I felt sure that my belief from before that I could trust him was a lie, he rasped, "She deserves more than just the satisfaction of bringing them down. You routinely go wild, Giulia. Why shouldn't Amara? Doesn't she deserve to get relief from the past as well?" His words, his defense of me, made me want to cry. "I get that she can't do every one of the fuckers," he said carefully, "but you need to make this up to her, Rex."

"I know I do." The Prez raised his hands. "But we're talking about an organization that spans so many facets of society and government that I can't even begin to calculate—" He reached up and rubbed his eyes, and his contrition appeared genuine as did his exhaustion. Enough that the solid block of ice that had taken root in my heart felt like it was thawing some. He sighed, like he had the weight of the world on his shoulders, then rumbled, "Vengeance can be served in different ways." He leaned forward, deeper into my personal space. "I need it too, Amara. My dad's a broken man because of these bastards. They killed my mom. Took down my uncle. My family is torn apart because of them. We need to find a way to bring them down, to take away the threat forever."

"And I need to find a way to sleep at night," I told him woodenly.

He reached up and rubbed the back of his neck, his guilt clear. "I know."

With a part of my brain still stuck in the past, I focused on the faces of those who'd hurt me the most. Some had just fucked me and left, others had whipped me and made me bleed, I'd been a toilet, I'd been cut, I'd been scarred for their amusement, and I'd been caged like a wild animal. Five faces drifted to the forefront.

Five

Three were dead now.

Jeremiah. Donavan Lancaster and his son.

But there were two more.

Two that I hated.

That made the ice inside me melt with the force of that hatred. With the heat of my anger.

"Let me find my peace from two people," I stated calmly.

His jaw worked. "The worst of them?"

"Yes."

Hawk's hand tightened on mine.

"We need to know who they are."

"One is the wife of the congressman."

Rex and Nyx shared a look. "She's a van der Brand, isn't she?" Link muttered down to Lily.

"She is. I know her. The family was friends with Father."

Link sighed. "Your father knew the best of the best, huh?"

"Scum attracts scum."

I cast her a look, saw the guilt in her eyes, even though she'd been hurt too, and I glanced away, intent on eking out this deal for myself.

The trouble was, I'd need protection, so even though I'd decided I'd manipulate them, I couldn't do that.

Not if Hawk was intent on being at my side like he'd said he'd be.

Quin had almost died because of me.

I couldn't let Hawk go through that too.

"The other one is not as powerful as her. You asked for the most powerful first."

"Why did you send the second one over? He's only a cop?" Rex queried. "I'm not taking away from what he did, Amara, I'm just curious."

"He had a lot of power over which girls went where. He knows a lot of people, but even more, he knows a lot of places where there are more women like me." I shrugged. "That is power, is it not?" I knew of other businessmen who came to me wearing expensive suits and platinum cufflinks with emeralds embedded in them, and I'd describe them next. But sometimes gofers had more power than those at the top realized.

I'd seen that man kill girls who he'd transported.

That was power.

"There are others like him?"

"Yes, but he seemed to run this area. Others would take over from him when we moved across the country."

"Like a relay," Rex muttered. "Makes sense, I guess." He sighed. "Who's the other guy? High up like the congressman?"

I shook my head. "Liliana ran the place where we all lived."

"The madam?"

I shrugged. "*Tak*. If that's the title for her job, then yes."

"Those two hurt you the most?"

"The first one hurt me, the second hurt us all. She allowed it." And Sarah had been so weak because of her.

"We need to find this fucking brothel," Nyx muttered under his breath as he cracked his knuckles.

"We sure as shit do," Giulia agreed, her voice like death itself as she stared at me, a cocktail of emotions in her eyes, a strange bewildering mixture that had me glancing away.

I didn't need her pity.

I turned to Hawk, casting him a quick glance as I half expected him to look at me the way she did. But he wasn't.

There was heat in his eyes.

Heat.

For a second, I tensed, then I realized his anger had entwined with something else—pride.

He was proud of me.

My tongue felt thick in my mouth, and when he squeezed my hand again, that was the only way I could break our extended glance.

"I'll let you have those two, Amara," Rex agreed. "But we need you to keep on identifying the faces. We need names."

"I will." I sucked in a breath. "There is something I must tell you, though."

"What is it?"

"The attacker... he didn't come for Quin. He came for me."

TWENTY-SIX

HAWK

INDY, Nyx, and Giulia were in with Quin who'd finally woken up, and while I'd been trying to get Amara to leave the hospital for hours now, she refused until she saw Quin.

I got it—she felt guilty, but it wasn't her fault she knew too much, was it?

I cast a look at her, my heart too full of weird discordant emotions that I didn't know what to do with.

She'd conked out a little while back. Falling asleep sitting up. She hadn't even leaned against me, had just sat there, straight as a fucking ruler, and had fallen asleep.

It would have been weird if it hadn't broken my fucking heart.

She'd relied on herself for so long. Too fucking long. It made me want to fix things, but I wasn't a natural fixer. I didn't know what I was to be honest. I'd never really known what to do with myself.

Bounty hunting had seemed like a great option for someone like me. I was well aware of what I was—street smart. But world smart? No. I could never be a cop because I wasn't a pig, but being a doctor was too much for me, and when I was a kid, though I'd dreamed of being a firefighter, I'd flunked all the entrance requirements.

Bounty hunting let me help like I wanted to, but even that had been too much for me.

I was too much of a Sinner not to see the world exactly as it was—more gray than black and white.

Helping Amara felt right, though. Felt like there was no gray. It was all black and all white. For the first time in my life, I could see a path ahead and there was another person who wasn't North in it.

My twin's abandonment stung less at that moment than it had before. Too much had happened of late, too much that fucked with my belief system.

He'd let go of me, not the other way around, and maybe I was reaching for that tie that had always kept me grounded, but it was too easy to curve my arm around Amara's shoulder, to encourage her to rest against me.

To hold her up, to come to her defense. To protect her while she slept, to stand by her and be proud as she negotiated with a bunch of hardened killers like my brothers.

This was a woman like no other.

I'd seen that today when I found her strangling her attacker.

What woman would do that?

I couldn't even see Giulia's instincts kicking in that way. Amara did more than impress me—she bewildered me. Confused me. Intrigued me.

"Quin's asking for her."

I blinked drunkenly, realizing that I'd been staring straight ahead like a dumbass for only God knew how long because my eyes stung and watered.

Rubbing them, I yawned and muttered at Giulia, "Is he doing okay?"

"Concussion headache, but throw in that with everything else..." She shrugged. "We're lucky we didn't lose him."

"He's staying in longer?"

"Probably a week to ten days depending on how he progresses."

I cast a look at Amara, and knew, somehow, that she wouldn't want to leave.

And though it might be founded in guilt, I wasn't a fool.

I saw how he'd looked at her.

I'd also seen how she looked at him.

I just wasn't sure how I felt about that.

Pinching my bottom lip between my fingers, I just stared at Giulia when she asked, "Is it wise to get close to her, Hawk?"

My brow puckered. "What kind of a question is that?"

She shrugged. "I don't know. I'm just concerned for you, that's all."

"Well, you don't have to be," I retorted.

"I do," she argued. "She's not like the other women you and North fucked around with. She's..."

"Don't even think of saying broken," I rumbled softly, trying not to disturb Amara with our bickering.

"She's stronger than she looks, " Giulia said, "but she deserves more than for you to fuck her over."

Something inside me settled, because I'd been half sure that she was about to say that Amara wasn't good enough for me.

Instead, it was the other way around.

I almost laughed.

I preferred the hit to my character than Amara's, which was when I accepted I was in this way deeper with her than I'd realized.

"I won't screw her around," was all I said.

Giulia just harrumphed. "Can't see you being in the settling down frame of mind, Hawk. Not that she might want that. God, if I'd—" She swallowed. "I'm not sure how she even lets you touch her."

No, I wasn't sure about that either.

Maybe some men would be freaked out about a woman who'd been through what she had, but I didn't see that in her.

I saw something else.

To others, she might be tainted. To me, she was powerful, and it made me want to erase her past. To erase every man who'd hurt her, and to show her how it should be.

How it could be.

I gnawed on the inside of my cheek, and admitted, "She might never want me that way, but that's fine."

"Don't make out like you're self-sacrificing, Hawk—"

I glared at her. "I'm not. But this is different. What she's been through? She deserves to have someone at her back. If that's all I can be, then that's all I can be.

"If all she can take is friendship, then why shouldn't she have that?"

Giulia shot me a disbelieving glance. "You've never had a friend who was a woman before. You weren't interested."

"I'd never been without North before."

Her frown cleared, but she bit her lip. "I guess I should have asked how you were doing without him."

"What's to talk about?" I denied.

"A lot if it's made you grow up enough to be able to have friends who are chicks and not friends with bennies."

I had to snicker. "I ain't a changed man, Giulia. She's fucking beautiful. Of course I want her that way." I sighed. "I just see more than that, that's all."

Her frown was less disbelieving, but she reached forward and pressed her hand to my forehead. "You got a fever or something?"

"Fuck off," I grumbled, leaning away from her touch as I batted her hand away.

She grinned, then retorted, "You gonna wake her up? Nyx or Indy will be in otherwise. What baby bro wants, he gets."

"Jealous?" I countered dryly.

"They're better elder siblings than you and fuckwit were," she agreed. "Think it's to do with how ill he was as a kid though."

"He was ill?" I questioned.

She nodded. "Something with his kidneys. He was going to need a transplant and then—"

"Then, what?"

She pulled a face. "Not sure I believe it, but they do, and neither of them are particularly spiritual."

"What happened?"

"Their grandmother healed him."

"Like Dr. Quinn, Medicine Woman kinda thing?"

Giulia grinned as she took a seat at my side. Her hands curved around the edges, and she muttered, "Quin was semi-raised by their grandmother in Quebec."

"He was?" I blinked, trying to think back to when he'd been born. I'd been around but I hadn't been interested in my own kid sister never mind someone else's kid brother.

"Yeah. After Kevin, you know?" At my nod, she continued, "The family broke down, but Quin was sick so I think he got shepherded up there because his grandmother could care for him there. Anyway, she pulled some shaman shit on him—"

I laughed as I interrupted, "Is that what they call it?"

Her nose crinkled. "I don't know, Hawk, maybe it is? Spooky ass shit to me. Modern medicine don't heal the kid, but some fucking herbs do?" She shrugged again. "He came back down to West Orange when she died. But Nyx and Indy always felt bad."

"Why? Not their fault he was sick."

"Think they tried to make up for being distant, you know?"

"Then he comes back and gets his ass landed in jail—"

"Which Nyx didn't respond very well to. He's barely visited him, so I guess he's in guilt trip mode."

"Why you telling me this?"

She smirked. "You're family with these fuckers whether you like it or not. Plus, as far as I know, you're still *my* brother. Even if you are fucking useless at it."

The words actually stung, even though I didn't think she'd intended for that to be my reaction.

What could I say though?

I *was* fucking useless as a brother.

I'd only ever 'seen' North, never Giulia. She'd been the pain in the ass, the thing that always cried and shit herself. Always too mouthy, too annoying. Hating on Dad, hating on Mom.

Frowning down at my feet as I accepted that neither of our parents had deserved gold medals, I muttered, "I'm gonna try to be a better brother, Giulia."

"Why? I'm a shit sister."

My lips twitched at her candor. "Maybe you can try to be a better sibling as well? Even with partners, we're the only family we really have left."

"Habits of a lifetime are hard to break."

Despite myself, and despite the fact I meant every word, I couldn't stop myself from chuckling. "True. You've always been a pain in the ass, so why stop now, huh?"

"Got me where I am, that's for sure." She stretched her arms out, hands tucked under to pull on the muscles in her forearms, and it was quite by chance that I saw the grazes on her knuckles.

I snapped out my fingers to snag hers, and asked, "What have you been doing?"

"Rats need to be dealt with."

"Against council orders? Jesus, Giulia. Rex will only cut you so much slack."

She shot me a smug smile, which had me rolling my eyes.

"You'll piss off Nyx one day too. You hand him his balls one too many times and you'll lose him," I warned.

"Why? Because I love the men who make up his sanctuary as much as he does? My loyalty to this MC is tied to him. The club is his sanity. It was his only solace.

"I fucking hated the Sinners. All my life, I grew up loathing them. The second I got here, you know I was intending on leaving. Getting out, going to NYC. But he changed that.

"Instead of moaning about it, instead of trying to get him to leave, I'm embracing his family. If I squeeze a little too hard, then how can he complain?"

"You don't know how men work, do you?" I shook my head at her. "He'll start getting shit about being pussywhipped."

"You think he's pussywhipped and I can't get him to do the fucking dishes or his laundry." She huffed out a sigh. "Okaaaay."

"I'm being serious, Giulia."

"I know." Her lips twitched. "If you think my man's whipped, then you're insane. We're on the same wavelength, that's all. I don't know why it's hard for people to recognize that we have similar opinions on the same shit. I don't have a right to think it because I've got a pussy? Well, that's BS."

I cast her a wary glance when I saw the same expression on her face that I'd been seeing since she was a kid trying to have a crap in the potty—determination.

"What's that look for?" I queried warily.

"I want a cut."

My eyes flared wide as I snorted. "That's never gonna happen."

She just hitched a shoulder. "I'm gonna try. I'm not the only bitch who deserves one. We've bled for this MC too. Why should you get one just because you've got a dick?"

"You want to go on runs, is that it? You want to get your ass landed in jail?"

"I want the right to have a say in how my life is managed. We obey the council but why? Sometimes, they're fucking wrong. They make no sense some shit they do. Just because you have cocks doesn't mean your brains are wired better.

"Lily taking on some of Mav's work is insane when it's just until he's better. She should manage the club finances full-time. She's got more fucking diplomas than the shop that prints 'em, but you're okay with her being on the side?

"Why wouldn't you want her to be integral to the running of the place? You think she might be untrustworthy? Then tie her into the club. Make her trustworthy.

"Why can't I be an Enforcer? These past couple weeks have proven that you got a problem with cunts. Women make up half the world, so why wouldn't you want someone close at hand to deal with that shit? Instead you want to just shove me in the kitchen?" She scowled. "This ain't the sixties, Hawk. I ain't gonna take the crap Mom did just because I love Nyx.

"Maybe we can't do the same shit as the brothers, but that don't mean we don't have a place. We're more than just Old Ladies."

"You're talking about changing shit that's integral to the club."

She tipped up her chin. "Don't care. Shit needs shaking up."

"You're destined for disappointment."

"Maybe, but I have to try, don't I?"

I blew out a breath, because though I'd warned her, she wouldn't take it well when Rex said no.

Rather than argue with her some more, aware that this was a dead end conversation in more ways than one, I turned to Amara and gently squeezed her shoulders.

"Amara?" That was it. All it took to wake her up. For a second, I wasn't sure if she'd been pretending about being asleep, but then I saw the dazedness in her eyes as she scanned her environment.

"You're safe," I assured her. It took all I had not to kiss her temple, to reassure her physically that she was out of danger. "I'll always keep you safe."

"Nyx ain't the only one looking pussywhipped," Giulia whispered in my ear as she got to her feet. "Quin wants to see you, Amara."

She jerked upright. "He's awake?"

"Yep, bit dopey. Keeps talking about sky girls and fucking buzzards. Maybe that cunt knocked some brain cells out while he was clobbering him on the head."

Amara blinked at her, then yawned. "I want to see him."

"Will you go home then?"

She shook her head at Giulia. "No. We have things to do."

"He ain't ready to draw tonight," Giulia cautioned. "I ain't got a clue what a *monetoo* is but he keeps whispering about it. Nyx only wants you in there because he thinks you'll calm him down."

She straightened up with an elegance that spoke of her years of dance training, then turned to me, her hand outstretched.

I stared at it in surprise, thinking she'd leave me behind, but she didn't. If anything she frowned at me, and flexed her fingers in a silent prompt as if saying, 'Well, come on. I don't have all day.'

My lips curved into a smile as I slipped my fingers against hers, entangling them, then ignoring Giulia's pointed stare, we walked out of the waiting room and toward Quin's ward.

It looked much like it had earlier—nothing out of place, just Quin had a couple more bandages on him.

He did look dopey, his eyelids flickering as if he was hammered but the second he saw Amara, he calmed down. The tension in his frame, the way his muscles bulged, how he was sitting straight up, ready to leap off the bed even though he'd probably fall flat on his face if he did, all of it lessened.

He sagged back into the pillows, slumping as he smiled at her.

"My savior."

I cast her a look, saw her blushing cheeks, and not for the first time today, wondered what the fuck was going on here.

She wanted me with her, at her side, but she looked at him like he...

I wasn't unaccustomed to sharing.

A part of me had always felt sure that I'd end up in a triad with North because we were so close that women always tried to get between us—and hadn't that happened this time and he'd fucking betrayed me, the cunt?—but I'd never have foreseen needing that without him.

Of course, this was me leaping way ahead into the future.

As much as I wanted more from her, I was well aware that I might never get that with Amara. She might only ever be able to accept me as a friend, and as much as that sucked, with her past, I wasn't sure if I could go all possessive on her ass when that was the last thing she needed.

Like the little bird I called her, she needed to soar high, fly free.

I couldn't tether her to me even if that was what I wanted.

Did that mean I'd let her go to Quin?

Christ, was I that selfless?

Gifting her with an orgasm was one thing, but that was something else entirely.

I'd always been good at sharing because of North, but Amara wasn't a toy, a bike, a club snatch.

She was different.

In more ways than I had words to describe.

"I am hardly your savior," Amara rasped gently after she tugged me toward the bed.

Indy was in the armchair Amara had been using earlier so she couldn't take a seat, and I noticed she fidgeted, unsure of what to do or where to stand when I sensed that all she wanted was how it had been earlier.

The three of us in here.

Maybe not raking up her past, but the gentle camaraderie of us eating a sandwich together, of us getting her to try a slushie and Checkers' fries.

Normality.

That was hours ago, but it felt like weeks.

Everything about club life felt as if time was turbocharged.

Years had passed so goddamn slowly when I was in Salt Lake City. But here, I'd barely been back any time at all and it felt as if a decade had spun by.

This was probably what people meant when they talked about hard living.

Living fast and dying young too.

Well, I didn't intend on dying young, but the other shit I was fine with.

Especially if...

Shit, I didn't have a right to think those thoughts.

Not yet.

Maybe not ever.

I squeezed her hand, needing her to accept and embrace that I was here, that I wasn't going anywhere, but mostly, it was for myself.

She'd chosen to tether herself to me in this moment.

Of her own volition, her own free will.

This might be the only time she ever chose to do that.

"—should have seen her," Quin slurred, breaking into my tangled web of thoughts. "The guy comes in and I'm so deep into the drawing that I don't even fucking notice—" He spoke so slowly it was like he was a YouTube video buffering. "He smashed me in the head and, out of nowhere, like fucking Batwoman, she's there. Gets the call button cord, whips it around his head and tugs on it like it's a lasso. Never seen nothing like it," he repeated, his grin dopey but pleased. "My sky girl's got claws."

Indy arched a brow at Nyx, who just shrugged. "The cops will be by tomorrow, Quin, so you might want to watch how detailed your statement is."

He blinked and slurred, "Detailed?"

Shaking her head, Amara reached out and placed her hand on Quin's. "Go to sleep. You need the rest."

Quin's fingers tightened about hers, much as mine did, and he muttered, "Don't go."

"That's not fair to her," Nyx intoned softly. "She needs the rest too, Quin."

His baby bro scowled, then squinted at Nyx. "You can't tell me what to do."

The VP snorted. "I can when you're too punch drunk to keep your eyes open for long."

"Amara's mine," Quin groused. "*Aashaa monetoo* told me."

Nyx heaved a sigh. "I'm sure Amara would like a say in things."

"Why would she?" Quin rumbled, sounding like he'd been drinking three bottles of vodka back to back. "*Aashaa* said it, so that makes it so."

"Amara, do you mind sleeping here?" Indy asked.

"She can sleep in bed with me," Quin said with a pleased grin.

"Cots in prison are smaller than this. This is like a California queen by comparison."

Indy snickered. "Again, you might want that but Amara needs some rest too. She ain't like you, Quin, remember?"

Amara chimed in, "Quin, I won't leave, but I'll sleep in an armchair."

The other guy's bottom lip popped out in a pout. "No fair."

Amara's mouth curved into the tiniest of smiles, which lit up her eyes in a way that made my heart skip a beat.

"You need all the room to yourself. What if I hurt you?"

"You can't hurt me. You're my sky girl," he repeated stubbornly, but as he muttered that final endearment, it was punctuated with a round of snores.

Amara cast Nyx and Indy a look. "What's a sky girl? It isn't the first time he called me that."

Nyx reached up and rubbed the back of his neck. The fatigue lining his face looked like it was there to stay—and this was before he had a shitting, pissing, screaming mini-Giulia on his hands.

God help him.

As a baby, Giulia had more than shown her true colors for what lay ahead as an adult. Restful she was not.

"It's something he talked about when our grandmother died."

Amara frowned. "It's a bad thing?"

Indy pulled a face. "Not necessarily bad, neither is it good." Cruz slipped into the room behind me, and as he approached his woman, she smiled at him tiredly, then curved her hand about his as he pressed it to her shoulder when he stood at her back, behind the armchair. "It's not a bad thing or a good thing," she repeated doggedly, "It's just a... well, I'd say a Quin thing, but it's more of an Algonquin thing."

"Your tribe?" I asked softly.

She snorted. "I ain't got a tribe."

Nyx grinned sheepishly. "Me either. We don't exactly live on a rez, Hawk."

I frowned. "Don't mean you ain't got the heritage."

"We don't live by it, and we weren't raised to either." Indy cleared her throat. "We call her grandmother, but Quin calls her *nòkomis*. She took him in when he got real sick, to the point where we thought he was going to die, and after Carly, well, shit wasn't good. He needed the stability that Mom and Dad weren't capable of bringing to the table."

Something about her tone had me wondering, "Your grandmother petitioned the courts for him?"

Nyx dipped his chin. "She did. She was right to. He needed the stability, plus whenever she was around and came to visit, he always seemed to get better, only getting worse when she left.

"She moved him into her home on the reservation up in Quebec. He was there for a good chunk of time."

"What does this have to do with him calling me sky girl?"

Indy shrugged. "He went on a vision quest."

"I've heard about those. It's where teen boys get high on weird plants, right? Then have to survive in the woods?" Giulia peppered, making Nyx grin as he hauled her into his side and kissed her on the temple.

"Something like that," he said with a chuckle.

"Wish I could have gone on a vision quest if it was like that," Cruz joked softly.

"Quin wasn't into the whole spiritual side of things, but he was very much into pleasing his *nòkomis*. She healed him when modern medicine couldn't," Indy added.

"How?"

"I don't know. She just did. Fed him plants and herbs and shit. To this day, he drinks her special tea. I got it sent to him inside, had to get Rachel to petition for him to have access to it.

"Anyway, however she did it, Grandmother was close to the tribe's shaman, and they worked to heal him. He's a walking fucking miracle to be honest. So when she asked him to do something, he tended to do it."

Nyx bowed his head. "His vision quest ended when Grandmother died. He got called back when she was found dead."

Amara's brow crumpled. "That's so sad."

"It was. For us all, but mostly for Quin. They were really close, and the vision quest was only important to her. He was only out there for her," Indy murmured, sighing sadly as she cast her brother a look.

"When we went across the border for the funeral," Nyx murmured, "Quin rattled on about his sky girl, and how *Nòkomis* would want him to find her."

"We just thought it was the Wysoccan," Indy said wryly.

"What's that?"

"A drug they give the guys before the quest starts." Nyx rubbed his nose. "To be honest, I thought it was the drug too. He was still coming down off that high. The shaman said he'd had an allergic reaction to it or something. But that was the last time he mentioned a sky girl. Hell, it's the last time he mentioned *Aashaa*." He cast Amara a glance. "Until you." His gaze drifted down to our joined hands, but it didn't make me drop my hold on her, if anything, it made me tighten my grip.

She squeezed back, then said, "I understand if you don't want to leave him because you think I'm dangerous for him, but I'd like to sleep here tonight."

Before they could answer or maybe argue, Giulia tugged on Nyx's arm. "You need to get some rest, babe. You're dead on your feet. I don't even think we should ride back to West Orange. We should crash in a local hotel or something."

Nyx scowled at that, but when Giulia scowled back, even harder, he scrubbed a hand over his chin. "It would be a lot easier if you were frightened of me."

She smirked. "We bypassed the fear a long time ago, Nyxypoo."

He grumbled under his breath. "Fucking Nyxypoo."

She grinned, then said, "Come on, I'm dead on my feet too. I think if you got me on the back of the bike I'd fall off."

Nyx straightened at that. "Why didn't you say something?"

"I just did," she said mildly, but when Nyx started grabbing his shit together, she turned to me and winked.

I shook my head at her version of managing her man, then turned to Amara and queried, "You okay if I stay here with you?"

She frowned. "Of course. Why wouldn't you be here?"

A cough sounded from across the bed, and I saw Indy was hiding a laugh. To be honest, I was just as amused, even if her surety came as a surprise.

Was this it then?

Was I a part of her inner circle?

Along with Quin, evidently.

As I eyed the kid who'd been sick as a baby, and who, before he'd even been able to be a man, had been locked up on a charge he was innocent of, and then, the second he was free, had almost died, I couldn't find it in myself to be mad if she did want to be close to him.

If anyone deserved a friend, it was Quin.

Indy clambered to her feet when Cruz murmured, "Think it's time you got some rest too, princess."

She hummed when he curved an arm around her shoulders, snatching her purse from the nightstand as she raised Quin's hand and pressed a kiss to his knuckles. "Sleep well, baby bro." She shot us both a look. "You'll contact us if anything happens?"

"It won't but of course I will," I confirmed, and with Nyx grunting at my sister as he shuffled her ass through the door, Cruz and Indy leaving us behind too, we were left alone with a sleeping, semi-concussed man.

"They'll probably be in every hour or so to wake him up," I informed her calmly.

"Why? He needs the rest."

"He's concussed," I explained. "They need to make sure he does wake up."

She blinked, then muttered, "I'll check myself."

I tipped my chin to the side at that, then asked the question that was burning on the tip of my tongue. "What's happening here, Amara?"

She didn't play coy, much as I'd expected her to. She just angled her chin, jutting it out with an obstinacy that was impressive considering the day we'd had and how exhausted we both were, before she said, "I trust you."

Though the words filled me with glee, I just asked, "And? What does that mean for you?"

"I don't know. I haven't trusted someone for a long time." She frowned. "Do you mind that I trust you?"

"I'm glad you do," I countered. "I just—"

"You want to have sex with me."

My lips twitched. "I'd like to at some point, but no, not right now. I also accept that that might never happen." I shrugged when she shot me a disbelieving glance. "Accepting and being happy about something are two separate things."

"I would like more orgasms," she said bluntly.

"Attached to me, or just orgasms in general?" Though my tone was level, I couldn't deny that a burst of irritation welled inside me at the idea of her getting that from someone else.

Jesus.

I didn't do possessiveness, so why was she proving that I totally did?

"I just told you I trust you, Hawk. Why would I want them from anyone else?" She frowned again, then turned to me. "I heard the last parts of your conversation with Giulia."

"You were faking sleep?"

"No, I was just... I don't know. Neither asleep nor awake." She sighed. "I wish I was normal for you but I won't ever be that."

"I don't need you to be normal, I just need you to be you."

She reached up and pressed her hand to my cheek. Her fingers traced across the grooves at the side of my lips before she said, "You make me feel safe. You make me feel like a desirable woman. Who knows what else you will make me feel—with time."

And that, I knew, was as much as I could ask for.

In a handful of days, she'd gone from being closed off, always looking like she was preparing to run away, a mouse scurrying around the edges of the walls to evade notice, to this: a predator. No longer the prey.

She was right—a lot *had* changed in such a short space of time.

Who knew what would happen in a week or a month?

I, for one, was looking forward to watching her spread her wings...

TWENTY-SEVEN

LODESTAR

TWO DAYS LATER

LODESTAR: *I got news for you.*
 aCooooig: *Good news?*
 Lodestar: *The best. Turn on Channel 5.*
 aCooooig: *The mayor? I heard. Someone sneaked into his office, right? It's an active shooting still.*
 Lodestar: *Stay tuned. I promise, it'll be fun.*

THOUGH HE CARRIED ON TYPING, I didn't engage, just turned my focus onto the big screen in Lily's kitchen.

All around me, there were brothers and councilors, their women and even Kat, squealing as she did some cartwheels in the outer hall, and though the noise was chaotic, it was also good.

I was glad this was happening here.

Glad we would see the first card tumble down...

"You sure Coullson was a Sparrow?" Rex demanded at my side. "Quin's not ready to start drawing yet so I don't know how you—"

I raised a hand. "aCooooig told me the other night. I wanted to check the facts before I came to you yesterday."

He pursed his lips as he cast a glance at the live footage on the TV. "You think this is going to work?"

"I set it up like Jason Young was behind the hit. Lacey thinks he's killing Coullson on Sparrow orders. It should have been an in and out job. But here he is, locked in the Mayor's office," I said wryly, "with helicopters flying overhead, and armed police surrounding the building. In his position, do you reckon he thinks he'll make it out alive?"

Rex hissed out a breath. "It's a risk."

"Most shit is in life."

"Not all lone wolf shooters are shot in the field. Most of them stand trial."

"Most of them aren't stooges. He's gonna be bitter. He'll think the Sparrows set him up to fail. Let's face it, that's what he helped them do to others. Why wouldn't he think they've turned on him too?" I grinned at him, eagerness filling me. "Anyway, you think Cin isn't there to shepherd him to St. Peter's gates if things go wrong?" I winked. "I told her to aim for the gut. Nice and big caliber. Let him have a slow, painful death. Thought that would please Amara and Quin."

Rex grunted, but leaned forward, resting his elbows on his knees as he stared over at the screen. "What the fuck is taking so long?"

"Why are you so nervous?"

"Because this has to work." He grabbed his chin and jerked his neck to the side.

"I can break it clean off if you want," I offered. "Take all your problems away."

He cut me a look, but his lips twitched. "You'd be so kind, huh?"

"Oh yeah, that's me. Kindness itself." I crinkled my nose. "Trust me. I wouldn't have set this in motion if I didn't think it would work."

Though he heaved another sigh, I turned the screen on, and feeling a little like NASA when they sent a rocket through the exosphere, nerves and excitement bubbled inside me.

This was it.

Rex wasn't wrong.

The catalyst.

I sat up straighter in the wheelchair, wondering how the hell Maverick had hidden in one of these things for so long when they hurt your ass like no one's business, and when the reporter started frowning instead of regurgitating the same-old same-old news, I shouted, "Everyone shut the fuck up. The game's about to start."

Nyx snatched the remote from the side and turned it on full blast.

As he did, everyone settled down and turned to watch the beginning of the end for the Sparrows.

"News just in. Craig Lacey, the detective who is currently sequestered inside the Mayor's office with the, we assume, deceased Mayor Coullson, has sent out a video message to his wife, Dana Lacey.

"'This video message has been passed on to over two dozen news' agencies. This footage may contain scenes that are disturbing to some."

The reporter disappeared, City Hall behind her did too, and instead, a man showed up on the screen, squatting in a corner, his back to the wall.

Aside from his location, Craig Lacey looked like a regular kind of 9-5 guy. Wearing an Oxford shirt and a sports coat, he even had a tie slung around his neck. His chin was cleanly shaved, and in his eyes, he was calm, even though I could see his pulse beating just above his ironed shirt collar.

He was dressed for a regular Monday... unluckily for him, nothing about this Monday was regular.

My lips curved into a smile as he said, "My name is Detective Craig Lacey of the 42nd Precinct. Yesterday evening, I received a call on my burner cell from Congressman Jason Young." He grabbed something from the table, turned it around to display the Caller ID log, which showed that a Jason Young had indeed phoned him. "At nine-twenty-four, he made the request that I dispose of Mayor

Coullson as he had broken ranks and was in talks with someone who was working against the organization.

"When I speak of an organization, I'm talking about the New World Sparrows, a body of people for whom I have worked since my first year at the NYPD Police Academy.

"Congressman Jason Young is also a member of this group, and I have been in contact with him for some years."

He switched onto an app, and there was a soft hushed voice, faintly masculine but androgynous that whispered, "Coullson can no longer be trusted. Those on high say he needs to be silenced. The usual payment will be made once the job is done."

Lacey's mouth tightened as Young spoke. I'd anticipated he'd record the conversation to protect himself but was even more impressed at my skills when Young's voice sounded as authentic as it did.

It had taken me hours to whip that together, but it had been worth every moment of stress now it was done, and now I was listening to it on the news.

When the recording was complete, he said, "This morning, I realized this was a trap. I was never meant to make it out of this room alive. If they think they can take me down for knowing too much, then they can think again.

"The Sparrows are everywhere—"

There was the sound of a faint explosion, as if a glass door or a window had been smashed, and he jerked like he'd been hit. But his head twisted to the side as he looked for the source of the bullet's entry, then he snarled, "Those bastards—" He gave his phone a quick glance, then his hand moved to the screen and the video cut off.

When the scene reverted to the newsroom where a panel of people were sitting, it was clear they were stunned at what they'd witnessed.

"We've had confirmation that Craig Lacey was shot dead at the scene of this extraordinary crime," one of the anchors stated, but that was all I heard as a wave of cheers roared around the kitchen, and I cut Rex a glance, and saw his face was blanched, his relief clear.

"You pretended to be Young to get him there?" Sin asked, swooping into my side so he could hear me over the noise.

"I made some software that scanned the internet for all the video recordings he'd been in over the years. I input the words I wanted him to say, and it pieced them together."

When he raised his fist to me, I shoved my knuckles into his and beamed at him.

"Round one to us," I declared.

Scum shouldn't walk the earth.

Lacey knew a lot that I could have gotten out of him through advanced interrogation techniques but, truthfully, when I'd hacked into his computer and phone, I'd gotten everything I needed.

Well, I would once I broke his code. And I wasn't talking Malbolge here.

Once my program figured out the key, I knew I'd be dealing with data that was more precious than the man himself. He had terabytes of the stuff, and I couldn't wait to dive in.

"Was that Cin who shot him?"

"Probably." I shrugged at Rex's question. "It doesn't matter, does it?"

He wriggled his shoulders. "I don't know. It would have been good if he'd spilled more about the Sparrows."

"People will already start tossing around the words 'conspiracy theory,' Rex," I pointed out. "At least this way, I've got access to all Lacey's files. I just need time to process what I found on his hard drive and cloud. Plus Young is going to be hauled in for conspiracy to commit murder."

"But he didn't do it," Sin remarked.

"The evidence says otherwise. I used his number, and speech recognition will prove that it's him doing the talking—the software I built is good enough to withstand testing.

"Even if it doesn't work, even if Young gets out of the arrest, he'll lose his career, and that means Amara can have her revenge." I shrugged. "Win-win situation because now, everyone will be talking about the Sparrows and that's exactly what they don't want."

Lacey, Coullson, and Young were collateral damage today.

The biggest hit scored was against the Sparrows.

It might only be a tiny dent in their armor, but that was more than we'd achieved since we'd taken down their mob front.

"She has a point," Sin commented, his eyes on the screen.

"She has a name," I replied, before I ignored them all and sent Conor O'Donnelly a message.

Lodestar: *It's not the priest, but you're welcome.*

aCooooig: *You're behind that?*

Lodestar: *What do you think?*

aCooooig: *I kinda want to be mad at you because we could have milked him for a while, but... I'm not my brothers. Thank you. <3*

Lodestar: *A heart? You going to send me some flowers next?*

aCooooig: *If that's what the lady wants, then that's what the lady shall get.*

I grinned to myself, and didn't even *gently* remind him that I'd done him a favor.

This came with no ties.

The Mayor thought he could dick around with Conor O'Donnelly's sensibilities?

He'd just had his ass handed to him as a result.

No one, and I meant, *no one* hurt my friends without regretting it at the moment of their death.

The Irish had turned Coullson in an attempt to begin identifying Sparrows with a view to taking them out, and all he'd given them was a name—that of a priest who'd abused Conor O'Donnelly as a boy.

Coullson had no way of knowing I'd take it as a personal affront, but it was to his detriment that he'd shoved Conor's abuser in his face.

The Mayor of NYC hadn't needed to die today.

But he'd made an enemy.

And in my case, I didn't believe in keeping my enemies close. I liked them firmly where they belonged—in a casket.

TWENTY-EIGHT

QUIN

SIX YEARS EARLIER

I WAS DELIRIOUS.

Exhausted.

Starving.

But I knew Nòkomis, *my grandmother, would send me back out onto the prairie until* Aashaa monetoo *spoke with me.*

Normally, boys my age would be taken into the woods, isolated and fed Wysoccan, a drug that was more powerful than LSD. They had to survive the harsh environment, all while dealing with amnesia, a racing heartbeat and hypothermia, all to prove that they were strong enough to become men. Men worthy of being a part of the tribe.

This vision quest BS sucked monkey balls.

I hadn't eaten in a week. I was freezing. I kept on seeing shit that I knew wasn't there, and I was pretty certain that I was going to die before Aashaa monetoo *decided I was worthy of chatting to.*

Mostly, I was angry about being out here period.

She hadn't made Nyx go through this shit, but here I was, my balls turning into ice cubes because she said, and I could quote, "You need to be cleansed, Winnange."

Winnange was the name she'd chosen for me when I was born, one of my secret names, and it was the only one she'd call me by. I hated it, because I knew what it meant.

Buzzard.

Not a majestic eagle for me or a grand owl or anything like that, a fucking turkey vulture.

That *was* the name she'd given me.

A name that was derived from the word 'win' which meant filth.

If I needed cleansing, it was because she'd picked a shitty ass name for me.

My eyelashes fluttered when a gust of wind made my mìkiwàms shudder, and the temperature seemed to drop a couple more degrees.

Nyx hadn't had to freeze his ass off, but then, Grandmother said it was too late for him. The Aashaa monetoo, her version of God, had already given him his path, and had set him on it.

I wasn't sure why Nyx had been blessed and I hadn't, especially when she was insistent that her Devil, the Otesho monetoo, had whispered in my ear as a kid.

Everyone knew Nyx was a pedo murderer, whereas I found it hard to kill fucking mosquitos. But here I was, the one in need of cleansing, while my brother went around the country slaying pedophiles like he was in an MC version of Grand Theft Auto.

I sucked in a sharp breath as I huddled deeper under the thin hide blanket she'd given me, but another gust of wind had my shitty wigwam collapsing all around me.

The thin birch branches splatted me in the face, the crappy structure I'd built providing me with more covering now it was down than when it had been erect.

As I peered up into the bleak winter sky, wondering if I had the energy to try to reconstruct it, I blinked when I saw a bird soaring overhead.

Maybe it was because I was weak, or maybe I was just so fucking hungry that I was seeing shit, but another bird appeared too, seemingly out of nowhere, blinking into being as if I'd made it come, moving around the first bird like it was dancing.

Squinting, I shielded my eyes with my hand, trying to get a better look, but I knew a lot about wildlife thanks to Nòkomis. She'd taught me many things over the years, from how to find and brew the mayflower infusion I should drink at least once a week to keep my illness at bay, to how to recognize the different animals on her land so I didn't get my ass killed.

Buzzards and hawks weren't exactly buddies, but I knew what I was seeing.

The hawk was stoic, soaring along the air currents like he was king bitch of the sky. The buzzard was... playful?

This was weird.

Really fucking weird.

"Your sky girl will come," a voice whispered in my ear, the accent strange enough to have me twisting around in the pile of birch branches to see if someone was sneaking up behind me as a joke. "She will need you, Winnange, as well as her Sakwatamo. You will ground her, keep her from soaring to the sky before her time. She is your purpose. Your reason for surviving, for being a man. What you go through, you will endure for her."

"Is this some kind of prank?" I grumbled, rubbing my ear as I heard scampering behind me. Pretty sure it was Paul or that asshole Hank messing with me, I twisted around to see if I could make anything out, but my eyes flared wide when, instead, I came face to face with two goddamn birds.

I quickly looked up and saw the sky was empty, so I twisted back to look at the hawk and the buzzard who were peering at me like they knew shit I didn't. No way they could have landed without me knowing—

What the hell was happening here?

Wide-eyed, I rasped, "She didn't just dose me with Wysoccan, she overdosed me." I mean... There were hallucinations then there was this.

A soft laugh seemed to echo in the wind. "You have your purpose, Winnange. She is your reason for being. Your sky girl. Otesho monetoo *will whisper in her ear, tempt her into the path of the windigo, but you will save her broken soul, and she will save yours, and if you fall, your hawk will save you both."*

The birds' wings flapped to punctuate the spirit's voice and I let out a girly scream as they flew at me. Pretty sure they were going to rip out my eyes, I shielded my face, but I felt no claws tearing at my flesh, so quickly lowered my arms and peered around me.

They weren't there.

As quickly as they'd come, they'd gone.

"My sky girl," I whispered under my breath, coughing when the wind sent dust flying into my face.

Because this was like the start of a paranormal romance book—the shit that Indy said she didn't read but totally did, because I'd seen her binge-reading Twilight before the movies came out—I was half certain Hank really was messing with me. But would he come up with something like this?

A woman who needed a buzzard and a hawk to save her?

Then I remembered that old story Nòkomis had told me. Something to do with porcupines and hawks, buzzards and turnips.

God, I needed to eat because none of this was making sense. And ratty turnips were starting to sound like gourmet grub.

"Caleb!" I heard the call, half-wondered if it was the Great Spirit again, but it wasn't.

It was Paul. I should have known. We had a pact that we called each other by our English names.

I jerked to my feet when he came running toward me, moving so fast he was windmilling his arms for balance. My head spun, white dots pinging into being around the edges of my vision as my empty stomach made itself known to me.

"What is it?" I called out weakly, staggering as I took a few steps toward him.

"It's your grandmother. The midew says she's dying. Come quickly! She's in the medicine lodge."

Any thoughts of hunger disappeared like I'd eaten a seventy-two ounce tomahawk steak.

The quest I'd been set retreated to the back of my memory banks in the face of losing the one stable link I had in my life—the grandmother who'd been with me through the trauma of dialysis, who'd guided the family when my parents had broken down, who'd taken me in when I'd done stupid shit, who'd brought me back to life, who'd shown me another way.

If she died, I'd be untethered.

Lost.

When I made it to the medicine lodge, she'd already passed over, Aashaa monetoo had taken her even as she'd sent me a vision.

That was the last time I stepped foot in Quebec.

The last time I thought about Aashaa monetoo.

The last time I answered to Winnange, and the last time I thought about the sky girl who needed grounding.

But of course, everything happened for a reason, and only the monetoos knew what that reason was.

TWENTY-NINE

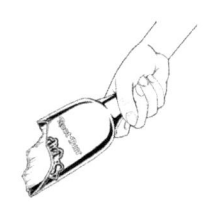

AMARA

PRESENT DAY

IT TOOK five days for Quin to wake up properly, to stop looking at me through beer-goggles as Nyx called it. Whenever he *was* conscious, he'd shoot me a dopey smile and call me his 'Sky Girl' again.

He did this for so long that I was concerned for his mental capacities—or lack of them. Had the Sparrow-sent guard really hurt him? Caused brain damage?

Hawk kept saying that he was fine, that Quin was just needing so much rest after what had happened to him with the stabbing and all the blood loss, but to be so out of it for five days or more seemed ludicrous to me.

When he finally started being normal again, on the following Friday after one of my tormentors had been killed by a bullet to the gut, he woke up, blinked at me sleepily, and murmured, "Hey, sky girl."

I wasn't sure if it was guilt or need that had me glued to his bedside all this time. I hadn't returned to Rachel's place once. Instead, there was a hotel around the corner that the Sinners were camping out in and which we used.

We were with Quin around twenty-three hours a day. Hawk would get cleaned up first while I sat with Quin, then the only time he was without us was when Hawk would return and walk me to our room so I could get showered and changed there. All the while, there were guards outside Quin's door, and they were on a rolling schedule too.

He was a lot safer now the Sinners knew one man wasn't enough to protect me and Quin.

Still, this particular morning, it felt different. He seemed different. Not as dopey or sleepy. His eyes were clearer, his voice less rumble and more murmur.

I shot him a smile, hoping that I wasn't jumping to conclusions, and teased, "It's about time you woke up, sleepyhead."

He blinked at me, then muttered, "Huh?"

For a second, my hopes sank because I thought he was just the same, hadn't gotten better like I'd thought, but then I realized, like a fool, I'd spoken to him in Ukrainian.

"Sorry," I rumbled, rubbing a hand over my face. "I'm very tired."

He blinked again then whispered hoarsely, "You need to get some rest."

I yawned. "I do."

I made no move to leave though, and that had nothing to do with the fact that I was the only one in the room and that Hawk had gone for a shower.

Putting down the romance novel Quin had bought me and which Indy had brought over during her last visit, I got to my feet and handed him a full glass of water.

Watching as he downed that then another, and munched through the Jell-O cup like it was a beautiful dessert, I told him, "Me and Hawk haven't left you since the attack. Well, only to shower."

Quin tipped his head to the side. "Why?"

I didn't have an answer, not a logical or a rational one at least. It was easier to be trite, to simply tease, "Because I'm your sky girl?"

However he didn't take it as a joke, just nodded at me, his expression serious. "I understand."

He did?

I didn't, that was for sure.

Then, he surprised me by mumbling, "Do I stink?"

"You've been washed by the nurses."

"Did you look away?"

I had to grin. "I did."

"Shame," he said with a sigh. "I'm packing."

I arched a brow. "Packing what?"

His nose crinkled. "Gotta be literal with you. I get it. You speak such good English I forget that you won't understand all the slang."

"Hawk is teaching me."

"You have two teachers now," Quin informed me with a smile so bright it reminded me of before the attack.

"I need all the help I can get. You have a lot of slang."

"We do." He hummed. "Anyway, I meant I have a big dick."

"And did you think I'd be impressed by that?"

"Well, I mean, it's not something to be *un*impressed by, is it?

I pondered that a second. "No, I suppose not. It's irrelevant though because I gave you privacy."

"I don't need privacy with you."

I shook my head. "Of course you do."

"I dreamed of you," he said softly. "I've been dreaming of you for years. I swear, some nights in the joint, that was all that got me through. My sky girl."

"You call me that but I might not be your sky girl."

"You are. Your voice. I know it like it's my own. I heard it when I was sixteen."

"Not possible—"

"I didn't think so either but it was..." He sighed. "Never mind."

I shot him a disbelieving look, which morphed into something else when I yawned wide enough to split my face in two.

He frowned at me, then muttered, "If you don't think I stink, then you can rest here." He raised the bedsheet, revealing nothing of himself, just the cot on the bed.

It wasn't the first time he'd made this particular suggestion, but it was the first time I'd considered it.

Quin was still weak, even if he appeared stronger today. He was injured, and had been suffering from those injuries all week. Though I clearly wasn't his sky girl, he thought I was—would he hurt his sky girl?

Men hurt their loved ones all the time, but I didn't get that vibe from him. Just like I didn't with Hawk for that matter.

When I'd shared what the men I'd described had done to me, their outrage and disgust had been like a warm embrace.

Maybe I should compare people to the ones I'd come to learn over the years, but that was a depressing way to live, and already, I'd been shown a different path.

The Sinners did things that were wrong, dark, but their path was like no other's. They were scum to the police—I'd seen their response to the cuts the brothers had worn when the NYPD had come to take our statements—and I knew the nurses were scared of them. But they'd not only saved my life, they'd brought me back to one, they'd fed me and clothed me and sheltered me, and were trying to help me now.

It wasn't because of Quin that I got to my feet and sat down on the edge of the cot, twisting slightly so that I could fall back against the soft pillows—it was because of his brothers. Because of what they'd shown me.

Those sinners who declared themselves as belonging to Satan had shown me more affection and loyalty and protection than I'd had since I was a child.

That gave me faith, but it was Hawk who made me trust.

When I curled onto my side, Quin didn't haul me into him, didn't do anything other than drag the blanket up higher so that it covered us to our shoulders. I even giggled because he pulled it so high it covered half my face.

He remained on his back, I stuck to my side, turned away from him, and I stretched out as much as I could without falling over the edge of the bed.

It felt like a lifetime since I'd slept in a real bed, and I'd grown used to some home comforts during my time with the Sinners, so this felt really good.

What felt better?

The heat at my back.

It felt forged in a different kind of fire—one that was protective rather than a threat.

Sounding less sleepy, he asked, "What happened to the guard? The one who attacked us?"

"You don't remember giving the police your statement?"

"No," he muttered. "Christ, I don't remember that at all."

"Well, he's been arraigned. I'm not sure what that is. Hawk told me three times, but I still don't understand it."

When I yawned, he sighed. "Can I tell you a story?"

"I'm many things but not five, Quin."

"Please?"

The lights were dim in here because it was late, almost eight, and Hawk and I preferred to sit with them like this, otherwise it was tiring on the eyes. So, stretched out, comfortable, and with pillows that felt like clouds beneath my head, I mumbled, "If you don't think it will tire you out, go ahead."

"There's this story that my *nòkomis* used to tell me. I heard it so many times because she told me once I was destined to fly."

"A plane?"

He snorted, and I tensed when he wriggled beneath the blanket, but he made no move to drag me into him, just seemed to get more comfortable. "I doubt it. *Nòkomis* didn't agree with planes. She didn't live far from an airport but would always drive down to West Orange when I needed her."

"I don't like planes, either," I mumbled.

"Why not?"

I shrugged. "Why is anyone scared of anything?"

"Well, *Nòkomis's* reason wasn't irrational, she just thought only birds should have wings. She belonged in a different era.

"I used to have a love-hate relationship with her house because she refused to have telephones and TVs, and anything in anyway modern was considered evil." He harrumphed but it morphed into a laugh. "She never made toast in a toaster but on a wood-fired stove, and water was boiled on there for baths too. It was insane. Like going back in time, but for all that, I never resented going. I loved it, in fact."

"You loved her," I murmured, aware I spoke the truth, and not just from what Nyx and Indy had told me but because it was in his voice.

Affection, tenderness, gentle amusement.

"I did. I still do. She taught me a lot, and still not enough." He heaved a sigh. "I was really sick as a kid, and when modern medicine failed me, Mom and Dad contacted *Nòkomis* and asked her for help.

"She moved down to be with me and it took a while, but she did what the doctors couldn't. When things got rough with the family, I moved with her, and she tried to teach me the way she'd been taught."

"Was she your maternal or paternal grandparent?"

"Maternal. My dad is a Heinz 57 American—German, Irish, probably even fucking Russian. Anyway, Mom was six gazillion generation Algonquin—"

"It must have been hard for your *nòkomis* to accept that her daughter took such a different path to the one she did."

Quin's hand moved beneath the sheets, while I tensed a little, I knew what he was doing—even though I had no idea how I knew—and I moved my hand from under my cheek and rested it on my shoulder. He placed his on top of mine, and we made a loose, and very awkward, bridge with our fingers.

"It hurt her a lot, yes. She didn't understand, and for a long time, they were estranged."

"That's why Nyx and Indy call her grandma and not *nòkomis*?"

"Yes. I was the only one who really knew her. Anyway, she gave me a name when I was young."

"What kind of name?"

"It's not uncommon for kids to get a name and then a secret one that only their mothers know. She called me Winnange."

"What's that mean?" I asked, twisting on my side so I could look at him.

"It's not a nice name," he said dryly.

I frowned. "Then why did she pick it?"

"Because of this story. She said, 'One day you'll find your hawk and one day, together, you'll meet your sky girl.'"

I tensed up. "She said that?"

"Those words exactly. Unfortunately for me, she said so much crazy shit that I didn't think much of it at the time," he said wryly. "When she died, I experienced something that made me realize she could be right, but I stopped thinking about the Algonquin half of me. I shoved it aside but fate can't be shoved aside forever. I didn't even register Hawk's name until you walked through that door with him. That was when everything changed."

"I doubt I'm really your sky girl," I repeated, and though it was mad, a part of me wished I was.

"We'll see."

Hope whirled to life inside me, but I dampened it down, asking instead, "What's the story?"

"A beautiful woman one day saw a porcupine near her wigwam." He paused. "Do you know what a porcupine is?"

"No. I don't know what a wigwam is either." He explained. "Okay, I understand now."

"They hunted porcupines because they used to decorate their clothes with the spines, so she chased the creature and it went up a tree. She followed it, climbing higher and higher—"

"How big was this tree?" I asked suspiciously.

"Very big," he told me, his amusement clear. "It was a magical tree. It grew and grew until it penetrated the sky lands."

"Heaven?"

"No. Just the land of the sky." He sighed. "*Nòkomis* used to tell this so much better."

My lips twitched as I closed my eyes, oddly content as he told me something from his past. "You're doing a good job. Carry on."

"Well, she chased him into the sky lands, and when she got there, he turned into a man. An ugly one, who'd seen her down below and had wanted her as his wife."

I tensed. "He trapped her?"

"Yes. He made her his wife and put her to work. He told her she would never see her home, her family again.

"One of her tasks was that, every day, she had to go find these turnips to feed them, but he warned her to never dig too deep."

"Why?"

"Because he didn't want her to know what was underneath."

"Underneath what?"

He clucked his tongue. "You ask a lot of questions."

I smiled. "Sorry."

"Not sorry." He sniffed, then squeezed my fingers. "Anyway, one day, she finds this massive motherfucker of a turnip, and when she yanks it out, there's a hole. She looks through the hole and sees her home. Sees trees and grass and the prairie and everything she'd come to miss being away from it.

"She knew that was her salvation. Her way of getting home, so every day, she gathered things together to make a lariat that would help her climb down to the ground. She found a tool to place over the hole so she could dangle the makeshift rope from it to stop it falling through, and on this particular day, she decided to descend to her rightful world."

"Did it work?" I asked when he took a breath.

"She got to the end of the rope but it was nowhere near long enough."

I clucked my tongue. "That's sad. Did her husband find her?"

"Yes. She swung there for hours at the end of the rope, not wanting to go back, but not wanting to die either, and then he appeared, and she thought he was going to make her come back and he'd punish her."

"What did she do?" I asked in a hushed voice.

"She prayed. She called on the Great Spirit and pleaded with Her for help. A hawk appeared, just as her arms grew weak from holding on, and he helped take her closer to the ground."

"That's so nice." I bit my lip, unable to deny that I felt a parallel with the story at that moment. Which was, I assumed, why he was telling me this tale.

The porcupine man was my past, my captors, and Hawk was helping bring me back to the real world—to the real me.

"But she was too heavy for just the hawk who grew tired, and the Great Spirit sent another bird. A winnange."

"A winnange, like your name?"

"Yes. Together, they helped get her back to the ground."

"Were her friends and family happy to see her?"

"Very happy," he said, turning onto his side, and this time, I felt the heat of his front against the full length of my back.

I didn't feel scared, though, just protected.

With his story in my ears, I held myself still as he whispered, "When I was sixteen, I went on a vision quest. I wasn't like the other boys in the tribe. They could survive in the wilderness, but *Nòkomis* insisted. She said I had to find my way and only the Great Spirit would help me." He snickered. "I nearly died. My wigwam was shit, it caved in with every nasty gust of wind, and I found out later that the drug they give you triggered an allergic reaction in me.

"I heard from the Great Spirit that day, but I always thought it was a hallucination—until you, Amara."

"Why? What did the Great Spirit tell you?"

"That I had to cling to life, no matter what, because my sky girl would need me. And I heard her again, Amara, just before I was transported into the ambulance. She told me you needed me, and that I had to hang on. For you. No one else. Just you.

"And the craziest thing of all is that she spoke to me in your voice.

For years, I've heard you in my dreams, Amara, and I've been waiting for this moment without even knowing it. Waiting for you to come along and to prove that my grandmother wasn't crazy, that I wasn't either. This is our truth, sky girl. *This. Here. Now.*"

A tidal wave of emotion hit me at that. Irrational or not, tears began pricking my eyes, great shuddering sobs began wracking my body, making me shudder and judder against him. They were so powerful that even the heavy-duty bed itself rattled, and then Quin's arm slipped over my waist, holding me to him, grounding me even as I sank beneath the emotional tide that tried to keep me under.

Gently, he pulled me into him as he settled his face beside mine on the pillow and whispered, "I'll always bring you back down to Earth, sky girl."

"What about Hawk?" I sobbed.

"You're his sky girl too."

Which was when I sobbed harder.

And why he held me harder.

Wrapping me up so tight that I knew, somehow, I'd feel that embrace for the rest of my life.

If I chose to accept it.

THIRTY

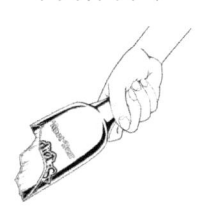

QUIN: *What's with Hawk?*
    Indy: *Man, it's weird having you back on FB.*
    Quin: *Good weird? Bad weird?*
    Indy: *Excellent weird. Glad to have you home, baby bro.*
    Indy: *Anyway, what do you mean?*
    Quin: *I'm ecstatic to be home.*
    Indy: *Imagine when you're not in that clinic.*
    Quin: *Trust me, I'm imagining.*
    Quin: *Re. Hawk, I mean, I want the lowdown.*
    Indy: *Oh. He works as a bouncer at the club's strip joint.*
    Quin: *Shit, we have a titty bar? How didn't I know that already?*
    Indy: *Probably because you've been locked up a while, and probably because you've been looking at a certain someone's set of tits so you're more interested in them?*
    Quin: *Shut up.*
    Indy: *You're the one who texted me.*
    Quin: *Shut up twice.*
    Indy: **snorts* Brat.*
    Quin: *You know it.*

Indy: *Hawk used to be a bounty hunter too. Back in Utah. I don't know if you remember his mom and dad.*

Indy: *Dog? Lizzy Fontaine?*

Quin: *I remember Dog. I didn't have long as a brother in the club but the Sinners ain't that big that I'd forget him.*

Indy: *Thought that bang to the head might have made you lose some brain cells.*

Quin: *Oh, it did, lol, but not that many.*

Indy: *Hawk and his twin brother North moved with Giulia to Utah. They came back earlier this year.*

Quin: *Why?*

Indy: *Their mom died.*

Quin: *Oh. Shit.*

Indy: *Their dad's dead too now.*

Quin: *It's not their year, is it?*

Indy: *Depends on how you look at it.*

Quin: *Lol. I guess.*

Indy: *They Prospected from the start, and then North cut and run with Dog's new Old Lady, and then Dog was murdered.*

Indy: *As far as I know, the council thinks North did his dad in.*

Quin: *Holy fuck! That's intense.*

Indy: *Yup. Hawk took it hard. Not just his dad, but losing North, I think. Giulia says he mopes a lot.*

Quin: *Must be hard losing a twin.*

Indy: *I can ask about him if you want?*

Quin: *No. I was just curious.*

Indy: *About what? If he's competition?*

Quin: *Lol. You know me too well.*

Indy: *I saw you eying Amara up like she's buttered popcorn fresh out of the machine.*

Quin: *I'd like to lick her up, that's for sure.*

Indy: *Yuck. Be careful with her.*

Quin: *She's not as fragile as you guys think.*

Indy: *Isn't she? I guess you'd know best, ya know, because you've had a handful of conversations with her.*

Quin: *I've had long, in-depth conversations with her.*

Quin: *Plus, I saw her handle herself. She's not made of glass. I think she needs to be reminded of that.*

Indy: *Maybe. Just don't hurt her.*

Quin: *I have no desire to do that.*

Indy: *Oh yeah, I forgot, because she's your sky girl.*

Quin: *I can feel you rolling your eyes at me.*

Indy: *Good.*

Quin: *Bitch.*

Indy: *You know it. You can't say shit like that to her. It'll freak her out.*

Quin: *See my earlier answer. She's not as fragile as you think.*

Indy: *Okay, oh, wise one, I'll bite. Why do you think she's your sky girl?*

Quin: *Because I heard her voice on my vision quest. I thought it was the Great Spirit but it wasn't. It was her voice.*

Indy: *You remember it that well?*

Quin: *Of course I do. It was fucking memorable.*

Indy: *Hardly. You were doped up on a hallucinogen.*

Indy: *One you were allergic to!*

Quin: *Well, I remember that. Whether it was a hallucination or not, I remember it. I thought it was weird, but ya know, spirits aren't going to talk like us, are they?*

Indy: *No. Not unless they're in Pocahontas.*

Quin: *Yeah, Indy, because we all live in Disney flicks.*

Indy: *:P*

Quin: *I'm telling you, I know it's her.*

Indy: *So what? What does it even mean? That she's your soul mate?*

Quin: *No. It means she's my sky girl.*

Indy: *So why are you interested in Hawk then? Did you switch to the other team?*

Quin: No.

Indy: If you had turned to the other team, I wouldn't mind, Quin.

Quin: I'm not gay.

Indy: If you're sure...

Quin: Jesus.

Indy: I'm here if you need me.

Quin: I don't. Well, I mean, I do, but not for your support as I come out. Christ.

Indy: Then, because you think Hawk's competition?

Quin: No.

Indy: You're not going to tell me?

Quin: I'm not even sure what I'm thinking.

Indy: Bullshit. You always know what you're doing.

Indy: You get that bullheadedness from Mom.

Quin: Gee, thanks.

Indy: Hah, you're welcome.

Quin: I think... God, it sounds crazy.

Indy: What does?

Quin: I think we're both meant for her.

Indy: Like in a threesome?

Quin: Yeah.

Indy: But you mean, permanently, right? Or just as a fling? I don't think Amara will ever be ready for that, Quin.

Quin: For a fling or a permanent relationship?

Indy: Jesus, I'm not even sure. She's... a lot of people did wrong by her.

Quin: That's exactly why she needs us. We'll always keep her from hitting the ground hard.

Indy: I guess that means something to you, but as far as I know, she isn't constantly sky diving.

Quin: Never mind. Is tomorrow the day you're heading to the TV studio?

Indy: It is. I'm nervous.

Quin: I'll bet. You'll kill it.

Indy: *I doubt it. It's just talks tomorrow. As far as I can tell anyway.*

Quin: *Let me know how it goes?*

Indy: *Depending on how late it is, I'll be by to see you afterward.*

Indy: *I might stop at the hotel first and get some rest. I have a feeling it's going to be exhausting.*

Quin: *I think it will be too. I know how stressed and pissy you get when you're trying to impress someone.*

Indy: *Shut up. I don't.*

Quin: *You do. And I know how much you respect Trade.*

Indy: *I really do. I can't believe they've invited me on his show.*

Quin: *I can. You deserve it.*

Indy: *Thanks, baby bro.*

Indy: *We ain't talked about this yet, but you're coming to train with me after you get home, aren't you?*

Quin: *Finish training. You and I both know I'm ready to work.*

Indy: *You need to do some exams first.*

Quin: *Fun.*

Indy: *Yep. But it's just certification to make sure you're all set to work at my ultra-respectable establishment.*

Quin: *Lol. You know I won't let you down.*

Indy: *Good. I'm looking forward to having some kind of a life again. The hours are crazy.*

Quin: *Good to know there's enough work.*

Indy: *I've earned quite a rep for my mandalas. God only knows what'll happen when they catch sight of what you're capable of.*

Quin: *o.O*

Indy: *Don't be coy. I never did tell Nyx that you came up with that design for his demons.*

Quin: *Good. I don't think he'd have wanted it back then.*

Indy: *Where did you get the idea from?*

Quin: *You don't want to know.*

Indy: *Probably not. Tell me anyway.*

Quin: *It's what I think Otesho monetoo looks like.*

Indy: *I know he's like the Algonquin devil... I shouldn't find that funny, should I?*

Quin: *Nope.*

Indy: *So, you were trying to ward off evil spirits by inking him with the biggest, baddest spirit around?*

Quin: *No. It's not a ward, more of an offering.*

Indy: *Each tattoo represents a soul Nyx took, and that's an offering to Otesho?*

Quin: *Yep.*

Indy: *It didn't work, did it?*

Quin: *Didn't it?*

Indy: *You mean... Giulia?*

Quin: *I do.*

Indy: *Christ.*

Quin: *Ha. Don't you mean Aashaa?*

Indy: *Moving swiftly on...*

Quin: *Before I tell you that Cruz is a gift from Aashaa too?*

Indy: *YEAH. So, what are you going to do about Hawk and Amara?*

Quin: *None of your business.*

Indy: *You made it my business.*

Quin: *I asked you a question.*

Indy: *And I answered.*

Quin: *You're a pain.*

Indy: *You know it.*

Indy: *BTW, what did you think of Cruz?*

Quin: *I've met him a lot in the past.*

Indy: *Yeah, but not as a brother-in-law. It's different as a brother.*

Indy: *Plus, you barely had a chance to get to know anyone before you were tossed in jail.*

Quin: *I think that I like how he looks at you.*

Indy: *Really? You're not just saying that?*

Quin: *Trust me, I'm not just saying that.*

Indy: Good. I'm glad. I want you to like him. How do you find Giulia?

Quin: She's a little out there, but I like how Nyx is around her. He's calmer.

Indy: It's funny, really. You wouldn't think that throwing two sets of fireballs onto each other would quench the fire.

Quin: No. You wouldn't. But it does.

Quin: I guess it's like in math. How two negatives make a positive.

Indy: Don't talk about math. It makes my eyes bleed.

Quin: You're still as much of a drama queen as ever.

Indy: You know it. BTW, I have some gear at the studio for you.

Quin: Like?

Indy: Phone, Mac. Shit like that. You can't use my iPad forever, lol.

Indy: Not sure what's going on with your living arrangements right now. You might end up with Nyx at Rachel's, or they might put you up in the motel the MC bought, so I figured we can get you what you need afterward but I know you need your tech.

Quin: You don't have to do that, sis.

Indy: Course I do. Anyway, you can pay me back by helping me rake it in when your portraits go wide.

Indy: I swear, I'm gonna plug the fuck outta your ink on TikTok. They'll dig that shit so hard.

Quin: Lol. Your faith in me is endearing.

Indy: Always.

Indy: Baby bro?

Quin: Yeah?

Indy: You sure you're not pushing too hard for something you can't know that you need yet?

Quin: What do you mean?

Indy: You're fresh out of prison. You sure you don't want to sow your wild oats or something?

Quin: I do. Just with her.

Indy: Didn't take you for a head over heels kind of guy, tbh.

Quin: Me neither. And I wouldn't be. But I'm telling you, Indy. I remember her voice.

Indy: I don't want to argue, but I'm telling YOU, she will need more reasoning than that.

Indy: A woman needs to know that she's wanted. Not just that you remember her fucking voice.

Quin: You ever looked at someone and known in your soul they belong to you?

Indy: I didn't feel that way at the start with Cruz.

Indy: But yeah, you're in luck. I feel it in my bones that we're right together.

Quin: Well, that's how I feel.

Indy: You don't know her.

Quin: I do.

Indy: You don't.

Quin: I do.

Indy: Jackass.

Quin: Yup. But it's true. I do know her. It might seem crazy to you, but I really fucking do.

Quin: Want to hear something crazier?

Indy: Of course. I didn't lock Nyx up in an asylum for what he did.

Indy: I think I can handle whatever you throw my way.

Quin: Gee, thanks x 2.

Quin: We're meant to be together. All three of us. I know it.

Indy: You sure you didn't read too much paranormal romance in the joint?

Quin: Positive. Tolstoy was more my thing in there.

Indy: Good God.

Quin: Lol. No joke.

Indy: No wonder you've gone weird on me.

Quin: Hardly. I was weird before. I think I knew, back then, that this was how it was meant to be.

Indy: *How are you gonna convince an ex-sex slave to be with two guys?*

Quin: *I don't know. I'm hoping that Aashaa is on my side.*

Indy: *You know if this is all mumbo jumbo to me, then it's gonna be weirder to Amara, right?*

Quin: *I'm sure. But everything happens for a reason. I have to have faith in that.*

Indy: *When she wraps a call button cord around your throat, tries to strangle you then castrate Hawk, expect me to say I told you so.*

Quin: *We'll never hurt her. That's not what this is about.*

Indy: *Never said you would. You think I'd let you anywhere near her if you were gonna hurt her physically?*

Indy: *Quin, she's not like regular women.*

Quin: *What is she? An alien?*

Indy: *No. I'm just...*

Indy: *I know Nyx talked to you about this. I know he did. You're well aware what I went through, and Cruz had to be careful around me.*

Indy: *I did a lot of destructive shit before I let him anywhere near me.*

Indy: *I just don't see why she won't be the same.*

Quin: *She will be. But don't you see, Indy? You did let Cruz in. What if Hawk and I are her Cruz?*

Indy: *Don't make me cry.*

Quin: *I don't mean to. I'm just telling you what I know in my bones.*

Indy: *It's so weird hearing a biker talk like this. You're not supposed to fall in love this fast.*

Quin: *This isn't love. It's fate.*

Indy: *Fuck, that's even weirder.*

Quin: *:D I know. Lol.*

Indy: *You're a nut. But you're my nut. *sighs**

Quin: *Sis, what Nyx told me... if I could kill him again, I would.*

Indy: *I know, Quin. xx*

Indy: *Gotta go, client just walked through the door.*

Quin: *I'll be thinking of you tomorrow, sis. I know you'll rock it.*

Indy: *Thanks, baby bro.*

Quin: *Stay safe and kick butt.*

Indy: *I don't need to. Cruz will be with me. He'll do all that for me.*

Quin: *I want to do all that, BE all that for Amara too.*

Quin: *Ttyl. x*

Indy: *xoxo*

THIRTY-ONE

RACHEL

"SHIT'S FUCKED UP, Dad. I swear, things'd be so much easier if you weren't in here."

The words weren't a whisper. More of a low murmur. But from my position by the window into the room, I could *see* them anyway. Reading lips was something I'd picked up as I made my way through criminal cases and depositions, and it came in handy now.

Rex.

My one weakness.

Not even Rain could get to me like he could.

I wasn't sure why God, Satan, or whoever in between had made him my Achilles' heel, but I'd stopped worrying about it a long time ago. Instead, I just got on with it. Got on with shit in general.

I didn't have the time to wallow, to worry, or to wonder.

Rex was Rex.

I was Rachel.

He was crime.

I was law and order.

Of a variation anyway.

It was simpler to shove him aside, to move on, to focus on the future, but here, now, that wasn't possible. The lines between the past, present, and future were blurring in a way I couldn't control, and I hated things that were out of my control.

Seeing Bear so broken was devastating. It was difficult to see anybody in the state he was in, but a man who was like family? Who felt as if he was my blood?

The blast had left him a ragged mess. There were no two ways to describe it. He was broken and battered not just bruised, and I had a feeling he'd never make it out of the coma the doctors put him in.

Rex visited every day, and invariably, I came here to watch him at first, then to sit with him.

Why?

Because I was a weakling.

Because Rex, as a caring, loving son, was like my version of puppies and flowers and boxes of chocolates.

It was the sight of the Rex I'd wanted him to be, instead of what he'd become.

I pursed my lips at the thought, then because I was getting sappy and I didn't have time for that, I barged into the room, stepping over to Bear's side and pressing a kiss to his forehead.

For a long while, we'd had to wear special protective gear, now, we just had to make sure our hands were clean and that our shoes were covered in those disposable paper socks.

I let my fingers drift over Bear's forehead, where bumps and bruises, cuts and scrapes from the blast were still healing, and ran it over the grizzled locks of a man who was more than just a bear by name, but nature too.

I cast Rex a look, saw the longing in his eyes, the pain in his heart, and asked huskily, "Any updates?" even though I knew there weren't any.

He knew too, but he still shook his head.

It took everything I had in me not to go to him, not to comfort him, not to sit on his lap and to bring his mouth to mine, to make our foreheads touch...

The thought was an acute form of agony.

I retreated from the bedside and moved over to the other armchair. Plunking my ass in it, I settled my briefcase on my lap and started going through some papers, rifling through them as I got some reading done.

I spent two hours in that room with Rex, and neither of us said a word after the start.

That was how it had to be.

We weren't broken. We just weren't meant to be, and our silence was proof that both of us knew it.

Amara's legal situation wasn't as cut and dry as I'd like. It'd be a lot easier if one of the brothers would fall for her and marry her, because the visa options open to her, well, the odds sucked, and after what she'd gone through, I didn't like the idea of her being deported.

She might not realize it yet but she'd become a part of the Sinners' family—whether she liked it or not—and that meant she'd have a form of protection that few ever experienced.

Of course, that came with many inherent dangers, but for someone like her, she needed the family. She needed that wall of security, and I didn't want it to be denied to her because Uncle Sam was a cunt where sex trafficking victims were concerned.

Sure, these poor women could service hundreds of thousands of good ole' boys who had the Stars and Stripes dangling from their front porch, but God forbid the victims were allowed to put down roots, to be safe in the so-called Land of the Free.

Pursing my lips at the thought, agitated and aware I had to make some calls if Amara was ever going to find any justice, I got to my feet, and said, "See you later, Rex."

He grunted but I felt his eyes on me.

I could have worn dress pants, sweatpants, yoga pants... but I rarely did around him. I almost always wore a skirt because they were his kryptonite.

I wasn't sure why I dressed to tease him, whether it was because I was a bitch or not, but I never met up with him in trousers if I could help it.

Aware his gaze was on my ass, I sauntered out of the hospital room once I grazed Bear's temple with another kiss, then I strode through the wards, heading into the parking lot before I climbed into my SUV, and drove home.

Rain wasn't back from wherever he'd been taking himself since Cyan's kidnapping, that goddamn bike of his was nowhere to be seen, but there were a couple of other bikes and cages parked here and there.

It was hard sharing my personal space with this many people, but God help me, they were family. What was I supposed to do? Let them live on the street?

Grunting at the thought, I parked, headed into the kitchen where the one good aspect of having people living in was usually found— Giulia. Goddamn, that woman could cook. She was a major pain in the ass, had an attitude the size of Mount Rushmore, but her skills in the kitchen made me understand why Nyx thought the sun rose and set on her.

I picked up some leftovers in the fridge, nuked the shit out of them, then retreated to my office which was at the other side of the property, and had views of the hills and the back end of West Orange.

When I was settled there, I got to work. My PA had already left for the day, and I had a crap ton of stuff to go through, so I worked and ate at the same time.

A knock sounded at my door minutes or hours later, and I blinked, then rubbed my bleary eyes that had been staring at the computer for far too long, and grimaced when I realized it was dark out.

"Come in," I hollered, and when the door opened, I tensed.

Rex stood there, his face grim. His pain clear.

Heart in my throat, I jerked into a standing position. "Bear? He's—"

He gritted his teeth but shook his head. "He had a cardiac arrest. They got it under control, but they don't know why—" He made a fist with his hand and smacked it into his palm. "If it happens again, that's it. He's gone."

I closed my eyes. "Jesus."

Pain fell like a landslide inside me, slipping down my bones, sinking into my muscles, penetrating my very soul.

I didn't stop him when he came to me, didn't shove him away when his arms slid around my shoulders and he hauled me into him.

I didn't do anything other than let him hold me, let him touch me, let us reconnect after so long apart.

It felt so good. So fucking good to be back here again. The agony of having Bear's time on Earth be shortened because of his health didn't lessen in Rex's arms, but it made it bearable. Made the tears that burned my eyes sting less as I burrowed into him, finding comfort and offering it.

How long we stood there, I didn't know, but what I was hyperaware of was his strength, his leanness, his power. So ingrained in him, so inbuilt. In another world, with his charisma, his smarts, and his acuity, he'd have made a fantastic politician.

He was born to rule.

I just couldn't believe he wasted himself on an MC.

But right now, our differences weren't at the forefront of my mind.

The man was.

My kryptonite was at the front and center of everything.

When things changed between us, I felt it. When a simple hug changed into something else, I knew the exact moment it happened.

There was the tiniest shift in the air.

The veriest whisper of our heart rates surging as he shifted his head, drawing it back so that he could press his mouth to mine.

He wanted to escape reality, I knew that. He wanted to hide from the truth. He needed comfort. But like always, men merged all that with sex and fucked everything up.

The only difference was, I needed this too.

I needed him, so I let him in.

I opened myself up to him when I'd always vowed I wouldn't, because this was the path to heartbreak. Devastation. Decimation.

But at that moment, I had confirmation that a man who was like a second father to me, a man who I loved as much as Rex did, wasn't going to live if he had another heart attack. If his brutalized body had to endure yet one more strike against it, that was it.

Game over.

His situation had always been precarious but this felt like the end of the line, and I knew Rex was hurting because he believed that too. Our abilities to be realistic, even when it hurt, was a trait we both shared.

My thoughts were dragged away as his hands came to cup my ass cheeks so he could draw me deeper into his hold. His strength overwhelmed and cosseted me, making me feel like I was seventeen again, winding back the years when he'd been my everything and I'd been his.

His tongue thrust against mine, his lips biting and ravaging me, filling me with an urgent need to have him plunder everywhere he touched.

I fought back, like I always did. Bite for bite, kiss for kiss, thrust for thrust, and it felt so good. So right. So natural.

This was how it was supposed to be between us.

Hunger, always hunger.

Need, always need.

Neither sated or quenched until we could be back in one another's arms again.

I groaned as he started shifting my skirt up my thighs, higher and higher until his hands were grazing the bare flesh of the back of my legs. When his fingers dug into my butt, sliding underneath the line of my panties, I didn't stop him.

What was the point?

This was inevitable.

It always was.

I moaned into his mouth when the tips flirted with the join between thigh and groin, and when he slid a finger along the length of my pussy, the moan turned guttural with want.

He growled under his breath, ripping free of my mouth so he could sink down to my throat, kissing and nipping me there as he sucked and lathed my pulse point before burrowing between my breasts.

Arching my back when he speared his finger inside me, I released a shocked cry at the abrupt move. Normally, he teased, but there was nothing normal about today.

This was about feeling—anything other than grief or loss, just pleasure. Relief. Escape.

He nuzzled the lapel of my blouse away with his nose and drifted over, shoving the delicate lace of one bra cup away so he could find my nipple.

As he sucked on that, he thrust his finger into me, fucking me with it until he growled again and shoved me back against the desk.

I let him.

I goddamn let him.

He spread my legs as he pushed his zipper down, his fly popped open as he grabbed his dick from between the folds of denim, and then his cock was there.

Pressing against me.

Pushing into me.

And it felt so good, so fucking right that my head tipped back, throat arching as he filled me full.

He dragged me nearer, his hard hands at the back of my thighs as he dug his fingers into the soft flesh, urging me to ride him as much as he was fucking me.

All around me, I could feel my solid desk judder and shake with the force of this thrusts, and nothing felt as good as this.

I'd missed it, *him*, so goddamn much.

With a cry, I slid my arms around his shoulders, hauling him closer as I hid my face in his throat, riding out the ferocity, jerked into pleasure so fast that I couldn't have expected it.

When the orgasm pummeled me from the inside out, tearing down walls as it blew me apart, I cried out, my mouth gaping wide, eyes clenched as he roared his own ecstasy.

In the aftermath, he didn't pull away, if anything, as I sobbed out my grief, he held me tightly, painfully. He clung to me as much as I clung to him, and the union of our bodies, his hardness softening inside me, didn't ease the agony of mourning that was coming my way, but it reminded me of one hard, solid, inarguable, unquestionable truth—that life was short and we, for all our sins, were alive, well, and utterly in denial.

THIRTY-TWO

QUIN

"YOU KEEP TOUCHING YOUR HEAD. Is it aching?"

I cast Hawk a glance. "A little."

"It's stupid that they won't give you any meds." He scowled at me, even though it wasn't at me, just hospital policy that would ultimately prevent me from dying—LOL—but which kept me up with a banging migraine that had stalked me solidly for three days on the run.

Amara reached over and did what she'd taken to doing—rubbing my temples. I tipped my head against the pillows, loving that she touched me so freely and wondering when that had started happening.

Had it been when she slept for twelve hours straight in bed with me? Not even moving when the nurses came in and checked my wounds?

Had it been the story of the sky girl?

Or was it seeing me suffer? Did it bring out the need in her to make me feel better?

I hoped it wasn't a maternal urge—she was younger than me, for fuck's sake, but still, the last thing I felt for her was maternal.

As she rubbed my temples with gentle fingertips though, I sighed, letting the weight of my head sink into the pillows some more as she leaned over me to start dragging the tips over my scalp.

As she did, I felt her shuffle closer, twisting to sit on the side of the bed, her butt against my hip. When I opened my eyes, I got an epic glance at her tits in the tee she wore.

Though she dressed like Mother Teresa, a desperate man saw things he wanted to see. Like the bulge at the top of her shirt, the way the fabric pulled taut, and how her nips would make an appearance when she was touching me.

I cast Hawk a glance, as I usually did when she touched me, and found him watching us both.

He brooded a lot.

I'd noticed that too.

Brooding looks, smoldering glances, stoic silence. He was the kind of guy who didn't say much, but somehow, didn't blend into the background.

After our initial introduction, where he'd done nothing but speak for ninety minutes solid as he updated me on the goings on in the MC, I'd thought he was a chatty Cathy, but he wasn't. If anything, he'd spoken more during that first conversation than he had, period, since I'd woken up.

Amara was a quiet one, too, which made it weird for me because I was a talker. I talked to fill awkward silences, and could keep up a conversation with myself.

Even with a goddamn migraine.

"Your pants getting tight?" I asked Hawk, watching his eyes flare wide in surprise at my question, but I figured if we were going to spend a lot of time together—which we would definitely be doing if I had my way—he needed to get used to this side of me.

"Hawk is not getting fat," Amara scoffed, tutting at me as she started making circles on my scalp that had me drooling like Homer in the Simpsons.

"Didn't say he was," I retorted.

"Then why would his jeans get tight?" Amara frowned. "You ask strange things, Quin."

My lips curved into a smirk, and Hawk flipped me the bird, scowling as he did so, before he settled back in his seat, a boner definitely tenting his pants as he looked at Amara's swaying tits.

She didn't wear a bra.

I wondered if she wore panties.

I'd have thought she would keep those bad boys locked up tight, maybe even wear a chastity belt, because her clothes were her first line of defense, but she didn't.

Praise *Aashaa*—the Great Spirit was clearly on my side.

I bit my lip as I watched the sway, kind of entranced by the sight, then when I recognized my head was capable of caning me with a migraine while sending blood south, I rasped, "Amara, honey, thank you, I feel so much better."

She hummed with satisfaction, then leaned back to stare at me. "There is less pain in your eyes," she declared.

Was there?

Maybe because it was all concentrated in my balls?

A man, fresh out of the joint, really needed to get laid, but after what I'd gone through, I shouldn't be this desperate.

Of course, Amara changed things.

And the way Hawk watched Amara changed them even more.

Did he get off on watching?

Or did he like being watched?

The prospect had me pursing my lips, but a knock at the door ruptured the thought process as James Dean opened it up, and let in a nurse with a tray of food.

James' eyes drifted from the nurse's ass, and over to Amara, who didn't even take notice of the nurse, never mind the brother.

I remembered James Dean from before and knew he had an eye for the ladies, knew they had an eye for him too, so it amused me that she didn't even notice him when the giggling nurse totally did.

Amara was more focused on making me comfortable as she

leaned over to resettle my pillows and fiddled with the button on the bed that made the incline on the back rest steeper so I could sit up and eat.

"Thank you, sky girl." She smiled at me, but the smile died a little when I also thanked the nurse: "Thanks, Janie."

"You're welcome," Janie chirped, her interest in me dying as she quickly twisted around to flutter her lashes at James, making it clear she'd give him some medical attention if he wanted it.

The stupid fucker was checking out Amara though, which had Janie's come-hither looks disappearing, and Hawk pivoting his arm to send his fist into James' stomach in a warning he compounded with, "Keep your eyes at neck-level, fucker."

James coughed and spluttered a bit which had Janie smirking at him before she sailed out, loaded with attitude, muttering, "If you want her, then you can sniff around her."

"Janie, don't be like that," James coughed, punching Hawk in the shoulder or, at least, aiming for that. Hawk twisted which had his fist colliding with the armchair backrest, and we all felt the thunk as he obviously hit a part of the wooden frame rather than the soft cushioning.

Hawk boomed out a laugh as James turned white. Clearly recognizing that he was in danger in this room, he scuttled away, leaving me and Hawk snickering, and Amara frowning at us both in confusion.

"What was that about?"

Though he was snickering, he managed to get out, "Nothing."

I shrugged. "She's got a crush on him."

"He was—"

Hawk, before I could say a word, retorted, "Never mind. Toss me the pudding cup, little bird."

She frowned, because she wasn't an idiot and knew something had happened, but because she didn't have eyes in the back of her head and because she never looked at James Dean, she didn't know he'd been checking her out.

She huffed under her breath and grabbed the pudding cup which they both knew I hated and passed it over to Hawk.

As he peeled back the lid, he asked, "What do you want tonight?"

Staring at the grim food on my plate, I muttered, "Anything but this."

Amara scoffed. "It is not so bad."

"I ate prison slop for years, sky girl, trust me, it's bad." I wafted the fork in my hand after I prodded an annihilated carrot. "Anyway, you can't judge. Your food probably made my slop look like Michelin-star dishes."

She blinked at me, her mouth working a second, and I knew that was the first time someone hadn't taken her plight seriously. I mean, I took it very seriously. Incredibly so. I wanted to hurt the motherfuckers who hurt her as much as Hawk did after hearing her stories, but I'd decided that we needed to desensitize her.

If she could stab someone in the eye with a key and slice someone's throat open—yes, I'd had story time too and knew all the details of Amara's attack on a club enemy—could also choke someone with a call button cord instead of cowering in a corner, then she was brave enough and big enough to deal with talking about her past without it triggering an atmosphere that belonged on an episode of *Oprah*.

Hawk studied her and then me, a glint of disapproval in his eyes, but he didn't rush to rectify the situation. He just waited for her to say, "You are right. This looks like a five-star meal by comparison." Her brow puckered as she stared at it. "But that does not mean I need to eat it. *Tak*." Her brow puckered even more, like she was trying to solve the hardest math puzzle in the world, then she whispered, "I don't have to eat this."

She didn't like the waste. Not when it was good, solid food and she'd been fed only fuck knew what before. That was why she finished off my dinners even though we always grabbed take-out.

But things were different now.

She was my sky girl.

The past was exactly that—ancient history.

I pushed the straw into the juice box and took a slurp. "Nope, you don't have to eat this shit. So, what's on tonight's menu?"

Technically, I wasn't supposed to eat the take-out, but I'd just get James Dean to finger Janie to soften her up when she came back and found a full tray of food.

"Pizza."

I nodded. "Good choice. Pie in New York is the bomb."

"This is good, no?"

"Very good," I agreed. "You want plain cheese or with toppings?"

"I've had it before, but very seldom. I wasn't allowed it when I was training. You know the..." She pursed her lips. "The yellow fruit."

I gagged. "You don't mean pineapple. You want that?"

Hawk rumbled, "If that's what she wants, that's what she'll have."

I rolled my eyes. "Yes, Daddy."

He snorted, but he pulled out his phone and murmured, "You want ham and pineapple, babe?"

She bit her bottom lip, eying the mush that was supposed to be potatoes, carrots, and some unidentifiable white meat that could have been either chicken or fish or fucking both for all I knew.

"*Tak.*" She blinked. "Please."

I hummed. "We need to rectify this shit. We gotta get you on the good stuff."

"What is the good stuff?"

"I'll go for fungi. I bet she likes the mushrooms. Hawk, do you like pepperoni?"

"I like ham and pineapple," he said with a grin.

"Okay, so you're both aliens and need to be returned to Mars." I gagged again. "Sweet lord, I think I'd prefer the chickfish here."

"Chickfish? What is this?"

"He's being a joker. I think I preferred you when you were concussed," Hawk muttered, squinting at me.

"I think I preferred you when your pants weren't as tight."

He scraped a hand over his jaw. "Speaking of, I'm going to get showered."

"I'll just bet you are," I mocked.

"I shall shower after you, *tak?*"

I cleared my throat when a glimmer of pain that only a man would understand flashed across Hawk's face. "Yeah. I'll grab the pies on the way back instead of ordering in. There's a busy place around the corner from the hotel. It looks good. I'll take you to the room once we've eaten."

I nodded, then said, "Whack one off for me."

I knew I was pushing it, but when he shot me a glance, I didn't see anger, just begrudging amusement.

"Did you get your ass beaten a lot in the joint?"

"Not once I beefed up," I told him smoothly.

He got to his feet as he put down the untouched pudding cup and murmured, "More by chance than anything else then."

I grinned at him as he stalked over to Amara who eyed him with the bewilderment in her eyes that told us both she knew something was being said without her understanding it, without us wanting her to understand it, but she arched her head back for him to press his lips to hers.

They had an odd relationship.

When he left for the hotel, or she did, they kissed like an old married couple. Otherwise, they rarely touched aside from Amara gripping his hand in hers from time to time if she was concerned or nervous or scared—that happened when the doctor came in to check me over.

I didn't think they'd had sex, but there was something that connected them. Something that was maturing as the days locked together in here passed.

I wasn't sure if that would fuck me over in the long run or not. She'd been touched by my sky girl story, but I wasn't sure if she understood. If she *wanted* to understand.

Indy was right. Destiny or not... What ex-sex slave would be happy at the idea of taking on two men?

And Hawk didn't look to be the kind of guy who was happy

about sharing.

He let me get away with stuff because I was sick, I thought, but like with James Dean, he quickly stomped out any competition. Fox had been in, one of the old guard who rarely acted as a soldier for the club anymore, and when he'd slid an arm around Amara's shoulders and dragged her into him, hauling her around like she was a clubwhore, Hawk's face had bled free of all color, and he'd bit out, "If you want to lose that hand, Fox, you'll keep it right where it is."

I'd wanted to beat the shit out of him too, but Amara's reaction had been the most interesting of them all.

At first, she'd hunched her shoulders and ducked her head. Then, from out of nowhere, like she was mentally tapping out in reverse, rage had flashed in her eyes, and I knew that she'd take off Fox's hand before Hawk even had the chance to get to it.

As my MC brother sauntered out now he'd gotten his kiss, I watched as Amara moved into the armchair she only sat in when Hawk departed.

As she curled her feet up beneath her, tipping her head to the side against the rest, I waited for her to ask me if I was up for drawing like she usually did.

Only... she didn't.

Instead, she asked, "What is 'whacking off?'"

Though I had no problem helping her out with her English, it wasn't the first time I registered just how fucking frustrating it must be for her having to translate everything all the goddamn time.

That didn't make me easier on her though. Not when I wanted answers: "Why do you kiss Hawk goodbye?"

It wasn't that I was averse to answering her question, quite the contrary, but I wanted an answer for an answer.

"Because it feels right," she said slowly, quite clearly seeing that I wasn't about to explain anything without payment in kind.

Immediately, I said, "Whacking off is, well, do you know what masturbating is?"

She blinked. "You talk of these things so freely?"

"Well, only because we know you won't understand. Or, well, knew that. Now you do, we might still do it."

"But, why?" she asked with a frown.

"Because we're comfortable around you. Do you not want us to be comfortable around you?"

"So, I'm one of the men?"

My eyes bugged. "Sky girl, no, when I'm talking about comfortable, I don't mean that kind of comfortable." A laugh burst out of me. "You're definitely not one of the guys."

"Then why do you talk of these things?"

"Because I was trying to push a conversation."

"With me?"

"With Hawk." I shrugged. "And you, if you bit, which you did."

"What kind of conversation?"

"About sex."

She tensed. "Why?"

"Because I'd like to have sex with you and I'm sure Hawk would like that too."

"I'm not ready for—"

I raised a hand. "And I'm not about to push the topic."

"That entirely contradicts what you just said."

"With Hawk, it's different." I sensed her anger, and recognized that gleam in her eyes. Because I didn't feel like being strangled with a cord, I said quickly, "You've seen how stoic he is." The way she tipped her head to the side was her way of showing she didn't understand. "He's all serious. Doesn't say much."

"I like this about him. You talk a lot."

I grinned. "I know." God, I smiled so much around her. Didn't she know what she did to me? I felt like a kid in class with a new girl who was from France, had triple Ds, and wore those socks that cut off at the mid-thigh point.

She heaved a sigh. "That wasn't a complaint," she said, but I could tell it was begrudging. "I just mean he's—"

Before she could finish the sentence, I did so for her: "Different, I know. That's why I wanted to push the topic. I'll be leaving the hospital soon." I shrugged. "I want to know what's happening."

"With what?"

"With us."

"There is no us," she grumbled.

"Isn't there? I know you stayed with me all week. I know Hawk did as well. I know you cried and slept in my arms, and I know that you wouldn't do that with someone you weren't learning to trust." I shrugged. "Seems like a massive deal to me."

"We are friends, aren't we?" she retorted, cocking a brow at me as her cheeks started to turn red with her anger. "Isn't this what friends do?"

"You barely knew me before. My sister and brother wouldn't spend all day every day with me. Things are different between us. Whether you accept it or not, they are."

She quieted at that, remained frowning at me, but though her squinty eyes made me feel like she was Mrs. Poindexter, glaring at me to make sure the one Native American kid in class didn't cheat on his science paper, I merely watched her back.

I had no idea what I wanted from her.

An orgasm, sure.

Conversation, definitely.

Friendship, you bet.

But this went deeper.

"In the joint—" I started, needing to express myself because if *I* couldn't express myself then how could she? "—it's actually weird. We look forward to going home, we crave it, and it's like this day that's never going to come, and you always think something is going to happen to have it taken away from you. But as it approaches, we're all on tenterhooks for other reasons.

"And I'm talking regular guys. Like men who aren't stabbed before they leave, and who aren't almost killed the second they make it outside."

"Why are they so frightened?"

"Because the world out here is frightening. Sure, the joint is literally a dog eat dog world. We're caged in, and it's hell. We're with people who want to hurt us just so that they look big and bad enough to rule the roost—" Her head tipped to the side. "To rule over the place, beneath the guards' noses, but in there, routine is everything. We're told when to shower, when to eat, when to sleep and when to wake up. When to work, when to clean, when to call our friends and family. What to wear, what to eat, and to some extent, what to think. Everything is controlled. Out here, nothing is. Freedom is delicious but it's like a maze."

She blinked at that. "Why are you telling me this?"

"Because I need you to understand something." I licked my lips as I leaned forward, resting my arms on my knees as I did so, ignoring the twinge of pain that came along my abdomen and down my side. "Before I was released, Nyx came to visit with me. Did you know that Indy was abused as a child?"

Her eyes flared wide before she sank back into the armchair like she could hide from what I was telling her. "I knew Nyx's sister..." She shook her head. "I mean, your sister had..."

I raised a hand, understanding that she had no words at that moment.

"Carly was a lot older than me, she died when I was really young." Then, I admitted something to her that I'd never share with Nyx or Indy, "Amara, I don't even remember her, but the bastard who got to her was our uncle, and, he got to Indy too." I clenched my jaw as the pain walloped me worse than my healing wounds did. "I never knew that. It was enough that he hurt Carly. That tore our family apart, and to be honest, if it weren't for *Nòkomis*, I'd be fucked.

"Mom and Dad were shredded to pieces by what happened to Carly. It changed everything, and for a little boy who was always sick, always in and out of the hospital..." I blew out a breath, the memories enough to make me feel that whirlwind of rage that had overtaken me that day Nyx had come to visit. "It was a hard time. Enough that *Nòkomis* petitioned the state and had me taken into her care. They didn't even fucking fight for me, Amara. They just let her take me away."

She bit her lip. "I'm sorry, Quin."

"Don't be. I know it was for the best, but it's hard. You know? To accept that your parents didn't think you were worth fighting for."

"They didn't think that!" she snapped.

"Didn't they? Why didn't they try to keep it together? Not only for my sake but for Indy and Nyx's? They abandoned us."

"And that's on them, not you," she said forcefully, straightening up in the seat and glowering at me.

I wasn't surprised when she got to her feet and strode over to the bed, glaring all the while at me as she hopped onto it. Once seated at the foot of the bed, she crossed her legs in the lotus position, and just that proximity helped soothe me.

"I started doing stupid stuff after *Nòkomis* died," I said with a sigh. "Jacking cars, going joy-riding. I was dumb, acting out, but I wasn't suicidal. I always picked clunkers, never anything expensive, and always in West Orange where the cops were in the Sinners' pocket." I gnawed on the inside of my cheek. "I'm not an innocent, Amara, and maybe I deserved a slap on the wrist, some time in juvie, shit like that, but not what I got." The case against me had involved an expensive car in Manhattan—what kind of dipshit would I be to have taken that for a ride?

"I'm sorry, Quin."

I shrugged. "Remember I told you my secret name?"

"Winnange?"

I smiled a little, touched that she remembered. "Yes."

"You said it was a bad name."

"It's an animal that eats dead things."

She pulled a face. "Your *nòkomis* called you that?"

I grimaced. "She did, and now I know why."

"Why?" she whispered, her eyes wide.

"Because she knew what was in my future, and she knew the day would come when I'd feel *Otesho monetoo*. When he'd whisper in my ear, and when he'd encourage me to do what I wanted to do when I left the joint."

She hunched her shoulders as she leaned forward. "What did you want to do?"

"You heard about what Nyx does?"

Amara nodded.

"I wanted to carry on his work."

Her mouth rounded. "Really?"

"Yes. *Nòkomis* knew Nyx's demons would haunt me. To her, it was better that I be a *winnange* than a *windigo*."

"What's that?"

"A type of soulless creature. Half man, half beast that eats the flesh of the living." She gasped. "*Aashaa* told me that was your path too, sky girl. That it was my duty to keep you safe."

"Me?" Amara breathed, pointing at herself like there was another sky girl in the room.

"Yes, you. But we're safer now we're together."

"We are?"

"Yes, because we'll keep each other's demons at bay." I gritted my teeth. "Before I got out, Nyx visited me to ask me if Kevin had abused me. I don't have any damage like that so I doubt he touched me in that way." I raked a hand over my head, feeling violent and explosive, like a bullet that had been thrown into a fire and was just waiting to explode. "Nyx always talked about hearing these whispers, and suddenly, I was hearing them too." I tapped my temple. "He talked about voices that spoke to him, that made him seek out those particular things he hunted." I chose my words carefully in case the room had been bugged. I didn't need to give the Sparrows any ammunition. "For the first time, I knew *Nòkomis* was as right about me as she was about Nyx. I also knew he'd never believe me when I explained what was happening to him."

"Why?"

"Because they weren't raised with the belief system I was. Not even I believe it half the time. Most of what I learned, I learned for *Nòkomis'* sake, but that's it. She was always rambling on about these things, and it's only now that I've heard Nyx's demons, and that I've met you, I realize she wasn't a mad old bat.

"If I thought she was crazy, well, can you imagine what Nyx and Indy thought?

"Anyway, Nyx didn't have the same relationship with her as I did. She stayed in Quebec until she came to Jersey, and even then, she was at the hospital more than anything, helping me."

"Why? Why wasn't she there for Nyx and Carly and Indy?"

I shrugged. "She wasn't welcome. My dad said she spoke bullshit that was bad for us, but when I kept getting sicker, Mom said she could help me. She did.."

"That's sad. He used her."

"He did, but her coming into my life changed everything." I shrugged. "It's sadder still because my brother and sister needed her. They don't even know that, but they did."

"You call them demons, but really, you mean one of her spirits talks to Nyx?" she whispered, and her tone was haunted, like she wasn't dissing me, but truly believed what she was saying.

That she understood me at all was a miracle.

"There are a lot of evil spirits, and they encourage us to do bad things. Nyx is... *was* a lost soul. Until Giulia. She saved him from *Otesho.*"

Her lips curved. "Giulia is many things but she's more likely to tell a bad spirit to fuck off than to be frightened of it."

Having seen my sister-in-law in action, I could stand behind that.

I also could see the admiration in her voice as she spoke of Giulia.

Like I'd explained to Indy, I explained to her, "In math, two negatives can make a positive. When I look at Nyx and Giulia, that's what I see."

"That is a good way of thinking of it."

"In Rikers, those spirits were talking to me, Amara." I reached for her hand, and was heartened when she didn't pull back. "Then, I got hurt. *Aashaa* spoke to me, and then I met you. You stopped them."

"They talk to me as well—"

"Exactly. We're two negatives. We make a positive. And with Hawk watching over us—"

"He isn't."

"Yes, he is. He watches you all the time. Don't you see that?"

She pulled her hand back. "Don't say things like that. I don't want anything to change."

"That's my point, Amara. I don't either. When I leave, things *will* change. I won't be always in bed, and you won't always be at my bedside with Hawk watching you."

Her gulp was audible. "You are right."

"I know I am," I said softly. "But you have to ask yourself what you do want. Because we can't make the choice for you."

Her gaze flittered from me and over to the armchair where Hawk usually sat.

I could see what she was thinking—she didn't want to choose between us, which gave me hope.

As far as I knew, I was just someone she pitied. Some sad fucker who'd been thrown in jail on trumped up charges, who'd been shivved on the brink of leaving prison, and who'd been leveled like I'd been hit with a Mack truck while a girl defended me...

Yeah, I was shit hot material.

I plucked at my bottom lip as she murmured, "Why can't I have two friends?"

"You can."

She straightened a little in surprise. "Then why are you asking me this?"

"Because..." I sighed.

I didn't want to be her friend.

Well, I did. I just wanted to be more.

And I knew Hawk felt the same way.

It was in how he watched her. How he touched her, kissed her, held her hand.

Indy had told me that he worked security, and I could see that, but he wasn't eying Amara like she was a potential danger.

More like she was something precious he needed to secure, and not because he was getting paid for it either.

THIRTY-THREE

HAWK

WHEN I RETURNED with the pies, I knew something was different.

The atmosphere had changed.

But, considering the better Quin was, the cheekier he became, it didn't come as much of a surprise.

In the time I'd known him, his personality had done a complete one-eighty. The raw wildness in his eyes, even when he'd been doped up that first night we met, was to be expected from someone who was not only fresh from serving hard time, but who'd nearly died in a shiv attack.

But call me crazy, I'd sensed the same demons in Quin as the ones that haunted Nyx, ones that made any sensible man keep a wide berth from him.

In a short space of time, however, Quin had changed. I didn't think that had anything to do with the drugs he was being fed, more like it was to do with Amara. I knew that sounded whack after everything that had happened, but I was starting to believe it.

Amara was...

Magnetizing.

She wasn't aware of it, didn't seem to recognize this quality she possessed because she never tried to draw any attention to herself whatsoever, but whether she knew it or not, men saw her.

And when I said *saw*, I meant it.

Now she was eating junk food as well as Quin's dinner portions, she'd filled out properly, and when I said properly, I fucking meant *that* too.

Sweet lord, what the burgers and fries she'd been enjoying did for her shape was criminal. And I'd know, seeing as I was one.

She was like sin and candy wrapped together, making me realize that though she'd been hot before, that was nothing to now.

The taste of her on my lips was becoming a distant memory and I resented that. I resented that so goddamn much but I wasn't going to push things.

If she saw me as a friend, then…

Christ.

I wasn't sure I could deal with that.

I wasn't a fucking pussy, so, sure, I could deal with it if I had to, but the difference was, I didn't want to.

My teeth ached as I clenched them, physically rejecting the thought of simply being a friend to this marvelous woman as she eyed me, then the pizza boxes, and stated, "You were very fast."

Quin snorted, and shot me an impish look. "Sometimes fast is all you need."

I scowled at him, unsure if I liked how he was dropping sexual innuendos or if I appreciated it.

I had no idea how to raise the topic of sex with Amara. The topic of more or of any-fucking-thing with her.

Around her, I was like a tongue-tied boy again.

She wasn't my usual kind of woman.

She wasn't like any woman I'd ever fucking known.

I wanted to grab her hair and drag her into me, pull her lips to mine as my hands slipped over her luscious curves. I wanted her so goddamn badly to grind into me, to want me as much as I wanted her but...

She wasn't capable of that.

Was she?

And after what she'd endured, after the memories she spilled when she described a face, I knew I'd never be able to treat her like a regular woman I was banging. Knew she might never be able to take what I needed to give her.

At Quin's teasing, she shot him a reproachful glare, complete with lip purse as she let her fingers drift over the logo on the pizza box.

Was she committing that to memory?

She pulled back to flick the tab and sighed at the sight before her.

I'd gotten four pizzas—mushrooms, pepperoni, ham and pineapple, and a meat lovers.

There were selfish reasons for my actions.

Watching her eat was becoming my idea of porn.

She sighed with delight—making me wish I was back in the shower, my fist around my dick again—then grabbed a piece of ham and pineapple. The second it collided with her tongue, she groaned, deep in her throat, and the guttural sound had me looking away.

Fuck.

How couldn't she know what she did to me?

I cast Quin a look, and though it was weird, we shared a glance that was loaded with camaraderie—that of two men who were suffering in silence here.

Sweet fuck.

A moan escaped her, followed by a hum as she chewed. Her butt wiggled and she did a little shimmy with her hips too.

That she was enjoying her first taste of cheesy sin was clear. What was also clear? That she was giving me an erection without even fucking touching me.

Jesus wept, things were getting desperate if her eating pie could get me hard.

Turning away, I adjusted myself, then moved over to the armchair so I could cross my legs and hide my erection.

"Let me try," Quin rasped, his voice hoarse as she frowned at him.

"You said it was gross," she argued, clutching at the box like he was going to try to take it away from her.

My lips curved as he huffed. "I might have changed my mind. I haven't tried this in years."

She pouted a little but handed over a slice from the twenty-fucking-four inch pie like I'd bought her a kid's sized pizza.

When he took a bite, I knew I was feeling jealousy for the first time in my life because I was envious that he could taste what she had.

I wanted to share a lot more than saliva and pizza with her but Christ... I was desperate.

Dick aching for real now, I sat back and watched as she sampled each pizza, and with each moan and groan, I was transported to a place that was my personal heaven and hell.

"Aren't you going to eat yet?" she asked me, frowning at me.

I shook my head. "I prefer mine cold." I also preferred to watch her eat, and I also preferred for her and Quin to get their fill.

Both of them were starving, like they hadn't eaten in years. I knew prison wasn't that bad, but the way Quin scoffed down everything in sight reminded me of how I'd been at his age, always eating but never gaining any weight.

She shrugged, reaching for a piece of pineapple that had fallen off a slice and into the box, then popping it into her mouth, and I felt sure I was going to come.

She slurped the pineapple between her lips, the juicy flesh a contrast to *her* juicy flesh—lips that I wanted to drown in—and hummed again as if the flavor delighted her.

Bursting to my feet had her jumping in surprise, but even though I tried never to move suddenly in her presence because she was still very jumpy, I ripped off my cut and hoodie, stripped down to my wifebeater and fell forward onto my hands.

I ignored her shriek, knowing she'd understand when I started doing push-ups. I felt like an ass but seriously, if I didn't get this out of my system then I'd be watching her even more than I already had, and it was getting to beyond stalker levels.

I knew whenever she fucking shifted on her seat, and didn't need to monitor the movement of her eyes as well.

Amara squeaked and scampered out of my way, the pizza in her hand as she retreated to the armchair that I considered her territory and sat down to eat.

A knock sounded at the door three-hundred push-ups later, and when I didn't answer, Quin did. "Come in."

When Janie made an appearance—I recognized her bright pink Crocs with the little 'big bird' patches on them—I ignored her, just carried on.

Push-ups were getting me through this fucking nightmare, but I usually did them at the hotel. My body was aching from the five hundred I'd done back in the room, but tormenting myself by feeding Amara required more punishment.

Better that than beat off in the fucking toilet next door.

"Wow, what's the show for?" Janie purred.

"Is there a reason you're here?" Amara retorted, her tone waspish, harder than I'd probably ever heard it.

"Just for the tray," Janie replied, and I heard her surprise too. Amara barely spoke to anyone here, and never with anything other than a toneless voice.

Amara's chair squeaked as she stood, the force of her movement enough to push it back and have the feet scraping against the floor.

I heard her grab the tray, and imagined she shoved it at Janie.

"Want a slice, Janie?" Quin offered.

Amara grunted under her breath, and I saw her feet move over to the window—the place she usually stood—only her toes were pointed toward the room and not the outside world.

Was she watching me?

This hadn't been about giving her a show, just self-flagellation and an effort not to treat her like she meant nothing more to me than a sexual entity.

In the time we'd spent together, she'd become a friend, and without North, I needed friends.

It had always been me and him against the world, but without him, it was like trying to function with one lung or one fucking eye.

Bastard.

Thoughts of my twin brother made my temper surge, and I threw myself into more push-ups as Janie ummed and aahed over the pizza. I knew James Dean or Fox would be watching, didn't give a damn what they thought about why I was doing this, just knew that Amara's eyes were on me.

I knew it.

I could feel them.

Just like I'd felt them all those nights ago when I'd been showering.

Janie giggled at something Quin said, mumbling, "I like it cheesy."

Was that supposed to be a pick up line? She sounded as if she was *trying* to be coy, at any rate.

Refraining from rolling my eyes, I focused on keeping my body aligned because otherwise, I'd hurt myself, and waited for her to fuck off and the brother who was guarding the door to back away as well.

A few more giggles, some flirty mutters, and Amara grumbled something under her breath in Ukrainian.

"What, Amara?" Quin asked, his attention apparently shifting from the nurse to her.

I'd say he was trying to make her jealous but Quin was an odd duck. He could talk to himself and have a fully fleshed out conversation. He spoke with all the orderlies and the doctors and the nurses, whether they were man or woman, as if he was flirting with them.

I'd noticed that with me and Amara he was worse, though. He teased. He joked. He said inappropriate shit, and waited for our reactions, finding his amusement in how we responded.

"Nothing," Amara bit off.

Quin hummed then wheedled, "Don't tell the doctors, Janie. I can't eat this slop."

She tutted around a giggle. "Don't worry, I won't say anything. You'll have to watch it when Bellamy comes in though. She's a stickler for the rules."

"You're telling me," Quin groused, but continued, "Hawk and Amara will erase all the evidence before she comes in."

"Can I take another slice?"

"Sure," Quin offered. "Hawk looks more interested in the floor than he is in pizza."

Janie crooned, "I can see that for myself."

More mumbled Ukrainian filtered across from the window where Amara was standing, and a few minutes later, Janie trudged out, taking her pink Crocs with her.

"Is everything okay, Amara?" Quin asked, his tone of voice so innocent that I doubted he'd sounded so naive when he was five.

"Were you doing that on purpose?"

I heard her irritation, even more, I recognized her confusion.

Had she been hurting, I'd have stopped and beaten into Quin. But the confusion was good.

Satan himself knew I was confused too.

"I didn't do anything on purpose," Quin replied calmly. "She came in for the tray."

"You were—" A huff escaped her, and that was enough to make me tip my head up and locate her in the room from my position.

From her scowl, I saw she was genuinely put out. Definitely not happy with what Janie and Quin had been doing which, essentially, was nothing more than sharing a couple of slices of pizza.

The thought made me want to smile, but I withheld it.

Maybe Amara needed to be confused.

Maybe she had to be to accept that she wasn't dead from the waist down.

I knew she wanted pleasure. I knew that because she'd asked me for it, but the past was haunting her, biting at her ankles.

We'd learned, however, that Amara was strong enough to bite back.

The difference was, in this case, did she want to?

"What was I doing?" Quin asked, his tone reasonable.

She replied in Ukrainian, then hissed under her breath. "I don't know the words in English."

"I'm sure you can explain it."

I snorted out a laugh at his calm, placid tone.

"This isn't funny, Hawk!" Amara burst out. "Would you stop doing this, *this*, this whatever it is," she growled, and I knew the words weren't processing how she wanted. Not for the first time, I felt her frustration at the language barrier. "It is very distracting."

I could deal with distracting her.

"It's either watch his ass bob that way or have him head back to the hotel and jack off again," Quin said conversationally, like he was talking about the next game between the Knicks and the Celtics.

I didn't even have it in me to groan, and not because of the pushups. I'd been doing enough fucking push-ups on a daily basis not to wind me.

"Why are you talking this way today?" she demanded, and I watched her feet move over to his bedside again. "You are being strange."

"We talked about this. I told you why," he replied easily.

Quin had spoken to her about something?

I mean, of course I knew they talked, but this sounded oddly specific. I couldn't find out what those specifics were unless I listened in, and as this was starting to get interesting, I let my knees connect with the floor, then, chest heaving, twisted around to sit with my back to the wall so I could see what was happening too.

"Things will not change that much tomorrow. You will stay with us at Rachel's home, and we will—"

"We will *what*?" Quin asked quickly. "Indy said there probably isn't enough room for me at Rachel's."

"He has a point," I rasped, the weight of that truth sinking into my bones.

I hated hospitals, had done for a long time and figured that was normal—they were no one's favorite place, were they? But I liked the dynamic we had going on here.

I liked how chill it was in between the high-emotion moments where Amara would describe one of the faces from her past, as well as what she'd been through.

I hated change, but I hated the prospect of this changing more.

Why was Quin pushing this though?

He clearly wanted her for himself, but where did that leave me?

The notion had me getting to my feet and I stormed over to Amara's side, muttering, "Things will be different tomorrow, but we'll still be here for you, Amara."

She frowned at me, then stunned me by hurling herself against my chest. She didn't appear to care that I was sweaty, my undershirt a little damp, my skin gleaming with exertion, my muscles bunched and hard from what I'd been doing. Instead, she came to me, for protection. For warmth. Affection.

Ever since I'd walked into this room the other night and found her sleeping beside Quin, I'd felt like things were out of balance.

I'd felt as if I was slowly being pushed out.

But here, now, I didn't feel that way.

I felt like I was in the circle again, and I was only just realizing how badly I wanted that.

Blowing out a breath, I slipped my arms around her waist and hugged her close, needing her to know that I was here for her.

Always.

Because I was.

I didn't want to be anywhere else but with her.

The admission, even though it was only in my head, rang true, and rang hard.

I didn't want to be anywhere else but *with her.*

Here.

I released a shaky breath and tucked my face against hers. She was hiding, but I wasn't. I was just enjoying the moment. Enjoying the feel of her in my arms. Of her hiding from the world but not me.

When I cast a glance at Quin, I expected to feel triumphant, expected to see resentment, instead, I saw his glee.

Almost jerking back, I shook my head instead, mouthing, "What are you doing?"

He just smiled. "Amara, don't be a baby. Come and eat your pizza before it's cold."

She rocked her face from side to side, and though it wasn't supposed to be sexual, Christ, my skin lit up just from the feel of her lips accidentally brushing me there, the soft flesh dragging against the cotton shirt.

Feeling like a priest who'd abstained for a lifetime when, really, it was probably only six weeks since I'd last gotten laid, I knew the exact moment she felt my erection.

She tensed, turning to stone in my arms, but just as quickly, she relaxed. I half-expected her to push away from me, to pull herself free of my hug, but she didn't.

She stayed put, and somehow, I knew that was a massive step forward.

Not backward. Not sideways.

Surprised, I kept my gaze glued to Quin's, and watched as he took a large bite of pizza like the little shit knew, and, like the fucker was telling me that his work here was done.

THIRTY-FOUR

AMARA

WHEN A BLAST of cold air hit me in the face, I tucked my arm into Hawk's as we stepped through the hospital doors and I huddled against his side.

It was freezing, and while Giulia had bought me a coat on her last visit, it still tore through the heavy-duty fleece as if the chill wind was intent on grinding my bones to dust.

He jostled me a little, squeezing my hand before he pulled his arm away, then he tucked me beneath it as he curled it around my shoulder so he could drag me into him.

His heat felt good. His scent was heaven. There was the faint trace of sweat from his working out and the delicious essence from his aftershave.

As we waited at a cross-walk, he pressed his lips to my temple and graced me with a gentle kiss.

How could something so simple feel so good?

My mother and grandmother had kissed me that way. Always on the temple, never the lips as I tucked myself into their tight embrace, but Hawk didn't trigger the same feelings in me as my family did.

Hawk stirred things inside me I wasn't sure I'd ever be able to deal with.

I tensed at his side as I thought about my reaction to Janie tonight, and knew that it wasn't the first time I'd felt that flash of rage when one of the many nurses that filtered through Quin's door gave them soft looks or come-hither smiles.

I didn't trust women or men for various reasons, but I knew those smiles and those looks and viewed them with suspicion.

A client—or monster, depending on your preference—who requested to see a few girls before he made his decision for the night, would have a sample displayed for him. I'd seen so many womanly wiles mobilized against him in an effort to be chosen for the night, and I'd even taken part in it myself when a client was known not to be cruel.

When pitted against one another in a battle of survival, 'all's fair in love and war' was exactly how it worked.

The one thing I'd learned from my time as a slave and after, when I was enjoying my freedom?

To live was to be at war.

When Hawk started shuffling me across the street, I asked, "Do you like Janie?"

He stiffened a little. "The nurse?"

"Do you know more than one Janie?" I grumbled.

He shook his head, which made the lower layers of his shaggy hair brush my cheek. "No, and no."

"No and no?"

"No, I don't know another Janie—you're right. And no, I don't like her."

"She likes you," I said gruffly.

He shrugged. "Don't mean I feel the same way."

I bit my lip, because I wanted him to say that he felt that way about me, but he didn't.

I prompted, "She has big breasts."

Hawk snorted. "So?"

"Men like big breasts." I knew that to my own detriment.

"They do," he agreed, but I knew he was trying not to laugh.

Scowling, I grumbled, "Nothing is funny."

He shrugged. "If I wanted her, I'd have had her. I don't want her. I haven't had her."

"It is this easy for you?" I argued. "You click your fingers and women come?"

"In my experience, sure. Although I don't think clicking my fingers is what gets a woman off."

"You and Quin. What is it with you tonight? You are both using these phrases I recognize but don't understand." I growled. "It is like you are talking a different language."

"It's called subtext," he advised me softly. "You know what he was talking about earlier, Amara. Though he shouldn't have talked about that shit, he wasn't wrong about me jacking off when I was having a shower. If you reckon I'd jack off if Janie was willing to spread her legs, if I wanted *her*, then you're thinking all kinds of wrong shit about me."

My nostrils flared at his words. I wanted to be satisfied by them, especially as it meant that bitch hadn't gotten her claws into him, but how could I be?

It meant that if he saw someone he wanted, then he'd take them.

I bit down hard enough on my bottom lip to make my entire mouth throb with the move, but I carried on, needing that to act as a barrier, to stop the words from spilling free as they bubbled in my mouth as if I was gargling with acid.

My stomach churned at the same time, making me very aware of the fact that if I didn't say something, *anything*, I'd end up with an ulcer. I could already feel the acid in my mouth burning through my gut, intent on destroying everything in its path if I didn't spew it out—

So I let it run free.

I told him that I wanted him even though I didn't know what it was to want someone.

I told him that I hated the idea of any woman touching him. I didn't want anyone's hands on him but mine, and I wasn't even sure if I wanted *my* hands on him.

I told him that he was a bastard for confusing me, for making me think about things that weren't possible, and as I spat the words at him, my hands were flying. Wafting around my head, arms soaring as I vented. All my rage, all my *out*rage zapping through the words on the side of a busy street in New York City.

Through it all, he just stared at me.

His brow furrowed, confusion in his eyes.

"...*pizda rulu*," I rasped at the end, irritated even more by the fact he didn't understand *why* I'd be outraged.

Of course, when I heard the curse, I realized that I'd hurled all that at him in Ukrainian.

He hadn't understood a word of it.

Boday by ty kachka kopnula.

"Are you okay, little bird?" Hawk asked softly, his concern as ripe as his confusion.

My mouth twisted into a snarl, because *no*, I wasn't all right. I was anything but.

I was lost, and I'd only recently started feeling like I was *found*.

Eyes burning with tears of anger, I snarled at him, "Do I look okay?"

"No. You look pissed off, but I have no idea what you were talking about." He frowned, then attempted to reassure me, "Amara, I don't want Janie."

I raised my hands to cover my face, needing to hide from him because, at some point, he'd want someone.

It was inevitable.

It was what men did.

He reached for me, tried to hug me, to hold me, but there was no making this better. He was a man. I wasn't a woman. I was three holes to be filled... and I didn't want that anymore. Did I?

I wanted to be free.

So why didn't *this* feel like freedom?

This man, this good man, who guided me to the hotel so I could shower, who sat with me and Quin, listening to all the vileness I discussed, who made sure I was covered with a blanket when I slept, who always had food for me before I recognized I was hungry... he wasn't like the others. He didn't make me feel like three holes, but a living, breathing woman.

And that was dangerous.

He was dangerous.

With his slow smiles that made my heart race, and the gentle brush of his hand over my cheek when he thought I was asleep; with his deep brown eyes that looked at me as if I was a beautiful woman who mattered to him, and the way his fists would ball when I discussed something heinous that had happened to me...

He was too much for me, but he was the freedom I knew I craved. A freedom I wasn't sure I'd ever have.

He didn't let me hide from him, didn't let me pull away as he hugged me tight. His palm cupped the back of my head as he thrust my face into his chest, and even though everything inside me rejected the move, a move that had been used against me so many times, in this, I knew he wanted only to give me comfort. I'd had precious little of that in my life. Even when I'd been at home, I'd been a potential meal ticket, one that could take the family out of poverty...

At that moment, Hawk was as out of reach to me as the Kyiv Choreographic College, and much like my teenaged self had craved a position there, I craved him.

But Hawk wasn't out of reach. Unlike the college, he was here. Holding me. Grounding me.

I released a shuddery breath, and finally let my arms drop. I didn't just stand in his embrace. I tucked myself into him as much as he tucked himself into me, and it was then that I realized I was made up of more than three holes.

There were others. They weren't physical, but emotional, and like a jigsaw puzzle, one of those was Hawk-shaped. That, somehow, was more terrifying than anything else that had happened in the past year.

THIRTY-FIVE

QUIN

"YOU AWAKE?"

I hummed. "Yup." The slow beeps of the machines, not just in my room but in the ward in general were starting to drive me mad, and this half-darkness, half-gloom made me want to turn all the lights on, but I wasn't that selfish. Not when Amara and Hawk were in here too. "I think I might get Indy to bring me some ear plugs." Did it make me a wimp if I wanted a night light too?

I sighed because I knew she'd never let me hear the end of that.

I loved my sister but she was such a bitch sometimes.

"Why?" Hawk asked, breaking into my mental diatribe. "I'll just head to a CVS and pick some up for you."

"I don't want to disturb you."

He sniffed. "Not stopped you before."

Despite my unease in the hospital room, I grinned a little at his waspish tone. He didn't sound happy about that, but neither did he sound annoyed.

Hawk, I was coming to see, was usually grumpy but gracious, and very generous. Not just with his time, but with his money. In fact...

"Were you born first?"

Amara had told me all about Hawk and North, especially North's disappearance from West Orange.

"Yes."

Humming, I told him, "Figures."

"What does?"

"Nothing." It just explained why he was so comfortable taking charge and looking after everyone.

"Why do people say that? Say nothing when it clearly means something," he grumbled, shifting in the seat. I got it. Those chairs looked like fucking torture, but I appreciated the sacrifice, not only because he was keeping my ass safe but Amara's too. "You gonna spill or not?"

"Not," I said promptly, smirking in the semi-dark.

It was neither dark nor light in here, which put me even more on edge. It was more gloomy than anything else, as if fog had sunken down in the room like a blanket, so it hindered my night vision and my regular vision, meaning I was defenseless.

At first, my head hadn't given a shit, but fuck, I hated the dark too much for it not to bother me now I was feeling better. The concussion headache was still there, but nothing I couldn't deal with. The dark? Well, that was another matter entirely.

A soft whispery breath escaped Amara, and though I got the feeling she'd be good at pretending to be asleep when she wasn't, that sounded like a genuine sleepy sigh.

"What was your game tonight?"

It wasn't altogether surprising that Hawk's attention was exactly where mine was—her.

"Pushing her out of her comfort zone." I rolled onto my side, able to see a lump in the dim lights that was him. "She's gotten comfortable here. Tomorrow, things change. In more ways than one."

He grunted. "I wish I could deny that, but I can't."

"My wisdom always surprises everyone," I complained. "I'm a fucking under-appreciated Yoda."

"Baby Yoda," he corrected. "You ain't old enough to be the other one."

"Does that mean you think I'm cute?" I snickered when he grunted at me. "Either way, I thought it was best to prepare her. I've been wanting to do it for the last couple of days but she's been pushing herself with the drawings, you know? I didn't want to make things worse for her by keeping her unapprised of the sitch."

Hawk didn't immediately reply, but he slowly asked, "You want her, don't you?"

"Fuck yeah I do." Before I got his back up, I quickly said, "I know you want her too. Ain't no reason we can't both have her."

"She's not ready for one guy, never mind two."

Curiosity struck me. "You've been with her?"

"No. And I ain't gonna tell you what went down between us either."

I smiled. "A gentleman never tells."

"You come out with some weird shit," he said gruffly.

Maybe I did, or maybe what I'd said resonated.

"Gentlemen can wear cuts," I remarked. "I'd know. I'm a gentleman to my fucking core."

He snorted. "Yeah, really fucking chivalrous of you to talk about my bobbing ass. That was how you phrased it, wasn't it?"

"You think you're gonna be okay with her not wanting you that way?" I scoffed. "Amara ain't dead from the waist down, Hawk. She might want to think she is, but you saw what she was like tonight with Janie. All predators go into heat."

Hawk grunted. "You make out like she's some kind of feral beast."

"Isn't she? You didn't see her with that guy who attacked me." With my focus on the iPad, my mind on the drawing I was creating, and so sure that I'd be safe here, my guards had been lowered.

Pathetic.

I'd learned in jail that nowhere was safe, but Amara had tilted my world on its head. In good ways and bad.

It wasn't her fault that I relaxed around her, but that day had taught me a lesson—safety was relative whether you were on the inside or the out.

"She was just hyped up. You know how things are when you've got an adrenaline rush," he argued, shifting in his seat again like he was uncomfortable with the conversation.

But why would he be?

Didn't he already know this?

"If you think that's just adrenaline at work, you're slower than I thought, Hawk," I pshawed.

It took a long while for him to admit, "I want, for her sake, for her to try to get some normality."

"Why would you want that? Being normal sucks donkey balls."

"Maybe, but she deserves that, doesn't she? A nice home, a good man, some cute kids—"

My eyes widened. "Are you deluded? Amara ain't ready for kids. Hell, a good man would drive her insane. She doesn't need any of that, Hawk. What she needs, whether you like it or not, is us.

"She needs two guys who know the darker side of life, who'll have her back when the world goes to shit. She needs a nest, somewhere safe, but she needs to focus on finding peace.

"Peace ain't gonna be found under a roof with some squawking kids. She needs to let her rage burn off."

"She deserves more," was all he said, confirming that he was a gentleman as well as showing me he was the oldest sibling in his family rather than just telling me.

These fucking older brothers were so goddamn self-sacrificing.

Every time he looked at her, he got goo-goo eyes, yet the asswipe thought he could give her up? What a dipshit.

"Yeah, she deserves two guys, a comfortable nest, and acceptance. Not what you think she needs, but what she actually has to have without losing any more of her mind." My voice lowered. "She's one of the strongest people I've ever met, but Hawk, you've seen how fragile she is mentally."

"Yeah," he admitted after a second, his tone deep and gruff and filled with worry.

"Even though she's been focused on describing these cunts, she found some peace with us. Why don't you want her to have more of that?"

"It's not that I don't—"

I didn't let him finish. "That's why I pushed things tonight, because I know you're too much of a martyr to recognize the truth. You want her, so do I. We work well together where she's concerned. She runs to you for some things, comes to me for others. We can make this work."

I heard the passion in my voice and was concerned it came across as fucking desperate, but, in a way, I guessed I was. For Amara. She needed this, *us*, but if Hawk wasn't on board... well, it was a non-starter.

His tone was grim as he said, "You say I'm putting things on her, but what about you? I'm telling you, she ain't ready to have us that way. As friends, it's one thing—"

"She wouldn't have bitten off Janie's face tonight if she didn't have feelings for us. Just be patient, man. You heard her grumbling away in Ukrainian. Fuck, I wish I spoke the language so I knew what she was saying.

"Either way, Rome wasn't built in a day, but look what happened when it came together—a cradle of modern civilization."

"Wasn't that Greece?"

"Maybe. Who the fuck cares? You know I'm right, Hawk. I know you do."

He was silent for so long that he could have fallen asleep for all I knew, then, just as I was about to drift away in the Sandman's creepy arms, he argued, his voice soft but raspy, "We don't rush her. We be what she needs. We let her decide the pace. You in agreement?"

If it meant that my sky girl would have her wings, I'd have signed my soul over to *Otesho* himself.

Which made it easy to say, "I agree."

THIRTY-SIX

AMARA

THE 'WELCOME HOME' committee waiting for Quin charmed me.

This was what it was like to be a part of a family.

I hadn't been a part of one for so long that I had almost forgotten what it felt like to have people care for me, aside from Sarah.

She was the only family I'd had in too long, and she wasn't really family. We were bound by a shared misery, a sisterly affection that came from knowing the same things and experiencing the same hurts. Yet, for no other woman would I have put myself out there, would I have allowed myself to be in danger, and that was, I thought, a form of family.

Quin was embraced like a soldier coming home from battle, and I hung back, confused over my place now.

Things had been so simple in the hospital.

Just last night, I had known what to do, where to sit, what to talk about.

Hawk had been there, but he'd have to return to work soon, and I knew he worked in the club-owned strip joint.

As he started to heal, Quin would move on with his life too. I knew he intended on working with Indy in her tattoo parlor. Would he meet someone there? Someone normal? As their friend, like I claimed I wanted to be, what would I do? Just watch from the sidelines? See them get together with other women?

Women who weren't me?

The thought triggered a pain inside me that was like being stabbed in the gut.

I had no right to either of these men, and yet, I wanted rights.

Last night, seeing Janie drool over both of them had triggered something in me I didn't know I was capable of—*possessiveness*.

Not the friendliest of characteristics.

Plus, for a woman who had been owned, I shouldn't want to own someone else—even if it was only figuratively.

And two men?

How ridiculous was I?

They weren't mine. I wasn't theirs.

Yet I'd heard them talking last night. I knew what their intentions were, and as much as I wanted that, I wasn't sure if I could cope. If I'd be able to unlock that part of me.

Just the thought had me biting my lip, and instead of focusing on something I wasn't sure I could change, I watched Nyx embrace Quin long and hard, in fact, so long and so hard that I felt the real emotion in the hug.

I'd come to learn that Quin was quite the joker. At first, I hadn't sensed that in him, but over our time in the hospital together, that part of him had been revealed to me.

I half-expected him to tease Nyx out of whatever it was that had him hugging his brother for this amount of time, but it seemed both needed it.

Nyx was a hard man.

Quin wasn't, but I knew he'd had to pretend to be.

He'd been forced to. His will taken from him. We both knew what that felt like.

Did he finally feel safe?

Back in the bosom of his family?

I hoped, for his sake, he did.

And found myself envious that he had that. Not in a begrudging way, just a wistful one.

A hand slipped around the back of my neck, and for a second, I froze. My brain kicked into gear, tensing up my body as I expected to be shoved to the floor, forced to do only God knew what, to suck and fuck and...

Then I released a shaky breath.

Hawk.

He squeezed me there slightly, just with the tips of his fingers in a soft salute of welcome.

He didn't grab my hair and force me to deepthroat his *khuy*. He didn't slam me into the car fender and fuck me over it.

He didn't hurt me.

A shaky breath escaped me as I expelled the thought.

No one would ever do that to me again.

No one.

Not unless I wanted it.

My body finally unfreezing, I tilted my head to look up at him, and saw he was grinning at something Giulia had said. His hand moved down to my shoulder, his arm sliding around me, drawing me toward him.

It was so uncomplicated for him.

So easy.

For me, it was a minefield.

He hadn't meant to frighten me. Didn't even realize he had.

My jaw tensed with resentment at my inbuilt defense system that was sabotaging me.

"Got news for you."

I blinked, then realized the voice came from below—Lodestar, in her wheelchair.

She shoved something at me.

A newspaper.

I frowned as I saw the headline, my eyes flaring wide before a deep satisfaction surged inside me.

It boomed out of nowhere, my resentment over my past fading, joy over what I was seeing flooding me.

Jason Young in handcuffs.

Seeing him triggered a strange cocktail of emotions inside me. Hatred and rage, bitterness as the memories threatened to bubble over like a volcano that was ready to blow. Then a sweet joy overtook that as I saw the house I'd been jailed in. The door wide open, his *pizda* of a wife watching on with surprise in her eyes, trepidation in the slack lines of her mouth.

"What will happen to him?"

"I don't know," Lodestar replied, her head tipped to the side as we watched brother after brother make an appearance, each one slapping Quin and, as he called it, 'shooting the shit' with him.

"You don't think he'll stay in prison?"

"I think his wife is rich enough to pay for very good lawyers."

My contentment faded. "Oh."

She smirked up at me. "Don't worry. He'll die before he takes a single step out of a jail cell."

My brow puckered. "You can promise this?"

"I can fucking guarantee it better than Bed, Bath & Beyond."

I blinked. "Good."

She dipped her chin. "You keep those images rolling in, yeah? You and Quin?"

I wasn't about to argue with something that would push us together.

"Of course. They are helping?"

She beamed at me. "Very much. Faces and names, they've been so difficult to pin down until now. Until you." Her eyes flared wide, a strange emotion burning in them... "Who'd have thought that one of their cum sluts would be their downfall?"

The harsh words might have stung, but I knew she'd gone through what I had. Giulia had told us that a while ago.

Plus... I had to be less touchy.

Quin had shown me that last night.

"Satisfying, isn't it?" Lodestar continued.

"Very," I murmured. "What are you going to be doing with the people you have identified?"

"I'm putting feelers out."

"What does this mean?"

"It means," Hawk interrupted, making *me* aware of just how aware *he* was of me. "That she's trying to see who would be most interested."

"As far as I can see, Amara don't need no translator."

Lodestar's waspish tone didn't faze Hawk. "She struggles with some words."

Lodestar sniffed. "I can explain English as well as you."

Hawk just rolled his eyes.

"What are you waiting for?" I queried, trying to get the conversation back on track.

"The right journalist."

"Why?"

"Because we're going big or we're going home, Amara." At my frown, she sighed. "I mean, when I drop this news, it's going to be like splatting a whale in a swimming pool. I want to make waves."

What a strange woman she was.

"And finding the right journalist will do this?"

She shrugged. "Yes. Of course."

"Will you tell me when you pick one?"

"If you want to know."

"I do. I *need* to know."

Maybe she heard that need in my voice because she nodded slowly. "I should have kept you in the loop this week. Sorry."

I shook my head. "No. I was busy with Quin. It is fine. But things are different now." There was that word again. Different.

The question was, how different?

"I'll keep you updated." She winked at me. "I'm looking forward to your next picture."

As she wheeled herself away, Hawk muttered, "She wouldn't be if she knew what you went through as you described them."

I looked up at him and said, "It's worth it."

"It's painful to hear, so I can't imagine what you feel like having to actually describe it."

I shrugged, repeated, "It's worth it."

"He's moving onto a place on the compound."

I blinked. "Quin is?"

Hawk nodded. "Giulia just confirmed it for me. Nyx wanted him here, but Rex served some time when he was Quin's age. Vetoed it. Said that he needed some space."

I bit my lip.

The compound was just down the road. A comfortable walk away, so why did that feel so far?

"Storm, Keira and Cyan left last week as well, little bird. Just thought you should know."

So many changes...

I studied Quin, and picked up on what no one else seemed to— the strain around his eyes.

Maybe Rex was right.

Maybe being in a house full of people would be too much for him.

"He didn't get stressed with us around."

"No. But we're not a house full of people. We were quiet as well. It wasn't like we were the talkers in that hospital room," he said, deadpan.

Even though I didn't feel like smiling, I couldn't help it. He was right. Quin talked. A lot.

With my focus on Quin, it took me a few seconds to realize that Nyx had moved around the side of the crowd that had gathered in front of Rachel's place, and had made his way to my side.

I only knew that because he murmured, "I'm not sure what you two did to him, but I'm glad you did it."

Hawk's arm tightened around me, and he grumbled, "Didn't do anything to him."

"If you'd seen him that last time in Rikers, you'd know the difference." Nyx's voice was gruff. "I mean, I know freedom tastes good for anyone, but he was... Nah, you did something. I don't know what, but he's the same dipshit little fucker as always."

I frowned. "Is that supposed to be a compliment?"

Nyx cackled. "No need to get defensive on his behalf, Amara."

I wasn't. Was I?

Frowning harder, I told him, "Quin isn't a dipshit little fucker."

Hawk chuckled. "You didn't think that last night."

Nyx arched a brow. "What did he do?"

"Nothing in particular. He's just a shit stirrer."

Nyx snorted. "Sounds about right."

"He's getting tired," I told him, disgruntled by the conversation and disgruntled by Nyx's opinion of Quin. "You should take him to his place. He isn't used to all this."

Nyx hummed under his breath. "He does look tired."

"He's still in need of rest."

"Isn't like he's doing a ten-hour shift," Nyx grumbled, but he started to walk off.

Before he could, I asked, "Quin told me Indy had an interview for a TV program."

Nyx paused, turned back to look at me. "Yes. She did."

"Did it go well?"

"Ask her yourself," Nyx retorted, and when I scowled at him, he grinned.

The sight was almost disturbing.

I wasn't used to him smiling.

Was he that happy to see his brother?

"I'll get jealous if he bestows any more of those on you," Giulia muttered at my side, causing me to shoot her a glance. "His smiles belong to me."

"I didn't ask him to," I muttered waspishly. "Why was he smiling, anyway?"

"Because he finds you amusing."

My eyes widened. "Me?"

"Yes," she confirmed dryly.

"But why?"

"Because you spent so long hiding, and the second you stopped, you killed a guy, almost killed another, and are singlehandedly helping us bring down our enemies."

"It isn't singlehanded."

She arched a brow. "Quin's drawing—"

"No. Hawk and Quin help me." At her frown, I muttered, "They listen. I need that."

Hawk had settled his hand on the ball of my shoulder, and he squeezed me gently as Giulia said, "Well, okay, whatever. I mean, Nyx doesn't know that. He just thinks you're kickass."

I bit my lip. "I'm the opposite."

Why was I arguing?

Giulia had been...

I sighed.

I'd had strange feelings for Giulia since the beginning. She looked after us, knew stuff that no one else did, fed us, helped heal us, stuck by us while we were pains in the asses on the road to recovery. But through it all, I'd never forget that day when we were in the woods, and she helped clean us up, trying to make us human so she could drive us home.

If I tried, I could even remember the songs on the radio that day as she drove us to West Orange...

My throat choked at the memories, and I turned away from her, for some strange reason needing to find Quin, who, I saw, was looking straight at me.

His eyes were drooping with fatigue, and his shoulders weren't as straight, his spine a little curved like standing up was too much for him, but as he looked at me, as he watched me watch him, I knew all he saw was my sadness, how mixed up I felt inside.

I blew out a breath and, to Giulia, said, "I guess I *am* a little kickass."

"You bet you are." When she elbowed me in the side, carefully, not to hurt, she murmured, "We've got a place for you on the Posse when you're ready by the way."

I frowned, surprised by the offer, especially when I'd been one of the Posse's targets.

"Is it true you broke every single one of Tink's bones in both hands and wrists?"

"And a lot more," Giulia confirmed.

"I shall think about it."

I'd have said yes, but Hawk had been the one to out the fact that I had a crush on Giulia, and she'd been acting weird around me ever since. With the glance we shared, however, I saw her acceptance, and saw, also, that when she let her gaze drift between Hawk and Quin, a smile danced on her lips.

As she leaned into me, those same lips brushing my cheek in a way that would have made my heart pound a month ago, said heart almost stopped as she whispered, "You go, girl."

I had no idea what that meant, and couldn't ask her as she moved away, strolling over to Nyx's side like she was on a catwalk, so confident in herself, in her place at Nyx's side, in her position in the MC, whereas I felt the opposite.

"Go where?" I whispered to myself.

Hawk hummed. "Huh?"

I peered up at him. "She told me to go, girl."

He blinked, and I noticed exactly how long his eyelashes were.

Unable to stop myself, I reached up and touched the crest of his cheek, the bones so high that I felt the sharpness against my thumb.

He tensed, then smiled, his eyes twinkling like he was happy I'd touched him.

I nibbled on the plump part of my lip, right at the back, not wanting him to notice, to see how torn up I felt inside.

Quin was over there.

Hawk was here.

I felt like I was in the middle of something I didn't understand, something I didn't need to understand, but that simply was.

It existed.

I hadn't really done anything to make it so, but it was.

I thought of the sky girl Quin likened me to, brought to the earth, taken away from the monsters of the past by birds of prey who were at the top of the food chain, and I felt oddly tethered and free.

Like I could fly with them.

Only with them.

"What did she say?"

I realized Hawk had repeated that twice now, and I blinked at him, "She said, 'You go, girl.'"

He laughed. "It's just a saying. It means go for it."

"Go for what?"

His lips twisted. "Well, it depends on what you were talking about?"

"Nyx thinking I'm kickass."

"High praise," he said wryly.

"I guess." Dismissing that, I told him, "Quin's tired, Hawk. I am too."

"What do you want to do?"

I swallowed, feeling like I was at a crossroads.

I wasn't dumb.

I'd been involved in sex acts that'd make the Devil himself blush.

I'd done things I was ashamed of.

I'd been in orgies, and all kinds of scenes that I wished I could erase from my mind.

Two men could be with a woman for sex.

But Quin and Hawk...

I wanted more than that.

Did they?

How could they?

It wasn't normal.

And if they did want that, was it because they thought I was a slut?

Who was I kidding? I was.

A dirty—

"Amara? Will you come to my new place?"

Stunned to find Quin there, right in front of me, I jumped. Angry at myself for overreacting, I reached up, much as I had done with Hawk, and rubbed the line of his jaw.

Closer, he was even more tired than I thought.

I saw the strain in his eyes, the shadows beneath them, and murmured, "Of course I will." To Hawk, I asked, "Will you drive us?"

He nodded. "Sure."

"Okay, guys, I need to get some sleep. I'm fucked," Quin boomed out with a chuckle that everyone else believed, but I knew was contrived.

"The bunkhouse key's under the mat," Rex told Hawk as Quin was patted on the shoulder some more as he returned to the truck and hefted himself into the back of it.

"Well, that ain't a security nightmare, is it?" Hawk asked dryly.

"Nah, Steel and Stone only moved out this morning."

"Where are they living?"

"He got them a place near the hospital so she can walk home if she has a break."

Hawk nodded, and his arm tightened around me as he started to move us forward, shifting us nearer to the truck.

Rex came with us though, murmuring, "Thank you, Amara."

I shrugged. "We're working toward the same goal."

But Rex only shook his head. Before I could ask him what was wrong, Link grabbed him and they started discussing something I had no interest in knowing.

Hawk deposited me at the passenger side of the truck, before he walked around to the driver's.

The second the door closed behind me, Quin rasped, "God, I'm tired."

"I could tell," I told him softly. "Not long. We'll get you settled."

He sighed. "I doubt that."

Hawk pulled open the door and hopped in. A lot of hands clapped on the truck as he backed out of the yard and onto the road that ran all the way up the hill behind Rachel's property.

He drove down it though, heading toward the clubhouse.

"It'll be noisy through the day because of the construction work," Hawk groused. "I'm not sure this is a good idea for you to move in here."

"Nothing's noisier than a prison," was all Quin said. "I just want my bed."

I felt that, and I knew what he meant.

After ten days of sitting beside a bed, not in one, I was ready for a nap as well.

Yawning as we trundled along, I appreciated the quietness of the cab. Even Quin wasn't chatting away like usual, and I knew we were all feeling the pinch of the last few days, especially after sleeping in the armchairs for as long as Hawk and I had.

Once Hawk drove through the compound gates, along the driveway, Quin rasped, "Christ, it's good to be home."

"Not long until the clubhouse structure is complete. We should be back inside soon."

I blinked, then bit my lip.

Would they be living in?

Would they... the clubwhores would be back, wouldn't they? They could fuck them.

Anytime, anywhere, any day.

My stomach churned at the thought.

"It's going to be bigger than before?"

"Yeah. Space was getting tight, plus Giulia petitioned for, and didn't lose, the request for two bars."

"Two bars?" Quin asked, sounding sleepy.

Hawk chuckled. "One for where the Old Ladies can sit, and one where the brothers can go and fuck the clubwhores."

Quin snorted, but didn't reply. In fact, he didn't say anything until we were out of the truck, and Hawk was dipping down to grab the key from beneath the welcome mat.

Inwardly, I sighed at the sight of his ass as he bent down to scoop up the keys, then when he let us in, Quin mumbled, "Jesus, this is all for me?"

I'd slept in one of these bunkhouses for a while, a bigger one, but this was a lot nicer. Where I'd been, it had been decorated like we were still in the sixties, whereas this was modern and fresh. It also smelled good.

There was no construction noise because I thought most of the brothers had been at Rachel's to greet Quin, but I knew the thud-thud of the diggers and machinery would judder through the foundations. Enough to exacerbate the concussion headache the doctor said he might have for a while.

Quin didn't complain about that but he didn't really complain about much, period.

The thought had my brow furrowing with concern, especially when I thought back to the scene at Rachel's place.

He'd looked like he was the life of the party. Grinning, exuberant. Only telling me that he was tired once we were alone, only showing it on his face with me being the singular person who noticed.

I wasn't sure why that distressed me, but it did.

I stuck close to his side as we moved past a very comfortable-looking sectional with a massive TV in front of it. There was a single step that separated the kitchen from the living room, like it was on a platform, and as Quin clambered over it, I turned to spot the infinitesimal whisper of pain crossing his features.

He was hurting.

He just wasn't saying anything about it.

What else didn't he say anything about?

I bit my lip as I shuffled forward into the bedroom, aware of how much I didn't know about this man. *Korva,* these men. It didn't frighten me though, more intrigued me.

The room was quietly feminine, a little like Stone, really. Small touches of color in a very blank white space. They hadn't stripped it free of furnishings, though, so I figured they were getting new stuff for their place.

It took a second for me to realize that Hawk wasn't with us, which made sense seeing as we weren't in a hospital room anymore.

Should I have not come in either?

God, this uncertainty was driving me crazy.

I clenched my fists at my sides, then when I looked at Quin once more, and saw his fatigue, that was when I knew I'd done the right thing by coming in with him.

Clearing my throat, I waited for him to join me at the side of the bed, and asked, "Do you need help getting changed?"

The Quin I'd grown accustomed to over the past ten days would have joked with me. Especially this newer Quin, the one who teased me mercilessly, like the hit to his head had liberated a bawdy sense of humor that he didn't want to control. Only, he didn't tease me. He just sighed, and that sigh broke my heart.

"Would you mind?" he asked drowsily.

I found it odd that I didn't. Mind, that is. I wouldn't have offered if I did, but I knew, as with Hawk, that he wouldn't hurt me.

That he'd hurt himself first.

The confidence in them, the trust, was small, only a kernel of a seed, but I knew it would take root.

I had faith that it would, even if the belief was enough to steal my breath.

I didn't reply, just worked on stripping him down.

He wore his cut, something James Dean had given him this morning. When he'd passed it over, it was like he was handing the crown jewels to him. Next came a hoodie, followed by a tee shirt and a wifebeater. Every time he had to raise his arms, he grimaced, grunted, shifted on his feet, stepping from side to side like he was pulling on his wound but the bandages were clean, so he wasn't doing himself any real damage.

By the time the wifebeater was on the bed, he had a few beads of sweat dotted on his temples and above his lips.

I reached up and murmured, "Do you need some pain medication?" as I brushed those beads of sweat away.

He closed his eyes, tipped his head to the side so I took some of the weight, triggering a connection that staggered me.

I almost gulped at the trust he showed in me.

He had faith in me too.

He hadn't shown weakness to anyone else, not even to Hawk, but to me, he did.

I knew that meant a lot. These men were all so ridiculously overmasculine, swaggering around like they were John Wayne on bikes.

"I'm just tired," he rasped. "I don't want to get hooked on that shit. I just got out of one jail, don't want to get stuck in another."

"Are they addictive?"

His mouth tightened. "Everything is."

I didn't argue but made a mental note to ask Stone if there was a problem, and if I had to force-feed him the *chyort* meds, I would if he was going to be stupidly stubborn about it.

"It's okay to leave my jeans on, sky girl," he said tiredly. "I don't want to make you uncomfortable."

The ridiculousness of the situation hit me then.

He was wobbling on his feet.

Half asleep.

Eyes half-mast.

Body trembling with fatigue.

How could I be uncomfortable?

But I knew that if it was anyone else, not Hawk, but some other guy, I'd have been uncomfortable.

Even the weakest-looking man had strength...

I clucked my tongue like he was being silly, when he was uncomfortably accurate in his belief, and reached for his belt buckle.

The last time I'd done this, the man had whipped me with it. I knew I had scars on my ass from where the buckle had torn into my flesh.

But unlike before, the memory didn't settle like a heavy weight in my gut. It whispered away, the *suka's* face flashing in front of my eyes so that I could have Quin draw him later, and I shrugged it off.

That was the past.

This was the present.

Quin was my present.

Hawk too.

I bit the inside of my lip once more as I tugged the belt out of the loops, and then reached for his fly.

I had a feeling he was waiting to see how far I'd take this, and because I was tired of being stupid, when I wasn't weak anymore, I got on with it.

Dragging them down to his upper thighs, I straightened, saw his eyes were closed, and concern for him hit me, enough that I leaned over and shoved them to his calves.

When I stood again, I half expected for him to make a joke, for him to tease me, but he didn't. His eyes were closed, and a little like with Hawk, I noticed how long his lashes were. But these had a slight curl to them. I doubted he'd applied mascara before he left the hospital, so the curl was natural. Envy-inspiring too.

A smile danced on my lips at the prospect of him putting on make-up, because these guys were all like the aforementioned John Wayne on bikes instead of horses, and I murmured, "Quin? Take my hands."

His lashes fluttered, his eyes dazed which told me this was genuine and not a way for him to get me comfortable with him being half-naked—I wouldn't put it past him.

"Huh?"

"We need to get you into bed."

I settled my weight on my heels, then leaned back so that I could take more of the strain as he let me help him onto the mattress.

When he was there, he plunked backwards, his spine connecting with the bed in a way that had to hurt his injuries, and I quickly pulled off his sneakers then his jeans, and was left with an already sleeping Quin.

Surprised, and a lot worried, I heaved a sigh and made a cocoon of the covers with him inside it, wrapping him up so he'd stay warm.

He didn't look overly pale, so I had to think the morning had just tired him.

Biting my lip once I was done, unsure if I should get Hawk to put him in bed properly, I took a step back and had to smile.

Quin always did that.

He always managed to make me smile even if I was concerned.

He was swaddled like a baby, his face the only thing peeping out from amid the covers.

Goodness, he was beautiful.

His skin was so richly coppery that it made my fingers ache with the need to touch him. His hair, short and black, unforgiving in its straightness, offset his coloring, making him even more beautiful.

With those long lashes brushing his cheekbones, his tan lips barely parted in sleep, he was... tactile.

He made me want to touch him.

Made me want to have the right to touch him.

I walked away because I didn't have that right, not yet and maybe not ever, not unless I was willing to take the right for myself, and when I moved into the kitchen, I found Hawk there.

The TV was on, some basketball game playing, and he was making himself a sandwich at the table, where, I realized, there was the tiniest Christmas tree I'd ever seen. It was just under a ruler in length, and had been dusted with what looked like snow. It was so cute.

"Do you want mayo on yours?" he asked.

Still focused on how damn cute the little tree was, I blinked. "On my what?"

He grinned. "Sandwich. Cheese and tomato. Not gourmet or fancy, but it's good."

"No mayo, thank you," I said thickly, glancing around the room and wondering how to phrase this... "Quin fell asleep standing up."

Hawk shrugged. "He did too much. It's the first time he's been on his feet that long for a while as well." His smile was gentle, and it hit his eyes. "He'll be fine. You want to spend the night here?"

I did. How did he know that? "Yes. I think it's best."

He hummed as he slapped the bread on the sandwiches he'd made. He put one onto a plate, passed it to me, then after he took a massive bite of his own, murmured, "I can go back to Rachel's—" My heart, stupidly, sank. "—grab some of your stuff that you might need. I need some more clothes to be honest as well. I can bring a few days' worth of gear over." My heart soared.

He wasn't going to leave.

Relief had me reaching for the sandwich and taking a bite to hide my shaky smile.

"That would be good. I need to do laundry. I can do that later on when he's awake though." My lips twisted. "I'll do yours as well if you like."

He grinned. "I won't say no."

"I'll bet," I teased, feeling oddly buoyant, lighter, *happy*.

The sensations were strange, odd, but good.

Great, even.

As I made my way to the sofa, a soft noise outside hit my ears.

It was only faint. The tiniest of sounds, and I moved over to the door, curious as to what it was considering the compound was clear.

Hawk had locked it, but I opened it as he asked, "Where are you going?"

I shrugged. "Can't you hear that?"

"The game?"

I shook my head, then jumped when the door opened and I found three cats standing there.

Each of them meowed at me, one of them hissing a little as if they were asking what had taken so long for me to let them in.

Then, before I could shut them out, they charged in, surging forward.

"What the fuck?" Hawk bit off, and I watched him try to grab one, get scratched for his pains, only for the trio of cats to push onward toward the door.

I'd never seen anything like it.

Ever.

I'd closed Quin's door too, leaving it ajar just in case he called out, but they pushed into it.

That had me running to stop them, but when I reached the doorway, they'd already made their move.

Curled up in tight balls, the three cats had settled around him. One on his belly, two either side of his head.

"What the hell?" Hawk breathed in my ear, clearly seeing what I was.

Too surprised to even jump at his sudden proximity, I whispered, "Do we move them?"

He grunted. "Not if we don't want more bloodshed."

I cast a look at the arm he was peering down at, and winced at the sight of the scratch.

"Jesus," he muttered. "That stings."

Four perfect lines scored the back of his forearm, deep enough for blood to flow from the cuts.

"I'll clean it," I offered, but hesitating, I asked, "What if they're dirty?"

"Well, I ain't ever seen any cats around here so they have to be strays," he pointed out.

He was right.

I'd been here a while and I'd never seen any animals around this place.

Where had they come from?

"I'll ask Giulia if he has any pets."

Uncomfortable with leaving bug-ridden animals with a man who really didn't need to get an infection, I stepped into the room and found the tabby on his stomach glaring at me, her teeth on display as if she was telling me to back off.

"You win this round," I muttered in Ukrainian, then retreated to the kitchen, leaving the door ajar again so they could leave if they wanted, and moving over to the counter to grab a dish so I could fill it with water.

I placed it on the floor by the door for them to drink—I didn't like them being in here but I knew what dehydration felt like and wished it on no one—then moved into the bathroom and looked in the medicine cabinet.

Seeing some alcohol wipes and bandages, I grabbed them, then returned to the kitchen.

Hawk was twisting his arm back so he could see the scratches, grumbling, "Where did the fucking cats even come from?"

For a second, I thought he was talking to me, then I realized he was on the phone.

I gently grabbed his arm and gestured at the dining chair. He heaved a sigh but sat down, only wincing when I began cleaning up the cuts and doctoring him.

"Tell Nyx he's a fucker for not warning us," Hawk retorted.

I could hear Giulia laugh, and found my own lips twitching. She had one of those infectious laughs, which made sense. Everything about her was aggressive, even her laughter.

"It's not funny, Giulia. What do you mean he's an animal whisperer?"

"How the fuck do I know?" Giulia countered, her grumble loud and clear now Hawk switched her to speaker. "Nyx just called it that. Not me."

"What happened?" Nyx called out.

"Three cats were waiting at the door to be let in. They didn't even wait, just came in like they were the fucking English at Bunker Hill, and jumped onto the bed to sleep with him."

Nyx snorted. "Little fucker ain't lost his touch."

"What do you mean?" I asked softly.

"He came back from Quebec and was like Dr. goddamn Doolittle. I swear, he's always got animals around him. It's a fucking nuisance."

"You're telling me," Hawk muttered grumpily, hissing as I poured more alcohol onto his wounds. "So, they're strays then?"

"Yep. They're probably pregnant or something. He always gets them. Birds with broken wings, sick dogs, even had a gecko once that had lost an eye."

"So they're not his pets?"

There was a shrug in Nyx's voice. "Depends on your definition of the word 'pet.'"

"Didn't know it was a complicated word," Hawk rumbled. "So, we need to get used to animals all over the place. Great."

"Hardly," Giulia retorted, before her voice turned sly. "Ain't you just dropping him off?"

"He was very tired," I said softly. "I don't feel comfortable leaving him."

"Well, Hawk doesn't have to—"

"I'm staying as well," Hawk said gruffly.

Silence sounded on the line, before Giulia murmured, "Do you need me to bring you some clothes?"

"It's only a short drive away."

"Best not to disturb Quin if he's sleeping," Nyx agreed. I heard a smacking sound that was like a kiss rather than a slap. "Thanks, babe."

"Does this get me out of the shit for Tink?"

Nyx snorted. "Nope."

She huffed. "We got the information we needed—"

Hawk grunted. "Before you get into a fight, can I put in a request?"

"Sure," Giulia grumbled. "If you want me to shove it up your ass."

Hawk smirked. "I wouldn't dare then." He cut the call, and shot me a look. "I put nothing past Giulia," he teased.

"Me either," I said, only I wasn't joking.

I truly wouldn't.

"She invited you into the Posse, didn't she?" Hawk asked, tipping his head to the side as I wrapped a bandage around his arm.

"She did," I confirmed.

"Will you join?"

"Maybe. I'm not good in groups."

"They're not your average group," he said dryly.

"You think I should? Join, I mean?"

Hawk shrugged. "Might be good for you." His lips twisted. "Be a good reason for you to stick around as well."

Surprise had my mouth gaping. "Where did you think I was going?"

"I don't know. You were going to leave before. I'd prefer if you didn't now."

"Why?" I whispered, my gaze pinned to his.

He heaved a sigh, then let his free hand slide to cover my wrist. "Don't you know, Amara? Really?"

"We're friends—"

"We are," he agreed. "And that's fine."

Somehow, I didn't believe him.

"You would—" This was it. For a second, my brain froze, then I whispered, "Hawk?"

"Yeah?"

I reached up and pressed a hand to my chest. "I feel."

"You feel?"

Nodding, I muttered, "I feel. A lot. I didn't used to. I didn't..."

"But you do now?"

"Yes. For you," I whispered, then I tacked on the unthinkable. "And for Quin."

His smile was soft, gentle, amused. "Little bird, you don't think I figured that out already?"

I winced. "This is bad, isn't it? I barely know you."

"We know enough. We know the worst of each other." Hawk grabbed my hand as I jerked to my feet, and stopped me from moving away. "You don't have to fly away, little bird."

"I'm a whore," I cried. "I'm what they said—"

He scowled at me, surging to his feet as well. As he loomed over me, I realized that I didn't cower, I didn't fall back in fear.

"You're not a whore," he snapped. "You're fucking perfect. Don't you get that? I told you that already. You're the most beautiful woman I've ever fucking seen, and it's more than your looks. It's your goddamn heart." His nostrils flared. "I want it for my own, Amara. I want to own it, own you. I want you fucking period. Everything you have to give and more, but..." His head jerked to the side, his neck cracking with the movement. "I know you're different. You ain't a whore," he barked, like he knew what I was going to say. "You're fucking perfect. You're you, little bird. That's who I want."

"A woman doesn't want two men."

He squinted at me. "I don't like to bring other women into this, but North and I fucked dozens of bitches who'd disagree."

My eyes flared wide. "You slept with your brother?"

"I wasn't interested in his dick." He snorted. "That was sex though," he grumbled. "I don't think this would be."

"You don't want to sleep with me?"

He hissed under his breath. "If you were anyone else, I'd grab your hand and make you *feel* how much I want to sleep with you, Amara." He reached up and ran a hand through his hair. "All the usual shit I'd do, I can't. I can't treat you like I would another woman, not only because you ain't like them, but because of your past." He blew out a breath. "I want to kiss you, fuck your mouth like I want to fuck your body. I want you on your knees, your back, on top of me. Any which fucking way I can get you.

"I want your pussy on my face, on my fingers. I want to fuck you in every position under the sun, and..." His gaze jerked to the wall that separated the kitchen from the bedroom. "...I'm pretty sure that's what Quin wants too. I have no problem with sharing you so long as you're okay with that."

Heart in my throat, I rasped, "I want all that."

He shook his head. "I'm not pushing my desires on you—"

I reached up and pressed my fingers against his lips. "I'm not saying I can do all that, but I can want it. Wish for it."

He grabbed my wrist, but rather than lower it and my hand, he kissed my palm, then shifted it to the side and whispered, "You don't have to wish for something that's freely offered."

"I might not be able to—"

"We can take it slowly."

My face crumpled as I closed my eyes, but the desire to be normal, to want these odd feelings inside me to be allowed out, to be free, overwhelmed me. A lifetime of feeling like I was locked up was something I couldn't stand.

Sometimes, a jail cell didn't have to have bars to keep you locked inside. Sometimes, we were capable of doing that to ourselves.

I jerked back and raised my hands to cover my face but it wasn't because I was upset, wasn't because I was scared, it was because I was furious.

So mad, so goddamn mad.

"They took this from me," I rasped, throwing my hands down like they were scalding hot. I glared at him, but my anger was aimed anywhere other than him.

They'd taken so much, and I couldn't let them take this too.

The anger was healing rather than destructive.

Anger was good.

Anger made me strong.

Made me anything other than a victim.

It made me the survivor.

And I wanted to do more than survive—I wanted to *khuy* live.

Hawk started to speak, started to say something, but I wasn't interested.

He'd told me what I needed to know.

He didn't think I was a whore.

He thought I was beautiful.

He accepted that I had feelings for Quin.

He knew the worst things men and women had done to me.

He accepted *me*.

And as tears burned in my eyes, tears that felt like acid, that blurred my vision and broke me, I knew that the reason he accepted all of those things was because he wanted Amara.

The woman standing here.

The broken woman who was fighting back.

The sex slave who was bringing down a network of corrupt officials.

The child who'd been ripped from her life and who was determined to make a future for herself.

That was who he wanted.

Me.

Flaws and all.

Which made it so easy to move into him, to step onto my tiptoes and to bring our lips together.

To make that first step.

To him.

Forever, him.

THIRTY-SEVEN

HAWK

I GENUINELY THOUGHT she was going to back away. Back off. Hell, run off.

Not dissimilar from the little bird I'd likened her to, I was half certain she was going to fly away. Flutter far from me because I scared her. Because my needs, my desires, my urges scared her.

Truthfully, when she'd started to cry, I felt as if I could bawl too.

I'd pushed it. Pushed her.

Too much. Too far. Too soon. Too fast.

I'd been the one warning Quin about rushing her, but I was the one blowing it.

Then, she bound us together in more ways than she'd ever understand.

I knew, right then, right there, I was irrevocably hers.

In the face of her bravery, her strength, her fierce will, how couldn't I be decimated?

How couldn't I be hers when *she* claimed me?

Fear had me holding back, not wanting to scare her, not wanting to overwhelm her, but she was the aggressor. Not at all what I expected, not at all what I thought I'd ever need, but fuck, the way she went after what she wanted, how she took it, inflamed me.

I reached up and cupped her cheeks, stopping before my palms could connect just in case someone had hurt her that way before. She seemed to feel the heat of my hovering hands, though, and pressed hers over mine to guide them into place. Then, she moved hers to my back, shaping my spine, touching me, caressing me like I'd been dreaming of for what felt like months but was only days.

She speared her tongue into my mouth, thrusting against me in that awkward way I remembered so well, and I rubbed mine along hers, trying to remind her of what to do, of how this worked.

She whimpered, her body flattening against mine, one leg coming up to cock against my hip, opening her up in a way that pretty much stunned me.

I felt awkward, uneasy, uncertain, but so fucking horny I wasn't sure that when she put her hands on me, I wouldn't burst.

Having never been so fucking torn, wanting to ravage her but knowing that would terrify her, I felt stalled. Lost.

As she kissed me in that hungry way of hers, I pulled back and rasped, "Do you want this?"

She blinked, eyes bright, wide, loaded with a million emotions I didn't have the cerebral capacity right now to dissect.

"Yes. I want you."

There was the difference.

You. Not this. Not *it*.

I got it.

And I'd take it any way she wanted to give it.

She surged onto tiptoe again, reaching for me, but I moved back, rasping, "No. We need to—" I blew out a breath.

What?

I cast around for what I thought we needed, and spotted the bandages. I snagged them, turned to her and found her watching me, horror lining her face, and somehow, I knew she believed I was rejecting her.

"No," I rasped. "I want you. I just... I don't want to fuck this up."

Christ, I wanted nothing more than to twist her around, push her into the wall and fuck her from behind. The urge was there, at the forefront of everything else, but I couldn't.

Wouldn't.

That was for the future.

Not for now.

She had to trust me. She had to know I'd never hurt her.

But those big brown eyes of hers, Jesus, they tore at me.

I shoved the bandage at her, the one she'd used to cover up the scratches from that fucker of a cat, and rasped, "Tie my hands up."

She frowned. "Why?"

"Because I want to touch you, Amara. I want my hands on you, and I'm fucking scared that I'm going to do the wrong thing."

She swallowed. "This isn't right. You should be able to touch me."

"You have to learn to walk before you can run, little bird, and we can learn to fly together," I rumbled, needing her not to back out now. My cock was so fucking hard from those few fumbles I remembered what it was like to be a virgin again.

"True," she whispered.

Her nod filled me with relief, and it came even more when she unfurled the bandage and tied it around my wrists, knotting them together with a big bow once she reached the ends.

The crepe felt weird against my skin, and it was stretchy. I could still touch her, could still fuck this up, so I muttered, "Can we move to the sofa?"

I wanted her over the table so bad...

Not letting her choose, I moved over to the sectional without waiting on an answer, and picked up the remote, switching it a few bars away from mute because dead silence might freak her out.

There were so many obstacles. So many minefields...

I lay down on the extra wide sofa, grateful for the room, and rested my arms overhead. Pinning my wrists in place, I murmured, "Come here, little bird."

She stared at me with those big wide eyes, studying my form, the way I lay, and I watched something spark in her. The confidence I'd inadvertently bruised coming back, returning, and before she took a step forward, she grabbed the bottom of her tee and stripped out of it.

My nostrils flared when I had confirmation of what Quin and I knew to be fact—she wore no bra. Those gorgeous tits of hers swayed as she hunched her shoulders when she unfastened the fly of her jeans. Dragging them down her legs, she toed out of her shoes, then stood there in nothing but a pair of plain black panties.

I worked at a strip joint.

I saw a lot of strip shows.

Nothing beat what I just saw.

Nothing.

I had to pray there'd be a time when I could touch her how I wanted. Could God be that cruel? To hand me the perfection of this woman and never let me touch her without her cringing?

Fuck.

She slid the panties off next.

And stood there naked.

My cock went from tenting my jeans to a full on fucking yurt.

She knew too, and smiled, a catlike smile that was even sexier when she reached up and ran her hands through her floppy pixie cut.

That coy curve of her lips was for me.

"Siren," I rasped.

I wanted to tell her to get her ass over here, but I bit my tongue.

Like I'd told her, this was her taking her first steps.

There'd come a time when she was ready for a marathon, and I'd run at her side until she was ready for those twenty-six miles.

Releasing a breath, I watched as she swayed toward me, then knelt on the sofa and crawled my way.

Even in this, she was the Amara I knew.

No bullshit.

No messing around.

Almost masculine in how she did things—her hand went to my

dick and she shaped it through my jeans. She hummed as she found the zipper, then dragged it down. She didn't bother with the button on my jeans, just reached inside, through the briefs, and pulled out my dick.

Unlike her, I was fully dressed. I even wore my cut. She didn't seem to mind. If anything, I had a feeling this was how she wanted it.

I watched her, licking my lips, wanting more, not sure how to ask for it without fucking this up and I needed this so damn bad, needed her like I'd never needed another woman.

This wasn't a walking pussy.

This was Amara.

Amara.

Fuck.

My dick throbbed even harder and she eyed it, then me, and smiled again.

When she dipped her head, her tongue slipped around the tip of my cock, and I groaned, the muscles in my throat tensed as I tipped my head back, working hard not to blow my load as she lapped at me, before her mouth opened and she took the glans, just the glans, inside.

When she sucked, I groaned.

When she hummed, I moaned.

When she palpated the slit with her tongue, I panted.

She bobbed her head down, getting me wet, then pulled back.

I hissed.

She did it again, and again. Always pulling away.

Teasing.

I knew why.

She was testing me.

I gulped, and knew she wouldn't learn anything if my head was tipped back, so I rocked it forward, and stared at her. Watched her test me, taunt me.

She rewarded me with a long lick down the back of my cock, along that throbbing vein that needed in her pussy so fucking bad.

She nipped the base, humming when I jerked, then returned to the head, and sucked on it hard.

Hissing a little, I watched as she shifted, changing position so she was straddling me.

The move split her legs and let me see her cunt.

She was wet.

Thank Christ.

Not wet enough, but clearly turned on.

"Touch your clit, Amara," I ordered.

She frowned like I was talking Martian, but eventually reached between her legs and complied. I watched as she touched herself, nostrils flared as I saw her pussy lips flutter a little.

"Let me eat you out," I rumbled, mouth watering for a taste.

"No," she denied me, slipping a finger inside and thrusting it once, twice.

She bit her lip, then moved the slick digit back to her clit. The sloppy juices made it easier, and she rocked against me, grinding into me as she worked herself higher, and though I knew words could be as cruel as fists, I'd taken the threat of touching her away but my words wouldn't be stopped.

"You're so fucking beautiful," I told her, meaning it, meaning every goddamn word. "I want that pussy all over me, your juices on my face, my lips, my hands. My dick. Christ, I want you so much, Amara. You've no idea.

"Those tits of yours, I want to drown in them. I don't care if I never breathe again. I want them around my dick, you testing me and teasing me would be worth it just so I could cum on them."

Her breath halted, a shocked gasp escaping her. "Y-You'd want that?" she moaned.

"I want every-fucking-thing you'll give me." I jerked upward, sitting higher, moving closer. "I want you, Amara. Don't you know that yet?"

She groaned, her fingers working faster, and faster, and I knew from how she was arching her hips that she was close.

"I want that cunt squeezing my dick, Amara. I want to feel your pleasure because, baby, it's no fun if you don't love it too.

"Nothing tastes as good as your pleasure, nothing." And I meant it.

That's what blew my mind.

I'd been living off the memories of the taste of her ever since the last time I'd had my mouth on her.

Her head fell back, throat working as she moaned through an orgasm that sent a flush of color along her chest. Tits shaking, hips wriggling as she writhed atop me, I watched the show, loving every part of it.

Cock still throbbing, I wriggled my bound hands beneath her, and grabbed an awkward hold on my dick. Dragging it through her folds, I found her clit and rubbed it with the tip. She squeaked, tensed up, and just when I was sure I'd fucked up, her head rocked forward, fire in her eyes as she fell onto me.

Her mouth found mine once more, and this time, I knew she was ready for some of *me* to bleed through.

I kissed her how I'd been wanting to kiss her. How I'd been needing to.

I devoured her, and she let me. She met me stroke for fucking stroke. Accepting what I needed, giving it back, making me realize what an angel she was.

As much as I supped from her lips, she tore from me. Hungry, ravenous kisses made my cock pound harder, throbbing against the molten heat of her cunt.

She reached between us, angling herself and though I knew she wasn't a virgin, it felt like she was—spiritually if not physically.

I tensed, anticipating a bad reaction to the prodding of my cock at her pussy, but there wasn't one. If anything, she groaned, long and low in her throat, so deep that I felt it through the kiss while she slipped around me so fucking perfectly that I knew her cunt was made for me.

When she was full of me, her ass flat to my thighs, I lifted my legs, bringing her into the cup of them, and letting her rock forward so she was nearer to me. I needed her to know we were in this together. It was mutual. Not just me taking. Our pleasure mattered here.

Pretty certain that I'd never thought as much during sex as I did now, I thrust my tongue against hers, needing her to rock, to ride me, needing to encourage her natural instincts to flourish.

But she didn't. Instead, I felt her hands on mine, coming to my wrists, and the pressure of the bandage around them disappeared as she unfastened the bow.

As she sank into my kiss, not breaking that caress, her fingers slipped around my wrists instead, and she raised them to her breasts.

I knew this took a lot of trust, but I wished for the bandages because they hadn't been for her, but for me.

I was hesitant as I cupped the tits I'd been dreaming about seeing again for the past ten days, then when I rubbed her nipples and she finally rocked her hips, I pulled back to nip at her bottom lip, breaking the kiss just so I could drown in her tits as I'd told her I wanted.

My lips found her left nipple, and as I pinched the other, careful not to really hurt, I nibbled the turgid flesh.

She groaned, her hands moving to my hair so she could drag her nails through it, could rake them against my scalp in a way that sent shivers down my spine.

One hand carried on down to my shoulders, her nails digging into my back while the other guided me where she wanted me—sucking down on the sensitive nub.

Slowly, she started to ride me.

Her clinging pussy walls suffocating me in their chokehold as she writhed atop me, urging my cum from me, making it boil in my balls as I had everything I fucking wanted in my lap.

I sucked harder on her nipple, pinched harder, excitement making me rougher than I wanted, but she didn't freak out. If anything, her nails just dug deeper into my back and scalp. But I loved that.

My little bird had claws.

She hissed when I let go of her nipple, and reached between us, and every time she rocked against me, I rubbed her clit.

Within a minute, she was howling, her cunt clamping down on me, and I was a goner. I came. I was pretty sure I'd never come so hard or so long in my life as I spurted inside her, my cum drenching her pussy as I flew with her. Both of us soaring through the skies together as we celebrated this moment.

The first time of many when we'd fly together.

Her hips bucked against me, her pussy twitching as she drained me of every drop, and then she sagged into me.

And for all my exhilaration, for all that the relief of coming was there, as she collapsed into me, trusting me in that moment of vulnerability to hold her, I knew nothing compared to this.

Slowly, I dropped back against the sofa, needing not to jar her. Wanting her to stay on my dick like this. And I raised my hands to shape her back, to rub it, to hold her.

Feeling the goosebumps there, I dragged a blanket from the back of the sofa and positioned it over us so she was covered.

When her face found the natural nook of my throat, and she settled down, I knew, point blank, I'd never felt anything like this before.

I wanted to be her shelter.

I wanted to be her protector.

I wanted to stand at her side, have her back, and tear anyone's throat out who hurt her.

Mostly though?

I just wanted this.

Her trust as she fell asleep, the aftershocks of her second and third orgasms overpowering her, and leading her to rest in my arms.

Where she was born to be.

THIRTY-EIGHT

AMARA

THE SECOND WAKEFULNESS HIT, I knew where I was.

The bunkhouse.

Where I wasn't was on top of Hawk anymore.

The thought had me frowning, as did the scent of frying bacon and the soft chuckles of two men—

Gasping, I sat up.

The blanket covering me tumbled down so I snatched it up and dazedly, found both Hawk and Quin sitting at the kitchen table eating.

My gasp had them frowning and looking at me, Quin twisting around so he could check on me...in more ways than one.

His gaze drifted down to my naked shoulders, and a soft smile played on his lips before he turned back around.

Hawk's eyes were sleepy, redolent with remembered pleasure, and I felt my cheeks flush because I'd given him that.

Even better, I had felt it.

Sleepily, I reached up and rubbed at my eyes. Now I knew it was Quin and Hawk, I felt strangely more at ease even as I felt guilty for doubting Hawk.

What had I thought? He'd brought the Sinners in to take turns with me?

The thought had me biting my lip.

No, I didn't believe that, but it had happened to me before...

That was the past.

The past.

Swallowing down the memories, those fucking memories, I watched as Hawk got to his feet, wearing nothing more than his jeans, and moved nearer to the sofa.

Like this was normal, like it was an everyday occurrence, he leaned over the back of the sofa and pressed his lips to mine.

His smile was heaven sent. It settled in my bones as he asked, "Want something to eat, siren?"

Their names for me were strange, but I liked this one.

As much as I liked sky girl.

Of course, I wouldn't tell Quin that.

He didn't need encouraging.

"I'm hungry, *tak*."

Quin snickered. "When ain't you, sky girl?" He twisted around. "You had a BLT before?"

I repeated the letters. "What is this?"

Hawk perched on the back of the sofa. "Bacon, lettuce and tomato."

"*Tak.* I had this at home." I perked up. "I would like some more, please."

He grinned, then after getting to his feet, leaned down, and made me shriek as he hauled me over with him, like I weighed nothing, as if I was as light as a feather.

I clung to him even though I knew he wouldn't drop me, and when he perched me on the seat he'd been using, drifting over to the counter to make my sandwich, I stared at Quin from within the blanket, aware that I was naked, aware that he knew I was naked, aware that he knew I'd slept with Hawk, and equally as aware that he was naked apart from a pair of boxer briefs.

This was...

I blew out a breath.

Because there it was again—this was strange.

But right.

He tipped his head to the side as he studied me, but before he could say anything, a meow had me jerking in surprise before I remembered the cats.

Quin's nose crinkled as he peered over the side of the table and found the displeased tabby that had been perched on his belly earlier.

"You already ate half my sandwich," he complained.

I cleared my throat at his grumble. "Nyx said they were pregnant."

"He did? How did he know that?"

"Meaning they are?" Hawk questioned, his back still to us as he made my snack.

"Yeah. All three of them." Quin heaved a sigh. "I was kind of hoping this had faded a little."

"What had?"

His nose crinkled. "This animal thing. It stopped while I was in jail. To be honest, I'm glad. Can you imagine being visited by a million rats and cockroaches in a dormitory with thirty-two other guys?"

"You'd certainly have earned yourself a rep," Hawk said with a laugh.

"I thought there were two people to a cell in America?"

"There are, but when I was first there, I was barely an adult so they put us in dorms. Shit ones." He pulled a face. "It was crappy enough having to shower, shit, and shave all without any privacy, never mind having a Pied Piper beneath you in the lower bunk."

Despite the topic, and as angry as it made me that he'd been wrongly convicted, a smile danced on my lips. "You are popular with the animal kingdom, Winnange."

He squinted at me. "You gonna use the name against me?"

I grinned. "No. It's our secret, isn't it?

"Well, not now Hawk knows too. But I'm okay with that," he ended as he caught me in a stare that had my cheeks burning once more.

Silently, he told me he knew, he understood, and it was how it was supposed to be.

How he made me aware of that with a look, I'd never know, but I guessed that was the power of him.

And yes, he had power.

I knew the longer we were together, I'd come into contact with that more and more.

"How do you know they're pregnant? Were you a veterinarian?"

Quin snorted. "I didn't have time to be anything before I was locked up."

Hawk tipped his head to the side. "Why did they target you so young?"

He shrugged. "Probably because they thought I was a weak link." His mouth tightened. "They didn't realize I'm a stubborn fucker."

I had to grin. "They didn't hang around you for long, did they? They would have learned that fast."

Smirking, he leaned over, and tangled my fingers in his. "Not everyone sees the side of me that you do."

Even as I felt sure the clock froze, I didn't drag my hand away.

I'd told Hawk the truth.

He'd said he was okay with it.

And having Quin's hand knotted with mine felt right.

Right was good.

I had to chase the good.

I knew that now.

Squeezing his fingers, I murmured, "You're a flirt."

"I'm not actually. I'm charming, sky girl. There's a difference."

Hawk had taught me the word 'flirting' after yesterday's debacle with Janie, Quin's nurse.

The bitch had been drooling over both Hawk and Quin, and I'd admit, I didn't like it.

Not one bit.

Huffing, I grumbled, "Charming, flirting, isn't it all the same thing? Isn't he a flirt, Hawk?"

Hawk placed a plate in front of me, one loaded with a roll drowning in bacon, lettuce, and tomato. As he took a seat, he didn't answer me, just asked, "Do you bat for the other team? You're like that with everyone."

Quin scowled. "No."

"Which team?" I queried, aware a different game was on the TV now.

Hawk cleared his throat. "I was asking if he liked men too."

Oh.

Ohhhh.

I arched a brow at him, then at Quin who'd picked up one of the cats and was stroking it.

The tabby.

She was sweet, I had to admit. Less of a hisser than the other ones who'd slept either side of Quin's head.

The thought was an unwelcome reminder.

"Do they have—" I grunted. "Insects?"

"Fleas," Hawk tacked on.

Quin shrugged. "Probably."

"We'll need to clean everywhere!" I shrieked, jumping to my feet, sandwich forgotten.

Quin waved a hand. "A flea bomb will sort that out, plus... Never mind." He sighed. "I'll sort it tomorrow."

"You can't sort anything. You're still tired," Hawk retorted, eying the cats with displeasure now.

"They can't help it," he grumbled. "It's not like they asked to be homeless."

Guilt hit me, but I muttered, "I've fed a lot of fleas. I have no desire to be their dinner anymore."

Quin winced. "I'll deal with it tomorrow, I promise. Indy says I can use her Amazon account until I can get a bank account and shit sorted."

"Christ, I forgot about that."

"About what?" I queried.

"When you go inside, it's like..." Quin sighed. "It's like you die, for a little while. I was lucky though. Nyx and Indy covered the fine the court charged me, and then they paid my bills for me. At least I'm not in debt but I bet my credit score is through the floor."

"This is bad?"

"Yes. It's very bad. Everyone lives on credit," Hawk drawled. "Even if they have the cash, everyone has a card."

"I don't."

"You will. Lily will arrange that."

"Lily, Link's woman, yeah?"

Hawk nodded. "She's giving Amara and Alessa a trust fund."

"Blood money."

"Yes. I will take it though," I told him waspishly. "And I will let you use it when your floor-less credit score won't permit you to buy a magazine."

Quin hooted. "You have worse claws than Cassie here."

"Cassie?"

He shrugged. "Can't just call them cat, can I?"

"You're keeping them?" I asked warily.

"Not really. They keep me," he said with a huff.

"Where are the others?"

"They left."

Eying the flea-bitten cat, I slipped back into my seat after I thoroughly washed my hands at the kitchen sink, I returned, aware that I wouldn't be able to see any fleas, and that there were worse things in life than another flea bite.

Plus, I was hungry.

No excuse, but I was.

"How will you get rid of the fleas?"

"I'll overnight some stuff."

"They slept near your head," Hawk pointed out.

"I'm not itching." Quin shrugged.

"We need to disinfect the linens." I shuddered.

"A flea-bomb will work. I'll get some other stuff my *nòkomis* used. She was like me. Or, should I say, I'm like her. This started when she died."

His phrasing was odd. But Quin was precise in his way. He didn't waste words. "You mean... She passed it on to you?"

Quin grimaced.

Hawk frowned. "You being serious?"

"Sadly."

"Are Native Americans always like this?" I asked after taking a bite of my sandwich. "I thought they were just like other people."

"They are." He laughed. "They're not vampires or shifters. My grandma was different though."

"You too," I pointed out.

"Because of her."

"Nyx and Indy aren't," Hawk retorted.

"Nyx is in a different way. He's blessed."

"What do you mean?" I blurted out, his answer surprising me.

"I mean he killed all those fuckers and never got caught?" Quin arched a brow. "His path was righteous. *Nòkomis* insisted *Otesho monetoo* had whispered in his ear as a baby."

"*Otesho monetoo?*" I queried, repeating the words as he'd said them but not screwing up the pronunciation.

"Like, her devil. A bad spirit. *Aashaa* is the good one." He waved a hand which the tabby, Cassie, batted, before ducking her head beneath his palm in a silent command for him to carry on petting her.

My lips twitched at the sight even if she badly needed a bath and delousing and only God knew what else.

"Indy, well, she won't admit it, but we're both gifted with drawing. Hers is different than mine. But she chose to ink skin, that's her medium, but it's a storytelling gift.

"I don't think the spirits talked to her as much as they did to Nyx and me."

"That's not fair," I grumbled.

"The spirits aren't sexist," Quin retorted with a laugh. "They speak with those who need the help the most. Maybe they knew she was a boss ass bitch on her own."

Hawk chuckled as he picked up a bag of chips that was in the center of the table along with some other snacks.

"What's the game plan tomorrow?" he asked. "Aside from bombing the shit out of this place with chemicals?"

Quin winced. "I don't know. We won't be able to stay in here for twenty-four hours after we bomb the place."

"You can stay in my room with me at Rachel's," I informed him calmly, proud of that tone when, inside, I felt anything but.

He arched a brow. "I can?"

I nodded. "It makes sense. Then, when this place is clean once more, we make sure no animals come inside." I frowned. "I don't want to be mean, but I don't like being bitten by fleas."

"To be fair, I don't like it either," Hawk concurred.

"You'd be okay with me sleeping in her room, man?" Quin asked quietly.

"Well, I'll be there too, so I don't see that it's a problem," was Hawk's calm response.

Quin's eyes lit up. "I thought you'd fight it."

"You don't bat for the other team, I don't either. Why should I fight it?"

"Which bat?" I demanded, irritation prompting me to ask when I was wondering if I'd be able to deal with two of them in the same bed. "Why is this bat so important?"

Hawk laughed. "It's a euphemism, little bird."

"Well, I don't like it," I muttered, then I pointed a finger at Quin. "Don't complain. You said you wanted this."

"I do. I'm just surprised I'm getting it. People like me don't always get what we want."

There was no self-pity to the words, but still, I didn't like *that* either.

He made me want to change that.

After I chewed on my sandwich, I muttered, "I'm not sure if I can deal with sleeping between both of you."

Hawk shrugged. "You'll have your knife."

"What knife?" Quin choked.

"I gave her a knife. We have a deal—she can always use it on me. Not that you needed it tonight," he told me with a gentle smile.

"Good thing, seeing as it's back in my bedroom at Rachel's," I said, deadpan, but I'd had no need to draw out the weapon tonight.

Homicidal thoughts weren't what he'd inspired in me—just ecstasy.

Swallowing at the memory, something that I knew I'd be repeating soon if I had my way, I murmured, "Is your bed bigger?"

Hawk shook his head.

Heaving a sigh, I glowered at Cassie. "You and your friends have ruined everything." She hissed at me, so I hissed back. Which made both men cackle with laugher. Glowering at them, I muttered, "You won't laugh when I accidentally stab one of you tomorrow night."

Quin smirked. "I can keep to my edge of the bed."

"Me too," Hawk said quickly.

Even though I was mad, I snickered. "We'll see, won't we?"

"You guys can't be comfortable on the sofa. You might as well sleep in there with me tonight."

I swallowed. "I suppose."

Hawk hummed. "Only if you're ready, Amara."

Would I ever be ready for this?

Mentally, probably not. Didn't mean it wasn't a step in the right direction.

What was it he'd said earlier?

That I had to learn to walk before I could run.

I'd always hated running, but if it meant having more of *this*, this strange feeling of comfort, of being in the right place, with the right people, then wouldn't it be worth learning how to jog?

"We can try," I said cautiously.

"We have plenty of knives in the kitchen." A twinkle appeared in Quin's eye. "You're very relaxed about all this, Amara. You too, Hawk. I thought we'd have more of a fight."

"Amazing what an orgasm will do," he teased. "I wish I'd been around for the show."

"No, you were busy getting bitten by fleas." When he grinned, that infectious grin that had my own lips twitching at the corners, I clicked my tongue. "I'm not sure it's the right thing to do, but I like this." I waved a hand. "This feels how it should be, and..." I sucked in a breath, before I blurted out, "I don't want you to sleep with clubwhores. I don't want you to sleep with someone else. I don't want anyone to see you with no clothes on.

"If you're sick, I want to be the one to help you. If you're happy, I want to have been the one who made you smile." My heart raced as the words spilled from me. They were garbled, the pronunciations all wrong, and I knew I even threw in a few Ukrainian phrases, but I couldn't stop now I'd started. "I didn't want this, not really.

"It's too much, and I'm not..." My jaw clenched. "I'm not right. I can't handle one man, never mind two, but you're not just men, are you?" I gulped. "You're mine. My Hawk. My Winnange." As I said their names, a great weight shifted off my chest, letting me breathe easier than before.

There was a gentleness in Quin's smile that made me want to cry, but his words had me huffing out a laugh. "About time you figured that out."

"It's been ten days since I first met you," I argued.

"And I knew the first time I saw you," he retorted smugly.

"What did you know?"

Quin arched a brow at Hawk. "She didn't tell you the sky girl story?"

"I can keep secrets."

"It wasn't a secret," he countered. "It's Hawk's destiny too."

"Well, you tell him now while I shower."

"I'd prefer to watch you in the shower," he said crookedly.

Inside, something melted.

I could do this.

He'd help me do this.

His facetiousness would heal me where Hawk's gentleness wouldn't.

Today, I'd known he wanted to touch me, to be more... savage, I supposed the word was. Instead, he'd had me bind his wrists.

Quin wouldn't do that.

He'd push me.

He'd test my limits.

That was why I needed both of them.

I tipped my chin up. "When you don't fall asleep standing up, you can watch me in the shower."

"Is that a deal?"

"It is." My lips quirked. "Bearing in mind that I stripped you off today and you didn't get hard... I think that says it all."

Then, I did the unthinkable.

Again.

I got to my feet and I dropped the blanket.

I felt a little sick, my stomach twisting with nerves. I had scars, welts, broken skin, brands, so many physical reminders of the past, but I knew, then and there, that neither of them saw any of those things.

They just saw me.

Aware of that, I twisted around and, much as Giulia had, owning my position here, my place in this unusual situation, I sashayed to the bathroom, knowing full well their gazes were glued to my behind.

My show of bravado was exactly that, *a show*, but I didn't fall apart once I was hidden behind the door, leaving Quin to fill Hawk in on the story he claimed was our destiny.

Instead, I moved to the vanity mirror, and for the first time in years, I looked at myself. No coercion, no Hawk making me do this, I did it on my own.

I didn't see what Hawk said, but I felt it. Every word he'd spilled tonight, every desire, every need, I felt it like it was ink he'd tattooed onto my skin.

And I knew I always would.

Whether this situation lasted weeks or months, I knew I'd never forget what he'd made me feel tonight. I knew, also, I'd never forget how Quin made me smile, and how he tore down my barriers.

I reached up and touched my mouth—lips Hawk had kissed. I pressed my hand to my breast—to the nipple he sucked. I cupped my sex—the place he'd filled.

Each individual body part was no longer just a piece someone owned for a transient moment in time.

Instead, those pieces belonged to someone now.

To me.

It had just taken two sinners to make me see that.

THIRTY-NINE

QUIN

I WOKE up to my sky girl beside me.

I also woke up without a knife sticking out of a part of my body, so I considered it a good night's sleep all in all.

My wounds weren't aching, my body was mostly just tired, but I knew I could sleep longer. I simply didn't because watching her was far too enticing.

Asleep, she was unguarded.

She had more barriers up than Rikers, and even though I was tired of bars, if anything, I wanted to liberate her from hers.

To free her as much as she could ever be freed.

Resting on her side, her tits smushed together beneath one of Hawk's tees that Giulia had apparently brought over last night—her cage rumbling toward the bunkhouse had been an alarm call for me—Amara looked like the siren Hawk had named her.

I could hear him on the other side of the bed too, not exactly snoring, just breathing deeply.

It was oddly comforting.

A lifetime of wondering what the fuck was happening, whether I was going to live or not, whether I was ever going to be free or not, to suddenly finding my footing.

To suddenly finding my place.

It felt good.

Like a load off my shoulders.

I'd always been the odd one out. Amid my siblings, amid the tribe, amid the Sinners.

This, here, was where I was supposed to be.

"What you go through, you will endure for her."

Those words resonated.

Aashaa had spoken to me through Amara's voice, priming me for a future I could never have anticipated, and though I didn't want to live it again, for this moment?

For the promise of tomorrow?

I'd endure it all.

I smiled at the thought, wondering if I was fucking crazy, which was, of course, when she woke up, just as I started smiling like a loon.

Her eyes... goddammit. A man could drown in those eyes.

I reached over, and for the first time, touched her.

It felt like a big deal to me, probably was the same for her, but I'd just been somewhere where touch was verboten. Where every word was a potential weapon and the most basic of acts could be a trigger for war. People could say I had PTSD, and that it had no cure, but they didn't have my sky girl. She'd cure any woe of mine.

When my fingers collided with her cheek, I knew she wasn't too sleepy to react, so she did a good job in not freaking out. I appreciated it too.

She felt like silk.

My callused thumbs felt filthy. Too dirty for her.

"Do you think we caught fleas?" she whispered, making me smile wider because, here I was, thinking romantic shit, and here she was, thinking about bugs.

"Technically, you can't catch fleas. They're not a virus," I rumbled, my voice as low as hers.

"I was too tired to care last night." She yawned, then stretched, and I swore, all my blood shot to below my waist.

Her gaze was tender when our eyes clashed, and I smiled, well aware she'd caught me ogling her but there didn't seem to be any offense written into her expression.

If anything, she stared at me, the curl of her lips telling me everything.

"Why does this feel so..."

When her words waned, I shrugged. "Natural?"

Because it did.

There was no evading that.

It felt right to have her beside me, Hawk on the other half of the bed.

More than just natural, it felt good.

Like this was how I should have spent every day of my life waking up.

Maybe if I had, my adult years wouldn't have been pissed down the drain in Rikers, but what I endured was for her.

Aashaa had told me that.

It didn't mean I was happy about it, but what was done was done.

I'd survived.

Much as Amara had.

And we were here, now, together.

I'd never believed in fate even though *Nòkomis* had tried to force-feed me it, but this was different.

When a man came face to face with his destiny, he'd be a fool if he didn't open his arms and embrace it.

"Yes. But it isn't natural, is it?" Amara asked worriedly. "It's wrong."

Finding myself wanting to erase the wrinkle between her brows, I reached over to rub it with the pad of my thumb as I told her simply, "We have both experienced the real wrongs in this life. If this brings us peace, why does it matter?"

She thought about that for so long I wasn't sure if my logic would resonate but, finally, her smile peeped out again. "You are wise."

"Oh, yes, I'm a regular medicine man," I said dryly.

"I thought I would be scared falling asleep like this but I wasn't."

"Each day, you get stronger and each day, you'll come to trust us more."

"What do you get out of this?" she whispered, leaning forward, so close that her heat imprinted on the front of my body. "You and Hawk, I mean."

Did she seriously not get it yet?

"We get you."

"You have to share—"

"Threesomes aren't uncommon in this life, Amara. They happen all the time—"

"With clubwhores."

I nodded. "It's not as weird as you might think it is."

"But we're not like that."

"No," I agreed immediately. "We're not."

Shit, the last thing I needed was for her to equate herself with one of the women who serviced the brothers.

The second she made that calculation was the second she'd think this was about sex.

If she hadn't walked into my life when she did, I'd have had Nyx send over one of the bunnies to the hospital to break a dry spell that was years' long.

Hell, I'd have had a fucking *warren* of bunnies servicing me, using a tag team of sweetbutts to screw the anger and frustration and bitterness out of my system. Emotions that Nyx had inadvertently triggered when he'd revealed the truth of Indy's past to me.

Instead, Amara *had* come into my world. She gave me things that an orgasm couldn't solve. Things I couldn't begin to describe. Things that were way better than Prozac and killing pedophiles to exorcise my demons. A lot less risky too.

"So, it *is* unusual, *tak?*"

"Unusual but perfect." I smiled. "Don't focus on normal. Normal is boring. Have you ever watched a movie with a love triangle?"

She frowned. "What is this?"

"Where a woman has to choose between two men?"

"Two men she loves?"

"Yes. She has to select one over the other." I grinned a little. "You know Twilight?" At her nod, I peppered, "Well, Bella had to pick between Jacob and Edward, right? Wouldn't that have been cool if she didn't have to choose?"

"Well, no. She had to pick because—"

I raised a hand. "Okay, okay, it happened for a reason, but at the time, didn't it suck?"

"Yes. Jacob hurt very badly," she agreed.

"He did. And I'd hurt very badly too if you picked Hawk over me, and I'm pretty sure he'd feel the same way if you picked me. This way, it's the best of both worlds. We both get you."

She squinted at me. "I am nothing special."

"Well, we don't know yet, do we?" I teased. "You might give birth to the next Queen of the Damned."

She grinned at me, her smile morphing into a chuckle that lit my heart up from the inside out. "This is true. Maybe we make a child who rides bikes, draws, has cats stalking him, and bites people for food."

"Life goals," I concurred. "But seriously though, why wouldn't you think you're special? You're fucking kickass."

Her nose crinkled. "If you say so."

"I do," I grumbled.

"You don't know me."

"Do you know us?"

"Not everything."

"So why are you lying here then?" I questioned waspishly. "Why are we so special that you're willing to lower your walls? That you're willing to let us in?"

She frowned at that. "This is a good question."

Smugly, I nodded. "It is, isn't it?"

"Are you two going to talk all morning?" Hawk mumbled his complaint more into the pillow than at us.

"What did he say?" she whispered, his garbled words clearly difficult for her to translate.

"He's bitching about us waking him up."

"Sorry, Hawk," she said softly.

"It's too late now." He huffed. "Anyway, I've decided," he said as he spun around, making the bed frame wobble as he did so. When he was facing us, he caught my eye and winked. "Every time I hear you diss yourself, you owe us both a kiss."

"A diss is like a kiss?"

"No. It's when you say bad things about yourself," I explained softly. "And I agree. That's a great idea, Hawk. She's too hard on herself, isn't she?"

"She fucking is." He stretched, yawning as he did so. The frame wobbled again.

"We need a bigger bed," I said around a yawn, catching one from him now he'd started the yawn train.

"We don't—beds are expensive."

"You should have faith, Amara. We'll get every penny out of our investment into a new bed. Of course, you'll have to pay for it seeing as you're Mommy Warbucks."

She waged her finger at me. "Like Annie. I know this reference."

I reached over and tapped her on the nose. "We need to get you up to date with the cultural references. It's nice when you know what the hell I'm talking about."

She chuckled then, her amusement morphed into horror. Just as I started worrying, she shrieked. "Something bit me!"

"Tell me it was you, Hawk?" I groaned.

"No. My teeth went nowhere near that luscious ass of hers," he grumbled, not sounding perturbed about the fleas that had apparently infested the bed.

Amara, on the other hand, cared. She scrambled off the mattress, whipped off her tee then darted over to the bathroom.

"Well, that made today's shitshow totally worth it," I muttered under my breath as I watched her ass jiggle away. I just wished I'd gotten a full frontal view... Of course, my dick might be willing but my body still felt like I'd been through a train wreck.

Hawk rocked his head to the side once the sound of the shower turning on made itself known.

"You gonna be weird about this?"

I shrugged. "I'm weird by nature. It can't be helped."

He rolled his eyes. "Great." Another yawn cracked his jaw. "You really meant it about that sky girl and hawk and buzzard shit last night? It wasn't a dream, was it?'

My lips twisted. "Nah. A vision, sure, but definitely not a dream."

"It's no wonder she thinks this is odd." He scratched his jaw. "Anyway, you were right about one thing. Having her pick you over me would fucking kill me." His frown made an appearance. "She's... special."

Though I got the feeling he settled on that word because describing this situation was difficult, I nodded, completely in agreement with him. She was definitely special.

"I knew she wouldn't choose, though."

"Because this *Aashaa* chick told you so?"

"Yep." I'd never believed in *Aashaa*, not really. *Nòkomis* had tried to make me see her path, but I hadn't been able to. It just wasn't in my very Americanized, twentieth century-spawned ass.

Now?

She'd made a believer out of me.

"That simple?"

"Uhhuh."

"Look at you, master of few words this morning."

I yawned again. "Some shit doesn't need an explanation." I let a smile dance on my lips as I stretched as well. "She keeps the demons at bay," I told him, before tacking on, "That makes her priceless."

"Meaning you won't want to kill any pedo—"

"Fuck no, it don't mean that. It just means I know she'll help me clean the body up afterward."

Hawk snorted. "Figured as much. The apple doesn't fall far from the fucking tree where your family is concerned, does it?"

"Nope." We definitely had blood to shed, but the eagerness, the rapacious hunger that I remembered experiencing from within the prison walls, a rage so pure I'd felt like being locked up had only fueled it, had definitely lessened.

Vengeance was more important than spilled blood.

And vengeance, I'd come to see, could be canny. Sly.

Lodestar had handed me a newspaper yesterday, had shown me what Amara's ID had done.

Now we just had to topple an entire secret fucking society, bring it to its knees. I could think of no better way than to do that by Amara's side. Me on her right, Hawk on her left.

"A woman like her, with the task ahead of her, she needs two guys to ground her," I said softly. "You've seen how she's practically purging herself when she goes through the descriptions with me."

Hawk nodded, but his gaze shuttered. "We'll get her the peace she needs."

I hummed. "That we will." I grunted when I felt something on my ankle, and though I scratched it with my foot, I knew what it was as well. Heaving a sigh, I rumbled, "Shit. I'd best get that flea bomb ordered. I didn't buy it last night. Amazon's changed since the last time I was on it."

Hawk just snorted. "No shit, smart ass."

I flipped him the bird, then reached for the cell phone Indy had given me yesterday at Rachel's place.

Before we could kill Sparrow cunts, I had some fleas to annihilate.

FORTY

AMARA

MY DAY, which had started so well, tucked in a safe cocoon between two men I was learning to trust, turned bad almost the second I darted out of bed and was compounded when we left Quin's new home.

A dog was there, whimpering by the doorway, and because I'd gone out first, I saw the poor thing before Quin did.

My stomach churned at the memory, a memory which had me and Quin striding into the vet's office while Hawk tried to park.

Quin carried in the poor crying animal, murmuring to the receptionist, "We think he was involved in a car accident. He has a wound on his head that won't stop bleeding."

That was an understatement. The slash was one big mass of blood that was dripping everywhere.

The sight had me flinching every time he moved and the small mutt's mournful cries made *me* want to cry in turn.

Covered in blood, filthy too, he was the most pitiful little thing, and I was half-certain that he would die from blood loss.

The vet's office stank of disinfectant and wet dog, but the staff mobilized into gear, guiding Quin into the room where the poor thing would be treated.

As he dealt with that, I was faced with the receptionist, who asked me, "Is that Caleb Sisson?"

"Excuse me?" I had no idea who Caleb Sisson even was.

The older woman frowned at me, her brow furrowed as she tapped her pen against her chin. "I'm sure it is. He went to school with my Ashley. They were dating—"

Instantly, white hot jealousy flared inside me.

Ridiculous, sure.

Debilitating? Definitely.

I had no reason to be jealous, but I was.

Jealousy didn't have to be rational, did it?

I shot the woman a stony look and ground out, "His name is Quin."

She just hummed, her blonde fringe dancing on her forehead as she shook her head. "Those silly names they all have. Such a nice boy. I knew him as Caleb."

That was Quin's real name?

I wanted to one-up her, tell her I knew the secret name only a few people had *ever* known, but that was ridiculous.

Stupid.

Pathetic.

I cleared my throat, not understanding where this negative emotion was founded, and instead rumbled, "What do you need from us?"

"Any details on the animal you have. Caleb always did have a way with strays," she said with fond amusement.

"We have none. He was just waiting outside the house when we left."

"You're living together?"

Because she sounded so surprised, I bit off, "Yes. We are."

We weren't.

Not technically, but it was like she couldn't imagine us together.

What was the matter with me?

She couldn't see my scars, the brand, didn't know the damage—

"Didn't he just get out of prison?"

Oh.

Oops.

I cleared my throat. "Yes."

The door opened, a bell over it tinkling, and looking as out of place as I felt, in his cut, Sinners' hoodie, jeans and boots, Hawk strode in.

He moved toward me, past the waiting area of people sat with gloomy cats in those cones that stopped them from licking themselves, and birds in cages.

His hand came to my shoulder and he asked, "Are they seeing the dog?"

I nodded. "Quin's in there now."

"Dr. McCollister is used to Caleb popping in now." The older woman's eyes twinkled. "Was sure he'd be a vet, then of course, everything went wrong when he joined that awful club." She sniffed, and pointedly glared at Hawk's hoodie.

I stiffened at her judgmental tone and retorted, "That awful club houses the most generous men you'll ever know."

While her hands were busy straightening up the notepad and diary she had on her desk, she stated like her word was gospel, "They're filthy criminals."

If I'd needed another reason to dislike her, I just had it.

"Is their money too dirty to pay for surgery? Do you know many dirty criminals who would pay for veterinary assistance for a dog they don't even own?"

The woman, whose name tag declared she was called June, pursed her lips. "We don't accept credit cards here."

Her gaze drifted over the logo on Hawk's hoodie once more, and I got the feeling they didn't accept credit from Sinners, just from everyone else.

"What? Do you think the payment would be declined?" Hawk retorted, but he sounded amused whereas I was just furious.

My hands balled into fists at my sides, and I felt certain that if she carried on 'dissing'—as Hawk would say—the Sinners, I'd smack her right in the face.

Long, strong fingers curled around one of my fists, and I blinked as he squeezed them, then tugged me back into him.

The affectionate touch caught Judgmental June's attention, and her lips pursed tighter than my asshole, as she cast a quick glance at how he pulled me into him.

I didn't even notice that I hadn't tensed up at his unexpected touch, instead, I was just focused on how hard it was not smacking her.

I could see her notching me down as a clubwhore, but I wasn't.

I was no whore.

Not anymore.

I stiffened, my chin jerking up as I ground out, "We will pay cash. Do you have a manager?"

She blinked. "Excuse me?"

"Do you not speak English?" I told her, my Ukrainian accent thick.

Hawk snorted out a laugh, and his ease in this situation, by comparison to mine, had me even more outraged.

Before the blast, I'd never really left the compound, so I'd never come across the prejudice he evidently dealt with on a daily basis.

At the hospital, I'd seen the cops' reactions, and at first, the nurses and doctors had been wary of the bikers, but I'd thought that was because a bunch of massive guys were taking up real estate in their waiting rooms, and if bad news had filtered their way... well, I wouldn't want to deliver that news either.

But maybe it was because they were dirty criminals to the rest of the world.

These dirty criminals who had saved me and Alessa and Tatána, men who claimed their woman and protected them, who saved them from the worst crimes, who shielded them like they were princesses.

"Why would you want to know if I have a manager?" June asked.

"Because I wish to speak with her."

"What's going on?"

I turned to Quin, wincing when I saw how tired he looked but the dog had refused to settle on anyone else's knee but his, and though he wasn't big, the thirty-pound mixed breed would have been heavy after what Quin had gone through.

I didn't even want to think about his wound and if he'd pulled out the stitches—

"This woman is prejudiced," I declared loudly. "She is rude and has treated Hawk very badly."

Quin frowned, then turned to the woman and his frown cleared. "Mrs. Kinder," he murmured, his tone polite.

"It *is* you, Caleb," June replied. "I don't know why she's saying such things—"

"Because you called the Sinners an awful MC?" Hawk questioned drolly, his other hand coming to cup my shoulder.

Quin's eyes flared wide at that, and ice crept into those soft brown orbs that were like velvet for me. "You did?" He shook his head. "That's a real shame, June," he said pointedly. "I'm not sure the doc would like that, especially with how much business I bring to the place."

June's mouth tightened again. "Well, I didn't—"

"No, you certainly did not," I snapped. "Where is your manager?"

"I'm sure she realizes the error of her ways," Quin started.

"If Hawk and Quin were such dirty criminals, such hard mean men would they have accepted your rudeness?" I spat. "No. They acted with polite decency unlike *you.*" I folded my arms across my chest. "Manager. Now."

The woman scurried away, her eyes narrowed with annoyance even though she was trying to put on a polite facade, which was how

I ended up complaining to the management in defense of Quin and Hawk.

A few hours later, when I explained this to Giulia and Indy, they both chuckled like it was funny.

"This is not amusing," I snapped, suddenly furious that I was the only person taking it seriously. Even Hawk had been laughing at the time.

"It isn't," Giulia agreed. "You're right. She sounded like a real cunt, but you're the funny one, Amara." She grinned. "Look at you, defending the Sinners. I'm beginning to see why Nyx thinks you're hilarious."

Indy, snickering as she got to her feet, gently patted me on the back. "The Sinners don't need anyone defending them, honey."

"I don't care. I didn't like her," I groused, still annoyed.

"Well, you're in America, baby, customer service is the only thing we do right. You exercised your rights to put a bitch down." Giulia held out her fist, grabbed mine, ignoring my flinch, then bumped them together. "You did good."

Neither Hawk or Quin had said this, but I wasn't sure why. Because they were accustomed to being judged? Or had I embarrassed them?

"She also said Quin dated her daughter in school."

Indy gagged. "I remember her. Ashley Kinder. God, I ain't seen her in ages. She's one of those good girls who like 'em bad. She's married to the church deacon and is probably dreaming of Quin now he's back." She cackled, but her words merely inflamed me.

"She has no right to dream of him," I snapped.

Indy's lips quirked into a grin. "Giulia said you were possessive. It's good to see. No one's ever been possessive about Quin before. He'll like that. He's got Mommy issues." Her nose crinkled. "Understandably."

"I don't have Mommy issues," Quin argued as he came into the reception area.

After we'd found out that the dog was doing well and that his cuts had been stitched up, we'd also been given orders to collect him tomorrow, so we'd come to the studio for him to get cleaned up—he was covered in gore and blood.

Now wearing one of Cruz's tees, he grumbled, "I don't," when Indy retorted, "He totally does."

I walked over to him, rested a hand on his shoulder and asked, "Did you pull on the stitches?"

He shook his head, but he reached for my wrist, twisting it slightly and said, "You ready to hide this fucker?"

I looked down at the brand, and murmured, "Now?"

He shrugged. "I can come up with a design. Or Indy can—"

"No. You," I said immediately.

Indy grumbled, "Thanks, Amara. Way to back up a bitch."

Quin stuck out his tongue. "She's got good taste."

Giulia snorted. "I'm gonna like having you around, Quin. It's gonna be fun."

Indy rolled her eyes. "G, you're all fucking heart."

Giulia laughed, and moving away from the reception desk, asked, "Look, we gotta keep your head from getting too big."

Quin's gaze was warm on mine, like he was imbuing me with it, trying to act as my personal radiator, but at that, he shifted to look at Indy. "Oh? You got news from the TV show?"

"She's getting a twenty-minute feature," Giulia said excitedly. "Isn't that great?"

"You didn't tell me that," Quin complained.

"I only just got the email, and then Amara came in like Hurricane Ukraine, and that was funnier," Indy reasoned, sounding unapologetic.

He huffed out a breath, but grinned at the end of it, and said, "My sis, the TV star."

Indy snorted. "Hardly."

Quin, much as Hawk had done earlier, curved his arm around my shoulder. "This is brilliant news."

"We're gonna be busy as fuck," Giulia predicted.

"You need to start cramming for those tests," Indy warned Giulia. "We're gonna need a piercer full time soon."

Giulia grimaced. "I promise, I'm trying. I'm almost there. It's not like shit hasn't been busy for the Posse, Indy."

Quin pulled a face as well. "I hate fucking exams."

"Well, you're gonna have to cram too. Until then, you can help out on the desk and handle prelim designs."

Quin shrugged, which jostled me a little. "I don't mind that."

"Don't fucking procrastinate, Quin. I know you," Indy warned. "I want you working as an artist, you hear me? Not a fucking gofer."

Quin reached up and scratched his nose with his middle finger. "I hear you. Hawk ain't the only one with Mussolini for a sister."

Giulia smirked but when the phone rang, she picked it up and declared, "Indiana Ink. Giulia speaking."

Indy moved over to us, muttering, "Amara, I eradicated that brand from Alessa, so when you're ready, I'm here, okay?"

"I'll come up with some designs," Quin agreed. "Let's get that fucker off you."

I twisted my wrist a little so I could see the mark of ownership, and hummed. "I might have some ideas."

"Good. It's got to be what you need. No one else." Indy elbowed Quin in the side, not even being gentle.

"Hey. Injured man here," Quin muttered, wincing as he rubbed his side.

"It's the other side," Indy drawled, which had Quin grinning shamelessly.

Their dynamic was unusual, a lot less strained than it was with Nyx, but I was glad for that. Especially when Indy reached up, hooked her arm around Quin's neck and pulled him into a semi-head lock.

As she scrubbed her hand over his hair, scuffing up the straight black silk, he burst out laughing and said, "Want me to bench press you? Ya know, to remind you I ain't a kid anymore?"

"You're never too old for some sisterly affection." She grinned again, then said, "You need to get back home and rest. I ain't about to bring you in here until you're ready, but the sooner you're fit for work, the better."

"If it's just sitting at a desk, I can help now," Quin argued.

"No, go and get some rest."

I grunted. "We can't. We have to flea bomb the place."

"Jesus." She reached up and pinched the bridge of her nose. "Quin, you ain't even had the place twenty-four hours."

"We've had three cats and a dog." On the first night.

Indy patted my arm. "It gets worse—trust me."

"Great." I peered up at him. "What is this anyway?"

"Animal magnetism," Indy teased, but I didn't understand the joke though Quin did—he glowered at her.

Before he could answer, the door that led to Indy's place opened and Hawk sauntered through, Cruz at his back. I wasn't sure what they were talking about, but they appeared grim.

Switching interest between both pairs, I heard Quin say, "We're going to get a flea bomb and spend the night at Rachel's."

Indy huffed. "You can't keep doing that. Don't forget, they stop working."

"I know, I know. I'll have to figure something out. I thought it had stopped when I was inside."

Whereas Cruz said, "Lodestar thinks she's got someone who'll bite."

"Is she a big name?"

"She's..." His voice dropped so I couldn't hear.

"She was on TVGM?"

Cruz nodded. "Then that story broke about her and it kind of ruined her rep."

"That's why Lodestar wants her?"

"I think the story was BS." Hawk grunted, but Cruz murmured, "Rex just wanted me to tell you to encourage them to get back to the drawing board."

"I'm sure I'll get this speech tonight. We have to move back into Rachel's for the evening."

"Why?"

He explained about the fleas.

Cruz frowned, but said, "Don't bother with the flea bomb. I'll cook something up."

"You will?"

Cruz hummed. "I'll get it there tonight. You'll still have to spend the night away, because the place needs airing before you can go back inside, but you should be okay for tomorrow."

"Thanks, man, appreciate that."

Cruz shrugged. "Don't worry about it. Rex made it plain today—nothing is supposed to get in the way of Amara and Quin getting those faces down on paper."

"You fuckers don't know how hard it is on her. Hell, Quin too," Hawk argued, and his defense of me, his earnest anger on my behalf settled something inside me that had been a tangled mess since the vet's office this morning.

Even though I wanted vengeance as much as Rex, it *was* an exhausting process. I was willing to deal with it, but that didn't mean I didn't appreciate his caring.

Was this what it would be like belonging to them permanently?

To have them put me first? Above the MC?

There was no denying that I liked it.

Probably too much.

FORTY-ONE

QUIN

I WAS tired by the time we got back to Rachel's place, and was relieved when we didn't come across anyone on the way up to Amara's bedroom.

It was a little like being back at the hospital once the door closed behind us.

Somehow, it was both cramped and more spacious, which meant I laid out on the bed because I was hurting again, Amara moved over to the window and perched on the window sill which was wide enough to act as a seat, and Hawk slouched in a small armchair that he was way too big for in the corner of the room.

The pressure from the club to draw these Sparrows was intense, and it meant that I didn't roll onto my side and go to sleep like I wanted, instead, dragged my bag onto the bed and grabbed the iPad so I could get started when Amara was ready.

I didn't prod her, knowing that she took a while to get her thoughts together. Neither did Hawk. He messed around on his phone, I read some news and caught up with a friend from Quebec, Hank, just letting her chill out.

The day had been a lot more stressful because of the dog we'd taken to the vet's, then her meltdown with June Kinder, but it had sure as hell been nice to have her defend us.

I wondered if Hawk felt that way too.

After heading to Indy's, we'd grabbed some Italian subs from a local diner, eaten them there, then came back here.

With Cruz's promise to eradicate anything that lived in the bunkhouse, I knew I didn't have to worry about cleansing the place, so the rest of the day was ours to work.

I wasn't looking forward to it.

When Amara started, she started hard and fast, descriptions shooting from her like bullets. We worked nonstop for three hours and pulled out three faces that were about to be annihilated. Not the way she'd have liked, but there was more than one way to skin a cat.

By that point, I'd heard more shit that shouldn't happen to an animal, never mind a human, and I wasn't surprised when, her shoulders sagging, she mumbled, "I need to rest."

"Me too," I agreed, yawning.

It was dark out by this point, and Hawk groaned when his cell pinged. "There's been an emergency. One of the guards at the club just crashed his bike so I have to fill in." He got to his feet, stretched, then strolled over to Amara. "You gonna get some good rest?" he rumbled as he leaned into her.

She blinked up at him. "When will you be back?"

"I don't want you waiting up for me outside," he countered, a smile dancing on his lips as he pressed his finger to her nose. "You think I didn't see you, but I did."

She crinkled that cute ass nose, and mumbled, "You're not the boss of me."

"Jesus, you hang around Giulia for an hour and you pick up on her sass," Hawk teased, dropping down to press a kiss to her lips. "Please, little bird. Get some sleep and don't wait up—it's getting real cold out there at night now."

She huffed a sigh but nodded. "Okay."

He straightened up and, to no one in particular, declared, "I expect you to be the responsible one in the room."

Because I'd lay down my life for my sky girl, I assumed he meant me. "Sure."

"Wasn't talking to you."

I grunted. "Funny."

Amara laughed, and I flipped him the bird. He just winked and strolled out.

She watched him go, while I watched her, and when she worried her bottom lip between her teeth, I asked, "What's up?"

"Nothing." She shot me a bright, totally fake smile, got to her feet then ambled over to the bed.

Without another word and still fully clothed, she got beneath the sheets, and I turned to her after I put the iPad down. "Last night's practice run wasn't necessary, was it?"

She blinked. "No. He won't get back until five if it's a full shift."

"You jealous?" I knew he worked at a strip-joint.

For a second, I thought she was going to lie even though I could read her like a book then, with a rough mutter, she admitted, "Yes."

Such a simple answer.

For such a complicated emotion.

I wriggled down the bed, scooting so we were at the same level, then rolled onto my side. It hurt, but looking at her made it worth it.

"Hawk has probably fucked a lot of women in his time."

She frowned at me so hard I had to fight back a smile.

"I know this."

"You want him all to yourself?"

She narrowed her eyes at me before she closed them. "I don't want to talk about this."

"There are clubwhores everywhere," I argued. "What are you gonna do when they come onto him?"

I wasn't pouring salt on the wound, was just curious.

"Nothing. I have no right to be jealous, but right or not, I feel it."

I hummed. "Whenever James Dean ogled your ass, I wanted to punch him in the throat."

Her eyes popped open. "You did?"

I shrugged, but nodded.

A smile danced on her lips. "I would like to see this."

"Bloodthirsty, no wonder I think you're hot as fuck."

Amusement made her light up as her lips curved into a smile so bright it made my bones ache. "You know how to make me feel better. Why is this?"

"Because you're my sky girl."

She heaved a sigh. "I'm not certain I am. Is it bad that I don't want you to learn otherwise?"

I snorted. "Sounds human to me."

"I am definitely human," she agreed.

"A hot human," I tacked on.

Her cheek puckered inward as her smile faded. "I have to stop this."

I refused to feel panic. Panic wasn't sexy so with a calm I wasn't really feeling, I asked, "Stop what?"

"These feelings..." She released a hiss. "I did not like June for more than her calling you dirty criminals."

Oh.

I smirked. "Figured she mentioned me and Ashley, right? She did like us together. June might be a walking-phobe but surprisingly, she wasn't racist. If anything, she used to say we'd make beautiful babies together." I cast her a look, saw her disgust and burst out laughing. "I dumped her, sky girl. There's no need for jealousy."

Her mouth twisted. "I-I..." She paused, sucked in a breath, then whispered, "I want to skin her alive."

I arched a brow even though those demons she put to sleep rumbled with delight at her bloody declaration. "That's a little out there, baby. I ain't clapped eyes on the bitch since she gave me trichomoniasis."

Her mouth gaped. "She cheated on *you?*" At my nod, she snarled, "That *blyat'*!"

Because I'd thought that would please her, I could see that Amara definitely wasn't rational where I was concerned. Made sense, since I definitely wasn't where she was either.

"What is trichomoniasis?"

I wanted to smile because she garbled the pronunciation, but shit, it was a mouthful for me. "Sexually transmitted disease." My nose crinkled. "I got it treated though. Thank fuck she only gave me something that was curable."

Her top lip curled. "This is disgusting. She should be—" Her eyes narrowed, like she was trying to figure out the kind of punishment that befit the crime.

Even though, deep inside, her repeated defense of me felt so fucking good, I murmured, "What's in the past is in the past."

"The present is a concern too. The future even worse." She gnawed on her cheek now. "The way I feel isn't healthy." She scowled. "Nor is it attractive."

"Want proof I disagree?"

"What do you mean?"

"Lift up the covers and you'll see," I guided easily, not putting any pressure on her.

As much as I wanted her to bounce on my dick, I was exhausted. Our first time together, I wanted her to come so hard she saw fucking stars. Couldn't exactly do that when I was pretty sure I was so tired that my dick'd fall off afterward.

I thought she wasn't going to look, but she grabbed the edge of the covers, jerked it up and peeped under.

I snorted at her antics. "Bet you didn't get a good look." It was too dark in here for her to have seen the tentpole in my pants.

She stunned me by grunting, then sliding her hand beneath the comforter and placing it over my cock.

Her palm was so hot, even through the denim, and felt phenomenal against me. As her fingers flexed, I both wanted more and knew it wasn't wise.

Just coming home had been a tiring process, and...

My tongue about cleaved to the roof of my mouth when she shaped me again, her fingers finding the zipper of my jeans and slipping between the tines.

"You don't have to do thi—"

She bared her teeth. "This is mine, Quin."

The primal declaration, as well as the show of her teeth, should have been a turn off.

But between me and her, nothing was normal.

Our bond was forged by the most visceral, atavistic of spirits. They weren't afraid to go for blood, weren't shy about revealing their intentions. And those demons that she put to bed by being with me, started roiling around my soul at what morphed from simply words to a statement of intent as she continued squeezing my length in her palm.

I hissed out a breath, but needing her to know my backing her up, being here with her, wasn't just about sex, I repeated, "You don't have to do this—"

"Don't I?" she half-snarled. "I think I do. This is mine. You're mine. If I'm *your* sky girl, then you're my Winnange."

"I'm not arguing," I rumbled, pointing out, "I'm the one who told you about this in the first place."

She ignored that logic, but I found it interesting she fell back on my vision when she didn't trust in it. I guessed, in this instance, it created a tie between us that she didn't feel with Hawk.

One she wanted to feel.

She had rights over me, but with Hawk, he was still a free agent.

If my little sky girl was feeling insecure, it made sense that she'd get all growly with me.

And fuck, I was ready to sacrifice myself for the cause.

My Adam's apple bobbed as I tipped my head back into the

pillow, savoring the feel of a fist that wasn't fucking mine for the first time in way too long.

She seemed to know exactly what I needed, and when. Her hand palpated around my length, stroking it with a firmness that I wasn't used to with women, and my hips bucked as she pinched the tip of my dick between her thumb and forefinger, before carefully rubbing the slit where bubbles of pre-cum had escaped.

She used that to lubricate her hand, and all the while, her eyes were on me.

Hungry.

Needy.

Desperate.

She wanted to tie me to her, and boy, did I want to be fucking tied.

I didn't care that my head would probably pound in the morning—at least my dick wouldn't be. And if my abdomen and side felt as if I'd been backed into by a Mack truck, that's what pills were for—I'd take one where normally I'd refuse.

She was worth it.

This was fucking worth it.

I let out a sharp gasp as she sped up, her fingers flying over my length until she stopped. Abruptly. Leaning over me, her heat cosseting me in a blanket of warmth and need and desire that I hadn't felt in so long as she loomed above me. Her gaze dropped to mine, then she pressed a simple kiss to my mouth. Before I could respond, she nipped my bottom lip, then dragged it down before biting.

Hard.

Enough to make an imprint.

It hurt, fuck did it, but the delight that zinged around my body was better than anything Oxy could ever do.

My hips rocked back, my ass grinding into the bed as that pain sang through my veins and centered itself in my dick.

Her other hand messed around with my clothes, creating more

space, tugging my balls out from my fly, and when she palmed them, I was pretty sure *Aashaa* had sent me to the sky lands.

Sweet, sweet *monetoo*.

I almost drooled.

My balls almost burst.

I almost fucking came.

Like an untried kid.

Shit, I'd probably lasted longer when I was a fucking virgin, but the intent behind this got me hotter than having a pornstar grinding on top of me.

My sky girl was claiming me.

Declaring I was hers.

I wanted to be nothing fucking else.

She bit me again, hard and fast, before she breathed into my mouth, "Say it, Winnange, tell me this belongs to me."

I stared deep into her eyes, and pledged her something I'd known to be the truth since the first time we'd met—it was hers. *I was fucking hers.*

"My cock is yours," I rumbled, then knowing she was feeling smug, I reached down, placed my fist around hers and guided her in the ways of making me blow my mind.

She was a fast learner—had probably had to be—and I watched as she took the way I jacked off and made it a thousand times better.

"I'm gonna come if you don't stop," I rasped, warning her.

Her smile was deadly. "Why would I want you to stop?"

That hint of Slav in her accent made my cock leak more pre-cum. It was hard and unfeeling and determined and all the shit that made my wet dreams look like shitty softcore porn.

I closed my eyes for a second, intent on enjoying my first non-prison orgasm, then I stiffened when she let go of me, the bed shifting as her weight disappeared.

I scrambled onto my elbows, sitting up to goddamn argue about her teasing a very, very, very desperate man, and then my tongue cleaved to my mouth as I saw her standing beside the bed, scuttling out of her yoga pants, toeing them and her panties off as she dragged her tee overhead. When that went flying, I watched as she scrambled back onto the bed and straddled me.

"I shouldn't do this," she said thickly. "You're not ready. Your body—"

"My body is in fucking heaven right now," I countered immediately, shutting that thought process down.

Instead, I itched with the need to touch her but she was a walking minefield and I knew she'd have triggers.

Having been in her position, a position where choice was not an option, I tried to think logically but that was fucking hard when your cock was making demands of you. Little brain had definitely taken over big brain, and at the worst possible moment.

If I reached up to grab her hair, then that would probably scare her. But I wanted her to kiss me—

Fuck.

Tough.

This was her show.

For now.

She'd learn that I'd cut off my own balls before I ever did anything to intentionally scare her, and when she learned that, then I'd show her what it meant for a sky girl and her *Winnange* to fly together.

I growled when she parted her pussy lips with her fingers, reached for my cock to slot it between her labia, and then rocked her hips, coating me in heat, in slick juices that told me she'd gotten wet from going all cavewoman on me.

I definitely wasn't about to complain.

She put a little pressure on the tip so that every time she rocked, I nudged her clit, and her head fell back, her eyes definitely closed as her hips bucked, rocking against me in a rhythm that I knew I couldn't stand for long.

I had no idea what she was waiting for, but I focused on anything but exploding…

Of course, that was when I came.

White-hot spurts of seed blasted her cunt as a groan of agonized delight rippled from my throat, bursting forth just as wave after wave of cum drenched her folds.

For a second, I was blind, deaf, goddamn insensate, nothing working, everything broken as I experienced pleasure for the sake of pleasure for the first time in years. No fear, no worry, no force.

Just ecstasy.

I only just came back to me when I heard her moan. Or maybe that was why my brain started working again because it sure as fuck did *not* want to miss out on anything my sky girl did.

She rocked harder, faster against me, the sloppy mess I'd made of her cunt making it easier, slicker for her to ride me, to hit the right spot.

But, Christ—

"Amara?" I rasped thickly. "We need— My cum."

She knew what I was talking about, apparently able to translate post-orgasm male, because she shook her head, whispered, "On the pill," and that was when I knew I could just enjoy this.

Revel in every fucking second of paradise she showed me.

It had been so goddamn long that within thirty fucking seconds, my dick was hard. Back to the point of pain. I hissed as, with each roll of her hips, she almost took me in. Her slit was right there. Waiting on me, hungry...

Fuck.

How I didn't arch my pelvis, encourage the tip inside, I'd never fucking know. Anyone else, I might have done it, but here, this was different.

Amara was different.

She'd do shit at her own time.

Her own pace.

And that was the way to encourage the beast, to get her out to party, because she was exactly that—a beast.

A fucking beautiful one, but I knew a monster when I saw one, because I saw it every goddamn day in the mirror.

We were meant for each other.

All of us were.

Three birds of prey that were born to soar through the freedom of the skies together, seeking out creatures that offended our version of what was right and wrong.

I held back, or at least, I tried to, but the need to touch her was prevalent. I let one hand rest on her waist, before the other surged up to cup her breast.

A part of me longed to grab the back of her neck, drag her down against me so that she was low enough to kiss, but instead, I fingered her nipple, felt my mouth salivate at her tits bobbing and bucking with every thrust against me, and then, I knew I had to do something because I was about to have the world's second fastest orgasm—once, I figured was forgivable. Twice? Not so much.

I reached between her and started caressing her clit, rubbing it with the flat of my thumb, not flicking it like I'd used to. Ironically enough, Ashley had taught me this, and while I knew Amara would *not* appreciate where my mind had gone, I found a delicious satisfaction in using what I'd learned in my very short active sex life to make her explode.

Her eyes popped open the second I rubbed her clit, and she stopped moving, her breathing hard, tits jiggling, her body gleaming with sweat—

She sucked the tip into her pussy like it was the best fucking Dyson in the world.

I swore I knew what it looked like at the back of my eye sockets because my eyes rolled right back there and stayed as her molten heat cosseted my every inch.

A long, deep, hungry groan escaped me, morphing into a growl once I tapped out, filling her all the way.

That was when she fell forward, her hands on the flat of my pecs, her nails digging in deep as she ground into me.

Because I needed to see that, I got my eyes back in working order, and switched focus.

Her face was puckered in an angry snarl. It shouldn't have been hot. I mean, we weren't goddamn Klingons, but I knew I looked the same.

Ravenous.

Starving.

Two monsters meeting.

Two fucking glorious weirdos finally getting it together and relishing every minute of the connection.

She bowed over me, her forehead pressing to mine as I reached for her hips. She didn't tense up which told me she was with me, every step of the way, in the here and now, not in the fucking past. Using my grip on her and brute strength, I took most of the load and helped her ride me harder, faster, and together, we soared.

Like I knew we were born to do.

Hers came first.

A short, sharp cry exploded from her lips as she squeezed me to the point of pain. My cock was far too needy right now, so the second her cunt showed it some lovin', that was *it*.

Mic drop moment.

She ground into me, eking out every bit of pleasure she could, and all the while, we panted together, breathing through the exquisite joy of what we'd just given each other.

Amara was slick with sweat, hot from exertion, and she fell against me like the best weighted blanket ever.

This was all I needed for a good night's rest. Her. Ripe curves, luscious swells for a pillow, her body a warm, comforting beacon of pleasure and, dare I say it, *love*.

My throat choked a little, because I knew she wasn't ready for that, was still confused—rightly so—and instead, I cupped my arms around her waist and hugged her to me.

She didn't tense up, or back off, or roll away. Instead, she laid there, letting me take the wet spot and probably ruining a good pair of jeans in the process, but fuck, I'd missed this too. The sloppy after part, the messy stuff was just as much a part of the journey, and I'd needed it. Needed her.

Unfortunately, my body disagreed.

Even through the endorphins and the hormones and all that good shit, I knew, tomorrow, my head would make me regret this, but for now, I was in fucking heaven and I wasn't about to complain.

Hours, minutes, weeks, seconds later, she rasped in my ear, "I did not mean to do that." Before my heart could sink, she sighed, "I need to look after you because you are bad at looking after yourself."

Relieved—which made me feel like a dick—I snorted. "Don't listen to Indy, I'm not—"

"I am not listening to her. I have watched you for eleven days straight now, Quin. You are very self-destructive." She tutted, then wiggled as if she wanted to be let go.

Not gonna happen.

But, because of her past, and because I knew what it was like to be held down, I rolled us over, my hand on her ass to keep us close, so now we were both on our sides.

"See?" she grumbled. "You are in pain now. We need to swap sides. This is your bad half."

My nose crinkled. "It's all good."

She huffed, but reached over and pressed her hand to my cheek. I liked when she did this and angled my head so that I got maximum 'sky girl' connection.

My eyes were closed, so I didn't think about how long she did it for. A little like a puppy loving the heat of the sun on his small body, I just reveled in the moment. Just soaked up her attention, her affection, *her care*.

Christ, maybe I *did* have Mommy issues.

Before I could develop a full grown neurosis, my sky girl whispered, "This is too easy."

A snort escaped me before I could contain it. "Is it? I feel like I've been through hell to reach you."

That had her gulping. "Men don't... you aren't fighting this. Men fight these things, don't they?"

"Pansies do," I agreed. "Fuckers who don't know their own minds. What about me makes you think I don't know exactly what I want? Hawk doesn't look like he's confused either, does he?"

"No," she concurred.

"So why worry about the tits that'll be shaken on stage tonight? Yours are the only ones he wants to see."

"You don't know that," she chided.

"I know that I feel that way. I also know that if he touches another woman when he's with you, I'll separate his spine from his body."

She stared at me a second, then murmured, "I will help you."

I grinned, then reached up to cup her wrist. "Let's get some rest, yeah? Then we get a few more pictures out afterward if we wake up early?"

Her nod was firm, no hesitance. "Thank you for this, Quin. I couldn't do it without you or Hawk."

I shrugged. "Told you, sky girl, me and him are supposed to ground you. That's what we're here for."

"You say these things and it makes me wonder if you're insane," she said sleepily, "but if you are, I don't want you to ever change."

I smiled. "Don't worry, I won't."

She hummed, then did the sweetest thing—tucked her face under my chin. Her hot breath felt so good against me, reminding me of our union, even as I slept.

For a long time, sleep hadn't been a haven. In jail, havens didn't exist. But here, now, I remembered what it was to sleep truly, dreamlessly, tension-free and to wake up feeling rested...

Heaven.

Yet another gift she brought to me, one she didn't know about, and one that merely confirmed exactly what we were to one another.

Fated.

FORTY-TWO

CONOR

FOUR-TWENTY-FIVE.

I cracked my knuckles.

Four-twenty-five-twenty-two

I switched music playlists so random shit played.

Four-twenty-five-forty-six.

I had a sip of iced tea.

Four-twenty-five-fifty-three.

That was when *noxxious* came on.

That was when shit got real.

"There, fate made me do it," I muttered to myself, preferring to blame a streaming service for the massive mistake I was about to make than to actually take responsibility for it.

"Nervous? I'm not nervous," I told the cat I'd bought recently.

It wasn't alive or anything, at least, I hoped it fucking wasn't considering it was studded with lots of diamantés, but it didn't give me shit so I kinda liked talking to it.

Less backchat all round.

I connected the call.

"Who is this? How did you get this number?"

The bark of a question was so aggressive that I was pretty fucking sure my dick made a crashing sound like that of a gong mallet hitting the gong itself.

GOOOOOOOOOOONG.

How to get a boner in less than three seconds flat.

Because of it, my voice was a little thicker than usual, but I rumbled, "Star?"

A hesitation. "Who is this?"

Still as aggressive.

Ah, shit. Why did I always get so hot for the mean ones?

"It's Conor."

A pause.

"Conor? As in, aCooooig?"

"Yeah, as in aCooooig." My lips curved a little. It was a long time since I'd heard my handle really uttered out loud by anyone who wasn't family or law enforcement. "I just wanted to touch base." I wasn't going to tell her I'd been building up the fucking courage for this call ever since I'd 'accidentally' found her phone number.

She was silent for so long that I thought she was just waiting for me to cut the line, but then she rumbled, "I imagined you with an Irish accent."

"I'm a New Yorker," I said with a lopsided grin she couldn't see. "I mean, I can pretend to sound like the Lucky Charms' leprechaun if you want."

"I would, actually. It would help me feel like I was talking to an authentic Irish mobster."

"I'm a hacker for the Irish mob," I corrected. "Allegedly."

"It's all about the *allegedly*'s, huh?" She snickered. "Well, allegedly, I may have seen your photo on Page Six."

"Allegedly, hmm. Not sure you can allegedly type in someone's name and stalk them online."

"Better than turning up outside your door."

"True, but that depends on the intent." I grinned and rocked back in my desk chair. Four thousand dollars' worth of ergonomic ecstasy cosseted my body as I slipped my feet onto the desk. "I mean, if you were coming to visit me with murder on your mind, then that would change things."

"Murder, *allegedly*."

"I'd prefer a happy ending."

"Of the massage parlor variety or Cinderella?"

"I'd never be able to fit into her glass slippers."

She cackled. "Me neither. I've got big feet."

"You know what they say about people with big feet, don't you?"

"What they allegedly say?"

"Yup."

"Other than the big shoes' gag, nope. What?"

"Long toes."

She snickered. "My toes are short."

"Then you'd have pretty fucking weird feet."

"Goddamn, Conor, *allegedly*."

"Well, I'm about to make shit real. Irrefutable. Take a picture of these weird feet. Big feet but short toes? You're really Bigfoot, aren't you?"

"Yes," she murmured, "you've discovered my secret. I don't have shark week, I have Bigfoot week. I gush blood from my uterus and spray the forest with it."

"Marking territory, got it. Never took you for a hippie."

Did it make me a pussy to admit that her laugh made my heart race?

"Well, when you're raised partway on the road, I mean, let's face it, you've got to have some hippie in your genes."

"Speaking of, my streaming service actually played *noxxious* today without me telling them to."

"Poor you. What shit music my dad made."

"SHIT?" I declared. "Okay, you officially killed my boner."

"My voice gave you a boner? Christ, Conor, you really need to get laid."

"I probably do. You feel like stalking over to my place? I know you said you would before." I pouted. "But you never did."

"Awwww, shucks. Well, I meant to give you a hug, not a happy ending."

At that moment, I'd be happy with either.

"I have Disney Plus," I said wryly. "Lots of happy endings on command."

"Why do you have that?"

"Why wouldn't I?" I countered.

"Because it's for kids."

"So? Aren't we all big kids at heart?" I declared dramatically, rocking in my chair. "They're the only ones who show *High School Musical*."

She snickered. "You're into that kind of thing, huh?"

"It reminds me of when I was young," I told her tongue-in-cheek.

"Weren't you old when that came out?"

"Old, *allegedly*. I will never grow old."

"You're mixing up your stories. Singing at camp is completely different to Dracula."

"Now, that's a show I'd watch. *High School Musical* with vampires."

"You're weird. I like it," she declared.

My lips curved. "Happy to be entertaining."

"Yeah, you broke up my night too—"

When I heard retching coming from the guest bedroom, I grimaced, and hoped she hadn't heard it too.

No such luck.

"What's that?" she asked.

"One of my brothers," I said easily. "Puking his guts up."

"He eat bad seafood or something?"

"More like drank too much tequila," I lied.

She grunted. "Who knew the Irish couldn't hold their fucking liquor?"

Grinning, preferring that Aidan took the hit to his manhood than the truth coming out, I just told her, "Some of us have livers made of steel and some of us don't."

She clucked her tongue. "It's been one of those fucking nights for everyone, then. I'm trying to figure some shit out and I'm failing. Maybe I need tequila, too?" she mused.

Curious, and glad to change the subject, I asked, "About the Sparrows?" I also turned up the music so she wouldn't hear Aidan, who sounded like he was projectile vomiting across the Hudson.

Sexy.

"Kind of. You heard about the biker who got shivved inside? Quin?"

I owed my family everything. My loyalty, my trust. But I wanted, right then, right there, to be on the same page as someone who went through the same shit as me.

We were behind the screens, asses glued to our seats, brains breaking as we coded, stress weakening our hearts, providing all the intel and expecting to have all the answers to questions that hadn't even been asked yet.

I was my family's Google.

I knew Star was the MC's.

"How could I forget?" Then, tentatively because we never spoke about the family to anyone who didn't have an O'Donnelly name, I rasped, "It caused a shitstorm on our end."

She hummed. "You're lucky the MC didn't blame you, that's for sure."

"You trying to figure out who was behind it?" That was on my ever-growing to-do list pile as well. "I've been trying to get CCTV footage of the attack but Rikers is going through a security upgrade."

"I hit that wall too. It could even be how they covered the hit, so I'm going around it a different way."

"Which way?"

"I need to access some names of inmates who were Sparrow stooges."

My brain started firing to life as I tried to figure out why she'd want that. "You want to see if what happened to Quin is standard practice?"

"Yeah." She grunted. "It's shitty, but why wouldn't they try to kill the poor bastards the second they were allowed out?"

"Wasn't he attacked again in the clinic?"

"Yes. Heard about that, did you?"

"Eyes and ears are everywhere, Star. You know that."

She hummed, "Yes, but that attack was for a different reason."

"Which was?"

"A woman who was with him was the target."

"Why?"

"Don't know yet. In the grand scheme of things, to the Sparrows, she's a nobody."

"Apparently not if they went to the effort of wiping her out."

She cleared her throat. "It could be that they have eyes and ears in the clinic as well, I guess."

"What would be interesting in there?"

"The woman was one of their sex trafficking victims."

"Jesus."

"Yeah. She's got this skill. Every face she's ever seen, she remembers them."

"You're dicking me around," I rasped, sitting up as the ramifications of that hit home.

"By the sounds of it, being a Sparrow gains you access to their stable of women."

"Holy fuck. How are you identifying them?"

"Quin, the guy who was shivved, is an artist. He's drawing them."

"You think she was targeted because people figured out what they were doing together?"

"Quin was injured in the attack, so I think it might have been a two-fer. Get 'em both at the same time. I just don't think the prison attack and the one in the clinic were related."

"Star?"

"What?"

"Thanks for Coullson." The mayor had fed my brother Brennan a name of a supposed 'Sparrow,' instead he'd given him the name of the priest pedophile who'd violated me when I was a kid. A guy who was dead now, so Coullson had evidently been trying to stick it to me. Wanting me to hurt. Wanting me to know the Sparrows were well aware of what I'd gone through. Voice breaking a little, I rasped, "I appreciate the moral support."

"My pleasure." She grunted, and because I knew she was uncomfortable with my gratitude, she dismissed it. "It killed a couple of birds with one stone as well. Got rid of that bent cop. I enjoyed planning that. I'm going through the shit I trawled off his tech." She whistled. "Interesting stuff."

"You willing to share?"

"Maybe."

I grunted. "You have other IDs?"

"I do."

"Gonna share them with me at some point?" I asked dryly.

"If you share something with me."

Pursing my lips as I thought about it, I murmured, "I'm down for that."

"I'll also only share them with you if you agree to let *me* handle how the names are revealed."

"Only fair."

"Nothing's fair in hacking," she said wryly, and she wasn't wrong.

"I got out of the ego shit a long while back." I ran a hand over my hair. "I ain't interested in outing the names to get the credit. I just need to take these fuckers down before they take us down."

"Agreed. Amara's the reason Jason Young was arrested."

I laughed. "Did you see those photos of him crying in the cop car?"

"I did. Fucker. Amara was his personal sex slave."

My laughter died. "You're gonna make sure he dies in jail, right?"

"Allegedly."

Snickering, I told her, "Good. Okay, so, what's the deal?"

"I need names of stooges. I need data to correlate so I can see if there's a pattern."

I thought about Caroline Dunbar, the dirty FBI agent that was on our payroll now. "I'll speak with a contact we have and get as many names as I can to you."

"Thanks, I appreciate that, Conor."

"My pleasure."

"You at your desk?"

"Of course." I snorted.

"Okay, I'll send the images through. Get ready to shit a brick."

I smirked. "Looking forward to it."

FORTY-THREE

HAWK

THE FOLLOWING week passed by in a blur. Mostly because I had to continue picking up the slack for Jarrod who'd broken a couple of bones in a crash that was totally his fault.

That first night, though I'd told her not to, I'd found Amara waiting for me on Rachel's porch, smelling of sex and laundry detergent and all things delicious. She'd given me a single kiss, had taken my hand then guided us to her bedroom.

The scent of sex had been ripe in the air but call me weird, I liked it. Even if I wasn't the one who'd gotten his dick wet.

Exhausted, my cock didn't do much more than twitch at yet more proof her and Quin had fucked, and I stripped down to my boxer briefs just as she did, only, when she was naked, she dragged on my used tee.

Because she did weirder stuff than that all the time, I didn't even have it in me to raise a brow.

We'd clambered into bed without uttering a single word and had crashed beside a dozing Quin, who was evidently fucked because he didn't stir at all, and he was an edgy sleeper.

That wasn't the last time she ignored my orders to sleep the whole night through.

After Cruz had fixed our little pest problem and we returned to Stone's old place, I came back to the compound and found a light waiting on by the door. Inevitably, she was asleep on the sofa, and because she looked so fucking beautiful, she always took my breath away when I saw her.

I'd never expected this.

Could never have anticipated it.

Why would I?

I was only thirty. Barely a fucking adult, at least, in the MC world. Maturity wasn't our strong suit where relationships were concerned. I had years left of boning clubwhores in me, but I just didn't have the same need for them.

Chassity and Laroux, two of the club's hottest strippers, both had a thing for me, and usually tried it on whenever I had to break up a fight and entered the club itself, often inviting me back to their dressing room, but though I'd taken them up on their offers in the past, I just didn't need to right now.

Maybe not ever.

It was too soon to feel this much, but everything was cemented in place so that whenever I crossed the threshold, the outside world fell away, and all I could fucking see was her.

Tonight, she wore one of Quin's tees, was sleeping on her side, and her hands were underneath her cheek. Her legs were covered by a blanket that made me jealous because I wanted to be that close to her, and she just looked...

It was the welcome home I didn't know I needed.

I sluiced a hand over my head to wipe off the excess moisture from the rainstorm outside, and shrugged out of my cut, boots and jacket, hanging them on the peg beside the door.

As I did, the dog Quin had saved the other day peered at me from the bed we'd bought him. Tucked amid a bunch of blankets that made him look like the princess and the pea, the stitches on his head, the part of his ear that had been torn off, none of it created one beautiful-looking animal, but he was quiet, didn't piss in the house even though he knew a cat—Stone's ancient Mrs. Biggins'—had lived here before and that other frickin' animals regularly made appearances in the bunkhouse, rarely barked, so to my mind, he was no harm.

He yawned as I pulled off my wet gear, then ignored me and fell back asleep when I was dry enough to head over to her.

After turning the TV off, I slipped my hands beneath her thighs, under her knees, then under her waist and hauled her into me.

She immediately awoke, but she turned her face into me, breathing me in like she wanted to recognize me that way, then she whispered, "You smell wet."

"I wish you did," I said dryly.

"You wish me to go in the rain?" she asked, confused, and so fucking cute that I could have kissed her face off. When she was tired, she not only understood less English, her accent came thick and fast.

It was surprisingly hot.

My lips twitched. "My best lines are wasted on you."

"Oh. You mean between my legs?"

I snorted. "Yeah, little bird, wet between your legs." Then I yawned and muttered, "How's Quin doing today?"

This past week had been shitty. I went to bed as soon as I got in, woke up around three, ate dinner with Amara and Quin then had to fuck off to the club because they were still running short on bouncers.

Much more of this and I'd tell Rex we needed to pull some guys out of the ranks because I wasn't willing to work seven days a week for long. Not when Amara and Quin needed me here.

On one hand, Rex was fucking riding me hard to get me to encourage their productivity levels, and the next I was getting orders to head into the club.

While I slept, they went to Indy's tattoo parlor, and spent the nights recreating Amara's captors.

It had been tough all round, and I could see it was wearing on them both. Amara had tired lines under her eyes and either side of her mouth, Quin was always yawning.

"He's tired," she whispered, yawning herself. "The bird that was sitting on the windowsill this morning—he died."

I frowned. "He did? What was wrong with it?"

She shrugged. "I don't know. Quin seemed to know it was going to happen, but he was still sad."

"He feels a lot, doesn't he?"

"More than he'd like people to think," she agreed. Turning her face into my chest, she whispered, "How was work?"

"Shit," I grumbled. "I almost got puked on, had to split up four fights, one girl had her hair extensions pulled out by a customer who dove onto the stage, then it poured down when I started riding home from the hospital."

"You had to go to the hospital?"

She pulled back, her eyes wide with concern.

"The woman was bleeding. Head wounds gush."

She frowned, then settled back into me. I knew she didn't like my job, and wasn't sure if that was for obvious reasons, or if it was to do with the fact women were, essentially, a merchandise for men's pleasure.

Of course, most of the girls were working their way through college, had better benefits than me, and pulled better tips than I did as well.

Somehow, though I thought it should be the latter reason, I knew she was jealous.

I also had a feeling she sniffed me to look out for another woman's scent.

Any other bitch pulled that shit, I'd have been out of there. Instead, with Amara, I loved it. I needed her to feel as crazy about me as I felt for her. She was more of a free spirit than I'd like, and I wanted her tethered to me how I was tethered to her.

I could deal with Quin. Mostly because I didn't want her to choose him over me. But seeing any other bastard around her, even the brothers who had Old Ladies, made me want to break bones. Why shouldn't she feel the same about me?

If she didn't, then I'd feel like a fucking weirdo...

Well, more of one than I already did.

Nothing about our relationship was normal. Everything was irrational. It was too much, too fast, too soon. So why was I so fucking happy?

As I padded into the bedroom, there was a nightlight on in the corner. None of us said anything, and I wasn't even sure if it was Quin or Amara who'd bought it, but it was always on during the night.

As it illuminated my path, I trudged over to the bed, and carefully lowered her to it. She rolled into the middle, closer toward Quin. He didn't say anything, but I knew he was probably awake. He was still on edge from Rikers, after all, but I kept quiet, just got undressed, and stripped down to my boxers.

When I climbed into bed, I released a deep sigh as she turned into me, her legs tangling with mine, her heat warming me up after the cold outside. I should probably shower but I was too fucking exhausted to, and I closed my eyes once she nuzzled her face into my throat, and together, we fell asleep.

The peace that I found in her made me sleep better than I had in years, so even though I was still fatigued when I woke up later on, my body protesting the punches and hits I'd taken last night during those ridiculous fights I'd broken up, I somehow felt fresher than I should after a long night at work.

With the bed to myself, I stretched, yawned again, then stared up at the ceiling. An odd type of peace filled me. I had nowhere to go and nowhere to be other than right here, right now.

It was refreshing.

Most of my life, I'd been chasing after something. Whether it was the need to get back here to West Orange, where I was certain I was missing out, where I should have been a Sinner by the time I was twenty-one, where my dad was, or just a stupid urge in me to help, to do more... I'd always felt restless.

If it made me grumpy, well, so be it. I wasn't happy. What did I have to smile about?

The kernel of warmth in my chest that Amara had put there, felt like it had taken root.

That way lay danger.

Changing my status from single to 'it's complicated' hadn't been on the agenda, but I couldn't find it in myself to really care that my life was about to do a one-eighty.

If anything, it made me smile because at last, I had something worth smiling about.

With the world set to rights for the moment, I decided I needed coffee, so I clambered out of bed. When I was standing, I padded barefoot into the kitchen, fully expecting for the place to be empty.

Only, it wasn't.

Amara was standing there, peering out of the window.

She did that a lot.

I wasn't sure if I liked it or not. Was she dreaming about flying off? Was she looking at the outside world and pining? Or was she feeling closed off? Caged in?

If I felt the ties that were binding us together growing tighter and tighter, why wouldn't she? Not by one iota did I think she wanted a relationship, but when we were together, it just felt right.

Like this was meant to be.

She was so intent on whatever she was looking at that she didn't even react to my presence in the room. For someone so hypervigilant, always aware of wherever someone was in her vicinity, that took me by surprise, but when I approached her and managed to get a glimpse out of the window, my lips quirked.

I knew they'd had sex. I wasn't sure how much of it, because I knew Quin was still feeling pretty rough.

Was I jealous? Maybe.

They got to spend a lot of time together where, with the nature of my current work, I wasn't permitted that, but there was no point in being jealous. No use. Not when she did what she'd done last night and did every night—waiting up for me, making it a point to be there when I got in.

A woman didn't do that unless she had feelings for someone.

Quin was running around the yard. Back and forth, back and forth. From her position, it meant she could watch him, and even though I didn't like him that way, I had to admit, the fucker was stacked.

If he'd been on the outside world, I'd have said he'd been taking steroids or something. His muscles weren't ridiculously pumped up, but he radiated strength. It definitely saddened me that he'd had to become that way to stay safe.

What the fuck were we doing to people? Locking them up with other monsters and somehow expecting them to come out and be decent, hard-working citizens?

Quin had only been a kid back when he'd first gone down. Why would any judge think sending him to Rikers would make him turn his life around?

It didn't matter that he was biker spawn. Judges did this to kids every fucking day. Kids who were from regular families, kids who'd made one little mistake...

It was wrong. So fucking wrong.

"You enjoying the show?" I rumbled in her ear, needing not to think about the many injustices in our society. When she jerked so hard she literally bounced in front of me, I grinned.

Twisting around, she glowered at me a second, but her cheeks were flushed, and her eyes were a little glassy.

She was turned on.

"Hawk, I thought you were sleeping," she rasped, her voice low and husky enough that my dick twitched behind my briefs.

"I was," I informed her dryly. "Now I'm not." I tipped my chin up at Quin. "Why's he running back and forth?"

"I told him to."

My lips twitched. "And he listened?"

Her nose crinkled. "We argued about it."

"You won?"

"Of course, because he was being stupid." Amara groused, "He wanted to run into town. As if that was ever going to be possible with his wounds." She clucked her tongue. "He agreed so that if he fell, I'd be nearby to help him."

The brothers who were working on the clubhouse were close by as well, but that she wanted to be the one who helped, well, it said a lot about her.

"Inadvertently, you got yourself some free porn, huh?" I teased, grabbing her hips and twisting her around so that she was facing the window again and could see Quin jogging back and forward.

Dumbass looked pale, and from how his mouth was twisted, I knew he was hurting. Amara told me that Stone had warned him against pushing it too hard, too fast, when she'd checked him over two days ago, but if he was gonna be a prick about it, then he'd have to deal with the consequences.

Of course...

Fuck.

I'd have to talk with him.

His actions didn't just affect Quin now. Amara would be scared if he hurt himself.

Fucker.

Resting my chin on her shoulder, I placed one hand on her stomach and murmured, "You getting wet, siren?"

Her ass rocked back into me where my boner was making itself felt. I was surprised she was letting me stand this way, looming over her, shadowing her, but she placed her hand atop mine and guided it down between her legs.

I liked how aggressive she was.

It figured that she was used to doing and never receiving, and that she was better at giving pleasure than accepting it because she'd been trained to do that rather than experiencing it for herself.

The difference was I wanted her to be selfish. I wanted her to expect, to fucking *demand* pleasure as if it was her right.

Which it was.

When I pressed my fingers between her thighs, her shorts diminished some of the heat but not all of it. She arched onto her tiptoes at the first touch though, and I turned my face into her throat, sucking down on it a little, raking my teeth there as I gave her the pressure she needed to grind down against me.

"You like seeing him get all sweaty?"

"He's in pain," she rasped, her disapproval clear but her head rocked back against my shoulder. With my head bowed the way it was, our cheeks brushed and I could feel that hers were burning up. "But I-I like him sweaty."

Taking a mental note about that, especially now her jealous reaction to me working out in Quin's hospital room made sense, I grinned to myself and hummed as I nipped along the join between neck and ear.

As I sucked on her earlobe, I shifted my other hand from her hip and let my fingers burrow beneath the thin waistband.

When I encountered no panties, my dick twitched, and then it just turned painful when I slipped the digits down to her core.

"Fuck," I rumbled against her throat, groaning at how wet she was, how fucking hot.

She was so responsive that it took my breath away.

I knew, whether she did or not, that her body recognized me, that it wanted me. It knew what it was getting when I was around, and though I hadn't had much opportunity to grant her the pleasure she deserved, I knew I'd spend every year I had left on this godforsaken planet making sure that her body always hummed to life around me.

As I found her clit, I pinched it slightly between my pointer and middle finger, delighted when she groaned. The sound vibrated in my ear because we were standing so near to one another, and I gritted my teeth as I rocked my hand back and forth, rubbing her until her hips bucked back against me.

Her breathy moans set me on fire and what I wanted to do was tell her to press her hands to the windowpanes, to fuck her here, against the glass. Only Quin would be able to see, because the other brothers were on the construction site at the east of the property. Unless they had eyes like a fucking owl, they'd see shit in here because the sun wasn't out. I wanted to be in her from behind, wanted to feel her this way, but I didn't want her to feel oppressed, to feel like—

She raised her hands and shoved them against the panes, doing as I craved without even asking it of her, and her ass began writhing against my cock as she rasped something in Ukrainian then hissed, "Stop teasing me, Hawk."

Brows high even though I was ecstatic, I growled, "You wanna feel me deep in your pussy, siren?"

She groaned. "Yes."

"You sure?" I asked again, when normally I'd just have fucking taken.

"*Tak*," she said thickly, her hands falling to her waistband as she dragged her shorts down.

Her confidence came as a surprise but I wasn't about to fucking complain.

Arching my hips, I shoved my briefs down, released my cock from its confines and grabbed it firmly in my fist.

Pre-cum had already gathered at the tip, and I felt like salivating when I pressed my length between her ass cheeks. She squeezed a little, making me grin, then I shoved it down, burrowing it between her thighs. She was slick and hot and so fucking perfect that it constantly astounded me.

Soaring onto tiptoe again, she demanded, "Put it in."

One day, I'd need to learn sex in Ukrainian just because I loved it when her accent came out.

I pressed the tip to her gate, let it stay there, then I bent down a little, and said, "I'm gonna raise your leg."

She sank back onto her feet, then helped me lift it. I pressed her knee to her chest as I leaned her deeper against the window, and then I slipped my fingers back between her thighs.

Slowly at first, I thrust into her, letting her feel me, letting her body know who was behind her, then I saw her hands on the pane, saw the knuckles tensing as she began to buck back against me.

As my cock was cosseted by every inch of that delicious cunt, I turned my face back into her throat and sucked down hard on the tender flesh there.

Hips rocking, I made love to her. With every stroke of my hand, I rubbed her clit, and with every thrust, I made her feel every inch, but I only let loose when I could feel her pussy clinging to me, grabbing at it, trying to milk me of cum as that greedy little cunt got to work on driving me insane.

My other hand went up to her tit, and I squeezed her there, harder than I should, but I got the green light when she cried out and she started rocking back into me, taking more, needing more, needing everything I had to give.

It morphed from love to fucking as she slipped her arm behind my neck, forcing us closer together.

I tilted my head to the side and bit down as I moved faster, harder, and from the corner of my eye, I saw Quin jerk to a halt. My hips didn't stop pistoning, but I'd admit to being concerned he was injured or something, only, he didn't fall to his knees in pain, if anything he changed course and I knew he'd seen us.

I knew he wanted in on the action.

She jerked in response when the door flew open, telling me that she hadn't noticed his change of direction, and she turned to look at him. I had no idea what he saw, but the way his eyes narrowed, his face tensing up, his jaw clenching, I knew she'd turned him on.

I didn't want to stop, my cock demanded I continue, but I knew he wanted in, and because I was more focused on her experiencing a pleasure overload, I rumbled in her ear, "I'm gonna take your weight so brace yourself."

She tensed up, and when I lifted her, I immediately twisted her away from the glass. Maybe I'd been wanting to give Quin a show, who the fuck knew? I simply knew that now the man himself was here, I didn't want anyone else seeing what was ours.

Quin wore nothing but a pair of sweats that had little droplets of perspiration beaded here and there. His dick made a tent pole at the crotch of his pants, but I was more interested in Amara's reaction to his presence.

Not only had her pussy tightened around my cock to an exquisite degree from the new position, Quin's presence had those delicious inner muscles doing the goddamn salsa.

I carried her over to the sofa, grateful it was leather and easy to clean, and I squatted down then rocked back so she wouldn't be jostled too hard. As I sat back, I encouraged her legs over my knees and spread her wide. Seeing what I was doing, Quin strode over, his hand delving beneath the waistband of his sweats, before he pulled out his cock.

I'd seen North's dick almost as much as I'd seen my own, and I'd rubbed up against it in a woman's pussy. It was weird. Not sharing with North—which, granted, would be fucking freaky to most people. But sharing with Quin.

North and I had done this so many times, we knew each other's limits. We never went down on a bitch if one of us was inside her, or if one of us had been inside her either—even though, until Amara, I'd always used condoms. I guessed, right from the start, I'd known she was different, and I wanted to claim her in the most basic way imaginable.

Grunting when Quin dropped to his knees, his pain threshold clearly shifting now he was about to get laid, he bent his head and pressed his mouth to Amara's pussy.

The second he connected with her clit, she went off like a light show. Her cunt clamped down around me, before she bucked and writhed in my hold—not to get free, but just in overload.

This was how I wanted her to be.

What I wanted for her.

Even if Quin's presence down there tested my comfort levels, it was worth it for her reaction. I needed her pleasure, needed it because... fuck, she'd had too little of it in her life, and her man, or men, should put that above everything goddamn else.

Quin's mouth was so close to my dick it had me tensing up whenever I felt his hot breath against the base of my shaft, but I shifted focus, loving how she was squirming on top of me because I got all the benefits without having to move an inch.

Reaching up, I cupped her tits, squeezing her nipples as she ground her pussy into Quin's face.

"*Ne valyahui duraka!*" Amara hissed, her voice hoarse as her hands burrowed their way into Quin's hair for added pressure.

As she clutched at me, I couldn't help but be reminded of that day on Rachel's porch, the one that had started all this.

What had she said to me?

'I want to growl.'

Here she went, proving me wrong again—she didn't squeak like I'd predicted.

She *growled* as she detonated. Outright fucking growled. Deep enough to make my ears ring, to make the hairs stand up on my nape.

Her back arched, the tension in her torso letting me know how graceful she'd have been as a ballet dancer, and she went utterly still. I'd have paid a fortune to have been able to see her face at that moment, but I couldn't. All I could do was hold her, keep her grounded. Tether her to the earth while a part of her went flying.

Of course, that was easier said than done when the pulsations of her pussy around my cock set me off too. I pushed the back of my head into the sofa cushions, pumping my hips from the bottom to eke as much ecstasy out of this as I could.

The noises Quin made as he sucked on her clit messed with me, teasing me and taunting me, making me ride the waves of glory higher and higher.

He enjoyed it. It was clear to me.

He didn't let her go, didn't stop until she was sobbing with fucking delight.

I'd never experienced anything like this before, and as she carried on coming and coming, never seeming to fucking stop, I was trapped in the same merry-go-round.

Aware that my senses were fried, uncaring that Quin's face was right *there,* I let myself go too, because I had no choice other than to ride this out. To suffocate in this unknown level of pleasure that was going to leave its mark on my memory banks for the rest of my life.

FORTY-FOUR

AMARA

I FELT HAWK COME.

I knew it was a technical impossibility. I'd never felt it before, and I'd been the cum dumpster for a lot of men, but I felt Hawk like no other. He was hot enough to brand me. For me to feel his mark on me deep inside, and I knew that was wishful thinking.

I wanted his mark.

I wanted for him to imprint on me like this. I needed it as much as I needed Quin to never, ever, *ever* stop what he was doing.

This guy, *pizda rulu*, he was born to do this.

Sweet hell.

With my eyes closed, my head pinned against Hawk's shoulder, I didn't see what happened, didn't understand what Quin asked Hawk because my brain was mush, just felt Hawk tense up, his cock disappear from inside me, and felt the thick rod of Quin's dick prod the entrance of my slick and sloppy pussy.

Aware that Quin must have pulled Hawk out so he could burrow into me, I wasn't about to complain.

They both filled me to perfection. Hawk hitting me deeper, Quin filling me to the brink of pain. My pussy lips spread around his girth, making my clit pop out, and when he ground against me, I felt his pubis bone brush up against the nub.

This wasn't my first threesome, but how I felt now in comparison to before almost made me want to cry.

Degradation.

Devastation.

That was all I'd known before these two wonderful men.

No pleasure. Never that. My reason for being was to provide it, not receive it.

Until now.

My eyes opened because I needed to look at Quin, needed to see him as he rocked into me. With my legs spread wide, his gaze was focused on the obscene way his cock split me in two, but the sight electrified him. I could almost feel the current throbbing through his skin as he reveled in me.

When he pulled back a little, his thumb moved down to my slit. He rubbed it beneath his cock, and I felt him gather some of Hawk's cum, before he slid it back to my clit. As he teased the nub, a shaky breath escaped me.

He should have fried my pleasure receptors.

I should *not* have been able to come again.

So why did my pussy clamp down around him?

Why did I leap forward to grab him, to haul him down, to dig my hands into his shoulders as I brought him nearer to me?

"No more watching," I growled at him. "More doing."

He chuckled, but I knew he didn't understand. I was incapable of English. Ukrainian was all I could speak, but he seemed to comprehend, and satisfaction, smugness too, crossed over his expression.

Finally, he gave me what I needed. Not too fast, not too slow, just letting me feel every inch, and then he bucked his hips at the last moment so my exposed clit got some lovin' too.

I groaned long and low when Hawk tipped my chin to the side, and as he bound our mouths together, I squirmed because Quin found my tits and he started sucking on the nipples.

Hard.

He nipped on the tip, not enough to make me scream with pain, but to whimper with need.

I wasn't as sensitive as I'd been before, the abuse had changed my body, but the way they worked me, with care, with affection, with need and tenderness, it seemed to right some of the wrongs of the past.

As Hawk plunged his tongue against mine, and Quin sucked on my nipple, I let out a hoarse cry as a second orgasm hit me, blindsiding me like nothing else could.

With a long, agonized whimper, I rode another high, soaring faster, harder, knowing that they were both here with me, their arms around me, their bodies keeping me in place.

I had nowhere else I wanted to be.

No place else I'd rather be than here, sandwiched between them.

When Quin growled around my nipple, I felt his seed too. This wasn't my first time with either of them, but it was the first time as a unit.

And that was how we felt.

Like a partnership, just with three instead of two. I had many concerns about our dynamic, but my body had none of them. It couldn't. Not when I felt *his* cum too. Not when it seared me from the inside out, so red hot that I knew he branded me as well.

When he sagged into me, I slumped into Hawk, knowing he would support us both, take our weight, the strain.

Which was when I realized that was how it was supposed to be.

Hawk was our backbone. Quin our wings.

I just didn't know what I was supposed to be yet.

But I was okay with that.

Really, truly, I was.

With them, I was even okay with flying.

The aftermath could have been embarrassing, but it wasn't.

Lazily, we got up, drifting into the kitchen to eat. Hawk, as usual, made us some sandwiches, and for the first time in my life, I didn't rush to shower off their seed like I would have done in the past. I was quite content with it filling me up, the slickness was comforting. A reminder.

We snacked in silence before Hawk grunted at the time and, after pulling me into a kiss that had me holding onto his arms to steady myself, went off to shower for work.

I didn't like it when he left, but I knew it was stupid. The poor man couldn't be with me constantly.

"*Zalupa*," I muttered under my breath as I tugged the throw blanket from the couch around my shoulders and scuttled over to the window to watch him leave.

As he kicked up his leg to settle on his bike, I stood to the side, uncaring that Quin was watching me sneakily watching Hawk. I only moved when Hawk had roared off, pleased that he gave the bunkhouse a backwards glance even though he didn't know I was standing there.

The brush of soft fur against my ankle had me jumping, but I smiled down at Petr, and leaned over to pat his head. "You want to go out?" I asked in Ukrainian.

"He's American," Quin informed me. "He no speaky the lingo."

I ignored him and moved to the door, opening it and letting the dog out.

Maybe Petr knew when he had a good thing going because he hadn't tried to run off even though there were plenty of places for him to explore. Instead, he headed out, did his business, then instantly returned to the bunkhouse and made his way back to bed after a sniff of his now-empty food bowl—I'd filled that up before Quin had gone running—and a quick lick of water.

It was almost easy to forget about him.

Apart from one thing—he didn't forget me and tended to follow me around. I didn't mind. It was quite sweet.

Casting Quin a look, I saw him pick up the remainder of the meat Hawk called baloney but which was spelled bologna on the packet—

English truly made no sense—and take a big bite of it before he tossed the last slither at Petr who snatched it up.

Quin looked cool and calm but, as usual, watchful.

He rested one arm along the back of the chair I'd been sitting in, his feet were kicked up against the sofa, and he tracked me.

There was no other way to describe it.

I was also used to that and couldn't deny that I liked it.

A lot.

Treading over to the fridge, I pulled out a bottle of the sweet tea they'd gotten me hooked on after eating at Checkers, then returned to the table.

"You'll pull on the wound if you sit like that," I chided after I filled up my glass.

Quin shrugged. "It's much better."

"It's still a fresh wound," I argued.

"You're bossy."

"You're obstinate." I grinned at him when his lips curved in a slow smile.

My relationship with Quin was different than it was with Hawk.

I didn't feel on edge with him.

Quin, I knew, believed the sun rose and set on me. That was because I was his sky girl.

Hawk knew I was human. We didn't have some strange spirit that had declared I was his. I wished we did. Even though I didn't believe in Quin's *Aashaa*, I liked how it tied us together.

"Why do you watch him leave?"

I arched a brow. "Why did I watch you run?"

He snorted. "I thought I felt someone tracking me. Every time I looked, you weren't there."

"I'm sneaky." I shrugged. "I like watching both of you. Especially when you're sweaty."

"Really?" He rubbed his chin. "Interesting."

"Is it?" I took a sip of iced tea. "Your muscles bulge when you sweat. Veins pop up." I hummed. "I like it."

"Good to know," he rumbled, but he was amused. I did that a lot—amused him. I wasn't sure how or why when I rarely told jokes, but he found me funny so who was I to complain? "You handled that well today."

"Handled what well? You?" I smirked at him. "You listened, didn't you? You didn't run past the driveway."

His nose crinkled. "I didn't mean me, but yes, you handled me too. Fucking guilt tripper."

"I didn't trip you!"

He rolled his eyes. "Never mind. I meant what happened on the sofa."

"Oh." I cast him a look. "Shouldn't I have?"

"I don't know. Maybe? You're a constant surprise though." He grinned, leaned forward so he was close enough to cup my chin. "I hope that never changes."

I tipped my head into his palm when his hand just hovered there, not connecting, waiting for me to consent to his touch. "My mind flickers. I won't lie."

"You never need to lie to me."

"I know." And it was remarkably freeing. "You know when I'm tired?"

"Yes, and you can't remember English words?"

"It's like that. But without being tired. My defenses lower, and I forget." I cast him a look from under my lashes. "Every time I flinch when you touch me, I want to scream."

"At me?" Concern flashed on his face.

"No," I said gruffly. "At me. If I could slaughter my demons I would but—"

"They're immortal?" He sighed. "I know how that feels."

He did as well. I reached up and rubbed his temple. "Why are you pushing yourself with the exercise?"

"Because it's my way of killing *my* demons."

"It works?"

"If I say yes, will you wear a sport's bra and those tight shorts to come running with me?"

"I hate running."

Interest appeared in his eyes. "But that's definitely not a no on the sport's bra and tight shorts." He grinned. "Watching you do squats will be better than porn."

I couldn't stop myself from grinning back at him. "You're a pervert."

"Who? *Moi?*" He gasped his outrage before he winked. "I've watched a ton of ugly fuckers do more squats than I ever need to see. You're going to be a pretty view."

"I should hope so," was all I said as I cast a look toward the window. Seeing that it was getting dark, and with little light coming in, casually, I got to my feet and headed over to the counter.

After switching on the light, I headed to the fridge and, as if that had been my intention all along, I reached for a bag of Butterfingers—I'd gone all out with the snacks ever since these two had introduced me to them. I also picked up the Thermos flask of mayflower tea which Quin brewed every few days. I'd learned that he'd gotten special dispensation to use the medicine in Rikers, and drank it religiously.

When I returned to the table, his lips were like a flat line. "Thank you," he said when I passed him the cold flask. "Why is it, do you think, that you're the one who was kept in the dark for weeks and I'm the one who's scared of the dark?"

I winced. "I tried to make it not obvious."

"You did a good job of it too," he said dryly. "But I'm the one with the fear."

"I have my things, you have yours."

"You certainly do." His gaze dropped to my breasts, and he winked at me, which made me grin before I bit into the treat. Then, he cleared his throat. "Have you told Hawk?"

I shook my head. "Why would I?"

He blew out a breath. "It's pathetic."

"Is it? I don't think so."

"You saw what happened yesterday in the tattoo parlor," he said gruffly, his gaze dropping to his tea.

"I saw you freeze for a split second, Quin. It wasn't that bad."

I'd taken to going to the parlor with him when he was helping out there.

In all honesty, it was easy to think that he'd spent most of his adult years in a summer camp. He wasn't dark and moody, depressed or anguished as one might expect now he'd come back to the real world with all its changes and chaos. Then, yesterday, a song had come on the playlist that Indy had booming around the place.

Like that, he'd disappeared.

Standing there, visible, but somehow lost.

I knew how it felt to be transported back to the past.

"You could check Indy's playlists. Make sure there are no songs that are bad."

"Most of Indy's playlists are bad. She has shitty taste," he said wryly.

"Stop joking, Quin," I said with a huff. "You joke too much about serious things."

"It's either laugh or cry, sky girl."

I glanced at him and though it was ridiculous, I saw a splinter there.

A fracture.

His soul was like mine.

Broken.

I swallowed at the sight, then leaned forward to tangle my fingers with his. Every part of me wanted to be his glue, but could a person be that for someone?

"Are you sure you want to go to Indy's tomorrow night?"

"It should be okay. Hawk will have to drive us though. I need to get my driver's license sorted out first."

"Why put yourself through it?"

"Because I'm not five?" He clucked his tongue. "It'll be okay."

"If I don't have to put on a brave face for you, then you don't have to do that for me," I chided.

He shrugged. "Giulia wants to go to the strip joint with Nyx. They deserve a date."

My lips curved. "Only that would be her version of a date."

His gaze darted from the glass in front of him to me. "Hawk told me you had a crush on her?"

"I didn't. I thought I did," I corrected, then feeling proud of myself for using a phrase I'd learned from them, I said, "Apparently she bats for that team too if she wants to see some women take off their clothes."

"I think it's more that she wants to make Nyx suffer."

"It's not his fault she has morning sickness," I pointed out.

"What part of Giulia seems rational?" His brow furrowed. "I know her a lot less than you but even I've come to see her logic is skewed.

"Does it bother you? The strip club?"

"Only that Hawk works there." Perhaps it should concern me that those women were being victimized, but I knew the Sinners too well to think they would use trafficking victims as a source of entertainment.

They were criminals, *villains* in any story, but their crimes weren't against humanity, just society.

His lips twitched. "We already talked about this. He's not interested in those women."

I sniffed. "I'm sure a lot of the wives of the men who used me thought the same thing."

"You don't see how he looks at you."

"I do. I have eyes."

"You don't say." He smirked at me. "Anyway, I mean when you aren't looking at *him*."

"How does he look at me?"

"Like I look at you."

I could feel my cheeks heat up. "Oh." Then I squinted at him.

"You don't know how you look at me. Unless you look in a mirror," I mused.

"I know how I feel."

I frowned. "How do you feel?"

"You sure you're ready for the answer to that, sky girl?" His hand dropped down to my wrist, and his fingertips brushed over my brand. "You should only ask me that when you're ready for the truth."

"I'm always ready for the truth," I said softly.

"Then you know that I love you and don't say that I don't, that it's too soon, that it's crazy, because that comes under the umbrella of not asking me if you're not ready to hear the truth."

He showed me he loved me in many different ways. It wasn't like I didn't know it already. Still, hearing it out loud... it was scary but good.

"What does love feel like to you?" I asked him softly.

"It feels like when I look at you I stop dying inside."

My stomach twisted. "I don't want you to die inside."

"Then always keep watching me," he said softly. "Be there so that when I turn around, I can find you in an instant."

I swallowed. "I can do that."

"Most women would say they can't."

"I'm not most women."

"No, you're my sky girl, aren't you?"

Slowly, I nodded. "I am."

"Aside from when you're teasing me, that's the first time you admitted that."

"I know."

"I'm glad you have."

"Me too." I gnawed on my bottom lip a second.

"What is it?"

"I feel the same way. I want to watch you. All the time. I want to know where you are and when." I released a shaky breath. "This is not healthy."

"Isn't it?" He shrugged. "We all have our coping mechanisms."

"Some are better than others."

"If this helps, then does it matter?"

"When I look at you, the demons can't touch me," I whispered, feeling insane for even verbalizing that, but if there was any sanity left in my mind then I thought it was more by luck than management.

He reached forward, his hand grabbing mine as he tugged me forward, not stopping until I was sitting on his lap. "Then we can keep them away together."

I swallowed. "I need Hawk too."

"I know you do." He didn't appear jealous. "But he's going to be harder to watch, sky girl."

My heart thudded in my chest at his acceptance. Somehow, it made my craziness feel more normal. "I know." A shaky sigh escaped me. "I smelled perfume on him yesterday."

"I'm sure you did. Strippers wear perfume. A lot of it." His brow puckered. "I bet they sweat a shit ton when they're dancing. Ain't exactly gonna make a guy drop some dollar bills if they reek of BO from across the stage."

I knew he didn't mean to make me laugh, but I couldn't stop myself from chuckling. "This makes me feel better. They probably stink."

He nodded, rather sagely. "You don't stink."

"I do now."

He leaned into me, burrowing his face against my chest. It was second nature to raise my hands and to drag them through his hair, to hold him close. It felt right. So goddamn right that I had to close my eyes. "You smell like the sky lands, Amara."

Because I knew what he meant, I tipped my head to the side and pressed a kiss to his temple. "I smell like sex."

"AKA perfect," he declared, smirking as I grinned a little at him. "We can always kill anyone he dares look at."

I arched a brow. "That's not practical. Also very unfair."

"It's good that you know that." Laughing, he nuzzled his nose against my cheek. "He doesn't want them."

"You don't know that." I sucked in a breath. "I can feel him holding back with me. How long before that gets boring?"

"If tonight was you holding back, then how the fuck could he get bored?" He grunted. "You were into it, Amara, I know you were."

I knew what he was saying. "I wasn't scared," I reassured him. "I didn't... well, I didn't let you do that because I was scared of not being enough."

"Good." He grunted. "If I ever find out you've done that—"

I heard the rumble of a warning in his voice and rather than set me on edge, it had me lowering my head and pressing a kiss to his mouth. "What? What will you do?"

"I don't know, but I'll figure it out if you do it."

"I loved every minute of what we did together."

"That's how it should be," he said gruffly as he reached for my hand. He tangled our fingers together, but his thumb stroked along my wrist. "I want to get rid of this tomorrow night." He tapped my brand. "I have an idea for some ink and I'm ready to give it a shot."

He'd been practicing on oranges to get back into the swing of things.

"Okay. I'm ready for it to go as well. You can decide on the design. Anything I think of I fall out of love with. I know you'll pick right."

"Just like that? Indy would probably do a better job than me."

"Maybe she would, but that isn't the point." Letting my gaze drift from the brand, I stared at him, straight in the eye. "It would be more than ink, Quin. Only you could remove it because only you have the power to replace it."

His eyes darkened at that. "Let's bring the thunder, sky girl."

I blinked. "What does that mean?"

"You'll find out soon."

FORTY-FIVE

AMARA

WITH THREE PEOPLE IN A BED, there was no space for Petr, but that hadn't stopped him from sneaking into the room when Quin had gotten up.

Dogs on beds... that was something my mother would never have allowed. We'd had cats around the place to catch mice, but they were animals. Dirty. Not allowed inside. Never mind in bed.

I found a strange amount of satisfaction in having him curl into me, slotting into me as I slotted into the curve of Hawk's stomach. His heat was at my back, ever solid, ever firm.

Reassuring.

Not even an event like Chernobyl would unsteady this man.

A hand slipped around my waist, and when he brushed Petr, the dog stretched with delight at being stroked, but Hawk jerked awake like he'd been tasered in the foot.

I laughed as he rasped, "What the fuck?"

I didn't mind that Quin attracted animals, but the best part was Hawk's reaction.

For the past two days, we'd had a rabbit showing up with

damaged paws that he'd tripped over, and a couple of pigeons who wouldn't leave their stoop on the roof that had crapped on him.

How could I be scared of birds when they did amusing things like that?

Where they loved Quin, they didn't like Hawk. Well, apart from Petr. He liked him.

I shouldn't have found the situation amusing, but it was hard not to.

"Where's Doolittle?" Hawk grumbled, his voice husky with sleep as he sank back in bed. He fidgeted a little, nudging a knee through mine like he wanted to get closer.

Who was I to argue?

"Amazon called."

"Oh, why?"

My lips curved in anticipation of his response. "With a shipment of dry food for the animals."

He groaned. "We'll never get rid of them if we feed them."

"Don't be a sport spoil."

"Spoilsport," he corrected sleepily. "We need a bigger place if he's going to keep bringing half of West Orange's wildlife into the bunkhouse."

"We'll need a bigger place just to store the amount of food he's bought."

He groaned again, then burrowed his face into my throat.

Beds had always been danger zones for me before, but I'd quickly learned that Quin and Hawk were cuddlers. They often woke me up in the middle of the night when they invaded my space, unaware that my heart was pounding with fear, but I didn't have it in me to move away.

I liked sharing a bed.

I liked being sandwiched between them.

For all that their jostling me in bed was a trigger, it was something I'd adapt to to maintain moments like these.

Hawk was busy at work a lot, so my time with him was rare. I wished it wasn't. I really wished it wasn't.

He fell asleep beside me, and to the sounds of Petr's snores, and Hawk's deep breathing, I dissected the odd bubble inside me, one that kept forming in these quiet moments.

His soft and gentle breaths brushed my throat, and I closed my eyes, so unbelievably aware of him at that moment that it was as if it was the first time I could see in years.

How did he make me feel like this?

Like everything was right with the world when it was the exact opposite.

Like I was normal when I was the exact opposite.

He made me hope for more, things that I might never be able to have, but instead of simply wishing for it, he made me want to *be* that way. To be the kind of someone who could lie like this with him, in silence, sleepy together, watching dust motes dancing in the air as the sunlight streamed in through a gap in the curtains. Someone who could be at ease instead of always restless and on edge.

I saw a future with him whereas, before, I saw nothing but a dead end.

The difference was remarkable.

As was the sense of stability he gave me, the feeling of being grounded where Quin made me feel like I could achieve anything...

Which, of course, was untrue.

I couldn't achieve anything I wanted.

I couldn't dance again and I couldn't redo my life so that, when my parents had yelled at me, demanding that I return to ballet school even though each step was agonizing thanks to my injury, I'd listened.

Instead of whining about the pain, I wished I'd danced through it because I wouldn't have endured what I had. Wouldn't have run away from home, wouldn't have cried myself to exhaustion and let my guard down. Wouldn't have been snatched and brought here. Wouldn't have been sold into sexual slavery and almost died in a cage like a wild animal.

Of course, I wouldn't have Hawk and Quin, either.

My jaw worked at that, a desire for a different past at war with the future I wanted for myself.

The idea of being without them... No.

Just, no.

Suddenly restless thanks to my warring thoughts, I wriggled away from Hawk, needing to get up but also needing not to disturb him. He was so tired, though, that he didn't even realize I'd moved.

Petr grumbled but didn't come with me, just shuffled nearer to Hawk, like the dog knew if he woke up, Hawk would tell him to go to his own bed, so Petr wouldn't be able to cuddle up to him.

As I stood watching over them both, the sight made that bubble stir to life inside me again.

What was this bubble?

It was so alien.

So strange.

So... *nice*.

Uncomfortable with this odd warmth, I moved over to the curtain to close them tighter. Hawk needed the sleep so I didn't want the light waking him up but as I peered outside, watching Quin moving bags of what he called *kibble*, I saw them down the driveway.

A group of them.

The warmth in my chest morphed into a searing, surging fire that made me feel like I was roasting in my skin.

There were three of them. Each wearing skirts and shorts so high that their legs were pink in the cold air. On their feet, they wore heels, and their skimpy jackets were the only concession to the biting temperature outside. Some were furry, others were fluffy. They were all bright in color, making them appear like a gaggle of geese who'd been doused in paint.

My hand crumpled the curtain I was holding as I watched them move nearer, their destination Quin.

Jaw tense, uncertain of what to do, unsure if I wanted to see him rebuff them or to know if he was as true to his sky girl as he said he was.

Doubt was infectious, but my desire to maim anyone who looked at them in a way that was sexual was stronger.

Quin didn't help matters by pulling off a sweatshirt. I knew he hadn't seen them because he was hefting the large bags that Amazon had delivered and drawing them inside.

Every now and then, I heard him huffing as he lowered a bag to the ground, so I knew he was working hard, probably when he shouldn't and still needed to rest.

He froze when he caught sight of the clubwhores, and I was relieved to see that his expression was stern as he propped his hands on his hips when they approached. His body language telling them to back off, even if they ignored it.

They talked. Nothing more, nothing less. Then one of them shimmied closer, hips swaying, butt shaking as she reached forward to rest her hand on his shoulder.

That was it.

The second I witnessed that, the heat inside me imploded, turning nuclear in less than five seconds.

I didn't care that it was crazy. Didn't care that I might look ridiculous. I grabbed the lever that opened the window, shoved it open, then hauled myself over it.

Wearing nothing but one of Hawk's tees and a pair of Quin's boxer briefs, too furious to feel the cold, I stormed over to them. My steps were silent thanks to being barefoot, and the grass crackled beneath my feet as I slipped into the scene without their awareness.

Quin knew, though.

I saw the amusement in his eyes.

Amusement that grew when I reached for the hand that had dared to touch him, drew it back and away, before I slammed my other fist into the woman's face. She immediately squealed as blood gushed, and while the other painted geese jerked back and away, not wanting to draw my attention, I grabbed her wrist with mine, drew her fingers back until I heard a snap, then I punched her again.

Before I spat on her, I snarled, "You do not touch him." I glared at them all. "Any of you."

One of them staggered back so fast and so hard that her heel snapped, where the other just squealed at Quin.

"Aren't you going to stop her?"

"OMG, this is horrendous."

"You broke her nose. Enya, are you okay?"

"I can't move my hand."

I stared at them all, unrepentant, uncaring, while Quin tucked his arm over my shoulder and murmured, "Feel better, sky girl?"

"She's crazy! OMG, wait until I tell Rex."

Quin grumbled, "Shut up, Peaches. Like he'll care. I told you to fuck off but you didn't listen."

"You need a guard dog now?"

"Fuck you, Kendra. In fact, you'd better get her to the ER. Enya looks like she's about to pass out."

"Aren't you going to help?"

Quin shrugged. "I value my balls too much."

"How whipped are you?"

"Kendra, I've heard about the shit you've been pulling. Maybe bringing yourself to Amara's attention isn't the smartest thing to do?"

She tensed, but I demanded, "What has she been doing?"

Kendra's nose, all beak and big nostrils, tipped up into the sky. Truly, you could see the Milky Way in those cavities. "Nothing." She bent down and helped the woman I'd attacked onto her feet. "Come on, Enya, let's get you away from this psycho."

"I'm totally gonna tell Rex," the one Quin had called Peaches declared as she shoved Enya's good arm around her neck. "We only came to say hello!"

"You have said it," I growled stonily. "Now fuck off."

As they staggered away, shooting me daggers and glares as they did so, my tension didn't ease as I turned to Quin.

Unapologetic, I rasped, "They touched you."

"I know, sky girl," he chirped, leaning forward to press a kiss to the tip of my nose.

As he did, I felt his erection brush against my hip, which told me my behavior aroused him.

He was a very odd man.

"Little bird?"

I tensed, then guiltily shot a look back at the bunkhouse. Hawk shook his head at me, but much like Quin, I saw amusement in his eyes.

He curled his finger at me, beckoning me toward the window, and even though it made me feel like a naughty girl, I squeezed Quin's arm, then trudged back the way I came.

At that moment, I knew neither of them would hurt me.

Ever.

I'd done something excessive—even for me—but this bleating monster inside of me had seen that *suka's* hand on Quin, and it had demanded she be made to regret that.

And if they'd even seen Hawk standing there, that necklace he wore, his compass tattoo on display, his pecs and abs all delineated from the way he was leaning against the window, then I'd have had to pluck their eyes out.

As I approached, he held out his hands and I realized he was going to pull me back in the way I'd left.

Frowning at the unorthodox entrance—not that I could say much as I was well aware this was what doors were for—I let him pull me through. Petr stood on the bed, tail wagging with glee now I was back, and then Hawk rumbled, "Come on, little bird, let's get some more sleep. Someone's cranky."

That had me grumbling, "I'm not tired."

"You will be soon. Your adrenaline will crash."

Because he was pulling me into bed, I almost tensed up, then, I realized he hadn't made me feel bad for what I'd done. Hadn't even chided me. If he was angry, he'd have shouted. I hadn't heard either man shout. Ever.

He must have sensed my confusion, because as he plunked on the bed once more, around a yawn he muttered, "You forget I'm Giulia's brother." Then, he wrapped his arms around my waist, and grumbled, "I need to start working a more regular job."

Because that was off-topic, I asked, "I don't understand."

He sighed. "So I can sleep with you at night, of course."

I wouldn't argue.

Him working at a strip joint was my idea of hell.

I hummed. "I would like this," was all I said.

He snorted, like he knew I'd *love* it, before he rumbled, "I only work there 'cause Rex asked me to fill in. I'm on Sin's crew, little bird." I knew Sin was the MC's Enforcer. "I go where I'm sent." His voice was sleepy, and when he yawned, I caught it and yawned too.

"You worked there before Jarrod's accident," I pointed out.

"They're always short on bouncers." He yawned once more. "Sleep, siren. You need to preserve your energy for the next cat fight."

While that wasn't reassuring, it also made me realize that darker tactics were required.

As I started to drift to sleep, I knew that breaking every woman's wrist in West Orange wasn't doable. I needed something contagious. Something that spread like wildfire.

And I knew I had it.

Gossip.

FORTY-SIX

QUIN

AMARA HAD A POINT; I needed to vet Indy's playlist.

Not just for songs that triggered me, but for fucking shit songs too.

Music was a rare commodity inside. We could buy MP3 players from the commissary and could stack some music onto them if we were 'model' prisoners with enough cash on the hip to afford it.

While Indy had hooked me up when I was inside, the commissary cost a fortune, and music wasn't as important as ramen—currency within the bars of Rikers. The only songs I'd heard were if my cellmate let me listen on his player, and Rodrigo had worse taste in music than Indy.

Fuck, I hated EDM.

Just listening to Martin Garrix right now was sending me back there.

When I was on the compound, inside with Amara and Hawk, I was okay. I could even deal with being bombarded by ads and colors, bright lights and loud jingles. But the second I stepped out, it was hardcore impossible not to freak the fuck out.

I felt like my brain was frazzled, and it resonated with me even more how Amara had leveled me out. If I hadn't met her, I was pretty sure I'd have been a head case by now.

As I listened to Troy Sivan talking about the past year taking its toll on him—because yeah, he'd been stuck in jail on trumped up fucking charges—I shifted my head to the side and found Amara.

She was watching me.

Another guy might find it creepy. Maybe Hawk did, I didn't know. But fuck, I loved it.

Those deep brown eyes made me feel like she was peeling back my skin to see beneath it, to see the real fucking me. The muscles and the marrow, the bones and the blood.

She wasn't doing anything special, just sitting with her legs up on the low coffee table, her hands in her lap as she described another monster for me to convey onto paper, but I felt like she was a magnet. Drawing me out of the weird flashback the song had made me face plant in with that intent stare.

"I bet you were a wolf in a past life."

She blinked, breaking the stare. "A wolf?" Her brows met in the middle. "Why?"

I could feel the cold sweat on my back, but shrugging it off, I muttered, "You're good at staring me out."

"At least you did not say dog."

I cast Petr a look as she dropped her hand over the side of the sofa to stroke him.

He had his own basket here now, blankets and shit too. I wasn't sure when we'd gotten a pet, but yeah, it had happened. Mostly, I was just glad he'd taken a liking to Amara. I was a pussy person all the way. And I wasn't talking about felines.

"Nah, you're too feral to be house-trained."

"There is compliment in there, I think," she grumbled, dropping her articles which told me more than anything that we were done for the night.

Steadily, ever since I'd returned to West Orange, we'd been working on purging her of her demons.

Every day, we were pulling out four or five faces from her memory banks. Today, we'd achieved an amazing six, all of which had been sent to Lodestar. I'd been set to work on unlucky number seven when Martin Garrix came on and ruined my vibe.

Now I knew she was tired, plus I wasn't feeling all that great what with the urge to claw at my skull—ya know, shit like that—we definitely weren't going to carry on with the drawing tonight.

Well... drawing *these* cunts, at any rate.

"Where is your mind tonight?" Amara asked softly, and it was only then I noticed that she'd gotten to her feet and was standing right in front of the reception desk.

A creepzoid used to work here. David, I thought his name was. Apparently, he'd disappeared, and ever since, Giulia had been working on the front desk. She was also training to be a piercer.

Why the fuck anyone would trust Giulia with one of their body parts was beyond me.

"I don't know," I admitted when she sidled even closer, and I parted my legs, spreading them so she could step between them. Resting my hands on her hips, I leaned forward, and pushed my face into her belly.

"You will suffocate and die," she murmured, but I heard her amusement as she started to scrape her nails over my scalp. Christ, that always felt so epic. Little tingles ran down the length of my spine, making me want to shiver in a good way.

"I won't," I said, voice muffled as I suffocated.

"You will." She snickered. "And I have much use of you." She tugged on my shaggy locks, pulling my head back so we could look at each other. "Inhale and exhale." Her voice had turned soothing. "Inhale deeply, hold your breath for a count of two, then release on a count of two."

My eyelashes fluttered to a close as she carried on stroking my hair, but I did as she asked, and after a few moments, I started feeling better.

"Do you know why I was in jail?"

"Because you were wrongly tried?"

"I had a rep," I admitted. "I used to jack cars." Then, when I knew she wouldn't understand what that was, I explained, "I'd break into them, disarm the alarms, and I'd race them. I almost always got away with it."

"Until you didn't."

"I used to hijack shit cars, not expensive ones. They fitted me up for that crime."

She stroked my hair. "I'm sorry, Quin."

"Money is worth more than a life in the system," I rasped. "Because the car was worth half a million, I was fucked right from the start."

Amara pressed a kiss to my head.

"I hate this song," I said thickly.

"You hate where it takes you," she corrected.

My mouth tightened because I could feel it start to fucking quiver. "You can never let your guard down in there," I rasped. "Ever. Even when you think you're safe, you're not." Her hand hesitated for a millisecond before she carried on stroking my hair. "I was stupid. It was about to be lights out. I thought—" I shook my head. "My cellmate back then had an MP3 player, and I was listening to it. That was when they came in."

Her fingers moved down to the back of my neck. She started palpating the muscles there.

"They?"

"Yes."

She hummed. "You got them back for it?"

"In a way. It added to my time inside, but I'm no one's bitch. I wasn't about to set up fucking shop as the go-to screw in my block." I swallowed back the memories.

"Have they been released?"

"One has."

She hummed again. "I think we should visit, don't you?"

I bit my bottom lip. "There are people out there who are more deserving of death."

"Aren't there always?" Amara asked wryly.

"I wanted..." I pushed my forehead into her stomach again for a handful of seconds before I told her, "When Nyx told me Indy was abused as a kid too, and then that he was hanging up his hat on the rampage front because Giulia and the baby needed him not to be in jail, all I could think was that the minute I got out, I was going to carry on in his stead."

"We can do that," she murmured, her hand pulling my hair back again so I could look her square in the eye. "I am more than okay with this."

"Now I'm out, sky girl, I don't think I can go back in."

"So we don't get caught. We be like Nyx."

"He was blessed."

"By *Otesho*, I know." She shrugged. "Maybe you were as well."

"I got put inside on trumped up charges, babe. Not sure I have his luck."

Her nose crinkled. "You know what I mean."

"I do, but I know that if I get hauled back inside, that's it. Game over."

"So, no revenge?"

Did she sound disappointed?

I heaved a sigh. "Some revenge is necessary. I just don't know if—"

She scowled down at me. "Don't you dare say that you don't deserve justice," she snapped. "I deserve it because of what I went through but you don't?" She scoffed, the sound derisive and angry—on my behalf. "What kind of logic is this?"

I grunted. "Sensible logic. *Chivalrous* logic."

"Chivalrousity—" She grunted, evidently floundering for the noun.

"Chivalry," I told her.

"Thank you. *Chivalry* has no place in our life or our decisions.

What you endured deserves as much punishment as what I did. You undersell yourself, Quin."

My brow puckered as I looked up at her, well aware that she believed that. That she truly felt that way.

"How are you so selfless?"

"I am not," she discounted instantly. "I'm very selfish."

She wasn't. She was generous. With herself as well as in other ways. That she didn't see that disturbed me.

Because Rome wasn't built in a day, I merely said, "Thank you."

"For what?"

"Thinking that I matter." I hadn't mattered to anyone other than family for way too long. Society had really fucked me over. In more ways than one.

Even though it was awkward because of our proximity, she bowed down over me to kiss my forehead before muttering something in Ukrainian.

"What does that mean?"

I felt her smile against my forehead. "Are you sure you're ready for the answer to that, Winnange?" My heart started racing. "You should only ask me that when you're ready for the truth."

"I think I can deal with it." I gulped, knowing where she was going with this, how she was parroting my words from last night back at me.

"I love you, Quin," she breathed. "I should have told you last night but—"

Drawing my arms around her hips, I hauled her tighter into me, squeezing her a little to make sure she didn't disappear.

When she'd asked what love looked like to me last night, I wasn't sure—

I should have known though.

She *was* generous with herself. How could a woman like her have learned *not* to love? Especially with the men who were born to give her wings?

Still, life had let me down too many times to have total faith, but hearing her now, fuck, I almost wanted to goddamn cry. In the face of what I'd just shared, of... My throat closed. She loved me anyway.

Though I'd been weak.

Though I'd been taken by force, gang-raped...

"Quin, do you think less of me for what I went through?"

I immediately tensed and pulled back, booming, "No! Of course not. How could you think that?!"

Amara smiled a little, her hand cupping my cheek, the thumb drifting back and forth just beneath my lower lip. "Then why would I think less of you?"

She had a point.

Before I could say another word, Indy drifted out from the backroom, her client in tow. I gave Amara another squeeze, mouthing the words back at her, "I love you, sky girl." Her smile set my heart on fucking fire as she shuffled away, not moving back to the sofa where Petr was watching on with disapproval—possessive little fucker—but behind me so that I could deal with arranging another *pro bono* appointment for the woman who was having her mastectomy scars covered up.

Indy stretched out her arms and hands when the customer went away, and after she yawned, Amara asked, "How did it go today, Indy?"

When we'd arrived, she had already been in the studio with her client so this was the first time we'd been able to ask.

"Great," Indy said with a sleepy smile. "I'm just tired."

"How's it working?" I asked.

"They'll be in to film within the next few weeks," she said, some excitement bleeding into her tired voice. "But so far, it's more about the designs."

"It's a competition, right?" I asked, feeling bad for not having delved into this with her before. It was a massive deal for her career but since I'd been let out, it hadn't exactly been quiet.

"No. A showcase. Basically these people come in for tattoos, and we have to create their designs. The cameras track the whole process, and we learn why the person wants that particular design, and what led to it. Then they watch me come up with the drawing and go through the inking process.

"Only four tattooists are having their studios featured on the show."

"That's fantastic, Indy," Amara told her, beaming at her. "I can't wait to watch it."

Indy's nose crinkled. "Well, I'm not looking forward to that part. You guys can watch it and tell me if it's a pile of shit."

I snorted. "As if."

"Cruz is under orders that he can watch it anywhere but here." She grunted, and an expression I couldn't read whispered across her face. A combination of amused thoughtfulness. Like she hoped he'd listen, but doubted it, which she sort of confirmed by muttering, "He'd better listen."

Another yawn escaped her, prompting me to say, "Look, why don't you go upstairs and clock out for the day? We'll stay open until closing time, but I can just take appointments."

She pulled a face. "Rent's due next week."

"So? The rent won't be paid if you do a shit design because you're exhausted." I didn't say that Cruz wasn't about to let her take the burden of a late payment... at least, not if he didn't want to eat my fist.

Brothers were on good money.

"True." She yawned again. "Stop being wise. I don't like it. It's freaky."

My lips twitched. "Fuck off."

She grunted, waved a hand at Amara, and muttered, "Night, guys. See you tomorrow."

When she trudged toward the door to the staircase that led to her apartment above the studio, and we could hear her footsteps, I murmured, "Lock the door, Amara."

"Is that wise? You just said you'd stay open—"

"We will, the lights will be on, and I'll keep the door to the backroom open so I can see if someone tries to come in, but I want to show you something."

She frowned. "What is it?"

I grinned. "You haven't seen this before."

That had her rolling her eyes, but she drifted over to the door and locked it, displaying yet another wave of trust.

I wasn't sure why *Aashaa* believed I was good enough for her, and doubted Her judgment in all honesty, but I'd spend the rest of my fucking life making sure that I tried to be the man my sky girl deserved.

Even if it killed me.

FORTY-SEVEN

HAWK

IT HAD BEEN a weird night at the club, but then, this place was rarely fucking normal.

Working as a bouncer was something I hated, but it paid the bills and it wasn't like I could complain about that.

Just knowing my baby sister was somewhere inside amped up the weirdness factor though. Why the hell Nyx had brought her here was beyond me, but then, why he did the shit he did was too.

When news of a fight breaking out bleated in my ear piece, I told the other guy on the door, Hungry John, that I'd deal with it. Mostly because I was curious what was going on inside.

Was Giulia going to have a knife held against Nyx's dick if it twitched when he looked at one of the strippers?

I'd probably pay to see *that*, to be fair, so dealing with a fight just gave me a free excuse to go inside.

The club was neither low-key nor high-luxury. It was a clean place, especially in the dark.

Everywhere was black and red, the stage was silvery, almost reflective, and above it, there were mirrors too that added to the atmosphere, and the chairs were black vinyl, be they stools at the stage or club chairs in the background.

Servers wandered around in bikini bottoms and nothing else apart from garters on their thighs for tips, James Dean was behind the bar with a couple other brothers and they just wore cuts and jeans, no shirts. I figured that was for the surprisingly high number of women who came to the club.

Giulia was by no means the first woman to darken these halls, but her logic behind being here was definitely suspicious.

It sounded horrible, but I didn't trust her. She was a hand grenade with the pin pulled out. If Nyx didn't realize that hand grenade was tucked right between his dick and his balls, then that was his downfall.

There was the stage upfront which took up two thirds of the bar, then there was the seating area where 'personal' lap dances went down. These club chairs were cordoned off, and were considered VIP areas—patrons had to pay a surcharge to sit there.

The ongoing fight was happening in one such area, and I had to hide my grin at the sight of three fucking pansies going at each other like those guys from that flick Mom had made me watch years ago—*Bridget Jones' Diary*. I swore, they were slapping each other with their hands, not punching or aiming for hits.

Rolling my eyes when they all jumped as I barked, "What the fuck is going on here?" I folded my arms across my chest and snapped, "Well?" when no one replied.

They just stood there, wobbling on their feet from way too much —a quick glance at their table told me what their poison of choice was —tequila, while the guy who had a wedding veil on his head, the lucky groom, I assumed, had his head tipped back, snoring loudly, the private lap dance he was being given totally wasted on him.

When Laroux saw I was here, she twisted around with a coy smile and, with her eyes on mine, started twerking like she'd been born to flex that ass.

Disinterested, I looked at the other guys, the poor bastard's groomsmen, who were on the brink of pissing themselves.

"W-We're just discussing something," one 'brave' fucker replied.

"Didn't look like much of a discussion to me."

If they'd been smacking the shit out of each other, I'd have hauled them out, but these fuckers were too smashed to do much damage to the furniture, and that was all that bothered me.

"I said Brady couldn't whoop ass if he was a Buccaneer," another guy muttered.

God, this was about football?

Inwardly, I groaned. "Okay, you're gonna sit the fuck down, stop fighting, stop talking about Brady—"

"He's MVP," the only guy who hadn't spoken yet called, and for some reason, that set them off again.

As they merged into a cat fight, I waded in, pulling them apart, receiving some pussy-assed licks as they slapped me, and then I shoved one of them hard enough against his chair for the seat to rock back, while the others plunked on the floor, looking like kids in the middle of a tantrum in the grocery store aisle.

"That's it," I snapped. "You have five minutes to wake your friend up and you're out of here."

They blinked up at me, before one guy toppled back and fell asleep on the floor, while the others crawled onto their knees and tried to wake the groom up.

I could have told them that if Laroux twerking on him didn't wake him up, they weren't gonna be able to do shit.

Eying James Dean behind the bar, who called on Inked and Two Knives, we each hauled one of the dicks outside, tossing them in the back alley.

"Christ, they're asleep again," I muttered when collective rounds of snores moved around the circle like they'd been sniffing too much laughing gas.

"Leave 'em here. Serves their asses right if they get their wallets stolen," Two Knives grunted, flexing his hands as he stalked back inside to the bar.

Because he wasn't wrong, we returned too, and as James Dean joined Two Knives, me and Inked cleaned up the area they'd been sitting. Spotting a puddle of liquid I really didn't want to clean up, I grinned at Inked and said, "That's part of the barman's duty. I'm needed outside."

"Motherfucker," Inked grunted as I backed away, right into Laroux.

Her hands slipped around my waist and I rumbled, "Thought there was a 'no touching' rule in this place?"

She snorted. "That's to protect me, not you."

"Well, I disagree. Get your hands off me, Laroux. Don't know how many times I got to tell you I ain't interested before you get the picture."

The stripper pouted as she darted in front of me, her hands coming up to my pecs. "Is it true?"

"Is what true?"

"You got yourself an Old Lady?"

My mouth tightened. "Who's been spreading gossip about me?"

She huffed. "Does it matter?"

"Yeah, it fucking does," I snapped. "Who?"

The last thing I wanted was word getting out about me, Quin, and Amara in town. I already felt like she had one foot out the door because this situation was intense between us. If gossip started flying, then she might disappear. I thought the Sinners had already put two and two together where we were concerned, but the MC wouldn't judge her.

She heaved another sigh. "I don't know. I just heard is all." Laroux shimmied against me, her tits bouncing off my chest in a way that did zero for my dick. "Come on, Hawk, we were good together—"

"We fucked around once or twice, Laroux."

Her hand delved between us and I knew where it was going, but before I could stop her, someone was there. They snatched Laroux's wrist, twisted it around, then jerked her arm behind her back.

"There a reason you're sniffing around him, skank?"

It was my turn to sigh. "Giulia, I don't need you to protect my virtue."

"Fucking virtue, my ass," my baby sister snapped. "You always did watch too many of those Jane Austen flicks with Mom." She scowled at Laroux who towered over her without the five-inch heels on her feet. "You fucking know he's taken, right?"

Now wasn't the time to get into technicalities, was it?

Amara was probably the only person who didn't consider herself taken in our triad.

"I didn't know shit," Laroux snapped. "So, you're that insane bitch Nyx is with." She squealed when Giulia tightened the grip on her arm, jerking it higher up her back until I saw sweat pop out of Laroux's pores.

"Wouldn't call her that," Nyx advised, seeming to appear from out of nowhere. "She doesn't like it." His grin was twisted as he slid his arm around Giulia's belly, quite content for her to be assaulting one of our dancers. He pressed a kiss to her forehead. "Let her go, babe. She's on the clock."

Giulia grunted but did as he asked. "If she's on the fucking clock, then why's she sniffing around Hawk?"

"That's a fair question." Nyx cast Laroux a look, and she turned white. So fucking white, it made Casper look blue. Nyx's rep preceded him, and while everyone knew he wouldn't hurt a woman, everyone *also* knew that Giulia was not on a leash. "Why the fuck are you sniffing around a brother, Laroux? Ain't you supposed to be working?"

"I-I'm on a break," Laroux whispered, almost too low to be heard over the music as she cradled the arm Giulia had let go of.

"I think that break's over. Get your ass back on the fucking stage where it belongs."

Her mouth quivered but she darted away.

Giulia muttered, "So much wrong with that statement, Nyx. We really need to enlighten you to the ways of feminism."

"I'm a feminist," Nyx retorted. "She's fucking working. It makes no difference to me if it's on the stage or behind the bar. If she worked behind the bar, I'd have told her to get her ass back there."

Though she rolled her eyes, Giulia moved into him before she glowered up at me. "Why the fuck did you let her touch you, Hawk?"

"What was I supposed to do? Throw her on the floor?"

"She was gonna grab your dick."

I shrugged. "Wouldn't be the first time. I'm a big fucking boy, Giulia. I can tell her to back off myself."

Her mouth tightened. "Amara likes you."

"So? I didn't do shit. Anyway, since when were you her biggest defender? Wasn't that fucking long ago you were watching Alessa smash her face into the table."

Her scowl didn't lessen. "For the club. I had to make sure she wasn't a rat." When she turned to look at Nyx, I did as well and found him watching the bar. Not the strippers or the servers. The fucking bar.

Typical.

A few weeks ago, I'd have shaken my head at him, called him hopeless, but the weird thing was, now, I got it. I hadn't before, but tits and asses were great, but they were even better when they belonged to the woman you really wanted.

"What's up?" I asked.

"Inked's acting weird."

"I just made him clear up something questionable. He's probably got the stench of piss or puke in his nose."

Nyx tightened his lips. "Nah." He shook his head. "I'll let Rex deal with this shit. This ain't my problem."

Because I was curious, I wondered what he'd seen. "What is it?"

"Think he's on the take." He shrugged. "Never mind."

Surprised, I turned and watched the bartender a second, before

Giulia pushed me in the stomach. "Look, Nancy Drew, don't be shitting on Amara. I'm telling you, she's good for you."

Absentmindedly, I told her, "I know she is," all the while my eyes were on Inked.

"Huh?"

I scowled down at my sister. "I fucking know she is, all right? I wasn't gonna do shit with Laroux. She's been shoving her pussy in my face all fucking week and I haven't bitten once, and I won't."

"You getting serious?" Nyx asked, his own surprise clear.

"Maybe."

"How's that working?" he queried. "I mean… you and Quin and Amara have been at the bunkhouse for over a week now."

"We're together." I tightened my lips, because there I was, thinking the MC wouldn't judge us. "You got a problem with that?"

He shrugged. "Don't give a fuck. Just making sure my bro's all right."

"You're in a…" Giulia blinked. *"Threesome?"* Her brow furrowed. "How's Amara even dealing with that?"

"We're not forcing her if that's what you're—"

Nyx snickered. "Babe, you should have seen how she sliced and diced that fucker. Trust me, if she didn't want our brothers around her, then she could protect herself."

"Doesn't mean I shouldn't check." Giulia studied me a second. "I already asked her to be a part of the Posse, so you've been warned. Hurt her, and we'll hurt you."

Not mad at her because I knew she meant it, and Amara needed friends more than she realized, I simply shook my head at her. "You got an initiation ceremony?"

"No, but I'm thinking of making one up," she retorted. "Spill blood for the MC and you're in."

"Where the fuck did Mom go so wrong with you, huh? I swear you've got rabies."

"Watch it," Nyx growled, but he didn't tense up so I didn't prepare for a fight.

Giulia shot me a smug look. "You'd better not stop her from joining."

"Why would I? She needs friends."

The more she had, the more settled she'd feel. If she had ties here, she wouldn't fucking leave, and even though they'd been through a similar situation, I was well aware that Amara and Alessa weren't friendly, because I didn't think they'd sought each other out once. Of course, Alessa bashing her face into the kitchen table probably hadn't smoothed over their relationship any.

"You gonna brand her?" Nyx asked.

I shrugged. "Don't know what we're doing."

Giulia stomped her foot. "If you're just messing her around—"

"She's the one who's wary, Giulia. Not me, all right?"

"Understandable." Nyx squeezed her arm. "She's allowed to fool around, find her footing, babe."

Giulia grumbled, "I guess. Just don't hurt her, okay?"

I didn't say anything, simply muttered, "Giulia, don't get involved in shit that has nothing to do with you."

And with that, I stormed off because the last thing I needed was more shit from her.

When they didn't follow me, I was aware they stayed in the club, doing only fuck knew what, but I was grateful when the rest of the shift was quiet.

Just as we started closing for the night, the grooms' party wandered out from the alley behind the club and, looking worse for wear, staggered over to a car.

Were the dipshits really going to try to drive?

Jesus.

I stormed over there, not only because it could blow back on the club that we'd served them too much alcohol, but also because I couldn't let the fuckers go onto the road as drunk as they were.

Thankfully, they were still bickering and mostly wasted. So when I watched one of them move around the fender, keys in hand, I crossed the road to the parking lot, and ran over to them once they were all slouched in the car. Only the driver's door remained open, so I darted forward, grabbed that door, leaned in, snatched the keys away, shoved the door shut, and locked them in.

It was pretty fucking hilarious how they just gaped at me, all of them so drunk they didn't remember they could open the doors themselves.

Fuckfaces.

I stood there, arms folded across my chest, just waiting for them to come after me, but they didn't. A few fell asleep as I stared them out, so I tossed the keys in my hand, and as I passed a mailbox, I slotted them in there.

It was more than they deserved for even thinking about driving.

Hungry John grinned at me when I made it back to my post. "Think they'll remember anything of what just happened?"

"No. But as long as they don't kill someone tonight, I'm fine with that."

In the following thirty minutes, once the clean-up was over, girls drifted out to their cars in the lot over the road, and Hungry John and I waited until they were safely in their vehicles before we started closing the building down.

Inked, Two Knives and James Dean headed out, and when there was no sight of Giulia and Nyx, I didn't even want to know which part of the club they were violating, but I left them to it.

Hungry John and I headed out at the same time, him heading to a subdivision where he was shacked up with his baby momma, while I made my way to the compound.

It hadn't been too hard a shift, just fucking boring, and I knew Giulia was going to tell Amara about Laroux even though it had been perfectly goddamn innocent and I didn't do shit wrong.

Riding back to the compound was miserable in winter, required a lot of layers and heavy-duty winter gloves or my hands would feel like they were going to drop off, so I was relieved as hell to make it through the compound gates.

Like I'd come to expect, there was a light on in the... could I call it home? It had only been a week but it felt like it. There was no hiding from the truth, was there?

I pulled up on the small track beside the building, then stretching and yawning at the same time, I strode over to the door, unlocked it, then let myself in.

Amara was asleep on the sofa, with a book and her phone lying beside her head. She looked like an angel. So clean and pure and sweet that everything inside me ached at the sight of her.

As I closed the door, when I turned back around, I saw her eyes were open and she was watching me. I felt her gaze burn through me like a fucking laser. I knew, right then, right fucking there, my bitch of a sister had messaged her.

"I didn't touch her." I figured that was the best way to start things off. Especially after Quin had filled me in with the deets of this morning's clash between her and the clubwhores.

"She touched you though," Amara ground out, a strange pitch to her words that I couldn't read.

It wasn't cold. Neither was it angry. It wasn't lifeless nor throbbing with emotion.

"She did," I agreed quietly, suddenly knowing how it felt to have a fucking bear right in front of me, one that'd maul my face off if I so much as blinked.

Slowly, she rolled to her feet, the blanket dropping away, revealing a very naked Amara. With that, she stalked toward me.

Yeah, stalked was the fucking word.

And it was the sexiest shit I'd ever seen in my goddamn life.

When she was there, right in front of me, her hand went to my dick. I didn't flinch, didn't react, but when she squeezed her fingers around my shaft, I let out a hiss, especially when she pulled on the zipper, dragged it down, then delved between the tines.

"This is mine," she rumbled, squeezing again, and her nails dug into the side of my shaft.

I let out another hiss, but I reached down and covered her hand with mine so that the pressure grew fiercer.

"You can slice it off if I stray," I rumbled back as, with my other arm, I caught her by the waist, hauled her into me, then twisted us around so she had her back to the door. Shoving her against it, I rested that same arm above her head so I was looming over her, and snarled, "I didn't fucking touch her."

"You didn't stop her—" she snarled back.

"I didn't get the chance." I bent my head and bit her bottom lip. She hissed. "Don't try me and convict me without hearing what happened."

"I don't care what happened. She touched you." A flurry of Ukrainian escaped her as she bounced onto tiptoe and treated me to the same—she bit my lip, hard enough to fucking hurt. "I can't stand it," she growled, punctuating the statement with another squeeze to my dick that, oddly enough, felt fucking awesome. "No one's allowed to touch you but me."

It could be said that after what she'd gone through, what all the women had gone through, their sanity might be a little shaky, but it was right then, right there, that I saw the fissures in hers.

Fissures that I'd never be able to heal, Quin either.

She was broken.

She'd been betrayed. She'd been hurt. She'd been tortured. She'd been starved, and left to die like an animal...

There was no coming back from that.

No way to heal when someone had been exposed to the worst shit humanity was capable of.

She'd admitted to me that the only way she felt sure she'd gain any peace was through the murder of the people who'd hurt her, and denied that opportunity by Rex, I got the feeling she'd compartmentalized, shrunk everything down, turned it and twisted it inside a box of Pandora-like proportions.

I saw, then and there, Quin and me were in that box too.

Not because we were bad for her, but because we were volatile entities she couldn't control but needed to.

It was, I realized, a do or die moment.

I could walk out the door, head away from what I saw down the line, or...

My jaw clenched.

I couldn't do that.

I couldn't leave her.

Not when, despite those fissures, I could see a future in her eyes too.

A weird one, to be sure. A violent one, definitely. But one filled with something I'd never had before, something I'd never wanted.

"Hawk," she rasped. "Do you hear me? No one's allowed to touch you but me."

"Good thing I don't feel that way about Quin, ain't it?" Her nostrils flared, but before she could snap at me, I dropped my forehead to hers and rasped, "What do you want me to do, Amara? What do you want me to say?"

Her bottom lip quivered, breaking my fucking heart in the process. "I don't know."

"There's nothing *to* say. This world we live in, there are bitches everywhere that try to get it on with the brothers because they want to be an Old Lady.

"Fuck knows why. It ain't like they're gonna be the town's VIPs," I groused. "There'll be a fuck ton of bitches who will lie and will tell you that ABC happened, when jack all did." My nostrils flared. "You're gonna have to learn to trust me, Amara."

Her other hand moved around my waist, and she clutched at me there. "I don't know how to."

"You'll learn, little bird, because I'll show you, and I ain't going to give you any reason to doubt me."

"You don't know that." Her fingers lessened their grip on my cock. "I-I, what I feel for you, it's..."

"You're scared of losing it?" Maybe she wasn't the only crazy one here. My heart leaped at the possibility. "I know how that feels, siren. I swear to you now, I'm half sure that I'm going to wake up one day and you're not going to be here."

She tensed. "What? Why?"

"Because I don't see you sticking this out."

"I-I don't understand."

"Me either. I just know that I don't want you to go. I don't want you anywhere but here. Do you hear me?

"Why the fuck would I want another pussy? Another hand around my dick? Another mouth around it, a different set of tits in my face and an ass bouncing on top of me that isn't yours?" I reached up and cupped her cheeks, holding her in place as I pressed my mouth to hers. "Don't you get it? You had me in the kitchen that day. I looked at you and it was like a fucking bullet to the head, little bird."

She shook in my hold. "N-No, that's not—"

"Don't tell me how I feel," I rasped. "I'm telling you what I know. No one's made me feel this way before.

"You fill me up from the inside. Grief's left massive fucking holes in my heart, Amara. My dad, my mother, my brother... all gone. The only one I've got left is that fucking bitch of a sister.

"I've never been alone before. I've always had North. Without him, I felt like I'd lost half of me. We've done everything together my whole life. He even did a stint as a bounty hunter too but he got fired because he was shit at it." My lips quirked up into a grin at the memory, which was more than I'd been capable of before. "You make me see the truth."

"What's that?" she whispered, the aggression of earlier bleeding away as she stared up at me, vulnerability and need in her eyes.

"I thought North was my soul mate. I thought, when we were born, we'd been cut in half. I figured we'd go through life together, would do everything..." I blew out a breath then admitted, "I even figured we'd eventually share a woman.

"He's everything I'm not, Amara. He's kind and generous and capable of being gentle. I'm just a grouchy bastard—"

"No, you're not," she snapped. "You're not a bastard and you're not grouchy."

I shrugged. "I am though."

"Inside these walls you're not. Here is all that counts."

Though I smiled at her defense, it quickly died. "You'd have been better off with someone like North, little bird—" She barked, "No," but I ignored her, to continue, "But even though I know you're fucked up, and even though I'm pretty sure Quin is too, there ain't no way I'm giving you up." I pushed my forehead harder against hers. "North might be better suited for you, and I might have thought he was my soul mate, but I see it clearly now..."

I felt her brow pucker beneath mine in confusion. "I don't see it. See what?"

My lips curved. "He made me ready for you."

"Huh?"

"I've protected him all our lives. Did you know that?"

"No, you never talk about North. How could I know?"

That was because it hurt knowing how he'd fucking abandoned me the second he'd—

As soon as it surged inside me, I let the bitterness drain away.

In the here and now, there was no place for it.

Swallowing, I rasped, "I kept a roof over our heads when he lost job after job. I fed us, made sure we had our bills paid, I had his back. All of that happened though to make me ready for this moment."

"I will always have your back," she growled. "I am not like North."

"I know you're not, little bird," I rumbled, leaning down to press our lips together. "But I always thought he was the light and I was the dark. I thought that was how we were. You know, like yin and yang? Now, though, I know that I have light in me—it was just waiting for you to bother shining."

She sucked in a shocked breath, then her mouth was on mine. No longer was she tearing at my lips with her teeth, she plunged her tongue between them, thrusting against mine as she practically clambered up me like a goddamn monkey.

Not wanting to loom over her now, I picked her up then twisted around so I was leaning on the wall, and as I hefted her high, she clung to me, her knees digging into my waist.

She reached between us and pressed her pussy to my dick, but not sinking down onto it, she rocked against me, riding it, making herself wet, grinding into me like she knew exactly what she needed.

When she was ready, she reached down and though it was awkward, managed to fit the tip in. As gravity had her sinking onto me, filling her full with my shaft, our groans intertwined.

I grabbed her ass cheeks, pulled them wide apart, then dragged her physically up and down my length.

It was hard work, and my biceps were going to fucking ache in the morning, but talk about worth it. Her muscles sucked on the tip of my dick every time I nearly pulled her off me, and the second she was full of me, I felt like she'd pushed me into the deepest, darkest part of the ocean, where pleasure was as prevalent as fucking water.

Rocking my head back against the door, I let her thrust her tongue against mine, let her fuck my mouth as I concentrated on us, on this, on our union.

When she clamped down around me after barely any time at all, it was the most powerful moment of my life because she came without me touching her clit. It was just my dick and my mouth touching her cunt and her lips, nothing else, nothing simpler, but she still got off which told me exactly how she felt about me.

No woman who'd endured what she had would be able to let down their guard this much, be able to come as hard as she did, without it meaning that she'd caught feelings.

And that made me feel about ten fucking feet tall.

I growled into her mouth as she sucked me dry of cum, and as her chest dragged against mine, she sobbed into my mouth as pleasure sent her flying.

Lips still locked, I pulled back to peck tiny kisses along her Cupid's bow, and only then did I rasp, "I love you, little bird. I've been waiting for you for a long time, but now that I've got you? You ain't going nowhere."

At that, she pushed her face into my throat, and I could feel the tears dampen my skin, could feel her emotions throb through her as she reacted to my declaration.

As she sobbed against me, I felt like a solid weight, a root system that'd let her grow and grow, until she was able to become who'd she'd been destined to be before life had robbed her choices from her.

She gave me light. She gave me wings.

I just needed for her to know that, with me around, I'd never, *ever* let her fucking fall.

I didn't expect a declaration. Didn't need one. I just wanted her to know that she was it for me. It wouldn't take away her jealousy, wouldn't stop her from watching me, but I didn't particularly want her to.

I couldn't have said how long it was before she lifted her head, but finally, she did, and she pressed a soft kiss to my lips, one that tasted of affection and need and warmth, everything I knew I'd been missing for a long ass time, and she whispered the impossible.

"I love you too, Hawk." She sobbed. "I didn't think anyone would ever be able to love me, but—" She hiccupped. "I'm not sure what I did to deserve you but I promise to be worthy of you."

"That's easy, siren," I whispered. "Just be you. That's all Quin and I need."

FORTY-EIGHT

QUIN

AS I ROCKED into the makeshift office where Rex had set himself up, I frowned when I realized the full council was here apart from Storm, of course, who was back in Ohio now.

As a kid, these guys had all been my brother's best friends, the fuckers he hung around with. I hadn't known them, what with always being in Canada, but the second I'd come back was the second I'd missed the tribe.

If you'd asked my *nòkomis*, she'd have said that I was a bad Algonquin. I didn't like tribal life, hated not having power, rarely wanted to listen to the Elders, and yet, when I'd returned to West Orange, I'd missed them like a lost limb.

When I'd seen my brother's tribe, I'd wanted to be a part of that.

Which was what had led to the ensuing fuckfest. Of course, it was hard to be bitter when I knew that had all happened so I'd be ready for my sky girl, but that didn't make the bitter pill easier to swallow, it just gave me a few drops of water to lube up my throat as I deepthroated the craziness of the last years.

They were all older now, but the mantels of power settled well on their shoulders. I remembered them as lunatics, always getting drunk, fucking everything in a skirt, yet only one of them didn't have a ball and chain now. We hadn't had a party since I'd come back, and it made me wonder if things had changed that much.

Had the settled-down Sinners settled down in more ways than one?

"What's wrong?" I asked warily, not appreciating being summoned but knowing I couldn't ignore a dictate from the council.

Rex eyed me. "Why do you think something's wrong?"

"You brought me here." I squinted at him. "Or did I read your text wrong?"

Nyx snorted. "I'd have told you if you were in the shit."

"Well, I didn't think I was to be fair." I hadn't fucked up yet. Aside from the animals that were coming to the bunkhouse door like they were a Biblical plague. But they wouldn't know about that yet. Not really. Not until the clubhouse was complete.

But Amara? I'd imagined that little contretemps with Enya had made its way back to Rex by now.

The Prez shot me a narrow-eyed glance. "You need to watch Amara, Quin. I saw the damage to Enya's face. Amara gets a lot of slack because of what she's doing, but I'm not gonna let her beat the shit out of people. I'm telling you now to keep her in line."

Steel laughed. "Peaches bitched at you, huh?"

"She did," Rex said gruffly. "But that doesn't matter. It's not right. Enya said she only touched your shoulder."

"Amara's possessive," was all I said.

"More like fucking possessed. Enya might need a nose job. And I'll have to foot the fucking bill seeing as your woman did it."

Wow, I liked that.

Your woman.

Even though she wasn't officially branded, they saw that. The council knew.

Nyx smiled at me, which told me he'd spread the word and I was grateful. I didn't know if Amara would allow us to claim her in the ways of the MC, so this gave her a dose of protection if anything ever happened to me or Hawk.

"Keep her on a leash," was all Rex said.

"She was on a leash," I replied simply, folding my arms across my chest. "You think she can just describe these fucking Sparrows to you without feeling anything? You think she's a robot? She's been fine for months. According to Hawk, she was quiet as hell, and even let Alessa haul her around like a bag of potatoes when the Posse got in her face. If you can't see a correlation between her aggression and the drawings, then you're not as fucking smart as I thought, Prez."

"He has a point," Maverick rumbled, and as I cast him a look, I took in his pale face. I didn't really understand what CTE was, but it was definitely winning. I saw that.

"She doesn't just remember the face, she fucking describes the worst thing they did to her at the same time. *If* she doesn't do that," I spat, "then she can't seem to find the words. The anger fuels her."

"Christ," Steel muttered, rubbing the back of his neck.

"I didn't know," Rex said simply, but the apology in his eyes wasn't enough.

"No, because you didn't ask. You just think she can do it and that's it."

"She killed that London fucker before she started drawing the pictures," Sin pointed out as he took a sip of coffee from the mug in front of him.

"If you can't see the difference, then God help you."

"You're a mouthy little fucker now, ain't you?" Rex replied with a quick grin.

"I ain't afraid to hear my own voice, no, and when it comes to her, you'd better believe I'll get loud."

Rex smirked a little, but he just said, "Try to keep her contained. For my fucking benefit?"

"I'll try, but I make no promises. She's intense, and it's only going to get worse."

"Fucking hell," he groaned, reaching up to rub his eyes.

"If she isn't the reason you called me up here, then what's going on?"

"Couple of things." Sin grunted. "Just wanted to let you know that the police are officially saying they ain't got a clue who killed Martin London, AKA, Jeremiah Berlin, AKA whoever the fuck he is. Your woman's off the hook."

Relief had me taking a seat at the table without asking for permission.

To be honest, concern about that had been riding me hard, but I'd let it go, knowing that when there was news, Nyx would tell me.

"The guy who jumped you in the hospital—"

"What about him?" I inquired.

"Fucker 'mysteriously' killed himself in his jail cell." Sin even did the whole quote mark thing with his fingers.

"Jesus," I whispered. "The Sparrows are hard-fucking-core."

"One mistake and you're out," Rex said grimly.

"We also got news from Lodestar," Sin carried on. "Guys like you who refuse to be a patsy for the Sparrows end up dead in the last week they're behind bars. It's always a fight between inmates or someone gets shivved in a cell."

"They're cleaning up after themselves?" I rasped, oddly comforted and discomforted by that revelation.

It was nice to have a reason why, because I truly knew fuck all about the Sparrows, apart from what I'd learned as the guy who drew for Amara. But I was out now, the damage was done, so did that mean I'd be wearing a target for the rest of my life.

"Clean-up is a light way of describing it," Rex muttered.

"I guess. I'm still in danger, right? I'm still a loose end that needs tying up." Did that put Amara in danger too?

"Maybe. I won't be sending you on any runs across the country for the foreseeable future that's for sure. Sticking to the state might afford you some protection, but mostly, we just need to take these cunts down."

"We're on track to do that, aren't we?"

"We are," Maverick rumbled. "I don't know half of what Lodestar has planned." He rubbed his head again. "But I know she's planning something more complicated than Times Square on New Year's Eve."

"Good. I hope they all fucking burn." I tensed my jaw. "Don't forget, Prez, you owe Amara. Hawk told me what you promised her."

Rex scowled. "I didn't forget."

"She needs some fucking peace."

"If anyone understands that, it's me." He cast Nyx a look. "I let him have his head, didn't I?"

"Yeah, but you're cutting her off before she can even hurt those who hurt her the most." I didn't want to pull this card, but for Amara, I'd blow my hand out of the water. "Anyway, don't think I don't know I did the MC a solid by killing Fieri. If it means pulling in that favor, then I will. I want her to get her justice."

"She means that much to you?" Rex queried, his brow furrowed.

"Yeah, she fucking does."

"Look, I ain't forgotten what you did with Fieri. But Nyx riding around the country killing cunts that people want dead anyway doesn't make waves. Half the cops who were called to those cases probably confiscated evidence because even pigs hate pedos.

"We're talking about high-powered men, Quin. I get that you want to stick up for her, but think goddamn rationally. I'll do what I can, give her the peace I can, but I ain't about to let the MC burn because Amara's got a screw loose—"

"And do you fucking blame her?" I snarled, jumping to my feet as outrage filled me on my woman's behalf.

"No, I don't, but my hands are tied because I won't let the MC drown for her. I gotta think about every bastard in the MC, Quin. Look, those fuckers'll pay. *That* I can promise."

Because he made sense, I nodded, but I also understood where Amara was coming from. The urge inside me was strong too. The urge to wreak justice on those who deserved to have their faces rotted off with bleach.

"Nyx told me that he was gonna stop killing the pedos."

Rex nodded. "He is."

"We're implementing other techniques to bring them down," Nyx rasped as he cracked his knuckles. He bit off each word through gritted teeth and I knew how much it had to be hurting him to stop, but I respected him so fucking much for wanting to be a better man, for wanting to be the father his kids deserved to have protecting them, rather than visiting him in a cell once every couple months.

"I want to be involved," I said flatly, not about to accept any of their BS.

Rex shrugged. "That's why I wanted you here today."

I tensed. "Really?"

"You're Carly and Indy's brother, ain't you?" he queried, his brows high. "Your vengeance has to be appeased as much as Nyx's, so are you in?"

I licked my lips, stunned by this gesture of goodwill, before I growled, "Fuck yeah, I'm in."

FORTY-NINE

AMARA

TWO DAYS LATER

"GO ON. THEY WON'T BITE."

"You don't know that," Hawk muttered, his hands on the steering wheel as he stared at the mansion ahead of us.

"I do. They're not rabid," Quin retorted.

"Aren't they? You didn't see Giulia the other day." He yawned. "Siren, I'm sorry to rush you, but I gotta get to the club after I get Quin to the tattoo studio."

Everything about that sentence was wrong.

I hated that he was going to that place where a woman thought she could touch him.

I hated that Quin was going to be out in the dark without me.

But I couldn't be in three places at once, and Lily had called me here for one reason—money. I had millions coming to me, and though it was more about the principle, I felt like a sell out for leaving Quin on his own when he needed me.

Like Petr knew I was distressed, he shoved his face into my leg and, absently, I reached down and petted him on the head. He was turning into my shadow, always wanting to come with me wherever I went.

Sucking my bottom lip into my mouth, I muttered, "Can't you get a different job?"

Hawk snorted. "Think I haven't asked Rex?" Another yawn escaped him. "I'd be happy if he just brought more guys in on the staff, but we're short right now. Lots of brothers are helping out at the construction site. We're all having to do crap we don't want just to get the clubhouse rebuilt." He leaned over and though his initial touch was gentle, a soft reminder that it was him and for me not to be scared, when he gripped the back of my neck, he rubbed it a little roughly. "Thought I'd already told you you could slice it off if I strayed?"

"It's not you," I retorted. "It's everyone else."

Quin snickered. "It's a good thing we both like cray-cray, huh?"

I frowned. "What is this? Cray-Cray? Is it a fish?"

Laughing, Hawk shook his head. "Where did you get that from?"

"It's a blackbird, isn't it?"

His eyes turned distant. "Cray— wait, you mean, like crow?"

"I don't know. What is this cray-cray?"

"Crazy," Quin said with a laugh.

"I'm not crazy," I muttered. "Hawk said himself that women would come onto you both because you're bikers and they wish to be yours."

"What can I say? We're chick magnets?" Quin rumbled, but he shot me a wink when I twisted in the front seat of the truck to glower at him. "Doesn't mean we're gonna act on it."

"I've heard what the women say about the clubwhores. The Posse say they broke up Storm and Keira—"

Hawk sighed. "Really? Now? We have to discuss this now?"

"Yes, because otherwise I will be accused of being crazy when I pull out some *blyat's* hair by the roots instead of it being justifiable."

"Legit thought you were going to say 'pull out someone's nails,' sky girl. I'm actually relieved hair is how low you're willing to sink."

I narrowed my eyes. "That is act one."

Quin grinned. "Devious. I like it."

"Storm, allegedly, was having sex with clubwhores while Keira was pregnant." Hawk shrugged. "That's about as much as I know."

"Kendra—you met her yesterday, sky girl—she told Keira about Storm cheating on her."

"How the hell do you know that?" Hawk queried.

Quin shrugged. "Indy told me."

I knew this Kendra. She had big nostrils.

My brow furrowed with confusion. "Why is she still alive?"

Both men blinked.

"Huh?" Quin asked.

"Why is she still alive?" I repeated. "Why did Keira not kill her?"

Quin licked his lips. "Well, some women see a call button cord and just see a call button cord, babe. You see a deadly weapon."

I hummed. "You should probably remember that."

"Oh, I have. Trust me." He grinned at me in that strange way that told me he found me hilarious when I wasn't joking.

Grunting at him, I told them both, "If anyone did that to me, I'd have—"

"Yeah, yeah, butchered them while they were alive, but that's the difference. We aren't fucking stupid," Hawk retorted. "Storm's always been weird."

"He has? I thought he was cool," Quin replied.

"Yeah, but like, you know when he left for Ohio?" Quin hummed which was all the answer Hawk needed to continue, "He had me follow Keira."

"Why?"

Hawk shrugged. "I don't know. I wish I'd been following Cyan to be honest. Might have been best all round if I had.

"But yeah, I had to tell him where she was and when. If she was seeing guys and shit."

"That's intense."

I declared, "I would do this for both of you."

Quin smirked. "Better than a declaration of love."

"I mean it," I told him firmly.

"I know you do. But let's not waste money on brothers stalking our asses, yeah?" Quin reached over and patted the top of my head. "You're with me most of the time anyway."

"I'm not with Hawk," I pointed out.

"No, but Giulia spread the word among the staff," Hawk said dryly. "Apparently, my dick is more dangerous than Chernobyl."

I smiled. "I asked this of her. I told her to tell them that you had syphilis."

"What the fuck?" Hawk boomed.

Shrugging, I said, "I told her to tell them that I gave it to you."

His eyes bugged. "That's supposed to make it better?"

My smile made another reappearance. "You told me you love me."

He stared at me.

Then, he stared at me some more.

Then, he chuckled.

It started out small, then morphed into a laugh so loud and forceful it rocked the truck.

"I thought I was the crazy one?" I rasped, staring at him in concern as he hooted. Casting a look at Quin to see if he was worried too, I found him grinning at me. "I'm not lying," I informed them both, unsure if they were taking me seriously.

"No, that's quite clear to see," Quin said with a chuckle of his own.

"It isn't funny," I grumbled as Hawk *carried on laughing*.

Quin rocked forward so that he was perched between both seats. He reached for the arm nearest to him, which just so happened to be the one he'd recently tattooed. He twisted my hand gently, and stroked his thumb along the strong, bold lines of what he'd called a thunderbird.

It was a large tattoo, the body of which settled where the brand had been, while the bird's wings flared out to wrap around my forearm.

The shape was blocky, long strong lines, lots of bold black ink on the body, but the wings were magical. The feathers—he was a magician. Just as talented as his sister.

"Remember what this means?"

I nodded. "It represents power and transformation."

He grinned a little. "I didn't tell you some tribes think that thunder is a battle in the sky lands. Thunderbirds beat their wings together to create the storm. They aren't just birds of prey, they're *war*mongers."

"So?"

"So, my little sky girl, you just declared war on the women of West Orange."

Hawk, who had finally stopped hooting, in a voice that was hoarse from his laughter, rasped, "If I wasn't so fucking turned on right now, I'd be terrified."

I scowled. "You're not supposed to be turned on."

He grabbed my hand, placed it against his cock where, truly, there was an erection.

Though I was disgusted by his inability to take my claims seriously—didn't they know I had to brand them somehow? In an ideal world, telling everyone they had syphilis wasn't the best option, but there were, as Giulia called them, skanks everywhere. They were like weeds. I had to fight dirty from the start—I still shaped his shaft through his pants.

Pursing my lips in disapproval, I murmured, "If a clubwhore does to me what this Kendra did to Keira, you have been warned—I will fight."

"That's half the fun," Quin chimed in, leaning forward to give me a kiss. Then, he melted my heart by lifting my wrist and kissing my thunderbird.

When Hawk did the same, it made it a little easier to get out of the truck.

They knew I was serious now.

They also knew I wasn't rational, but I was fine with that.

Something about me gave them erections, I wasn't above using that against them.

"Go on, little nightmare," Hawk said cheerfully. "Go and bring home the bacon."

"Bacon?" I frowned. "She's giving me millions, not pigs."

He grinned. "I'll take both."

With a huff, I opened the door to let Petr out, then jumped out of the truck too. Awkwardly, I stood there. Alessa hovered in the doorway of the mansion, watching me. I'd never liked her, but we'd been through a lot together.

With my men at my back, the last thing I wanted was for them to leave, but I was a big girl.

Sort of.

"Sky girl?"

I jolted at Quin's voice, but twisted around and saw he'd gotten out of the truck and was clambering into the front seat.

"Yes, Quin?"

"Play nice? You might just find your people in there."

"You're my people," I insisted.

His smile hit his eyes. "I know we are, but wouldn't it be nice if you had people who'd go to war with you? Instead of waging it on your own, thunderbird?"

With that, he blew me a kiss that I instinctively caught and held to my heart. Hawk smiled at me too, and it was in a way that told me, tonight, if he didn't fuck me against the floor, it was only because he'd been hit over the head with a beer bottle.

Therefore, unlikely.

My man was wily.

"I love you," he mouthed, not saying the words out loud, but they meant more after my confession somehow.

If he could say that now, after being told the lengths I'd go to to claim him, I thought it was more powerful.

"I love you too," I replied just as noiselessly, before I sucked in a breath and moved to face the mansion.

Alessa, Stone, and Lily were there, all of them watching me now, and as the truck ambled to life, I stepped forward. Before I reached the door, I turned back to see their vehicle on the road, driving away, and though I wanted to run after them, and while this felt like the first day of school, I straightened my shoulders.

Time to be a big girl.

"Finally," Giulia muttered as, by the time I entered the house, she was in the hall too.

"How's the foot, Amara?" Stone asked. "Do you need me to look at it?"

I frowned. "My foot?"

She sighed. "I'll take that to mean that the massive fucking gash on your foot healed?"

"Oh." That. "*Tak,* it is fine. Thank you for asking," I tacked on, somewhat awkwardly because the wound hadn't been that bad.

As she rolled her eyes at me, Giulia scowled down at Petr, demanding, "What's with the dog?"

"Where he goes, I go," was all I said before I pursed my lips, then, asked, "Why is Kendra still alive?"

It was clear they hadn't expected that as a greeting, but Giulia grinned at me. "I like it. You're bloodthirsty. Tonight couldn't come soon enough for me so I know it must be killing you."

"What must be?" I frowned.

Lily shepherded me inside the hall, and said, "This isn't just about the money."

"It isn't?" I questioned blankly as she shuffled me forward, drawing me into a massive living room.

It was beautifully designed, the decorations impeccable, with an incredible chandelier made up of what seemed like thousands of glass baubles, but it might as well have been daubed in blood for all that it impressed me. I could see it for what it was, but knew that it had been forged on the misery of others.

I also saw that the room was full of women.

Old Ladies.

Uncertainly, I cast Tiffany and Indy a glance before Giulia, Alessa, Stone, and Lily moved over to the sofas.

"I will fight back this time if you try to shove my face into the table," I said woodenly, folding my arms across my chest.

Like he understood what I said, Petr growled, long and low.

Wondering if I could train him to go for the throats of people I didn't like, I whirled around when I heard a squeaking sound of wheels on the tiles, which keyed me into Lodestar's presence long before she spoke:

"You're not here for that."

"What's going on?" I demanded, uneasy with not understanding what was happening.

Lily shot me a soft smile and pointed to a large coffee table. On it, there was a tray loaded down with snacks, all kinds of them, chocolate, candy, chips, everything and nothing was there, and my newly-awakened hunger for junk food pinged to life, even as I registered another tray with beers and bottles of water as well as a few bottles of red wine, and a silver bucket for white. Between all this, there were two sets of papers. From here, I could see that one was signed.

"I'm supposed to tell you," Giulia said, "that Rachel agreed with the terms of the contracts. In her words, 'You'd be insane if you didn't sign them.'"

Considering I was sure I *was* insane, that didn't help me much.

Either way, I didn't care if it meant signing away my firstborn. I'd sign the contracts. I wanted the money I was—

I sighed.

Lily didn't owe me anything.

Her father did.

Her father's organization did.

My jaw tensed as I strode forward to the coffee table, muttering, "*Stiy*," at Petr to make sure he stayed put.

It seemed imperative that I spoke before I signed anything. "Lily, I was hard on you at first. I wish to apologize for that."

Lily smiled at me, her pretty features softening as she sank back into a sofa, a large glass of wine in her hand. "I understood, Amara." She took a sip of wine. "I'm lucky you didn't tell Link I had syphilis." She choked on her drink as she laughed, and the others did too.

I scowled at them. "Skanks will not take this seriously if you laugh."

Why was everyone finding this so amusing? Didn't they know I was serious? I wanted people to think they were diseased. It was my first line of defense.

Shrugging unapologetically, Giulia grinned. "I had to tell them. It's fucking genius. I don't know why I didn't think of it."

"Probably wouldn't stop the fucking whores," Indy muttered as she swigged some beer from a bottle. "They'll take the syphilis so long as they don't have to work for a living."

"You think?" I queried, my brow furrowing. I knew the depths women would sink to to lure a man. "Syphilis rots the brain. I googled it."

"Of course you did," Giulia drawled with a grin.

Stone chuckled. "Hate to burst your bubble, Amara, but syphilis is curable now."

"Not everyone is doctor, hmm?" I narrowed my eyes. "You are though. What disease would make them avoid Hawk and Quin?"

She arched a brow. "So, you're really claiming them both, huh?" I merely narrowed my eyes at her. "I don't know, Amara. I mean, Christ, Ebola? Maybe that'd keep them away."

"Can you catch Ebola in West Orange?"

"If you try hard enough," Stone said with a laugh.

Giulia grumbled, "Those bitches aren't the smartest. They probably don't even know what Ebola is."

"That's mean," Lily chimed in. "They're not all horrible. Cammie was nice."

"She was also fucking Bratva." Giulia rolled her eyes. "Can you believe that?"

I tensed up, and knew Alessa did too.

With our nationalities, we'd have been insane not to be scared.

"Bratva?" I asked hollowly.

Giulia grunted as she took a sip of water from the bottle, but at my tension, Alessa's too, she turned to me, head tilting to the side. "What is it?"

I ignored her and asked Alessa in Ukrainian, "Sarah was taken by the Bratva. Were you?"

"They promised me safe passage over the ocean. Did they offer you the same?"

"No. I was snatched. Sold." I'd run from home and had dared to go to the park. I'd sat down on a bench to watch the snow flurries fall to the ground, wondering about what I'd do with my life, and that was the last thing I remembered.

I had a feeling I'd fallen asleep and they'd hit me over the head or something. The next was the horror of waking up in a cargo hold of a ship, my head pounding with agony, the back of it bloodied from my injury, with dozens of other women in there with me.

Sarah, at my side, had puked all over me, but that was nothing to what we were sitting in. What we were—

God, the memories made the vengeance inside me surge forward.

It was quite by chance that I looked at my wrist, and saw the magic of Quin's work, though he couldn't have known this would happen. My pulse was so strong, so fast, the feathers of my wings shuffled like the bird was flying.

At that moment, I didn't need Quin and Hawk to soar through the skies, but I needed them to stop me from diving into chaos.

"What are you two talking about?" Lodestar snapped.

Alessa's voice was gruff. "The Bratva were..." She swallowed. "I went to them for help to get over here for Kati."

Lodestar's nostrils flared. "Son of a bitch." Her hand slammed down against the armrest.

"The old guard's dead," Giulia muttered. "I heard them talking about it in church. The Pakhan was murdered, and then the Sovietnik and Obschak, basically Rex's Maverick and Nyx, were killed too."

Gulping, I snapped, "It doesn't matter who's at the head. They're all monsters."

Lodestar gritted her teeth. "Okay, this changes things. We thought the *Famiglia* were their front. That's who Donavan was associated with—"

"Rex told me that there were ties to the Triads as well in China," Tiffany whispered, her hands coming up to cup her arms like she was trying to comfort herself.

"Why not the Bratva too?" Giulia agreed. "Why not every fucking cunt in the mafia?" She hurled the water bottle away from her, uncaring when it slammed into the wall, dropping down onto a console table where it knocked over a vase.

"What does this mean?" Stone whispered.

"I told Rex about the Triads, but when I checked them out, I found that their operations are mostly heroin, not girls, over here. Either way, this means we can only trust the Irish," Lodestar bit off.

"You don't know that we can trust them. Maybe they're in on it too—"

She shook her head. "No. My contact, he's good people."

Giulia arched a brow. "Good people?"

"What?" Lodestar snapped.

"Just never heard you say anything nice about anyone."

Lodestar flipped her the bird.

Tiffany murmured, "You know Sin and Declan from the Five Points are tight because he's family, right?"

Lily arched a brow. "What have you been eavesdropping on?"

Tiff crinkled her nose. "I found out Camille isn't just Bratva, she was the Pakhan's daughter."

"No fucking way," Stone rasped.

"Yes." Tiffany sat forward. "She's married Brennan O'Donnelly."

Indy hooted. "Oh Christ, just wait until he learns that Nyx treated Cammie like shit."

Giulia sniffed. "My man can hold his own."

"I don't think Cammie's a troublemaker," Stone said softly. "She was very quiet. You know that."

"She was," Giulia agreed gruffly. "I didn't like her but she was decent. I knew she loved Nyx but she wanted what was best for him. Me."

She said that part like it was a declaration.

I understood her need to claim her man.

My trouble was I had double the men to stake a claim on—there were only so many hours in a day.

"I can't see her telling Brennan," Indy agreed. "She wouldn't want to hurt Nyx even though he did treat her badly."

"They all treat the whores badly," Lily countered. "I'm not sure why anyone would want to be a bunny."

"Because some people don't want to work for a living?" Lodestar said, her tone disapproving.

"I don't think it is just that," Alessa retorted. "As much as I dislike the cruel ones, some must be desperate to put themselves in that situation. You have to ask why the daughter of the Bratva Pakhan would choose to place herself in that position."

"She has a point," Lily said softly.

"Because she wished to escape the Bratva," I rumbled, my tone low enough to make Petr ignore my command, amble over to me and nudge me in the calf, like he knew I needed comfort. "Why wouldn't she hide herself among the biggest, baddest men around?"

"She has a point," Stone agreed. "What else did you find out, Tiffany?"

"Maxim Lyanov is the new Pakhan. He's... well, I think he must be insane."

"Why?" Giulia queried, her interest clearly piqued.

"As far as I can tell, the O'Donnellys are supporting his takeover of the Bratva, but there was some kind of situation—I don't know all the details. Camille was kidnapped with her younger sister, Victoria."

"*Pizda rulu*, is she okay?" Alessa demanded.

It was quite by chance that I looked at Lodestar at that very moment.

Her face was wooden. Shifty.

She was hiding something.

About this kidnapping?

As Tiffany answered, I kept my eyes on Lodestar, "Brennan O'Donnelly got them both back, but Maxim Lyanov took it as a personal affront because he wants to marry Victoria..." She paused, then, eyes wide, rasped, "Lukov was the Obschak. Lyanov cut off his head and sent it as a gift to Victoria."

A few shocked breaths whispered around the room, but Lodestar didn't look in the least surprised.

So, she'd already known but was choosing not to say anything?

Having learned an important lesson about her loyalties to this group of women, I merely said, "That's my idea of romance," when a dead silence followed Tiffany's statement.

Snickering, Giulia shook her head. "Well, I'm not sure romantic is the word."

"She's only fourteen," Tiffany argued.

I shrugged. "He will keep her safe. This is important in our world."

"Christ, does it make me insane that I agree with her?" Lily groaned.

"Lily!" Tiffany gasped in horror.

"What?" She shrugged. "If Link had sliced off Luke's head for me when I was a kid, I'd have loved him forever."

Lodestar rolled her eyes. "Okay, if story time is over, the Bratva's involvement with the Sparrows definitely changes shit, but it doesn't change the things I've set in motion."

"Which are?" Giulia demanded. "You wouldn't tell me anything when I asked you earlier."

"Why tell you when I need to tell all of you?" she retorted, before she wheeled around the overlarge sofas and to the coffee table. I noticed then that she had a laptop on her knees.

Lily cleared her throat. "Amara, please, sign the contracts. Let's finish this business tonight, hmm? Each page needs your initials and a signature where there's an 'x.'"

Because she was right, and because I wanted the money, I leaned over, uncapped the pen on the table and shuffled through the papers, signing and placing my initials wherever they were required.

When that was done, she held out her hand. In it, there was a credit card.

"The money is in a trust for you. My people have set up bank accounts for you and the yearly dividends will go in there.

"You can draw up to five hundred thousand dollars in one shot in December, but I recommend you leave it in the account to accrue interest.

"This card draws off that account, but I've topped it up with a hundred thousand dollars to tide you over until the first dividends come in next month."

I stared at the piece of plastic in her hand, well aware that when Lily had told us of this plan, I'd thought of that money as freedom.

But now, I knew it wasn't.

Quin and Hawk were freedom.

They let me be me.

They always would—I knew that, just like Lily knew I'd never have seen that much money in a million years if she hadn't gifted it to me.

Swallowing, I reached for the card and rasped, "Thank you, Lily."

"You don't have to thank me," she discounted. "It's what you're due." Her mouth tightened. "As for the rest of his blood money, I'm hoping Lodestar can help me with that too."

I didn't understand her, but a light flickered on in the corner and I saw a massive console open up to reveal a huge TV. There was a blank screen on there right now with a drawing of a cartoon person which had me frowning.

"We'll be having a video call soon," Lodestar informed us.

"With whom?" Tiffany asked softly.

"The journalist I've picked to leak the IDs of the people Amara remembers." She flickered a glance at me. "I've found them all, Amara. That's how fucking good the renditions were. Every single goddamn one of them.

"I've not slept more than two hours at the kitchen table since the images started coming in, because I don't just want to give her IDs, I want to give her evidence."

I refused to cry. "I'm glad they were of help." Would this make the faces that haunted me before I slept disappear?

She tightened her lips. "I've come up with a game plan."

"Which is?"

"If you'd fucking listen, Giulia, I'd tell you. Jesus." She heaved a sigh. "Look, shit's been weird for a long time. It comes as no real surprise to me that the Bratva are involved because this operation crosses the fucking world.

"They'd need help from every corner of the planet, and where there are people desperate for better lives in other countries, there's money to be made.

"One of the reasons I got involved with this shit is because I was like you, Amara, Alessa." I could feel the thunderbird's wings start to flutter. "I was sent to the Middle East and ended up being trafficked. It's only because I'm a canny fucking bitch that I'm here today, and I promised myself as well as all the other poor bitches who were going through what I went through, that I'd take them down." She released a breath. "Along the path of taking these cunts down, I've made enemies, but, also, I've made friends. The Sinners are my family.

"The second they took Bear, brothers, and even those skank hoes down, the clubhouse too, shit dialed up a notch."

Giulia whispered, "I heard Rex talking about Bear today. They say he's dying."

A soft cry escaped Indy, but it was Stone, the Sinners' doctor, who explained solemnly, "His heart can't take much more."

Giulia released a shaky breath. "He saved me, you know? When

Luke..." She cleared her throat. "That night, Bear came in and killed that cunt for me. He's the only reason I didn't end up in that brothel or that cabin in the woods with you guys." She gestured at me and Alessa. "It's not fair that he saved me from that and is going to die like this."

I knew it wasn't helpful, but I couldn't stop myself from saying, "Life is not fair."

Giulia dipped her chin. "This is fucking true."

"Everyone thought you killed Luke," Lily burst out. "Wasn't that why the cops were investigating you? They were trying to bury you—"

"They were," she agreed, then she pressed her fingers to her lips. "Before he left, he asked me not to say anything."

"Why?" Stone muttered. "Why would he do that? Bear wasn't afraid of anything. He'd know the cops could be bought round here."

Lodestar cleared her throat. "I think I have the answer to that." When the focus was back on her, she explained, "Ever since the blast, I've been wondering why the Sparrows would target him. Was he just a Trojan horse? Did they use him to get into the compound?" She shook her head. "I knew that was bullshit when I watched Tink climb into that truck. London already had his in. He didn't need to target Bear, so what did he know? What did they want to eradicate?"

"You think they wanted it to look like it was a Trojan horse, but really, Bear was the target all along?"

Lodestar nodded at Stone. "That's exactly what I think. With a bit of digging that I'd prefer you don't mention to Rex or the rest of the council, I found Bear has an email that he rarely used other than to send himself pictures."

Giulia frowned. "Of what? Women? Sunsets? We all know he was traveling—"

"At first, I didn't know what the hell they were. Bikers aren't exactly the kind of guys who take snapshots for souvenirs, are they? Then, when I downloaded the images, I saw how massive the files were."

Lily frowned. "I've heard of this before. Steganography, right?"

"Two points to you," Lodestar said with a nod. "He was hiding data within the images."

"Shit," Giulia rasped. "That's so fucking cool."

"Spooky too," Indy rumbled. "He's helping from the other side."

When she shivered, I knew, whether she wanted to believe it or not, she was more in touch with her Algonquin side than she recognized—Quin would have shivered too.

"He isn't dead yet," Stone soothed, but Indy's arms still shifted, moving around her waist like she knew something we didn't.

Lodestar just grunted. "The data was encrypted, of course, so I know someone was helping Bear, and Maverick tells me it's not him. I have no idea *who* it is, but they're good. Very good."

"What data was he hiding?"

"Anything from drug shipments, to prison inmates he believed were Sparrow dupes." She cleared her throat. "Bear had Quin on there."

A gasp escaped me before I snarled, "And he let him rot inside?"

"Jesus," Indy whispered.

Lodestar nodded. "I don't know how he knew this shit, but he was doing something while he was traveling. Like I said, I've been monitoring shit through the net. He did it old school. All of his findings correlate with mine."

"What was he searching for?"

"The people who killed his wife," she said softly.

"It was a hit and run," Stone argued.

Lodestar shook her head. "No, Stone. It wasn't." She heaved a sigh. "The guy you killed, Amara, he was an assassin for the Sparrows. He killed Bear's Old Lady."

"Well fucking done," Giulia growled. "God, I'm so glad you fucking did that, Amara."

I staggered back a little, settling my ass on the side of the sofa, needing that to keep me upright because I had a feeling Lodestar wasn't done yet.

As I sat though, Alessa reached over to pat my knee, and Tiffany squeezed my hand before she huddled against me, like *I* could support *her*. It was such a complete 180, when she'd been the one who, pre-blast, had tried to help us through what we'd dealt with.

I didn't feel shaky in a sense that I was weak. I felt like if I didn't sit down, I'd take off.

Vengeance, whether Rex liked it or not, was very much back on the table. Petr, as if we were in tune, growled, and it echoed through the room, making the others cast a surprised glance his way.

"Bear, somehow, in the years he was active, uncovered shit that I *couldn't* find out, and along with what I'm uncovering in Lacey's files, they've given me the evidence that'll blow the whistle on these cunts and that will help the journalist I've chosen."

"Jesus," Giulia rasped, her shoulders slumping as she pressed her elbows to her knees. "What are we going to do?"

Lodestar murmured, "I wanted Amara and Alessa to meet with the woman who's gonna bring their captors to their knees."

At my side, a tremor rushed through Alessa, but I straightened up, ready to hear more. Ready to know everything.

Lodestar tapped a couple of buttons on her computer, and the TV screen changed, a ringtone sounded and then a woman appeared. I frowned at the face that I knew, but couldn't remember from where until Indy gasped, "Christ, it's Savannah Davies!"

Was she a celebrity?

Then, I recognized my brain wasn't at full speed because if she was a journalist and I knew her face, it made sense that I'd seen her on TV.

Stone sat forward on her seat, then said, "Savannah, can I just say it was shitty what TVGM did to you?"

For a second, the woman's lack of expression impressed me. Especially when I saw a turbulence in her eyes that spoke of her anger at whatever Stone was talking about. She smiled a little, the muscles in her cheek clenching down because she really didn't want to smile.

"What did they do?" Alessa asked.

Lodestar rumbled, "It doesn't matter. We're about to put Savannah back on top, while taking down the motherfuckers who've played God for far too long."

"You're sure about your facts here?" Savannah demanded, her tone edgy. "I've got very little professional respect remaining. If I fuck it up, throw it away on this, then I'm screwed in this town."

Lodestar sniffed. "Wouldn't have come to you if you weren't, Vana. I know you need my help. Of course, you won't admit to it."

The other woman pursed her lips at the nickname. "I picked up the phone because of our fathers, Star. Don't make me regret it."

"Regret it? I'm the one who's about to help you get your fucking name back. Maybe show a little gratitude?"

Savannah just squinted at her, then snapped, "I don't know you guys, and you don't know me, but is she bullshitting me here?"

Giulia snorted. "Lodestar is a Grade A bullshitter, but in this instance, she isn't." She pointed to me and Alessa. "Those women, we saved them from being starved to death when we found them in a cabin in the woods. They were kept there as punishment."

Savannah blanched. "Holy crap. It's all true?"

"It is," Lodestar rumbled grimly. "I wouldn't lie about something as fucked up as this."

Savannah's eyes widened. "Oh, Star, that means—"

"It's okay, Vana. I'm alive. I'm home. That's all that matters now."

The other woman's composure ruptured for the first time, her eyes watered and her bottom lip trembled. "Your daddy would be—"

Lodestar raised a hand. "I know. Look, I wanted to contact you about this from the start, especially after I saw that fuckfest with the papers, but I wasn't sure if you'd be open to the story. It's not your usual type of narrative."

"Injustice is injustice," Savannah dismissed, but I didn't understand what Lodestar meant. What was a narrative? Like a story?

"You're more accustomed to ass-licking the motherfuckers we're gonna take down."

"Either way, I have to do something. I refuse to run back to Dad for help."

Lodestar shrugged. "I won't release any information to you until I want it going live."

"Hang on a second, you never said—"

"I'm the one with the info you need, Vana, so I make all the calls."

She bit off, "You always were a fucking control freak."

"Like father like daughter," Lodestar said grimly. "Anyway, Congress shuts down for the holidays next week, but I want to wait until the 21st when it closes for Christmas."

"Why the wait?" Giulia asked. "These fuckers need taking down—"

"Because I want this to scar their families," Lodestar murmured. "I want the cops to come knocking on their doors on Christmas fucking morning and to take them away like the animals they are."

Tiffany fidgeted. "Those families are innocent."

"Not all of them," I rasped, my fingers tangling in Petr's fur. "Jason Young's wasn't. His kids knew me too. They were old enough to recognize certain things but they never spoke up."

Tiffany sucked her bottom lip between her teeth. "This is pretty harsh."

"As harsh as locking women in cages?" Giulia growled. "You weren't there that fucking day, Tiff. I was the one who smelled that —" She blew out a breath. "Sarah was decomposing right beside them, for Christ's sake. The families should be grateful we're taking those cunts out of their lives."

Alessa cleared her throat. "It does seem cruel—"

In Ukrainian, I barked, "Cruel? How many times were you raped, Alessa? How many times were you whipped and cut and beaten? How many times were you starved to make you do heinous things that decent people wouldn't put an animal through?"

"I haven't forgotten, Amara," she snarled back, her eyes alight with ire. "But why hurt the innocent?"

"No one is that innocent," I said grimly. "They're all tainted.

Every one of them. We were treated like a relay, shuffled across the country like we were cattle.

"They all deserve to burn. Every single one of them, because the money that funded the entire circus is what's putting food on their tables, and is putting their snotty kids in fancy schools."

Alessa dipped her head. "Have some heart, Amara."

"Why should I? They didn't with me." I tipped up my chin. "I agree, I think this is a good idea."

Though no one understood us, it was clear that they sensed by tone alone that we were not discussing Christmas gifts.

Savannah's gaze turned pensive. "A lot of people are tuning out around the holidays. They're not interested in the news."

"Just you wait, Vana. This shitshow's gonna make ratings surge over the holidays." Lodestar's smile was unholy. "You're about to make anchor, sweetheart. You can thank me later."

FIFTY

HAWK

"THINK SHE'LL BE OKAY?"

"You worry too much," Quin told me, his tone breezy.

If I didn't know there was a lot more depth to the man than he let on, I'd think he actually meant that.

As it stood, I knew he believed in all kinds of stuff that was a mystical mystery to me so, straight away, the supposition he was an airhead was BS. But he sure made it look realistic.

Always happy, always joking. Interminably fucking cheerful. If I wasn't used to North, he'd have driven me insane, but the difference was, Quin *did* have depth. I'd come to see that North was all fucking facade. No substance.

I scratched the stubble growing on my jaw before I asked, "I don't worry. I just know she's..." As per usual, I struggled with a way to describe Amara. "She's not exactly delicate, is she? But she's—"

"Temperamental?" Quin snickered as he stretched his fingers. "That's her."

"Fingers aching?" I queried, rather than pick up the conversation about Amara.

"Yeah, it's pretty fucking hard to get used to these phones. I feel all fingers and thumbs."

"Won't take long to adapt."

"It will. I need my fingers for more important things."

My lips curved as he guffawed like a loon afterward. "You're a dirty fucker, do you know that? You'd be a real creep if you weren't always laughing. Instead you're like a psychotic clown."

"Pennywise? Or Krusty?"

Grin deepening, I replied, "You ever killed anyone?"

"Once. I fed a few dudes their tongues too. That up my rep?"

I shot him a quick look. "Literally?"

"Nah. I mean, I tried. I couldn't get my sharpened spoon to do much. I shoved it up one of their asses though."

"Ouch." My butt clenched.

"That didn't do much damage, sadly."

"Who knew spoons weren't all that dangerous?" I grumbled.

"Probably for the best. I'd have gotten more time. They routinely added an extra couple months for fighting to my sentence."

"Sucks."

"It does," he agreed. "Mostly because they knew I'd defended myself, I think. Or I might have gotten longer."

"It's fucked up that we send kids into jail expecting them to get raped and beaten."

"More than fucked up. The shit I saw would make your hair turn curly." He chuckled. "Oh, wait, it already is."

"Screw you," I told him, little to no heat in my words. "My hair's not curly." It wasn't. More *wavy*, but I knew the fucker was trying to change the subject and I couldn't blame him.

It meant a lot to me that he was open about this stuff, especially when I doubted that Nyx or Indy knew the full truth.

"It kinda is. Do you use those curling irons on it?"

I rolled my eyes. "Yeah, of course I do. I even go to the fucking salon, Quin, and get it done."

A cackle escaped him but, abruptly, he hissed, "Stop!"

I slammed on the brakes. "What the fuck is it?" I demanded, concern making my voice harsh as horns screeched all around us.

"There's a flower shop over there."

A growl escaped me. "You shitting me? We almost got rear-ended!"

He shrugged. "You need to buy Amara flowers."

I scowled. "You did not just say that?" Deciding that sticking in the center of the road was only going to get the cage rammed, I pulled into a parking lot.

"Yeah, I did. You need to start wooing her, man. Chicks dig that shit."

"Is this a challenge? You and I both know that if I bought her some flowers, she'd be like—why do you buy me dead things?"

He snickered. "Might be worth buying her them just to see if you matched her accent."

My lips twitched—I had been trying for that Baltic accent that got my balls in a twist.

"I bet you fifty she likes them," Quin chivvied.

"I bet you a hundred she says that word for fucking word."

"Deal."

"Can't buy them now, though. I'm seriously late."

Quin tapped his nose. "I'll remember the terms of the wager."

I'd just bet he would.

"You really think she needs romance?" My brow furrowed as we drifted out of the parking lot. "Amara and romance aren't words that I'd necessarily put together. I get the feeling that if I showed up with a ring box in my hands, she'd open it and ask me where the finger was that the ring belonged on."

A snort escaped Quin. "You know her pretty well, don't you?"

Though I got that he was trying to help, his insinuation pissed me off. "I have to work, Quin. If I could spend all day with her, I would."

"I know, man. I'm just saying... there's more to falling for someone than giving them orgasms."

"Speak for yourself," I retorted.

"I'm speaking for her."

I huffed. "This is weird. You giving me advice on dating and shit. I'm, what? Nine years older than you?"

"Eight," he corrected. "And you're not dating. You're already living with her, Hawk. Whether things are official or not, I can't see you moving back to the clubhouse when it's ready, do you?"

His words flew across my mind then disappeared. Not one ounce of me wanted to live in the clubhouse, at least, not without her, at any rate. She was already on the edge about the strippers, throwing club-whores into the mix would make things incendiary.

"No," I agreed.

"Anyway, you'd tell me if I was screwing up with her, wouldn't you?" He shrugged. "We're all living under the same roof. It'd be nice if we could do that peacefully."

"Fucking Yoda at work again," I grumbled, even though I knew he was right. Heaving a sigh, I rumbled, "I guess we both have to keep each other accountable."

"We do," he said with a nod. "I know this is unorthodox for you, and trust me, I never thought it'd be like this, but it is. This was how it was meant to be."

When he talked like that, it always freaked me out even though, as time passed, I was starting to think he was right.

Quin pulled out his phone and started scrolling down the screen. "Which flowers?"

"You're getting them delivered?"

"Might as well. If we pay express, they might even have them for her tomorrow—"

They did, and later that following evening, Amara earned me the hundred bucks the expensive lilies had cost, with her, "But they are dead. Why you bring me them?"

FIFTY-ONE

QUIN

FIVE DAYS LATER

"THIS IS FOR ME TO BORROW?"

"No. It's yours."

I stared down at the bike, not sure whether to cry or grin.

After a miserable afternoon at the DMV, I'd just gotten my driver's license renewed.

With one flashback thanks to a fucking song that had played on the radio, the feeling that the walls were closing in on me when there'd literally been a line out of the door, I knew that if Amara hadn't been there to stop me, I'd have walked out. Fuck the license.

I could thank her later for having my back, in ways that couldn't be done in public.

Nyx shrugged. "Least we could fucking do." He rubbed his chin. "Got it at a discount anyway. We bought so many fucking Harleys from the dealer that his kids probably don't have to worry about student debt or getting a fucking mortgage on their first home."

I cast him a look. "Don't make out like the club was behind this. You were. Only you'd know I'd want her to look like this."

"Maybe it's a boy."

I cast Amara a look. "I ain't riding a boy hog."

"Why is it a girl hog?" she retorted. "Why should I ride a girl hog?"

"You ride two guys. Ain't that enough?"

"I wish to ride third," she declared with a smirk.

Nyx's lips twitched. "She still don't get why she's funny, huh?"

"Nope." I snickered. "How about it's a hermaphrodite?"

"What is this?"

"Both sexes."

She pursed her lips in contemplation, then nodded. "I like this. Equality for all."

"Pleased to help," I drawled, watching as she pulled out her phone when it rang. With her attention averted, I smiled at Nyx. "Only you'd know to grab me the Ultra Classic when I always wanted a Knucklehead."

He shrugged. "She wouldn't be able to ride bitch on that. Figured that would be more important to you."

"It is."

"She's the one?" He grinned. "Because I can exchange this for the Knucklehead."

Snickering, I shook my head. "I'll stick with the Ultra-Classic." I clapped him on the back. "Thanks, Nyx. You really didn't have to."

It wasn't my dream ride, but I'd prefer this with her clinging to me on the back than the Knucklehead any time.

He grunted. "Wanted to. Least I could do."

When Nyx reverted to sentences with very few syllables, I knew he was getting in his feelings.

As I rounded the bike, checking out the gleaming electric blue body, I asked, "100 HP?"

"Yup, but Link says he'll work on it—"

"Quin?"

I turned to look at Amara. "Yeah, sky girl?"

"Hawk says Lodestar might have found the brothel." She waved a hand at the bike. "Can we ride there?"

"Is that wise for her to go?"

Nyx's question had me chuckling. "Yeah. Like you'd be able to stop Giulia."

"I will come with you. Lodestar needs confirmation that it's the place we were kept."

Well, this wasn't exactly the maiden voyage I wanted my new hog to take, but I guessed justice didn't wait for a pleasure ride.

"Where are we meeting up with him?" I asked, because Nyx had brought the bike to Indiana Ink.

She passed her phone to me. "Wherever this is."

I nodded, recognizing the address of the motel the Sinners had purchased after the bombing.

"Do you need back up?" Nyx asked. "We can all ride together. Lodestar should have told Link anyway. I swear, she's a fucking pain in my ass."

Amara grumbled, "This is her gift to me. Stop spoiling it."

"Gift?"

She shrugged, but I recognized that shifty look. When she never dropped eye contact, I knew she was planning something fucked up.

I kind of liked that she was predictably unpredictable.

"What if there are guards there?" Nyx retorted. "This is insane for you to go on your own."

"We won't be. Hawk and me are brothers. It's not like you'd send a full troop out for this, is it?"

Nyx scowled. "I guess not. Just be watchful."

"Yeah, okay, Dad." I snorted at his grimace.

"I'm sure you used to be scared of me."

"You wish I was."

Nyx just grunted but his hands curled into fists. "I promised I wouldn't go too far, but I can help out, Quin. I don't want you going into this shit on your own."

I shook my head. "I appreciate it, bro, but nah. This is Amara's moment."

"*Tak*, it is," she agreed. "Now, be quick. I want to know if it is the right place."

"Did Hawk say how she found it?"

Amara shrugged. "I do not know, nor do I wish to."

I hid a grin, before I told Nyx, "Seriously, thanks for this, bro. I didn't expect it, but I'm really grateful."

"Enjoy it." To Amara, he said, "I bought you some gear to wear to ride during the winter. Indy has it. You can change in there." After she thanked him and headed into the studio, he told me, "The second you're on the road back, give me a call. I want to know you're all okay."

"Were you always such a worrier?"

He rolled his eyes. "It's the VP's lot in life."

"Yeah, I'm sure. Pussy," I said under my breath, but loud enough for him to hear. When he punched me in the shoulder, I accepted the blow with a laugh as I raised my hands in surrender and retreated to my bike before he took it back.

Amara made an appearance dressed in leathers, which had my cock hardening before she tossed me a jacket and some gloves too.

Now kitted out for the ride, I straddled my bike, and Amara hopped on behind me. I'd thought she'd be awkward, but I figured her excitement was giving her wings.

"Watch the pipes," I warned her. "They get hot."

When her arms were around my waist, and her face was tucked between my shoulders, her cheek pressed against my back, I knew I'd take a dozen wimpy passenger hogs over the kind of rides that gave me a boner because having Amara at my back was like a wet dream come true.

After waving farewell to Nyx, I pointed the hog in the direction of West Orange.

I didn't bother pulling into the motel because Hawk was there, waiting for us on his classic black bike, which meant he'd known about my gift. Either that, or Amara had told him what we were riding on. Whichever it was, he pulled out of the parking lot, and I revved my engine as I roared after him.

We headed toward the Pennsylvania border, which made me

glad I'd been pardoned otherwise crossing it would have breached my parole, and with each mile, I could feel her growing tenser behind me. I knew it wasn't a tension founded in fear, more like in excitement.

She wanted it to be the brothel.

She wanted to reach the madam today.

I wasn't sure if she thought she was indestructible, and could somehow wander into—what I assumed—was a secured house, make it past the guards and to the woman who ran the place, but she was destined for disappointment.

Not only was I not about to let that happen, I knew Hawk would back me up every step of the way.

I figured the sky girl's hawk and buzzard's principle job was to keep her alive. Today might very well be the day we'd been put on this fucking earth for.

When Hawk turned off at a signpost for a town called Greenwich on the border, I felt her sudden stillness, and waited for her to give me a clue as to whether this was the right place or not.

Greenwich was a small town, but it was nicely appointed. Lots of family homes, a big church in the center that was painted a bright, gleaming white like its maintenance was important to the town.

The roads were busy, as were the sidewalks, but we bypassed the shopping areas and headed toward the southwest of the town.

She grew tenser and tenser, her stiffness giving me more clues than I needed. When we made it onto the street that Hawk ultimately slowed down on, I already knew we'd found the right property, but the 'For Sale' sign outside the door said it all.

Hawk didn't outright stop, just skimmed past what appeared to be one of a few residential places on this street as the rest were businesses, and we followed until we were riding out of Greenwich again.

We'd passed a couple of bikes, but it was definitely more of a pick-up truck place, meaning our rides stuck out like sore thumbs.

When he parked up at a rest stop, I drifted onto it. The second we were still, Amara leaped off the back of the bike and began striding back and forth. I didn't bother getting off, because I was close enough to Hawk to comfortably converse with him.

"Guess that means Lodestar found the brothel?"

I nodded. "She tensed up the second we passed the church."

"They set the place up in Middle fucking America. Jesus. The audacity."

"How did they get away with it? I would have thought the traffic alone would cause eyebrows to rise in a place like that."

Hawk shrugged. "It's on the border of the town, and didn't you notice? The neighbors either side of it were commercial. After a certain time, they wouldn't know what went down in that house."

"True," I conceded. "How did she find it?"

"Dug it out of Lacey's files."

Before I could reply, Amara was there. I knew it sounded stupid, but it was like the wind pushed her forward, making her look like she was floating.

"I want to burn it down."

My lips curved. "Arson. I like it."

"There's a special place in hell for arsonists," Hawk retorted. "But in this instance, I agree. That fucking house needs to rot."

Before I could get excited, I muttered, "If we tell the cops about the place, do you think they'd be able to pull DNA from the site?"

Amara's hands balled into fists at her sides. "I need that place not to exist," she whispered, her eyes huge in her beautiful face. God, they looked like they were going to swallow her whole.

"They'd have cleaned it afterward, wouldn't they?" Hawk muttered, his hands tightening about his handlebars. "Surely?"

"They were a pro team. I can't see a CSI unit finding much."

"I need to see it burn," Amara repeated. She stepped forward, her hands parting, one coming to cover mine and the other to blanket one of Hawk's. "I need this."

Hawk twisted his hand beneath hers. "Tonight," he promised her huskily, and I knew he was just as much of a sucker for her as I was.

"Tonight," I vowed in complete agreement.

Amara wasn't going to be able to take down every single one of the cunts I'd drawn for her, but she needed some peace.

With the madam gone, potentially in the wind, it might take a long time before Amara got to her. And with Jason Young's bitch wife in the press right now, it wasn't like she could disappear without it becoming a matter for the public to dissect.

She licked her lips. "It's going to be dark soon, Quin," she told me softly. "You can go home—"

I tugged at her fingers until ours were bridged. "Maybe we'll make enough of a bonfire to burn away my fears too, hmm?"

Her smile was tight, but I knew there was no teasing her out of this mood. She wouldn't be at peace until the house was burning.

Which was why, three hours later, I used my lock-picking abilities—hard won after breaking into many cars during my misspent youth—to let us into the house.

We wore winter balaclavas and leather jackets, and had walked the ten-minute journey to the house from the turn-off to try to remain incognito.

It didn't take much to see that the gas was still connected, the electricity was even running as the clock on the stove ticked onward, and from the condition of the place, exactly how clean it was, I knew it was only newly vacated.

Amara did too, because with every room she explored, I heard her soft sobs and wanted to kill someone for every tear she shed.

Hawk and I trudged behind her, watching as she hovered her phone's flashlight over each room.

The bitch of it was, it just felt like a regular home. Nothing weird about it. I'd never have known that it had housed sex slaves. Would never, in a million years, think women were imprisoned here.

The weight of her emotions had her shuddering by the time we made it to the top floor—the attic.

"I slept here," she rasped. "Sarah too. We were always in trouble."

I wanted to tease her, say that didn't come as a surprise, but even me, the perennial joker, just couldn't crack anything humorous here.

"Why?" Hawk whispered, stepping forward for the first time so he could bridge their hands together.

"Sarah was always sick, and I was always trying to get them to see she needed a doctor," she whispered.

"Why aren't you close to Alessa?" I asked quietly.

"Because none of us were friends here. I wasn't even friends with Sarah. It wasn't like that. S-She was a link to the Amara I used to be. She saw me back then, and she saw me now. I don't know why, but that kept me going." She gulped. "This place used to smell so bad."

It didn't now.

It smelled of lavender and—

Christ.

That spray the realtors used to make it seem like someone had just freshly baked cookies.

Stomach turning, knowing I'd never be able to smell cookies without remembering *this*, she whispered, "The big bedrooms, on the second floor, they were the ones they fucked us in. It was smaller here. There was a bigger place. I don't know where, but it was in the middle of nowhere. Like an industrial park. We each had our own rooms there. I think I preferred this."

I squeezed her hand as I stepped nearer to her and rasped, "I think we need to see this burn now, sky girl, don't you? Let's sear it from your memories, huh?"

Her shivers transmitted to me, and I felt them in my fucking soul as I curved an arm around her waist and whispered, "If we let the gas run on the stove, it won't take much to make this place blow. Do you want it to burn or to go boom?"

"Boom," she repeated huskily.

So, we went to the kitchen, turned all the gas knobs on, then drifted out the way we came in.

After ten minutes, and standing on the other side of the road, Hawk pulled out the glass bottle we'd bought from a 7-11 for this purpose. We'd sucked out some gas into the bottom of the bottle, had torn up one of my socks and doused it in it, then set fire to it.

He hurled it across the road before we all ran another thirty feet back, taking cover behind a low fence.

As the house exploded, even beneath the bang, I heard her sob. Even though I wished it weren't so, I knew that freedom, for Amara, would not be as simple as destroying her demons. Much like Nyx, her past had transformed her.

Temporary peace was all we could ever hope for for her, and the only thing we could do was to stand by her side and support her no matter what came.

The way Hawk sheltered her beneath his arm gave me faith.

We were in this together.

For the long haul.

FIFTY-TWO

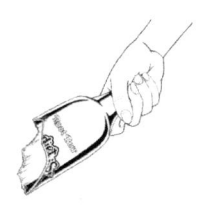

AMARA

I WAS aware of the fractures in my mind.

Some days, I felt as if shadows bled from them, entwining with the ones that Quin said spoke with him too. Mine didn't talk, they just acted as a shroud. Covering me, choking me, killing me.

Three things stopped the fractures from rupturing entirely.

Hawk, who I clung to on the way back to West Orange.

Quin, who rode at our side now that the traffic was quiet and we could ride this way.

The wind.

I knew that sounded strange, but on the back of the bike, I felt like I was flying. I felt free in a way that I never did. Beneath me, the world passed me by while I stayed still.

It was glorious, and exactly what I needed.

That house...

Those rooms...

The memories were thick, cloying, overwhelming because each one sent a face drifting through my mind.

A hundred more faces for Quin to draw.

More and more.

So many.

It felt like they'd never end.

Would he be drawing for the rest of his life?

Would I be haunted for the rest of mine?

When we slowed down as we headed off the freeway and into West Orange itself, I knew we were almost home, because that was what it had become. No longer a place to lay my head, to wait things out until I made a decision about what to do with myself.

This was my home because these men lived there.

They were my home.

My peace.

My loves.

I clung to Hawk tighter, needing more than this even though I was well aware it was wrong for me to want them at all.

The memories were like TikTok videos that constantly replayed over and over. Such powerful entities that manifested the physical sensation of hundreds of hands ghosting over my body, touching me when I didn't want them to.

It made no sense that I wanted Quin and Hawk right then, but it was more that I *chose* them. It was my decision. I needed their love, their affection, their tenderness, their need.

Their emotions were honest, pure.

Not a transaction that someone else received money for.

When they cut off the bikes' engines, the silence reverberated around the yard for a few minutes.

My ears were aching from the blast of before, and that unearthly quiet made them throb but not enough to stop me from moving fast as I climbed off the back of Hawk's hog, then strode forward to open the door.

I didn't wait on them, didn't even pet Petr who barked at me in a delighted greeting, just went straight into the shower.

Unsure and uncaring if water would ruin the clothes Nyx had bought me, I stood under the waterfall as I tried stripping out of them, growing more and more frustrated as the leather tore at my flesh. I didn't give a damn that the temperature was frigid and that it had turned my skin blue by the time Quin made it into the bathroom after me.

A few seconds later, he was there, helping my shaky hands take off the leathers. He burrowed me into the corner, murmuring, "Let the wall support you—"

Before I had to, Hawk was there to support me instead.

He stood at my back, all of us fully dressed, as he held me up while Quin stripped me down.

I should have been revolted by their touch. Those ghostly hands still trailed along my flesh, after all, but the heat of Quin's seemed to burn them away.

Soap was distributed between them, and my shivering, patchy-colored body was scrubbed clean. I didn't have to say a word—they did it three times, like they knew I needed that. Like three times was what it would take for me to feel the bare minimum of clean.

Hawk switched off the shower, then guided me away from the showerhead as he grabbed a towel and began to dry me. As he did, I heard squelching sounds, before the water came on again and I knew Quin was cleaning up too.

Hawk touched me like I wasn't a dirty cum slut. Like he hadn't just seen one of the many places I'd been abused.

He touched me like I was a *khuy* princess.

The need to tell him to stop hovered on the tip of my tongue.

I didn't deserve to be cherished.

Didn't deserve to be loved.

Didn't—

Didn't—

Didn't—

I screamed. My hands coming up to my head as I pulled at my hair, needing to shut up that inner voice, needing for it to stop, to go, to leave—

Arms came around me, and I didn't fight it. I knew who it was. I knew who they were. More than my body recognized them—my soul did. It knew where safety was and where danger lay.

I heard them hushing me, before I was guided into the bedroom. They dressed me like a child, in a shirt I knew was Quin's because it was baggy, and boxer briefs that were tighter around the hips so were Hawk's, and their tenderness tore at me, making the scream in my head reverberate once more.

I didn't deserve their tenderness.

I was dirty.

Used goods—

"Should we call Stone?" I heard Hawk whisper. At least, it sounded like a whisper to me. Above the scream, that was all I heard.

"She just needs us," was Quin's reply.

"We're not tranquilizers," Hawk muttered.

Quin was damp, his flesh sticky with water as he shuffled me forward. "Go and get changed," he ordered Hawk as he guided me to the bed. He helped me down onto it, then lay on his side beside me. He didn't touch me, just lay there, then he whispered something in a language I didn't understand.

It seared my ear drums like a hot brand. Each word did something. Made the tension in me die a little.

"What was that?" I whispered brokenly.

He gave me a soft laugh, that cheerful sound which was so intoxicating to me at that moment.

Quin was joyful in a way few people ever were.

"It was a song *Nòkomis* taught me. I should have known she taught it to me for a reason—to calm you down when *Otesho* won't leave you alone."

His surety of our connection soothed something inside me.

"Don't let them win, sky girl," he breathed in my ear, before pressing his lips to my temple.

"I don't—" I sucked in a ragged breath. "I don't know how to make sure they lose."

"We'll figure that out together." Another kiss to my temple. "Maybe there's no answer, but we'll always be here."

Hawk slipped into bed at that exact moment, and his legs tangled with mine just as Quin's did. All three of us were damp from the shower, but with the duvet pulled tightly around us, the temperature soon surged between the sheets.

"It's time we wore your brands and that you wore ours," Hawk rumbled.

For a second, I only heard the word: brand. But I remembered their odd customs. Ink. They tattooed each other in lieu of a wedding.

I thought about wearing their names on me, and wasn't revolted by the notion.

But the prospect of them wearing mine?

Triumph surged through me, and the best part of it, it drowned out the roar in my mind.

Women would know they were mine.

They'd know to back off.

They would know not to touch.

"Yes," I said thickly.

"I'll book some time off," Hawk rasped, "and make sure that it coincides with Indy's schedule." He pressed his lips to my shoulder. "You're ours, Amara. Ours. Not *theirs*. Ours. When you need to scream, remember *that*."

I swallowed. "I don't deserve you."

"We're not princes," Quin said dryly. "I'm an ex-con who's afraid of the fucking dark, with few prospects, whether he was pardoned or not, if his sister doesn't give him a job. Hawk, well, he's got weird brother issues—"

"Thanks, Quin," Hawk said with a short laugh.

"It's true," Quin retorted. "He works as a bouncer at a strip joint. Future kings we aren't, but we're yours and we'll slay any fucking dragon that comes at you.

"You deserve a kingdom, Amara. You deserve the entirety of the sky lands, but that's not your place yet. This is your home. With us. Don't let them take you away."

I gulped, because his words resonated with me.

Living was the one true way to get revenge.

Surviving.

Enduring.

Not only to take those bastards down, but to be *happy*.

To make Quin and Hawk happy.

Don't let them take you away.

I knew he meant that. Knew he needed me as much as I needed him, *them*.

"Go away, *Otesho*," I rumbled in Ukrainian, pressing my face into Hawk's throat, feeling him wrap his arms around me, squeezing me tight, like he was scared I was letting go. "I'm not yours. I'm theirs."

And that, I knew, was the one solid truth I had to live by.

The one thing that would keep me going when the fissures in my soul cracked wider and wider.

I was theirs.

Simple.

FIFTY-THREE

HAWK

AS INDY PUT the final flourishes on Quin's tattoo, he released a sigh like that was the most relaxing thing he'd ever gone through.

I shook my head at the crazy fucker before I cast a look at Amara.

She'd been depressed since we'd set fire to the brothel three days ago.

That wasn't why we were here, though.

I was here because she was the strongest human I'd ever met and I wanted her to know she was mine.

As for Quin, well, she was his sky girl.

I was almost envious for the ease in which he decided shit where she was concerned, but to him, fate had picked her out for him. For me? I chose her. Me. No one else. Maybe kismet had shoved us together, but this was my choice.

And that was why I wore her brand, and why she wore mine.

Her collarbone was pink from where Quin had wielded the ink gun. On either side, like epaulets, she wore our names, but on the balls of her shoulders, a little like pretty spider webs, she wore two of Indy's mandalas.

She hadn't cried throughout the process, even though I knew it had to fucking hurt, and I wished she had. She needed the release.

As for me, I already had ink on my chest, above my heart where I wore my brother's tattoo. The compass with the oversized 'N' for the fucker who'd tossed me aside without a second's thought, without a single call in months now.

I wasn't about to get rid of it, or to get ink over it, because traitor or not, he was still my twin. But I begrudged the position of the tattoo even if there was nothing I could do about it.

Instead, I wore her brand on my stomach, to the side. Much as Quin did. As similar as our ink was, it was also very different.

The Sun, to the Native Americans, was a powerful symbol. Especially the way they designed theirs.

There was a negative circle surrounded, at the compass points, by four single lines, which acted as the rays. The central two were the same length, the outer two were shorter, but of equal length as well.

Inside the circle, Quin had designed a hawk for me that ran along the same Native American-style. It sat in there, solidly, wings spread wide while, in its claws, Amara's name took pride of place.

As for Quin, he had a buzzard in the center of his, but the creature's wings wrapped around the rays unlike mine, while its claws also carried Amara's name.

For the first time in my life, I looked at a piece of art and understood the symbolism.

After I helped destroy that fucking house, after she told West Orange I had syphilis, after, after, after... I'd come to realize one thing.

What I felt for her wasn't going anywhere.

Much like the sun, it was eternal.

Much like the sun, she shone light on me.

And at the heart of every sun was power. For her, a hawk and a buzzard that would forever keep her from falling to her death.

Quin's story about the sky girl had seemed like bullshit to me, but the deeper into this fucking mess we tumbled, the more I recognized the truth.

Amara would sink without us.

She was a survivor, but even survivors could only take so much.

"There, done," Indy said, her tone satisfied as she looked over us. "My baby brother, claimed. Who'd a thunk it?"

Quin gave her a dopey grin, which told me he was the lucky kind of fucker who rode endorphins while being inked, but it also told me he was happy to wear Amara's brand.

I understood that entirely.

"She doing okay?" Indy asked me quietly as a yawning Quin sat up on the bed.

"She's been weird since the other day."

"Understandable." She pursed her lips. "I wonder if revenge will make her feel better."

"I hope it does," I rasped, because seeing her like this killed me.

"Tell her to come to Lily's tonight. We're having a girl's night."

"I'm not sure she's in the mood."

She shrugged. "Tough. She needs to be around maniacs like her."

"True. It could help." I pursed my lips. "Giulia says you're letting her in the Posse? Could you... I don't know, go and beat up Kendra or something?" Maybe that would cheer my little bird up.

"Why, Hawk, I didn't think you approved of our tactics...?" she teased, prompting me to roll my eyes.

"I don't, but..." I heaved a sigh. "There's no denying that Amara's bloodthirsty. Why shouldn't that work for the MC instead of being left to waste?"

She grinned. "Don't worry. Kendra will gets hers." When I arched a brow, her grin deepened. "Did you hear about Lodestar's plan?"

I hummed.

"You don't approve of ruining the Sparrows' families either?"

"No. But I get it. I don't have to like it to understand why. We didn't go through what they did."

"Alessa didn't approve."

"Alessa's kinder than Lodestar and Amara."

Indy grunted. "True. I have to admit... in their shoes, I'd want to watch the fucking world burn. Nothing else would do."

"And that's why I'm not going to try to get Rex to change Lodestar's mind."

She sighed. "I get it."

"You ready for Thanksgiving?"

"My first with Cruz."

My lips curved. "Our first too. Didn't think I'd be spending Thanksgiving as part of my own family."

She elbowed me in the side. "You've got a big family now. Giulia says she's making a feast at Rachel's. I'd ask if you're joining in but I thought I'd keep you in the loop with Quin. He isn't into Thanksgiving for obvious reasons," she said dryly. "Nyx celebrates it with the club, but I've never bothered that much.

"Mom was Canadian so that was when we got together as kids but we haven't done that in years." She hummed. "Maybe next year though? Now we're all together again?"

The thought, surprisingly, hit me in the feels. "Yeah. I'd really like that."

"While it's a sore subject for him, Quin will go to the party for Amara if he thinks it's best for her, and I really think you should go," Indy said. "I think it would do her good, bring her out of herself, you know?"

"This week's been tough on her," I agreed.

"We do this thing, Hawk, as a family. I wanted to tell you because I know Quin would like you both there but I don't know if he'd ask you—"

"You do know your brother, don't you?" I half-teased. "He's not exactly shy."

"No, but with this, he might be... It's tradition, at Thanksgiving, both the Canadian and American, and on Christmas morning, to go to the club's graveyard. We visit with the family."

The last time I'd been there, we'd been burying Dad.

I sucked my bottom lip into my mouth then let it out with an audible pop. "What time?"

"Eleven in the morning."

Nodding, I said, "Amara and I will be there. Even if he sneaks out and doesn't tell us or something."

She smiled. "Thank you."

"You don't have to thank me," I chided. "Like you said, we're family now."

My phone buzzed and I reached into my pocket. Because it pulled on my tattoo, I cast a look at Quin who, with his ear buds in, was bobbing his head to a song as he dragged on his shirt, giving me and Indy some privacy to talk and allowing me to check over the stab wound on his back without him giving me any shit for being a worrier. Now uncovered, it was healing nicely, the true bright pink of an aging wound.

As I studied it, I connected the call, not bothering to check the ID.

"Hawk?"

I blinked. "Rachel, hey. Is everything okay?"

"Not really. Can you come and see me at my place?"

"Sure. We're heading back that way anyway."

"Great. Just knock on the door."

"What's it about?"

She heaved a sigh. "Nothing that can't be fixed."

When she cut the call, I figured she didn't want to talk about it over the line but it pushed me into paying, then shepherding Quin and Amara out onto the street.

Quin and I had the day off, which was why we'd gotten inked and had picked up a new mattress. For all that my morning had started out nice, I had a feeling my afternoon was about to turn sour.

"What did Rachel want?" Amara asked, her voice lacking the luster I was used to hearing.

"To speak with me," I replied, rubbing the scratches on my forearm. They were itchy as hell now, mostly healed but four long lines still scored the flesh—fucking cats.

"Just you?" Quin asked.

"I think so. I'll drop you off at the compound—"

"No, I wish to speak with Giulia," Amara said gruffly.

"I can hang with Nyx," Quin agreed with a shrug.

Nodding, I jumped behind the wheel of the cage and drove us back to the road that led to the compound and Rachel's place. Once we pulled up, I grabbed Amara's hand and raised her knuckles to my mouth.

After I kissed them, she rasped something in Ukrainian.

"What did that mean?"

"It means I don't deserve you."

My smile was slow but sure. "You don't know what you deserve."

Quin chimed in, "He's right. Good thing you have us to show you."

Amara sighed, then leaned forward and pressed her mouth to mine. "Thank you," she whispered when she pulled back.

"What for?"

She hitched a shoulder. "Everything."

"Far too vague," Quin complained. "For being sex gods? For being hunkier than that guy in *The Witcher*?"

Her lips twitched, and it reminded me exactly of why we'd gotten the sun tattoos—because her smile made me feel like the sun was finally peeking out from a blanket of gray clouds.

I leaned over her again to taste that smile, and when she sighed into it, her head arching back as she gave me full access, I reached up and cupped her face between my hands.

"No matter what, we can overcome it, Amara. You just need to be patient."

She blinked, her eyes dazed as she whispered, "Patience is hard."

"You trained to be a ballerina," I told her. "You know what patience is."

"That was a long time ago, and I'm a very different person now."

"I know, but it will come. I promise you, Amara, it will fucking come."

She swallowed. "You can't promise that. Even I know that now."

"Does that mean you'll talk to Rex tomorrow and won't ignore him anymore? It *is* Thanksgiving," I wheedled.

Her nose crinkled. "I don't think he cares."

He probably didn't, but I did.

I reached up and rubbed her crinkled nose. "He's just trying to protect us all."

She blew out a breath. "I know."

"We've got a long life ahead of us, little bird. There's plenty of time to wreak the havoc you deserve."

Amara cupped my cheek, rubbed at the stubble that was growing there, then murmured, "Go and speak with Rachel, hmm?"

"I will." I nodded as I pulled back, and realized Quin had disappeared. That was unlike him but I appreciated the privacy he'd given us.

That was the thing with a threesome. Figuring out the dynamics was hard, but it was relatively easy for us seeing as I had to work so fucking much at the moment. Quin spent more time with her than I did, but he was good about disappearing, going to work or just working out so I had some time with her. Even snatched moments in front of the TV was better than sweet fuck all.

She waited for me as I rounded the cage's fender, and hand in hand, we walked into the house.

Squeezing her fingers when she moved toward the kitchen, shortly after, I headed for the back of the house where Rachel's office was located.

After I knocked and she called me in, I popped my head around the door and said, "Hey, Rachel."

"Come in, Hawk." She shot me a tight smile but wafted me toward the seats in front of her desk.

Much like the rest of the house, it was a swanky place. Behind the massive, masculine mahogany desk, she should have looked out of place, maybe even small. Instead, she commanded it. But that was her nature. She wasn't exactly a submissive kind of woman.

"What is it, Rachel? What's going on?" I queried, when her serious expression only added to my nerves.

"There are a few things..." She pulled out a document.

"What is it?"

"Your father's last will and testament." Her lips twisted with disapproval. "We should have read this sooner, but North is completely off the radar."

I frowned. "North and Giulia should be here!"

"Giulia isn't included in the will. North is, but like I said, I can't find him. I asked Lodestar to help but, understandably, she's got more important things on her mind."

"Do you think he's dead or something?"

Rachel reared back. "Why would you think that?"

"He hasn't tried to call me once." I shook my head. "That's not like him."

"If he is, we won't find out if Lodestar doesn't help us," she said, her tone resigned. "Maybe when her vendetta is complete she'll try to track him?"

"It's fucking horrible that I'd almost prefer him to be dead than to think he can cut me off like this."

"Family always lets us down," she said mournfully, her mouth tightening as she rocked back in her seat. "It's best to accept that and move on."

"And they say I'm a fucking grouch," I retorted, which had her lips twitching.

"I'm a realist," she corrected. "Anyway, Dog left you and North his house. It's divided between the pair of you—"

"Wait, not Katy? What about his wife?"

"He left her no assets."

"None? Christ, he was such a cunt."

She snorted. "That's certainly one way to describe him," she agreed drolly. "There's a sizeable monetary bequest, but with the house, it'll have to be transferred into both your names until you can reach North."

I shrugged. "Can you deal with that?"

"Of course."

"I didn't even know he owned that house he lived in."

"You haven't been since he died?" I shook my head. "Why not? You could have stayed there instead of here?"

I winced. "I guess I didn't want to be alone."

Her eyes softened. "It must be difficult to be separated from a twin."

Difficult? More like agonizing.

Amara had soothed that ache. Much like Quin and I were doing for her. We alleviated the pain, smoothed over the suffering, but none of us were fucking miracle workers. Life didn't work like that. It'd be nice if it did. Smoothing over, *alleviating*, that didn't take away the source of the agony, did it?

"Yeah," I said thickly. "It is."

"I'm sorry, Hawk," she replied gently.

"It's okay." It really wasn't. "Is that everything?"

"No. I wish it was." She reached up to pinch the bridge of her nose. "Look, I should have called you all in, but I didn't want to offend Quin or worry Amara."

"Why would you?"

"I don't know why or how or who, but the visa petition I put through for Amara, it's been denied."

Shock slalomed inside me. "What the fuck?" I jerked to my feet, hands slamming on the table. "She told me that you said it'd take years for her case to even come up!"

"It normally does. It can take dozens of months, but..." Rachel grimaced, "...I have to assume someone actively sought out her case file and made sure she was denied.

"Considering Rex informed me of the attack against her in Quin's hospital room, I have to assume there's a link between that and this. She's been targeted by someone."

Though rage filled me, my mind raced, hunting for solutions. "What are the alternatives? Marriage? Will that look like we're doing it for a green card?"

"Maybe, but she'll have more of a legal standing here if she's married. It'd be best if you were the spouse, Hawk. I understand you have an arrangement between the three of you—" Funny how that made something so natural, seem so dirty. *An arrangement.* Fuck. "But with Quin's record, even with a pardon, and—" She pinched the bridge of her nose. "—I hate to say this but his ethnicity, you'd be the stronger, more viable option."

The inked sun on my abs burned like it was a source of autonomous energy.

There wasn't a doubt in my mind that I'd marry her, but Rachel's reasonings stung.

"What a fucking world, Rachel," I hissed.

She dipped her chin. "I know, Hawk. It's disgusting. I shared the news with Rex and he's hiring an attorney who can help with the specialized circumstances of this situation, but marriage will protect her."

"How much time do we have?"

She scowled. "How much time do you fucking need?"

My mouth tightened. "Enough for it not to look shady. Enough for her to never know that this is the reason why I'm asking."

"There might be another way if you don't want to go through with a marriage," she said stiffly. "To be honest, I'll be pushing through with that as well but considering the circumstances, dual protection would be advisable."

"What's the other way?"

"Money is no issue for her now. There are visas that rely on the person applying investing in the nation."

"Do it. I want her safe on her own merit. I don't want her to think her freedom here is tied to me. Christ, I always was gonna propose anyway, just…"

"Just what?" Rachel asked quietly, her tone softer now.

I ran my hands through my hair as I straightened up. "At Christmas. After the shit with the journalist went down. It seemed fitting."

"Well, she won't hear it from me," was the attorney's reply. "I won't say a word."

"She'll figure it out eventually," I said, pissed at having my plans wrecked.

Why did the truth have to be so brutal?

"What will I figure out eventually?"

I twisted around and found Amara standing there in the doorway. She had that same vibe as *The Omen's* Damien when he entered a room sometimes. I could almost hear shrieking violins screech to a crescendo.

If I didn't love her so fucking much, I'd say she belonged in a horror movie with the uncanny way she had of nosing through shit and coming up with gold.

"Nothing. Rachel just read me my dad's will."

"He was also Giulia's dad. Why is she not here?"

"He didn't leave her anything," I replied.

She scowled and her accent was thicker than frozen custard as she sneered, "He was bad father."

"Yes, he was," Rachel concurred.

What the hell could I say in Dog's defense? He had sucked, even if North and I wished we could put him on a pedestal, he was a weak-minded wife-beater.

Christ.

Just thinking that made me want to reject every cent he'd given me.

"Why would this upset me if I found it out eventually though?" Amara asked, tipping her head to the side in confusion.

Rachel shrugged when I cast her a look. The desire to shield her was strong, but one thing I'd learned since me and her had gotten together was that she needed the truth.

"Your visa's been denied."

There.

Blunt.

She blinked then shrugged. "So? We will get married, *tak?*"

Rachel coughed to hide a laugh, but deep inside me, the relief was real.

I truly had believed she'd put up a fight over this, but she was so certain, so fucking sure. God... maybe this fear inside me that she'd fly away would finally disintegrate. I could only hope so.

Lifting a hand, I muttered, "You don't mind?"

"You will wear a ring?"

"Yes." I frowned. "Why?"

"Will Quin wear a ring too?"

"A three-way marriage isn't legal," Rachel pointed out.

"Legal or not, he can still wear a ring," Amara insisted.

"Yes, he can. If you want, there are special ceremonies for these kinds of relationships."

Amara shot me a smug smile. "I will still tell everyone you have syphilis, but the ring will make things far more formal. They touch you," she rasped, and her words were as much of a vow as if she was saying, 'I do,' "—they die."

My lips curved, even as I saw Rachel's shock at Amara's declaration. "I didn't need to hear that," she muttered. "Attorney-client privilege only covers so much."

"If he will wear ring, and you will wear ring, and every *blyat'* knows you're mine, then why should I mind if we must marry for a visa?" Her eyes narrowed. "The Sparrows have done their best to put stones in my path, and if they think this is one, then I will show them who they're dealing with.

"I'll kick each and every one of them out of my way and make them wish they were dead long before God sends them straight to hell."

The crazy thing was, I knew she meant it. Every word.

Crazier still?

The boner her words, and that deepening Slavic accent, gave me.

FIFTY-FOUR

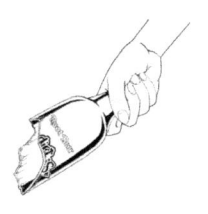

QUIN

FOUR WEEKS LATER

IT WAS FUCKING FREEZING in the graveyard just beyond the clubhouse, but we stood there anyway, heads tipped down as we paid our respects to Carly, our parents, Dog, and Sarah.

Only *Nòkomis* and Hawk's Mom weren't here, and while their presence was missed, it felt right that most of our roots were here.

Amara threaded her fingers through mine, making our rings clink. Neither of us were used to wearing them, and even though mine was only 'ceremonial' at the moment, I knew she got a kick out of them. I often found her staring at her rings, then glancing at Hawk's and mine too.

She was a possessive little thing, and in all honesty, if I was anyone else, she'd terrify me. Amara embodied the thunderbird I'd inked onto her wrist—quite willing and able to dive face-first into war with zero regrets.

She had no morals anymore, nothing that held her back. If either of us ever strayed, if we betrayed her? Well, surviving her would definitely be impossible. Dicks lopped off first, questions asked later. Probably when we were six feet under.

Maybe I was just as crazy as she was, because the thought

cheered me up, and to be honest, I needed it. Graveyards weren't the most cheerful of places, were they?

Giulia and Nyx drifted away first, followed by Cruz and Indy, leaving me, Hawk, and Amara to stand there in the cold.

As my breath misted in front of me, I raised my head and stared up at the sky where I knew *Nòkomis* was waiting for me. I smiled up at her, knowing she'd want me to be happy.

Aashaa had decided, *Otesho* had whispered in my ear, and as a result, my demons and Amara's were tangled quite neatly together, making a perfect little unit with Hawk making up for the sanity that the pair of us were so sorely missing.

A match made in the sky lands...

Hawk ruined my visual by muttering, "I think one of my balls just fell off."

"It's not that cold," Amara chided even as Petr shivered at her side. "In Ukraine, you step outside and your breath mists then falls to the floor."

"That happens here too."

"Not like in Ukraine," she insisted, as if it was a competition.

"Do you ever want to go back there? Your parents might be alive," I pointed out.

"No. I'm dead to them. They won't know me like this." She pursed her lips. "Do we have to eat at the clubhouse?"

There was a massive party going on, a kind of triple celebration.

Not only was the clubhouse finally ready, even if it was missing a lot of furniture, Amara's pictures had rocked the country, sending shockwaves through the political foundations of the US itself, and, well, it was Christmas. That merited a party.

"We should show our faces," was all Hawk said.

She wrinkled her nose. "You will have to go with the men, and I will have to go with the Posse—" Yeah, she'd been inducted into the 'hall of fame.' "—this does not sound like fun to me when we could be in the bunkhouse. Naked."

A laugh escaped me. "I mean, when you put it like that..."

Her eyes gleamed. "You are smart man."

"I try."

"I can live without turkey," Hawk agreed.

"Thought you might." Her brow puckered. "What about the kitten?"

Hawk grunted. "It'll be fine."

She shook her head. "It is yours."

"Fucking Quin," Hawk muttered under his breath, and even though I shouldn't laugh, I couldn't stop myself.

"It's not my fault she picked you!"

I'd gone outside to feed my wild menagerie of creatures this morning and had found a tabby kitten. Bright ginger, button-cute nose, she was definitely Cassie's. I'd thought Amara would love her, but instead, she hadn't left Hawk's side and had been hissing up a storm when he'd closed the door with her behind it.

"I don't even like cats," he grumbled.

"Well, she likes you," Amara said flatly as she watched Petr run off, barking, back toward the bunkhouse as we turned around to start walking back too. Hawk reached out and connected their hands as we made our way home. "You can't say no when they pick you."

Hawk heaved a sigh. "I don't have time for a kitten."

"Nonsense," she said briskly, and though it was dumb, it always made me feel better when she accepted the animals that came to the bunkhouse.

It wasn't a gift I asked for, but I couldn't turn them away, could I? Instead of giving me shit about it, she always accepted them, and even fed them or helped with giving them meds if they needed it.

At the moment, we had an injured squirrel and a hedgehog that wasn't doing so great, and she was the one giving them the drops the vet prescribed.

Grateful, I squeezed her fingers and, like she knew I was thanking her, she squeezed them back.

Amara took no shit from either of us, even if Hawk genuinely didn't have the time for a kitten.

When he was home, he was focused on being with us, not the zoo I had in the back yard. He didn't work as many hours now that Rex had some more men to work at the strip club, but he still had long shifts where he was away from Amara.

I knew she wasn't the only one who felt the distance.

She helped out at the tattoo studio too, especially as Giulia had finally gotten her certification to start piercing, and I was slowly spending more time apprenticing under Indy, so while we weren't always together, she could have her eyes on me constantly.

That, I knew, was something she needed to feel balanced.

Something I needed just as much.

Hawk working at the strip club didn't help with her possessiveness, so I knew he was excited about the brewery Rex was planning on opening as soon the permits came in for the motel to be demolished, and the licenses for the construction trickled in too.

As a unit, we wandered over the brittle ground, carefully stepping across icy patches on the path. Unfortunately for us, when we made it back home, it was clear that the Posse had foreseen our intentions.

They were all there, each of them.

Their Old Men were traipsing back and forth with shit from the clubhouse, hauling tables around, dragging chairs inside the bunkhouse, carrying dishes and hot pans and baking trays, all while Petr barked at them for disturbing our peace.

"Don't be a miserable cunt, Amara," Giulia hollered, evidently seeing my sky girl's grumpy face as she took in the jollity. "It's Christmas Day. You can fuck them later."

Laughter drifted around the place, but it was Lily who approached us first and who hugged Amara, whispering, "We know you don't like the clubwhores around Quin and Hawk."

Her nose crinkled, but she didn't deny it as she half-heartedly hugged Lily back before shrugging out of her coat.

It always amused me how affectionate she was with us, but wasn't with anyone else.

Five cats made an appearance, winding around our ankles, their pregnant bellies rubbing against us as they silently demanded more food.

The kitten Hawk didn't want but who wanted him whether he liked it or not, dug her claws into his jeans and climbed up him like he was a tree. He hissed and detached her from his pants, then propped her on his shoulder.

"She's a cat not a bird," I pointed out. "Long John Silver."

He flipped me the bird. "This is all your fucking fault," he grumbled as the kitten nuzzled into him.

Giulia drifted over to Amara with Tiffany and Indy, but only Giulia slugged an arm around her waist as Hawk and I backed off a little, letting them be as Hawk went one way, talking to the kitten about how she'd prefer Amara who was much nicer than him—outright lies, Amara was anything but nice. Well, okay, she was nice to us and to the animals—and I headed to the kitchen for more cat food.

As I did, I heard Giulia whisper, "She actually cried?"

Indy muttered, "That's weird. I don't think I've ever seen her cry. She's the fucking Ice Queen."

"Do you think someone upset her?" Amara asked, sounding lethal. And when Amara sounded lethal, that meant she was about to do something interesting with a corkscrew to someone's eyeball.

"Rachel's impossible to upset," Indy said with a scoff. "There must be some other reason. Do you think it's to do with Bear, and they're not saying—"

Before I could do much more than arch a brow in curiosity, Nyx called out, "Okay, you bastards, it's Christmas. It's the law around here that we have to enjoy ourselves, so keep your hands to yourself until after seven when you can go screw in your own beds, you horny fuckers.

"So let's eat, drink, and be merry and let's spare a moment to think of those bastards who are in jail and are busy trying to figure out if they can hang themselves with their bedsheets."

A cheer rang up around the bunkhouse, and while it wasn't exactly festive, it sure as hell was fitting.

I cast Amara a glance, saw her bloodthirsty sky girl smile, and as her gaze darted from me to another point in the room where I knew Hawk must be standing, I knew it was going to be a very merry Christmas indeed.

The first of many.

For an eternity.

TWO MONTHS LATER

IT WAS FREEZING in Providence when the woman opened the door to her house. The heat was on, but it was so frigid that even the intense warmth didn't thaw out her cheeks or stop the subsequent itch as heated air met cold flesh.

She shuddered as she closed the door behind her, and locked it up tight. Disengaging the alarm, she shrugged out of her coat and hung it on the rack, then toed out of her boots and slipped out of her gloves.

Only when she was fully divested of her outer clothes did she call out, "Carlos? Where are you?"

Upon receiving no answer, she heaved a sigh, told Siri to play her the national headlines, then trod down the hall toward the kitchen, in dire need of a hot cup of coffee and then something to eat. It had been a long day and the last thing she'd eaten was a *pain au chocolat* earlier that morning.

"In other news, the badly decomposed body that washed up along the Hudson River in Edgewater, has finally been identified as a missing man from West Orange, New Jersey.

"Kevin Sisson disappeared twenty-two years ago while out on a hunting trip.

"Police say there are signs that his death was suspicious.

"A murder investigation has begun, and Edgewater Police are confident that despite this being a cold case, there is enough evidence to make an arrest."

"In the sports' world…"

Flipping on the switch to the kitchen, she froze the second her eyes adjusted to the light.

Another woman sat there, right in the center of the room, on one of the kitchen chairs. As regal as a queen, as if the wooden seat were a throne, with a man at her back like a silent sentinel, an odd mutt at her heels, the three intruders watched her as much as a cat would watch a mouse it was about to bite into.

She twisted around, her intent to run out the way she came when she found herself coming face to face with another man who braced his arms on the door frame so she couldn't pass.

Nostrils flaring, she jerked back around, demanding, "Who the hell are you? What are you doing here?"

"Don't you remember me, Liliana?" Smoothly, the stranger got to her feet, and that was when Liliana saw the knife in her hand. "No?" she asked, her head tilting to the side. "Just one of many, wasn't I? Just one more cunt to sell, I suppose." She smiled. "It's such a shame that you made quite an impression on me…"

THE NEXT BOOK IN THE SERIES IS NOW AVAILABLE TO READ ON KU!
www.books2read.com/StormSerenaAkeroyd

AFTERWORD

STORM IS NOW AVAILABLE TO PREORDER!!
Grab it here: www.books2read.com/StormSerenaAkeroyd
Whether you love him or hate him, closure is coming...

So, my darlings, a few things.

Super recognizers are legit! Scotland Yard truly does have a team of them to scan CCTV footage. They're more accurate than computers—how fucking cool is that?

The sky girl is from a real Algonquin legend. You can read the original here: https://www.ultimatecampresource.com/uncategorized/the-girl-who-climbed-to-the-sky/ I took some creative liberty and twisted it around so that Hawk saved Sapana first. :)

Now, harsh fact time.

- Between 15,000 and 50,000 women and girls are trafficked each year into the US, with the global figures for modern slavery standing at somewhere between 20 and 40 million.

- 51% of active human trafficking cases in the US involved *only* children.
- Human traffickers earn over $150 billion a year.
- In the US, a teen enters the sex trade between 12-14, with many of those victims being runaway girls who were sexually abused as children.

Facts' source: https://www.dosomething.org/us/facts/11-facts-about-human-trafficking

Horrific.

I wish my story was founded on fiction, but the truth is often far crueler than reality.

In this universe, however, *I* am God, and people *will* pay.

I stand with Amara.

I stand with Alessa.

I stand with Tatána and Sarah.

I stand **FOR** justice.

Let's watch the NWS ***BURN***.

Are you ready for FILTHY HOT?

Preorder it here: www.books2read.com/FilthyHot

For a comprehensive reading order of the crossover universe, start here:

FILTHY
NYX
LINK
FILTHY RICH
SIN
STEEL
FILTHY DARK
CRUZ
MAVERICK

FILTHY SEX
HAWK
FILTHY HOT (Coming soon)

Thank you, so much, for your support. And, while you're here, if you'd like to join my Diva reader group on FB for all the latest news on my releases, especially if it's still release week, there'll be some goodies to grab in there. Join here: www.facebook.com/groups/SerenaAkeroydsDivas

Love you, guys, and thanks for reading!
Serena
xoxo

FILTHY

FINN

Obsessive habits weren't alien to me.

They were as much a part of me as my coal-dark hair and my diamond-blue eyes. Ingrained as they were, it didn't mean they weren't irritating as fuck.

As I rifled through the folder on the table in front of me, staring down at the life of one pesky tenant, I wanted to toss it in the trash. I truly did.

I wanted not to be interested in her.

Wanted my focus to return to the matter at hand—business.

But there was something about her.

Something...

Irish.

I was a sucker for my own people. When I was a kid, I'd only dated other Irish girls in my class, and though I'd become less discerning about nationality and had grown more interested in tits and ass, I'd thought that desire had died down.

But Aoife Keegan was undeniably, indefatigably Irish.

From her fucking name—I didn't know people still named their kids in Gaelic over here—to her red goddamn hair and milky-white skin.

To many, she wouldn't be sexy. Too pale, too curvy, too rounded and wholesome. But to me? It was like God had formed a creature that was born to be my downfall.

I could feel the beast inside me roaring to life as I stared at the photos of her. It wanted out. It wanted her.

Fuck.

"I told you not to get those briefs."

My eyes flared wide in surprise at my brother, Aidan O'Donnelly's remark. "What?" I snapped.

"I told you not to get those briefs," he repeated, unoffended. Which was a miracle. Had I been speaking to Aidan Sr., I'd probably have lost a finger, but Aidan Jr. was one of my best friends, as well as a confidant and fellow businessman.

When I said business, it wasn't the kind Valley girls dreamed their future husbands would be involved in. No Manhattan socialite, though we were wealthy as fuck, would want us on their arm if they truly knew what games we were involved in.

My business was forged, unashamedly, in blood, sweat, and tears.

Preferably not my own, although I had taken a few hits for the Family over the years.

"My briefs aren't irritating me," I carried on, blowing out a breath.

"No? You look like you've got something up your ass crack." Aidan cocked a brow at me, but his smirk told me he knew exactly what the fuck was wrong.

I flipped him the bird—the finger that I'd have lost by showing cheek to his father—and he just grinned at me as he leaned over my glass desk and scooped up one of the pictures.

That beast I mentioned earlier?

It roared to life again when his eyes drifted over Aoife's curvy form.

"She's like your kryptonite," he breathed, tilting his head to the side. "Fuck me, Finn."

"I'd rather not," I told him dryly. "Now her? Yeah. I'd fuck her anytime."

He wafted a dismissive hand at my teasing. "I knew from that look in your eye, there was a woman involved. I just didn't know it would be a looker like this."

I snatched the photo from him. "Mine."

My growl had him snickering. "The Old Country ain't where I get my women from, Finn. Simmer down."

Throat tightening, I grated out, "What the fuck am I going to do?"

"Screw her?" he suggested.

"I can't."

He snorted. "You can."

"How the fuck am I supposed to get her in my bed when I'm about to bribe her into selling off her commercial lot?"

Aidan shrugged. "Do the bribing after."

That had me blowing out a breath. "You're a bastard, you know that, right?"

Piously, he murmured, "My parents were well and truly married before I came along. I have the wedding and birth certificates to prove it." He grinned. "Anyway, you're only just figuring that out?"

I shot him a scowl. "You're remarkably cheerful today."

"Is that a question or a statement?"

"Both?" The word sounded far too Irish for my own taste. My mother had come from Ireland, Tipperary to be precise—yeah, like the song. I was American born and bred, my accent that of someone who'd been raised in Hell's Kitchen but, and I hated it, my mother's accent would make an appearance every now and then.

'Both' came out sounding almost like 'boat.'

Aidan, knowing me as well as he did, smirked again—the fucker. "I got laid."

Grunting, I told him, "That doesn't usually make you cheerful."

"It does. I just never see you first thing after I wake up. Da hasn't managed to piss me off today."

Aidan was the heir to the Five Points—an Irish gang who operated out of Hell's Kitchen. It wasn't like being the heir to a candy company or a title. It came with responsibilities that no one really appreciated.

We were tied into the life, though. Had been since the day we were born.

There was no use in whining over it, and Aidan wasn't. But if I had to deal with his father on a daily basis? I'd have been whining to the morgue and back.

Aidan Sr. was the shrewdest man I knew. What the man could do with our clout defied belief. Even if I thought he was a sociopath, he had my respect, and in truth, my love and loyalty.

Bastard or no, he'd taken me in when I was fourteen and had made me one of his family. I'd gone from being his kids' friend, the son of one of his runners, to suddenly being welcome in the main house.

All because Aidan Sr.—though I was sure he was certifiable—believed in family.

I shot Aidan Jr. a look. "Was it that blonde over on Canal Street?"

He rubbed his chin. "Yeah."

Snorting, I told him, "Hope you wore a rubber. I swear that woman has so many men going in and out of her door, it should be on double-action hinges."

He scowled at me. "Are you trying to piss me off?"

"Why? Didn't wear a jimmy?" I grinned at him, my mood soaring in the face of his irritation. "Better get to the clinic before it drops off."

Though he flipped me the bird as easily as I'd done to him—I was his brother, after all—he grumbled, "What are you going to do about little Aoife?"

I squinted at him. "She's not little."

That seemed to restore his humor. "I know. Just how you like them." He shook his head. "You and Conor, I swear. What do you do with them? Drown yourself in their tits?"

Heaving a sigh, I informed him, "My predilection for large tits is none of your business."

"And whether or not I wore a jimmy last night is none of yours."

"If it turns green and looks like a moldy corn on the cob, who you gonna call?"

"Ghostbusters?" he tried.

I shook my head, then pointed a finger at him and back at myself. "No. Me."

Grunting, he got to his feet and pressed his fists to the desk. "We need that building, Finn."

"The business development plan was mine, Aid. I know we need it. Don't worry, I won't do anything stupid."

He snorted. "Your kind of stupid could go one of two ways."

That had me narrowing my eyes at him, but he held up his hands in surrender.

"Fuck her out of your system quickly, and then get started on the deal," he advised. "Best way."

It probably was the best way, but—

He sighed. "That fucking honor of yours."

I had to laugh. Only in the O'Donnelly family would my thoughts be considered honorable.

"If I'm fucking someone over, I want them to know it," was all I said.

"That makes no sense."

"Makes for epic sex, though," I jibed, and he shot me a grin.

"Angry sex is always good." He rubbed his chin, then he reached over again and flipped through the photos. "Who's the old guy to her?"

"To her? Not sure. Sugar daddy?" The thought alone made the beast inside rage. I cleared my throat to get rid of the rasp there. "To us? He's our meal ticket."

Aidan's eyes widened. "He is?"

I nodded. "Just leave it to me."

"I was always going to, *dearthái r*." He tilted his chin at me, honoring me with the Gaelic word for brother. "Be careful out there."

"You, too, brother."

Aidan winked at me and, with a far too cheerful whistle for someone whose dick might soon be 'ribbed for her pleasure' without the need for a condom, walked out of my office leaving me to brood.

The instant his back was to me, I stared at the photos again. Flipping through them, I glowered at the innocent face staring back at me through the photo paper—if only she knew.

Hers was a building in Hell's Kitchen. Five Points Territory. One of many on my hit list.

Back in the 70s, Aidan Sr., following in his father's footsteps, had bought up a shit-ton of property, pre-gentrification, and it was my job to either sell off the portfolio, reconstruct, or 'improve' the current aesthetics of the buildings the Points owned.

This particular one was something I'd taken a personal interest in.

See, I was technically a legitimate businessman.

This office?

I had views of the Hudson. I could see the Empire State Building, and in the evening, I had an epic view of the sunset setting over Manhattan. This office building, also Points' property, was worth a cool hundred million, and I was, again technically, the CEO of it.

On paper?

I looked seamless.

The businessman who sported hundred thousand dollar watches and had a house in the Hamptons. No one save the Points and my CPA knew where the money came from. I liked that because, fuck, I had no intention of switching this pad for a lock-up in Riker's Island.

Still, this project cut close to home, and the reasoning was fucking pathetic.

I'd never admit it to any of the O'Donnellys. The bastards were like family to me, and if I admitted to this, they'd never let me hear the end of it.

Extortion?

I usually doled that out to someone else's to do list. Someone with a far lower paygrade than me, someone expendable. But the minute I'd heard of the troublesome tenant who was refusing to sell her lot to us? After not one, not two, not even three attempts with higher prices?

Five outright refusals?

The challenge to convince her otherwise had overtaken me.

See, I liked stubborn in women.

I liked fucking it out of them.

Throw in the fact the woman's name was Aoife? It had been enough to get me sending someone out to follow her.

If she'd been fifty with as many chins as she had grandchildren, she'd have been safe from me.

But she wasn't.

She was, as Aidan had correctly stated, my kryptonite. All milky flesh with gleaming auburn hair that I wanted to tie around my clenched fist. Her soft features with those delicate green eyes that sparkled when she smiled and were like wet grass when she was mad, acted like a punch to my gut.

Now?

My interest hadn't just been piqued.

It had fucking imploded.

Yeah, I was thinking with my cock, but what man, at the end of the day, didn't?

I'd just have to be careful. Just have to make sure I put pressure on the right places, make sure she'd bend and not break, and the old bastard in the pictures was my key to just that.

See, every third Tuesday of the month, Aoife Keegan had a habit of traipsing across Manhattan to the Upper East Side. There, at three PM on the dot, she'd enter a discreet little boutique hotel and wouldn't leave until nine PM that night.

Five minutes after she arrived and left, the same man would leave, too.

At first, when Jimmy O'Leary had told me that Senator Alan Davidson was at the hotel, I hadn't thought anything of it.

Why would I?

Senators trawled for donations in fancy hotels every fucking day of the week. It was the true luxury of politics. Sure, they made it look real good for the press. Posing in derelict neighborhoods and shaking hands with people who did the fucking work... all while they lived it up large with women half their age in two thousand dollar a night suites.

My mouth firmed at that.

Was Aoife selling herself to the Senator?

The thought pissed me off.

I couldn't see why she'd do such a thing. Not when I'd looked into her finances, had seen just how secure she was. But maybe that was why. Maybe the Senator was funneling money to her.

The only problem was that the lot Aoife owned—did I mention it was owned outright? Yeah, that was enough to chafe my suspicions, too, considering she was only twenty-fucking-five years old—was a teashop in a small building in a questionable area of HK.

I mean, come on. I loved Hell's Kitchen. It was home. But fuck. Where she was? What kind of Senator would put his fancy piece in *that*?

My jaw clenched as I studied the Senator's and Aoife's smiling faces as they left the hotel. Separately, of course. But whatever they'd been doing together, it sure put a Cheshire Cat grin on their chops— that was for fucking sure. Jimmy being a dumbass, hadn't put the two together, had just remarked on the 'coincidence,' but I was no fool.

How did I know they were together in the hotel?

Jimmy had been trailing Aoife for four months—told you I was obsessive—and every third Tuesday, come rain or shine, this little routine had jumped out, and when Jimmy had picked up on the fact Davidson had been there each and every time, I'd gotten my hands dirty, bribed one of the hotel maids myself—and fuck, that had been hard. Turned out that place made even the maids sign NDA agreements, but everyone had a price—and I'd found out that my little obsession shared a suite with the old prick.

My fingers curled into fists as I stared at her. Butter wouldn't fucking melt. She was the epitome of innocence. Like a redheaded angel. Could she really be lifting her skirts for that old fucker? Just so she could own a teashop?

Something didn't make sense, and fuck, if that didn't intrigue me all the more.

Aoife Keegan had snared one of the biggest, nastiest sharks in Manhattan.

She just didn't know it yet.

***

Aoife

"We need more scones for tomorrow. I keep telling you four dozen isn't enough."

Lifting a hand at my waitress and friend, Jenny, I mumbled, "I know, I know."

"If you know, then why the hell don't you listen?" Jenny complained, making me grin.

"Because I'm the one who has to make them? Making half that again is just . . ." I sighed.

I loved my job.

I did.

I adored baking—my butt and hips attested to that fact—and making a career out of my passion was something every twenty-something hoped for. Especially in one of the most expensive cities in the world. But sheesh. There was only so much one person could do, and this was still, essentially, a one-woman-band.

With the threat of Acuig Corp looming over me, I didn't feel safe hiring extra staff. I'd held them off for close to six months now. Six months of them trying to tempt me to leave, to sell up. They'd raised their prices to ten percent above market value, whereas with everyone else in the building, they'd just offered what the apartments were truly worth. Considering this place wasn't the nicest in the block, that wasn't much.

Most people hadn't held out because, hell, why wouldn't they want to live elsewhere?

Those who were landlords hadn't felt any issue in tossing their tenants out on the street. The tenants grumbled, but when did they ever have any rights, anyway?

For myself, this was where my mom and I had worked to—

I brought that thought to a shuddering halt.

Mom was dead now.

I had to remember that. This was on me, not her.

My throat thickened with tears as I turned to Jenny and murmured, "I'll try better tomorrow."

The words had her frowning at me. "Babe, you know I'm not the boss here, right?"

Lips curving, I whispered, "I know. But you're so scary."

She snickered then peered down at herself. "Yeah, I bet I'd make grown men cry."

Maybe for a taste of her. . . .

Jenny was everything I wasn't.

She was slender, didn't dip her hand into the cookie jar at will—the woman had more willpower than I did hips, and my hips seemed to go on forever—and her face looked like it belonged on the cover of a fashion magazine. Even her hair was enough to inspire envy. It was black and straight as a ruler.

Mine?

Bright red and curly like a bitch. I had to straighten it out every morning if I didn't want to look like little orphan Annie.

I'd once read that curly-haired women straightened their hair for special events, and that straight-haired women curled theirs in turn, but I called bullshit.

Curly-haired women lived with their straightening irons surgically attached to their hands.

At least, I did.

My rat's nest was like a ginger afro. Maybe Beyoncé could make that work, but I sure as hell didn't have the bone structure.

"I think grown men would cry," I told her dryly, "if you asked them to."

She pshawed, but there was a twinkle in her eye that I understood. . . . She agreed with me, knew it was true, but wasn't going to admit it. With anyone else, she might have. She had an ego–that was for damn sure. But with me? I think she figured I was zero competition, so she felt no need to rub salt in the wound, too.

I plunked my elbows on the counter and stared around my domain as she bustled off and started clearing the tables. It was her last duty of the day, and my feet were aching so damn bad that I didn't even have it in me to care.

This owning your own business shit?

It wasn't easy.

Not saying I didn't love it, but it was hard.

I slept like four hours a night, and when I wasn't in bed, I was here. All the time.

Baking, cooking, serving, and smiling. Always smiling. Even if I was so sleep-deprived I could sob.

Jenny's actually a life saver.

My mom used to be front of house before. . . .

I sucked down a breath.

I had to get used to thinking about it.

She wasn't here anymore, but just avoiding all thoughts of her period wasn't working for me. It was like I was purposely forgetting her, and, well, fuck that.

She'd always wanted to have a teashop. It had been her one true dream. Back in Ireland, when she was a little girl, her grandmother had owned one in Limerick. Mom had caught the bug and had wanted to have one here in the States. But not only was it too fucking expensive for a woman on her own, it was also impossible with my feckless father at her side.

I didn't want to think about him either, though.

Why?

Because the feckless father who'd pretty much ruined my mother's life, wasn't the only father in my life. My biological dad hadn't exactly cared about her happiness, but once he'd come to know about me, he'd tried. That was more than could be said for the man who'd lived with me throughout my early childhood.

"You look gloomy."

Jenny's statement had me blinking in surprise. She had a ton of dishes piled in her arms, and I'd have worried for the expensive china if I hadn't known she was an old pro at this shit. Just as I was.

We could probably earn a Guinness World Record on how many dishes we could take back and forth to the kitchen of *Ellie's Tea Rooms*. I swear, I had guns because of all that hefting. My biceps were probably the firmest part of my body.

More's the pity.

I'd have preferred an ass you could bounce dimes off of, but, when it boiled down to it, there was no way in this universe I could live without cake.

Just wasn't going to happen.

My big butt wasn't going *anywhere* until scientists could make zero calorie eclairs and pies.

"I'm not glum."

"No? Then why are your eyes sad?"

Were they? I pursed my lips as I let the 'sad eyes' drift around the tea room. I wish I could say it was all forged on my own hard work, but it wasn't. Not really.

"I was just thinking about Mom."

"Oh, honey," Jenny said sadly, and she carefully placed all the dishes on the counter, so she could round it and curve her arm around my waist. "It was only seven months ago. Of course, you were thinking of her."

"I just—" I blew out a breath. "I don't know if I'm doing what she'd want."

"You can't live for her choices, sweetness. You have to do what you think is right for you."

I gnawed at my bottom lip again. "I-I know, but she was always there for me. A guiding light. With Fiona gone and her, too? I don't really know what I'm doing with myself."

This business wasn't something that made me want to get up on a morning. It was my mom's dream, her goal. Every decision I made, I tried to remember how she'd longed for a place like this, but it wasn't my passion. It was hers, and I was trying to keep that dream alive while fretting over the fact my heart wasn't in it.

"I think you're doing a damn fine job. You have a very successful teashop. Your cakes are raved about. Have you visited our TripAdvisor page recently? Or our Yelp?" She squeaked. "I swear, you're making this place a tourist hotspot. I don't think Fiona or Michelle could be more proud of you if they tried."

The baking shit, yeah, that was all on me, but the other stuff? The finances?

I'd caved in.

I'd caved where my mom had always refused in the past.

With the accident had come a lot of medical bills that I just hadn't been able to afford. Without her help, I'd had to take on extra staff, and out of nowhere, my expenses had added up.

Mom had been so proud of this place, so ferociously gleeful that we'd done it by ourselves, and yet, here I was, financially free for the first time in my life, and I still felt like I was drowning because my freedom went entirely against her wishes.

"Is this to do with Acuig? I know they're still pestering you."

Jenny's statement had me wincing. Acuig were the bottom feeders who wanted to snap up this building, demolish it, and then replace it with a skyscraper. Don't get me wrong, the building was foul, but a lot of people lived here, and the minute it morphed into some exclusive condo, no one from around here would be able to afford to live in it.

It would become yuppy central.

I'd rejected all their offers to buy my tea room even though I didn't want the damn thing, not really. Mostly I wanted to keep mom's goals alive and kicking, but also, it pissed me off the way Acuig were changing Hell's Kitchen. Ratcheting up prices, making it unaffordable for the everyday man and woman—the people I'd grown up with—and bringing a shit-ton of banker-wankers and 1%ers to the area.

So, maybe I'd watched Erin Brockovich a time or two as a kid and had a social conscience... Wasn't the worst thing to possess, right?

"Aoife?" Jenny stated, making me look over at her. "Is Acuig pressuring you?"

I winced, realizing I hadn't answered—Jenny was my friend, but she also worked here and relied on the paycheck. It wasn't fair of me to keep her hanging like that. "They upped the sales price. I guess that isn't helping," I admitted, frowning down at my hands.

Unlike Jenny who had her nails manicured, mine were cut neatly and plain. I had no rings on my fingers, and wore no watch or bracelets because my wrists were usually deep in flour or sugar bags.

I spent most of my life right where I wanted it—behind the shopfront. That had slowly morphed where I was doing double the work to compensate for Mom's loss.

Was it any wonder I was feeling a little out of my league?

I was coping without Fiona, grieving Mom, working without her, too, and then practically living in the kitchens here. I didn't exactly have that much of a life. I had nothing cheerful on the horizon, either.

Well, nothing except for next Tuesday, and that wasn't enough to turn my frown upside down.

The money was a temptation. I didn't need to sell up and start working on my own goals, but that just loaded me down with more guilt and made me feel like a really shitty daughter.

Jenny squeezed me in a gentle hug. But as I turned to speak to her, the bell above the door rang as it opened. We both jerked in surprise—each of us apparently thinking the other had locked up when neither of us had—and turned to face the entrance.

On the brink of telling the client we were closed for the day, my mouth opened then shut.

Standing there, amid the frilly, lacy curtains, was the most masculine man I'd ever seen in my life.

And I meant that.

It was like a thousand aftershave models had morphed into one handsome creature that had just walked through my door.

At my side, I could feel Jenny's 'hot guy radar' flare to life, and for once, I couldn't damn well blame her.

This guy was . . . well, he was enough to make me choke on my words and splutter to a halt.

The tea room was all girly femininity. It was sophisticated enough to appeal to businesswomen with its mauve, taupe, and cream-toned hues, and the ethereal watercolors that decorated the walls. But the tablecloths were lacy, and the china dishes and cake stands we used were the height of Edwardian elegance.

Moms brought their little girls here for their birthday, and high-powered executives spilled dirt on their lovers with their girlfriends over scones and clotted cream—breaking their diets as they discussed the boyfriends who had broken their hearts.

The man, whoever the hell he was, was dressed to impress in a navy suit with the finest pinstripe. It was close to a silver fleck, and I could see, even from this distance, that it was hand tailored. I'd seen custom tailoring before, and only a trained eye could get a suit cut so perfectly to this man's form.

With wide shoulders that looked like they could take the weight of the world, a long, lean frame that was enhanced by strong muscles evident through the close fit of his pants and jacket, then the silkiness of his shirt which revealed delineated abs when his bright gold and scarlet tie flapped as he moved, the guy was hot.

With a capital H.

"How can we help, sir?" Jenny purred, and despite my own awe, I had to dip my chin to hide my smile.

Even if I wanted to throw my hat into this particular man's game, there was no way he'd choose me over Jenny. Fuck, I'd screw her, and I wasn't even a lesbian. Not even a teensy bit bi. I'd gone shopping with her enough to have seen her ass, and I promise you, it's biteable.

So, nope. I didn't have a snowball's chance in hell of this Adonis seeing *me* when Jenny was in the room.

Yet....

When I'd controlled my smile, I looked over at the man, and his focus was on me.

My breath stuttered to a halt.

Why wasn't his gaze glued to Jenny?

Why weren't those ice-white blue eyes fixated on my best friend's tits, which Jenny helpfully plumped up as she preened at my side?

For a second, I was so close to breaking out into a coughing fit, it was humiliating. Then, more humiliation struck in a quieter manner, but it was nevertheless rotten—I turned pink.

Now, you might think you know what a blush is. You might think you've even experienced it yourself a time or two. But I was a redhead. My skin made fresh milk look yellow, and even my fucking freckles were pale. Everything about me was like I'd been dunked into white wax.

But as the heat crawled over me, taking over my skin as the man looked at me without pause, I knew things had rarely been this dire.

See, with Jenny as a best friend, I was used to the attention going her way. I could hide in the background, hide in her shadow. I liked it there. I was comfortable there. Sometimes, on double dates, she'd drag me along, and even the guy supposed to be dating me would be gaping at Jenny. As pathetic as it was, I was so used to it, it didn't bother me.

But now?

I just wasn't used to being in the spotlight.

Especially not a man like this one's spotlight.

When you're a teenager, practicing with your mom's blush for the first time, you always look like a tomato that's been left out in the sun, right?

I was redder than that.

I could feel it. I could fucking feel the heat turning me tomato red.

When Jenny cleared her throat, I thanked God when it broke the man's attention. He shot her a look, but it wasn't admiring. It wasn't even impressed.

If anything, it was irritated.

Okay, so now both Jenny and I were stunned.

Fuck that, we were floored.

Literally.

Our mouths were doing a pretty good fish impression as the man turned back to look at me.

Shit, was this some kind of joke?

Was it April 1st and I'd just gotten the dates mixed up again?

"Ms. Keegan?"

Oh fuck. His voice.

Oh. My. God.

That voice.

It was. . . .

I had to swallow.

Did men even talk like that?

It was low and husky and raspy and made me think of sex, not just mediocre sex, but the best sex. Toe-curling, nails-breaking-in-the-sheets sex. Sex so fucking good you couldn't walk the next day. Sex so hot that it made my current core temperature look polar in comparison. Sex that I'd never been lucky to have before, so I pined for it in the worst way.

Jenny nudged me in the side when I just carried on gaping at the man. "Y-Yes. That's me." I cleared my throat, feeling nervous and stupid and flustered as I wiped my hands on my apron.

Sweet Jesus.

Was this man really looking for me while I was wearing a goddamn pinafore?

Even as practical as they were, I wanted to beg the patron saint of pinnies to remove it from me. To do something, anything, to make sure that this man didn't see me in the red gingham check that I always wore to cover up stains.

And then I felt it.

Jenny's hand.

Tugging at the knot.

I wanted to kiss her. Seriously. I wanted to give her a fucking raise! As I moved away from the counter and her side, the apron dropped to the floor as I headed for the man whose hand was now held out, ready for me to shake in greeting.

There are those moments in your life when you know you'll never forget them. They can be happy or sad, annoying or exhilarating. This was one of them.

As I slipped my hand into his, I felt the electric shocks down to my core. Meeting his gaze wasn't hard because I was stunned, and I needed to know if he'd felt that, too.

From the way those eyelids were shielding his icy-blue eyes, I figured he was just as surprised.

It was like a satisfied puma was watching me. One that was happy there was plump prey prancing around in front of him.

Shit.

Did I just describe myself as 'plump prey?'

And like that, my house of cards came tumbling down because what the hell would this man want with me?

I was seeing things.

God, I was so stupid sometimes.

I cleared my throat for, like, the fourth damn time, and asked, "I'm Ms. Keegan. You are?"

His smile, when it appeared, was as charming as the rest of him. His teeth were white, but not creepy, reality-TV-star white. They were straight except for one of his canines, which tilted in slightly. In his perfect face, it was one flaw that I almost clung to. Because with that wide brow, the hair so dark it looked like black silk that was cut closely to his head with a faint peak at his forehead, the strong nose, and even stronger jaw, I needed something imperfect to focus on.

Then, I sucked down a breath and remembered what Fiona had told me once upon a time. When I'd been nervous about asking Jamie Winters to homecoming, she'd advised me in her soft Irish lilt, "Lass, that boy takes a dump just like you do. He uses the bathroom twice a day and undoubtedly leaves a puddle on the floor for his ma to clean up. I bet he's puked a time or two as well. Had diarrhea and the good Lord only knows what else. Just you think that the next time you see that boy and want to ask him out."

Yeah. It was gross, but fuck, it had worked. Her advice had worked so well I hadn't asked anyone out because I could only think of them using the damn toilet!

Still, looking at this Adonis, there was no imagining *that*.

Surely, gods didn't use the bathroom.

Did they?

"The name's Finn. Finn O'Grady."

My eyes flared at the name.

No.

It couldn't be.

Finn O'Grady?

No. It wasn't a rare name, but it was a strong one. One that suited him, one that had always suited him.

I frowned up at him wondering, yet again, if this was a joke of some sort, but as he looked at me, *really* looked at me, I saw no recognition. Saw nothing on his features that revealed any ounce of awareness that I'd known him for years.

Well, okay, not *known*. But I'd known his mother. Our mothers had been best friends. And as I looked, I saw the same almond-shaped eyes Fiona had, the stubborn jaw, and that unmistakable butt-indent on his chin.

At the reminder of just how forgettable I was, my heart sank, and hurt whistled through me.

Then, I realized I was *still* holding his hand, and as he squeezed, the flush returned and I almost died of mortification.

CHAPTER 2

FINN

GOD, she was perfect.

And when I said perfect, I meant it.

I'd fucked a lot of women. Redheads, blondes, brunettes, even the rare thing that is a natural head of black hair. None of them, not a single one, lit up like Aoife Keegan.

Her cheeks were cherry red and in the light camisole she wore, a cheerful yellow, I could see how the blush went all the way down to the upper curve of her breasts.

She'd go that color, I knew, when she came.

And fuck, I wanted to see that.

I wanted to see that perfectly pale flesh turn bright pink under my ministrations.

Even as I looked at her, all shy and flustered, I wondered if she was a screamer in bed.

Some of the shyest often were.

Maybe not at first, but after a handful of orgasms, it was a wonder what that could do to a woman's self-confidence, and Jesus, I wanted to *see* that, too. I wanted a seat at center stage.

My suit jacket was open, and I regretted it. Immensely. My cock was hard, had been since we'd shaken hands, and her fingers had clung to mine like a daughter would to her daddy's at her first visit to the county fair.

Fuck.

Squeezing her fingers wasn't intentional. If anything, I'd just liked the feel of her palm against mine, but when I put faint pressure on her, she jerked back like she'd been scalded.

Her cheeks bloomed with heat again, and she whispered, "Mr. O'Grady, what can I do for you?"

You can get on your fucking knees and sort out the hard-on you just caused.

That's what she could fucking do.

I almost growled at the thought because the image of her on her knees, my cock in her small fist, her dainty mouth opening to take the tip....

Shit.

That had to happen.

Here, too.

In this fancy, frilly, feminine place, I wanted to defile her.

Fuck, I wanted that so goddamn much, it was enough to make me reconsider my demolition plans.

I wanted to screw her against all this goddamn lace, which suited her perfectly. She was made for lace. And silk. Hell, silk would look like heaven against her skin. I wouldn't know where she ended and it began.

When her brow puckered, she dipped her chin, and that gorgeous wave of auburn hair slipped over her shoulder.

If we'd been alone, if that brassy bitch—who was staring at me like I could fuck her over the counter with her friend watching if I was game—wasn't here, I'd have grabbed that rope of hair, twisted it around my fingers, and forced her gaze up.

Some guys liked their women demure. And I was one of them. I wasn't about to lie. I liked that in her, but I wanted her eyes on me. Always.

It was enough to prompt me to bite out, "Can we speak privately?"

She jerked at my words, then as she licked her bottom lip, turned to look at the waitress. "Jenny, it's okay. I can handle the rest by myself. You get home."

Jenny, her gaze drifting between me and her boss, nodded. She retreated to a door that swung as she moved through the opening, and within seconds, she had her coat and purse over her arm.

As she sashayed past—for my benefit, I was sure—she murmured, "See you tomorrow, Aoife."

Aoife nodded and shot her friend a smile, but I wasn't smiling. There were dishes on every table. Plates and saucers and tea pots. Those fancy stands that made any man wonder if he could touch it without snapping it.

Aoife was going to clear all that herself? Not on my fucking watch.

When the bell rang as the waitress opened the door, I didn't take my eyes off her until it rang once more upon closing.

Aoife swallowed, and I watched her throat work, watched it with a hunger that felt alien to me, because, God, I wanted to see my bites on her. Wanted to see my marks on that pale column of skin and her tits.

Barely withholding a groan, I asked, "Do you often let your staff go when you still have a lot of work to do, so you can speak to a stranger?"

Her cheeks flushed again, and she took a step back. "I-I, you're not—" Flustered once more, she fell silent.

"I'm not what?" Curiosity had me asking the question. Whatever I'd expected her to say, it hadn't been that.

She cleared her throat. "N-Nothing. You wished to speak with me, Mr. O'Grady?"

My other hand tightened around my briefcase, and though seeing her had made my reason for being here all that more necessary, I was almost disappointed. There was a gentle warmth to those bright-green eyes that would die out when I told her my purpose for being here. And her innocent attraction to me would change, morph into something else.

But I could only handle *something else*.

Some men were made for forever.

But those men weren't in my line of business.

I moved away from her, pressing my briefcase to one of the few empty tables. I wasn't happy about her having to do all the clearing up later on, and wondered if Paul, my PA, would know who to call to get her some help.

There was no way I was spending the rest of the night alone in my bed, my only companion my fist wrapped around my cock.

No way, no fucking how.

I paid Paul enough for him to come and clear the fucking place on his own if he couldn't find someone else.

I wanted Aoife on her knees, bent over my goddamn bed, and I was a man who always got what he wanted.

In this jungle, I was the lion, and Aoife? She was my prey.

I keyed in the code and opened my briefcase. The manila envelope was large and thick, well-padded with my documentation of Aoife's every move for the past few months.

It had started off as a legitimate move.

I'd wanted to know her weaknesses, so I could put pressure on her and make her cave to my demands.

Now, my demands had changed. I didn't just want her to sell the tea room we were standing in, I wanted her in my bed.

Fuck, I wanted that more than I wanted to make Aidan Sr. a fucking profit, and Aidan's profit and my balls still being attached to my body ran hand in hand.

Aidan was an evil cunt.

If I failed to deliver, he'd take it out on me. Whether I was his idea of an adopted son or not, he'd have done the same to his blood sons.

Well, he wouldn't have taken their balls. The man, for all his psychotic flaws, was obsessed with the idea of grandchildren, of passing it all on to the next generation. He'd cut his boys though. Without a doubt.

I knew Conor had marks on his back from a beating he refused to speak about. Then there was Brennan. He had a weak wrist because his father had a habit of breaking *that* wrist.

Without speaking, I grabbed the envelope and passed it to her.

She frowned down at it and asked, "For me?"

I smiled at her. "Open it."

"What is it?"

"Leverage."

That had her eyes flaring wide as she pulled out some of the photos. A gasp fell from her lips as she grabbed the photos when she spotted herself in them, jerking so hard the envelope tore. Some of the pictures spilled to the ground, but I didn't care about that.

Leaning back against one of the dainty tables once I was satisfied it would take my weight, I watched her cheeks blanch, all that delicious color dissipating as she took in everything the photos revealed.

"Y-You've been stalking me. Why?"

The question was high-pitched, loaded down with panic. I'd heard it often enough to recognize it easily.

I didn't get involved in wet work anymore. That wasn't my style, but along the way, to reach this point, I'd had no choice but to get my hands dirty. Panic was part of the job when you were collecting debts for the Irish Mob. And the Five Points were notorious for Aidan Sr.'s temper.

He wasn't the first patriarch. If anything, his grandfather was the founder. But Aidan Sr. was the type of guy that if you didn't pay him back, he didn't give a fuck about the money, he cared about the lack of respect.

See, you owed the mob and didn't pay? They'd send heavies around, beat the shit out of you, and threaten to do the same to your family, and usually, that did the trick. You didn't kill the cash cow.

Aidan Sr.?

He didn't give a fuck about the cash cow.

Only the truly desperate thought about borrowing money from Aidan, because if you didn't pay it back, he'd take your teeth, and your fingers and toes as a first warning. Then, if you still didn't pay—and most did—it was death.

Respect meant a lot to Aidan.

And fuck, if it wasn't starting to mean a lot to me. The panic in her voice made my cock throb.

I wanted this woman weak and willing.

I wanted it more than I wanted my next breath.

Ignoring her, I reached for my phone and tapped out a message to Paul.

Need housekeeping crew to clean this place.

I attached my live location, saw the blue ticks as Paul read the message—he knew better than to ignore my texts, whatever time of day they came—and he replied: *Sure thing.*

That was the kind of reply I was used to getting. Not just from Paul, but from everyone.

There were very few people who weren't below me in the strata of Five Points, and I'd worked my ass off to make that so.

The only people who ranked above me included Aidan Jr. and his brothers, Aidan Sr. of course, and then maybe a handful of his advisors that he respected for what they'd done for him and the Points over the years.

But the money I made Aidan Sr.?

That blew most of their 'advice' out of the window.

The reason Aidan had a Dassault Falcon executive private plane?

Because I was, as the City itself called me, a whiz kid.

I'd made my first million—backed by the Points, of course—at twenty-two.

Fifteen years later?

I'd made him hundreds of millions.

My own personal fortune was nothing to sniff at, either.

"W-Why have you done this?" Aoife asked, her voice breathy enough to make me wonder if she sounded like that in the sack.

"Because you've been a very stubborn little girl."

Her eyes flared wide. "Excuse me?"

I reached into the inside pocket of my suit coat and pulled out a business card. "For you," I prompted, offering it to her.

When she turned it over, saw the logo of five points shaped into a star, then read Acuig—in the Gaelic way, ah-coo-ig, not a butchered American way, ah-coo-ch—aloud, I watched her throat work as she swallowed.

"I-I should have realized with the Irish name," she whispered, the muscles in her brow twitching as she took in the chaos of the scattered photos on the floor.

Watching her as she dropped the contents on the ground, so she was surrounded by them, I tilted my head to the side, taking her in as her panic started to crest.

"I-I won't sell." Her first words surprised me.

I should have figured, though. Everything about this woman was surprisingly delicious.

"You have no choice," I purred. "As far as I'm aware, the Senator has a wife. He also has a reputation to protect. I'm not sure he'd be happy if any of those made it onto the *National Enquirer's* front page. Not when he's just trying to shore up his image to take a run for the White House next election."

She reached up and clutched her throat. The self-protective gesture was enough to make me smile at her—I knew what the absence of hope looked like.

There'd been a time when that had been my life, too.

"But, on the bright side," I carried on, "this can all be wiped away if you sell." As her gaze flicked to mine, I added, "As well as if you do something for me."

For a second, she was speechless. I could see she knew what that *something* was. Had my body language given it away? Had there been a certain raspiness to my tone?

I wasn't sure, and frankly, didn't give a fuck.

There was a little hiccoughing sound that escaped her lips, and she frowned at me, then down at herself.

"Is this a joke?"

"Do I look like I'm the kind of guy who jokes, Aoife?" Fuck, I loved saying her name.

The Gaelic notes just drove me insane.

Ee-Fah.

Nothing like the spelling, and all the more complicated and delicious for it.

"N-No," she confirmed, "but . . ."

"But what?" I prompted.

"I mean . . . you just can't be serious."

"Oh, but I am." I grinned. "Deadly. You've wasted a lot of my time, Aoife Keegan. A lot. Do you think I'm normally involved in negotiations of this level?"

Her eyes whispered over me, and I felt the loving caress of her gaze as she took in each and every inch of me. When she licked her lips, I knew she liked what she saw. I didn't really care, but it was helpful for her to be eager in some small way—especially when coercion was involved.

Aidan had called it bribery. I preferred 'coercion'. It sounded far kinder.

"No. That suit alone probably cost the mortgage payment on this place."

I nodded—she wasn't wrong. I knew what she'd been paying as rent, then as a mortgage, before some kind *benefactor* had paid it all off. Free and clear.

"I had to get my hands dirty, and while I might like some things dirty . . .," I trailed off, smirking when she flushed. "So, as I see it, we have a problem. I want this building. You don't want anyone to know you're having an affair with a Senator. Or, should I say, the Senator doesn't want anyone to know he's having an affair with someone young enough to be his daughter . . ."

If my voice turned into a growl at that point, then it was because the notion of her spreading her legs for that old bastard just turned my stomach.

Fuck, this woman, the thoughts she made me think.

Because I was startled at the possessive note to my growl, I ran a hand over my head. I kept my hair short for a reason—ease. I wasn't the kind of man who wasted time primping. It was an expensive cut, so I didn't have to do anything to it. Even mussing it up had it falling back into the same sleek lines as before—a man in my position had to look pristine under pressure. And very few people could even begin to understand the kind of strain I was under.

The formation of igneous rock had less volcanic pressure than Aidan Sr.

She licked her lips as she stared down at the photos, then back up at me. "And you want me to sell the place to you, even though this is my livelihood and the livelihood of all my staff, and then sleep with you?"

Her squeaky voice, putting suspicion into words, had me crossing my legs at the ankle. "We wouldn't be doing much sleeping."

Another shaky breath soughed from her lips, then, those beautiful pillowy morsels that would look good around my cock, quivered.

"This is crazy," she whispered shakily.

"As far as I'm concerned, all of this could be avoided if you'd just sold to me a few months back. Now you have to pay for my time wasted on this project."

"By spreading my legs?"

Another squeak. I tsked at her question, but in truth, I was annoyed at her using those same words I had to describe her with that old hypocrite of a Senator.

I didn't move, though. Didn't even flex my arms in irritation, just murmured, "Small price to pay. And, even though it's ten percent above market price, I'll stick to the last offer Acuig gave you. Can't say anything's fairer than that."

She shook her head, and there was a desperation to the gesture as she cried, "I need this business. You don't understand—"

"I understand that some very powerful and very dangerous businessmen want this building demolished. I understand that those same powerful and dangerous men want a skyscraper taking up this plot of land. I understand that a four hundred million dollar project isn't going to be put on hiatus because one small Irish woman doesn't want to go out of business . . ." I cocked a brow at her. "You think I'm coming in hot and heavy? These kinds of men, Aoife, they're not the sort you fuck around with.

"Take my check, and my other offer, before you or the people you care about are threatened." I got to my feet and straightened my jacket out. "This suit? These shoes? That briefcase and this watch? I own them because I'm damn good at what I do. I'm a financial advisor, Aoife. Take my word for it. You're getting the best deal out of this."

She staggered back, the counter stopping her from crumpling to the floor. "You'd hurt me?"

"Not me," I repudiated. Not in the way she thought, anyway. "But the men I work for?"

Her gaze dropped to the one thing she'd retained in her hand—my card. "Acuig," she whispered. "Five in Gaelic."

My brows twitched in surprise. She knew Gaelic?

"The Five Points." Her eyes flared wide with terror. "They're behind this deal."

I hadn't expected her to put one and one together, but now that she had? It worked to my advantage.

Nodding, I told her, "Any minute now, there'll be a team of housekeepers coming in here to clear up for the night." When she gaped at me, I retrieved the contract from my briefcase, slapped it on the table, and handed her a pen as I carried on, "I suggest you let tonight be your last night of business."

What I didn't tell her, was that my suggestions weren't wasted words. They were like the law.

You didn't break them, and, like any lawmaker, I expected immediate obeisance.

***

Aoife

SO, the beautiful man just happened to be an absolute cocksucker of a bastard.

Still, this couldn't be real, could it?

The dick could have anyone he wanted. Jesus, Jenny was panting after him like a dog in heat. She would have gone out with him if he'd so much as clicked his fingers at her.

But he'd had eyes for me.

Like he wanted me.

He thought he'd bought me. Or, at least, bought my silence, and yeah, to some extent he had. But . . . why buy me, why not just drop the price on the building if he wanted me to pay for the time he'd wasted on me?

The arrogance imbued in those words was enough to make me pull my hair out, but that was inwardly. I was a redhead. I had a temper. But that temper was mostly overshadowed by fear.

Senator Alan Davidson wasn't my boyfriend, my lover, as this dick seemed to believe. He was my father, and as Finn O'Grady had correctly surmised, he was aiming for the White House.

How could I put that in jeopardy?

My dad was a good man. He'd made a mistake one summer when he'd come home from college, one that only some careful digging by his campaign manager had uncovered. Dad himself hadn't known of my existence, not until his CM had gone hunting for any nasty secrets that could come out and bite him in the ass.

This had been five years ago when he'd run for Senator. Now, Dad's goal was the presidential seat, and I wasn't going to be the one who put a wrench in the works.

When Garry Smythe had approached me back then, I'd thought he was joking. I was out on the street, heading home from work. At the side of me, a black car had driven in from the lane of traffic, just to park, or so I'd thought. As he'd held out his hand with a card, one of the car doors had opened up, and I'd been 'invited' inside.

Had I been scared?

At first.

But when Garry had told me my country needed me, I hadn't been sure whether to laugh or tell him to fuck off. He hadn't shuffled me into the car, though, hadn't tried to coerce me. He'd just asked if I'd voted for Senator Alan Davidson in the elections, and because he was one of the only politicians out there who wasn't a complete douche, and that was the name printed on the card in my hand, I'd shuffled into the back of the car.

Where the Senator himself had been sitting.

Now, when I thought about that day, I realized how fucking naive I'd been to get into the back of a limo for such a vague reason. But I'd been fortunate. Alan *had* been waiting for me. Waiting to tell me a story that still shook me to my core.

I'd made a promise to my dad that I wouldn't tell anyone. He'd offered me money, and I hadn't accepted it. I guess I should have, but back then, I'd been haughty and proud, and because the good guy I'd thought him to be hadn't been so good when he tried to buy my silence, I'd told him to fuck off. I'd been disappointed in him, frightened by the lifelong lie I'd been living, and equally hurt that the man who'd sired me was just concerned that I was a threat to his campaign.

I'd walked out of that car never expecting to see my dear old Dad ever again.

Then, the day after he'd been elected, he'd been sitting in the booth of the cafe where I worked part-time to get me through culinary school.

Seeing him, I'd almost handed that table off to one of the other waitresses, but I hadn't. Not when every time I'd passed the table, he'd caught my eye, a patient smile on his lips, one that said he'd wait for me all day if he had to.

Ever since that second meeting, I'd been catching up with him every three weeks.

And this bastard thought he could use our limited time together against my father? The one politician who could make a difference in the White House? One who didn't have Big Oil up his ass, a pharmaceutical company sucking his dick, or any other kind of corporation so far up his rectum that he was a walking, talking lie?

No.

That wasn't going to happen.

Which meant I was going to have to sleep with this stranger.

Before this conversation, hell, that hadn't been too disturbing a prospect. Because, dayum, what woman wouldn't want to sleep with this guy?

Even with an ego as big as his, he was delicious. Better than any cake I could bake, that was for fucking sure.

More than that, I knew him.

And I now knew that the life Fiona would never have wanted for her son was one he'd been drawn into.

The Mob.

The Five Points were notorious in these parts. Everyone was scared of them. I paid protection money to them, for God's sake. I knew to be scared of them, and having been raised in their territory, it was the height of stupidity to think paying them wasn't just a part of business.

Still, Fiona had never wanted that for Finn, and her Finn was the same as the one standing before me here today. In my tea room, which looked far too small to contain the might of this man.

She'd be so disappointed. So heart-sore to know that he was up to his neck in dirty dealings with the Five Points, and as he'd pointed out, the cost of his shoes, his clothes, and his jewelry, was enough to speak for itself.

If he wasn't high up the ladder in the gang, then I wasn't one of the best bakers of scones in the district.

Like Jenny had said, I had five star ratings across most social media platforms for a reason. I was good. But apparently, this man wasn't.

Before I could utter a word, before I could even cringe at how utterly sorrowful Fiona would be about this turn of events—not just about the Five Points but what her son was making me do—the door clattered open.

Like he'd predicted, a team of people swarmed in.

Finn motioned to the floor. "Want anyone to see those?"

With a gasp, I dropped to my knees and collected the shots, stuffing them back into the envelope with a haste that wasn't exactly practical.

Two shiny shoes appeared before me, followed by two expensively clad legs, and I peered up at him, wondering what he was about. He held out his hand, but I clasped the photos to my chest.

"You're making more of a mess than anything else, Aoife." His voice was raspy, his eyes weighted down by heavy lids.

For a second, I wondered why, then I saw *why*.

He had an erection.

An erection?

I peered around at the staff, but they were all men. Not a single woman in sight, well, save for the seventy-year-old with a clipboard who was barking out orders to the guys in what sounded like Russian.

So that meant, what?

The erection was for me?

The blush, the dreaded, hated blush, made another goddamn appearance, and to cover it, I ducked my head, then pushed the photos and the envelope at him.

For whatever reason, I stayed where I was, staring up at him as he calmly, coolly, and so fucking collectedly pushed the photos back into the torn envelope—it was some coverage. Better than none at all, I figured.

Being down here was. . . .

Hell, I don't know what it was.

To be looked at like that?

For his body to respond to me like that?

It was unprecedented.

I'd had one sexual experience with a boy back in college, and that had not gone according to plan. So much so I was still technically a fucking virgin because, and this was no lie, the guy had *zero* understanding of a woman's body.

Craig had spent more time fingering my perineum than my clit, and every time he'd tried to shove his dick into me, he'd somehow managed to drag it down toward my ass.

I'd gotten so sick of him frigging the wrong bits of me, that I'd pushed him off and given him a blowjob. It had been the quickest way to get out of that annoying situation.

Yeah, annoying.

Jenny, when I'd told her, had pissed herself laughing, and ever since, had tried to get me to hook up with randoms, so I could slough off my virginity like it was dead skin and I was a snake. But life had just always gotten in the way, and I'd had no time for men.

Shortly after *that* had happened, we'd lost Fiona. Then, I'd graduated, and after, Mom and I had set up this place thanks to some insurance money she'd come into after her husband had died. It had been crazy building the tea room into an established cafe, and then mom had passed on, too.

So, here I was. Still a virgin. On my knees in front of the sexiest man on Earth, a man I knew, a man whose mother had half raised me, one who wanted me in his bed as some kind of blackmail payment.

Was this a dream?

Seriously?

I mean, I'd been depressed before Finn O'Grady had walked

through my doors. Now I wasn't sure whether to be apoplectic or worried as fuck because he wasn't wrong: you didn't mess with the Five Points.

God, if I'd known they'd been behind the development on this building, I'd have probably signed over months ago.

The Points were....

I shuddered.

Vindictive.

Aidan O'Donnelly was half-evil genius and half-twisted sociopath. St. Patrick's Church, two streets away, had the best roof in the neighborhood and the strongest attendance because Aidan, for all he'd cut you into more pieces than a butcher, was a devout Catholic. His men knew better than to avoid Sunday service, and I reckoned that Father Doyle was the busiest priest in the city because of Five Points' attendance.

"I like you down there," he murmured absentmindedly.

The words weren't exactly dirty, but the meaning? They had my temperature soaring.

Shit.

What the hell was I doing?

Enjoying the way this man was victimizing me?

It was so wrong, and yet, what was standing right in front of me? I knew he'd know what to do with that thing tucked behind his pants.

He wouldn't try to penetrate my urethra—yes, you read that right. Craig had tried to fuck my pee-hole! Like, *why?*

Finn?

He oozed sex appeal.

It seemed to seep from every pore, perfuming the air around me with his pheromones.

I hadn't even believed in pheromones until I scented Finn O'Grady's delicious essence.

It reminded me of the one out of town vacation we'd ever had. We'd gone to Cooperstown, and I'd scented a body of water that didn't have corpses floating in it—Otsego Lake. He reminded me of that. So green and earthy. It was an attack on my overwhelmed senses, an attack I didn't need.

With the envelope in his hand, he held out his other for me. When I placed my fingers in his, the size difference between us was noticeable once more.

I was just over five feet, and he was over six. I was round and curvy, and he was hard and lean.

It reminded me of the nursery tale Mom had sung to me as a child—Jack Sprat could eat no fat, and his wife could eat no lean.

Did it say a lot for my confidence that I couldn't seem to take it in that he wanted *me*? Or was it simply that I wasn't understanding how anyone could prefer me over Jenny?

Even my mom had called Jenny beautiful, whereas she'd kissed me on the nose and called me her 'bonny lass.'

Biting my lip, I accepted his help off the floor. My black jeans weren't the smartest thing for the tea room, but I didn't actually serve that many dishes, just bustled around behind the counter, working up the courage to do what Mom had done every day—greet people.

I wasn't a sociable person. I preferred my kitchen to the front of house, hence the jeans, but I regretted not wearing something else today. Something that covered just how big my ass was, how slender my waist *wasn't*.

Ugh.

This man is blackmailing you into his bed, Aoife. For Christ's sake, you're not supposed to be worrying if he likes the goods, too!

Still, no matter how much I tried, years of inadequacy weighed me down as I wiped off my knees.

"Do you have a coat?" he asked, and his voice was raspy again. "A jacket? Or a purse?"

I nodded at him but kept my gaze trained on the floor. "Yes."

"Go get them."

His order had me shuffling my feet toward the kitchen, but as I approached the door, I heard his strong voice speaking with the old woman with the clipboard: "I want this all cleaned up and boxed. Take it to my storage lot in Queens."

With my back to him, I stiffened at his brisk orders. *Was I just going to let him do this? Get away with it?*

My shoulders immediately sagged.

Did I have a choice?

If it was just him, just Acuig, then I'd fight this, as I'd been fighting it since the building had come to the attention of the developer. But this wasn't a regular business deal.

This was mob business, and it seemed like somehow, I'd become a part of that.

FML.

Seriously, FML.

CHAPTER 3

FINN

SHE WASN'T AS fiery as I imagined.

Did that disappoint me?

Maybe.

Then I had to chide myself because, Jesus, the woman had just been *coerced* out of her business. What did I expect? For her to be popping open a champagne bottle after I'd forced her to sign over her building to me?

Sure, she'd made a nice and tidy profit on her investment—I hadn't screwed her that way. But this morning, she'd gone into work with a game plan in mind, and tonight? Well, tonight she was out of a job and knee deep in a deal with the devil.

Of course, she hadn't actually agreed to my other terms, but when I guided her out of the tea room and toward my waiting car, she didn't falter.

Didn't utter a peep.

Just climbed into the vehicle, neatly tucked her knees together, and waited for me to get in beside her.

Like the well-oiled team my chauffeur and car were, they set off the minute I'd clicked my seatbelt.

The privacy screen was up, and I knew how soundproofed it was—not because of technology, but because Samuel knew not to listen to any of the murmurs he might hear back here.

And if he was ever to share the most innocent of those whispers he might have discerned? We both knew I'd slice off his fucking ear.

This was a hard world. One we'd both grown up in, so we knew how things rolled. Samuel had it pretty easy with me, and he wasn't about to fuck up this job when he was so close to retirement. If he kept his mouth shut, did as I asked, ignored what he may or may not have heard, and drove me wherever the fuck I wanted to go, Sam knew I'd set him and his missus up somewhere nice in Florida. Near the beach, so the moaning old bastard's knees didn't give him too much trouble in his dotage.

See?

I wasn't all bad.

Rapping my fingers against my knee, I studied her, and I made no bones about it.

Her face was tilted down, and it let me see the longest lashes I'd ever come across on a woman. Well, natural ones. Those fucking false ones that fell off on my sheets were just irritating. But as with everything, Aoife was all natural.

So pure.

So fucking perfect.

Jesus, Mary, and Joseph.

She was a benediction come to life.

I wasn't as devout as Aidan Sr. would like me to be, but even I felt uncomfortable thinking such thoughts while sporting a hard-on that made me ache. That made my mental blasphemy even worse.

"Why did you let him touch you? Was it for money?"

I hadn't meant to ask that question.

Really, I hadn't.

It was the last thing I wanted to know, but like poison, it had spewed from my lips.

Who she'd fucked and who she hadn't, was none of my goddamn affair.

This was a business deal. Nothing more, nothing less. She'd fuck me to make sure I kept quiet, and I fucked her so I could revel in the copious curves this woman had to offer.

Simple, no?

She stiffened at the question, and I couldn't blame her. "Do I really have to answer that?"

I could have made her. It was on the tip of my tongue to force her to, but I didn't really want to know even if, somewhere deep down, I did.

"You know why you're here, don't you?" I asked instead of replying.

Her nostrils flared. "To keep silent."

I nodded and almost smiled at her because, internally she was furious, but equally, she was lost. I could sense that like a shark could scent blood in the water. This had thrown her for a loop, and she was in shock, but she was, underneath it all, angry.

Good.

I wanted to fuck her tonight when she was angry.

Spitting flames at me, taking her outrage out on me as she scratched lines of fire down my spine as she screamed her climax....

I almost shuddered at how well I'd painted that mental picture.

"When you're ready, you have my card."

"Ready for what?" she asked, perplexed. Her brow furrowed as she, for the first time since she'd climbed into the car, looked over at me.

"To make another tea room. I've had them move all the stuff into storage."

She licked her lips. "I want to say that's kind of you, but I'm in this predicament because of you."

A corner of my mouth hitched at that. "Honestly, be grateful I was the one who came knocking today. You wouldn't want any of the

Five Points' men around that place. Half that china would be on the floor now."

Her shoulders drooped. "I know."

"You do?"

"I pay them protection money," she snapped. "Plus, I grew up around enough Five Pointers to know the score."

That statement targeted my curiosity, hard. "You did, huh? Whereabouts?"

Her mouth pursed. "Nowhere you'd know," she muttered under her breath.

"I doubt it. This is my area, too."

She turned to me, and the tautness around her eyes reminded me of something, but even as it flashed into being, the memory disappeared as I drowned in her emerald green eyes. "Why are you doing this?"

"Why do you think?" I retorted. "You're a beautiful woman—"

"Don't pretend like you couldn't have any woman under you if you asked them."

I wanted to smile, but I didn't because I knew, just as Aidan had pointed out to me earlier that day, that Aoife wasn't exactly what society considered on trend.

She'd have suited the glorious Titian era. She was a Raphaelite, a gorgeous and vivacious Aphrodite.

She wasn't slender. Her butt bounced, and when I fucked her, I'd have some meat to slam into, and her hips would be delicious handholds to grab.

If I smiled, I'd confirm that I was mocking her, and though I was a bastard, and though I was enough of a cunt to blackmail her into this when it hadn't been necessary—after all, before I'd told her who I was, I could have asked her out and done this normally—there was no way I was going to knock this glorious creature's confidence.

"Some men like slim and trim gym bunnies, some men like curves." I shrugged. "That's how it works, isn't it?"

Her eyes flared at that. "But Jenny—"

"Would you prefer she be here with me?" I asked dryly, amused when she flushed.

"Of course not. I wouldn't want her to be in this position."

I laughed. "Nicely phrased."

"What's that supposed to mean?"

Leaning forward, I grabbed her chin and forced her to look at me. "It's supposed to mean that you can fight this all you fucking want, but deep down, you're glad you're here. Your little cunt is probably sopping wet, and it's dying for a taste of my dick. So, simmer down. We're almost at my apartment."

And with that, I dipped my chin, and opening my mouth, raked my teeth down her bottom lip before I bit her. Hard enough to make her moan.

***

Aoife

THE STING of pain should have had me rearing back.

It didn't.

It felt. . . .

I almost shuddered.

Good.

It had felt good.

The way he'd done it. So fucking cocky, so fucking sure of himself, and who could blame him? He'd taken what he wanted, and I hadn't pulled away because he was right. My pussy *was* wet, and even though this was all kinds of wrong, I did want to feel him there. To have his cock push inside me.

Jesus, this was way too early for Stockholm syndrome, right?

I mean, this was . . . what was it?

It couldn't be that I was so horny and desperate for male attention that I was willingly allowing this to happen, was it?

Fuck. How pathetic was I if that was true? And yet, I didn't feel desperate for anything other than more of that small taste Finn had given me.

As a little girl, I'd watched Finn. It had been back in the day when his old man had been around and Fiona had lived with her husband and son. He'd beaten her up something rotten. Barely a week went by when Fiona, my mom's friend, didn't appear with some badly made-up bruise on her face.

I was young, only two, but old enough to know something wasn't right. I'd even asked my mom about it, wanting to understand why someone would do that to another person.

I couldn't remember what my mother had said, but I could remember how sad she'd been.

For all his faults, my dipshit stepfather had never beaten her, he'd just taken all her tips for himself and spent every night getting drunk.

Well, Finn's dad had been the same, except where mine passed out on the decrepit La-Z-Boy in front of the TV, Gerry had taken out his drunk out on Fiona.

And eventually, Finn.

Even as a boy, in the photos Fiona kept of him, Finn had been beautiful.

I could see him now, deep in my mind's eye. His hair had been as coal dark then as it was now, and not even a hint of silver or gray marred the noir perfection. His jaw and nose had grown, obviously, but they were just as obstinate as I remembered. Fiona had always said Finn was hardheaded.

When I was little, I hadn't had a crush on him—I'd been a toddler, for God's sake—but I'd been in awe of him. In awe of the big boy who'd been all arms and legs, just waiting for his growth spurt. Sadly, when that had happened, he'd disappeared.

As had his father.

Overnight, Fiona had gone from having a full house to an empty nest, and my mom had comforted her over the loss of her boy.

To my young self, I'd thought he'd died.

Genuinely. The way Fiona had mourned him? It had been as though both men had passed on, except we'd never had to go to church for a service, and there'd been no wake.

As kids do, I'd forgotten him. I'd been two when he'd disappeared, so I only really remembered that Fiona was a mom and that she was grieving.

We'd barely spoken his name because it could set her off into bouts of tears that would have my mom pouring tea down her gullet as they talked through her feelings.

As time passed, those little scenes in our crappy kitchen stopped, yet Fiona hung around our place so much it was like her second home.

One day, my stepfather died in an accident at work. The insurance paid out, Fiona moved in with us, and Mom had started scheming as to how to make her dream of owning a tea room come true. With Fiona living in, I'd heard Finn's name more often, but the notion he was dead still rang true.

Yet, here he was.

Finn wasn't dead.

He was very much alive.

Had Fiona known that?

Had she?

I wasn't sure what I hoped for her.

Was it better to believe your son was dead, or that your son didn't give enough of a fuck about you to contact you for years?

I gnawed on my bottom lip at the thought and accidentally raked over the tissue where Finn had bitten earlier.

"We're almost there," the man himself grated out, and I could sense he was pissed because the phone had buzzed, and whatever he'd been reading had a storm cloud passing behind his eyes.

"O-Okay," I replied, hating the quiver in my voice, but also just hating my situation.

This was....

It was too much.

How was it that I was sitting here?

This morning, I'd owned a tea room. Now, I didn't.

This morning, I'd been exhausted, depressed about my mom, and *feeling* lost.

Now?

I was the *epitome* of lost.

A man was going to use me for sex, for Christ's sake.

But all I could think was: *did I still have my hymen?*

God, would he be angry if he had to push through it?

Should I tell him?

If I did, it would be for my benefit, not his, and why the hell was I thinking like this? I should be trying to convince him that normal people did not work business deals out by bribing someone into bed.

But, deep down, I knew all my scattered thinking was futile.

I wasn't dealing with normal people here.

I was dealing with a Five Pointer.

A high ranking one at that.

It was like dealing with a Martian. To average, everyday folk, a Five Pointer was just outside of their knowledge banks.

Sure, they thought they knew what they were like because they watched *The Wire* or some other procedural show, but they didn't.

Real-life gangsters?

They were larger than life.

They throbbed with violence, and hell, a part of me knew that Finn was cutting me some slack by asking to sleep with me.

Yeah, as fucked up as that was, it was the truth.

He could have asked for so much more.

He'd have a Senator in his pocket, and to the mob, what else would they ask for if not that?

Yet Finn?

He just wanted to fuck me.

My throat felt tight and itchy from dryness. I wanted some water so badly, but equally, I wasn't sure if it would make me puke.

Not at the thought of sex with this man—a part of me knew I'd enjoy it too much to even be nervous.

No, at what else he could ask of me, that had me fretting.

Was this a one-time deal?

How could I protect my dad from the Five Points when . . . ?

I shuddered because there was nothing I could do. There was no way I could even broach any of those questions since I wasn't in charge here.

Finn was.

Finn always would be until he deemed I'd paid my dues. Whether that was tomorrow or two years down the line.

Shit, it might even be forever. If my dad hit the White House, only God knew what kind of leverage Finn could pull if my father tried to carry on covering up my existence. . . .

"We're here."

Something had *definitely* pissed him off.

He'd gone from the cat who'd drank a carton full of cream, to a pissed off tabby scrounging for supper in the trash.

"We're going to go through to the private elevator, and I'm going to head straight down the hall to my living room. You're going to slip into the first door on the right—that's my bedroom."

"O-Okay," I told him, wondering what the hell was going on.

"You're going to stay quiet, and you're going to try to not hear any fucking thing I say, do you hear me?"

"I hear you."

"You'd better," he ground out, his hand tightening around his cellphone. "Coming to Aidan O'Donnelly's attention is the last thing a little mouse like you wants."

A shiver ran through me.

Aidan O'Donnelly was in his apartment?

Fuck, just how high up the ranks was he?

. . .

CONTINUE
THE FIVE POINTS' MOB COLLECTION
HERE:
www.books2read.com/FilthySerenaAkeroyd

CONTINUE
A DARK & DIRTY SINNERS' MC SERIES
HERE:
www.books2read.com/StormSerenaAkeroyd

FREE BOOK!

Don't forget to grab your free e-Book!
Secrets & Lies is now free!

Meg's love life was missing a spark until she discovered her need to be dominated. When her fiancé shared the same kink, she thought all her birthdays had come at once, and then she came to learn their relationship was one big fat lie.

Gabe has loved Meg for years, watching her from afar, and always wishing he'd been the one to date her first and not his brother. When he has the chance to have Meg in his bed—even better, tied to it—it's an opportunity he can't refuse.

With disastrous consequences.

Can Gabe make Meg realize she's the one woman he's always wanted? But once secrets and lies have wormed their way into a relationship, is it impossible to establish the firm base of trust needed between lovers, and more importantly, between sub and Sir…?

This story features orgasm control in a BDSM setting. Secrets & Lies is now free!

CONNECT WITH SERENA

For the latest updates, be sure to check out my website! But if you'd like to hang out with me and get to know me better, then I'd love to see you in my Diva reader's group where you can find out all the gossip on new releases as and when they happen. You can join here: www.facebook.com/groups/SerenaAkeroydsDivas. Or you can always PM or email me. I love to hear from you guys: serenaakeroyd@gmail.com.

ABOUT THE AUTHOR

I'm a romance novelaholic and I won't touch a book unless I know there's a happy ending. This addiction is what made me craft stories that suit my voracious need for raunchy romance. I love twists and unexpected turns, and my novels all contain sexy guys, dark humor, and hot AF love scenes.

I write MF, menage, and reverse harem (also known as why choose romance,) in both contemporary and paranormal. Some of my stories are darker than others, but I can promise you one thing, you will always get the happy ending your heart needs!

Printed in Great Britain
by Amazon